The Goddess of Dance

The Spirits of the Ancient Sands

Anna Kashina

Dragonwell Publishing

This is a work of fiction. All of the characters, organizations, and events portrayed in this novel are either products of the author's imagination or are used fictitiously.

Copyright © 2012 by Anna Kashina
Cover art by Stephen Hickman
Design by Olga Karengina

Published by Dragonwell Publishing
www.dragonwellpublishing.com

ISBN 978-0-9838320-2-7

First edition

Contents

I. Tears of Stone

II. The Temple

III. The Dance

Wind sweeps over the ancient dunes of the desert, and the grains of sand rustle as they settle back over the wavy crests. One can almost hear the wind murmur and whisper as it passes through its endless realm. One can imagine voices, barely distinguishable in the wind's dry rustle over the sands.

"A djinn is free..."

"A djinn must never be freeeeee..."

"The one who freed him is a threat..."

"... to the existence of the world."

"She must be contained."

"She must not be allowed to stay in her world."

"She must become a slave for eternity."

The wind rushes on, straight into the crimson haze of the ever-setting sun. The desert is empty. There is no one around to listen to the voices in the wind.

I

Tears of Stone

Scent of Myrrh

*T*he rustle of the reeds on the riverbank has a threatening pitch, as if someone is crawling through the thicket.

Sobek, the crocodile god?

Thea desperately claws at the knot on her wrist. Why did mother tie her up and leave? Was she trying to teach her a lesson? Or had she finally tired of Thea's willfulness?

A wail of a night bird cuts through the air. *Only a few hours until dawn. Maybe then mother will come back!*

If she does, Thea will never be a bad girl again. She'll always clean up after herself, and comb her hair all the way down, and she'll never ever tease her sisters ever again. If only she survives the night. If only Sobek doesn't take her first.

Sleep, she thinks. *If I sleep, Sobek will think I'm dead. And if he still wants to take me, at least I won't feel it.*

The ground is hard and damp. Inhaling the fresh sweet smells of earth and lotus, Thea closes her eyes. *Make my death swift and painless, Sobek,* she prays as she sinks into a deep sleep.

Princess Gul'Agdar of Dhagabad opens her eyes. It seems that the air has just stirred in front of her bed. As if someone had been standing there and disappeared when she woke up, leaving behind a shimmering trace.

Hasan?

The princess sits up. The uneasy feeling of a powerful presence disturbs her. And something else, barely perceptible, hanging in the air. *A smell.*

She inhales, trying to recognize it. The scent is sweet and heady, like incense. And very, very faint. It quivers in the still morning air and disappears, just like the shimmer of a shape disappeared a moment ago. Only after it vanishes completely, replaced by the fresh spring smells of flowers and earth from the garden, does she finally put a name to it.

Myrrh.

Hasan's natural smell has always been juniper. A week ago, after his transformation from a djinn into a free wizard, this barely perceptible scent acquired a more substantial human touch, no longer a pure juniper essence. In its human quality the princess finds his scent even more intoxicating than before. But the smell that was hanging in her room a moment ago was nothing like that. *No human could have such a smell.*

The princess's skin tingles.

"Hasan!" she calls out softly, peering into the depths of the room. When they came back yesterday, after their sweeping flight over the world to celebrate Hasan's freedom, she was so exhausted that she didn't even say good night properly before falling down on her bed and sinking into sleep, still dressed in her outdoor clothes. She doesn't know where Hasan has spent his night and where he is this morning, but he should come when she calls him. He always does.

There is no answer. She peers into the air, trying in vain to see the familiar shimmer of air. Her heart quivers, filling her chest with a frightful emptiness.

He is no longer her slave. She has freed him by forsaking her duty to marry a prince and proclaiming to the whole city of Dhagabad that she loves her djinn-slave instead. Her wholehearted wish for his freedom shattered the ancient magic that had held Hasan in its bonds for almost two millennia. He is now free, an all-powerful wizard. He is no longer obliged to appear on her command.

There must be a perfectly natural reason for his absence, she tells herself firmly. Maybe he couldn't sleep, and left for a morning stroll in a distant, magical place. Maybe he went there to bring her something from a faraway land. Maybe—

Voices from beyond the door to her chamber draw her attention. The loud, commanding voice of Nanny Zulfia and the high-pitched one of the princess's youngest nanny, Airagad. *Arguing?* It takes a moment to make out the third voice, deep and low, whose powerful timbre creeps in through the door curtain, making the princess shiver. *Nimeth.* The mysterious slave woman from the desert land Aeth, the sultaness's companion since she was still a child.

There is only one possible reason for Nimeth to be here. She came on an errand from the sultaness.

The princess's heart sinks. She knows all too well what such an errand would be.

She hastily climbs out of bed and glances into the large mirror at the side of her chamber. In her crumpled clothes, with hair in disarray, she looks like a misplaced serving girl, not like the only daughter of the ruling sultan and sultaness of Dhagabad. She straightens her hair and draws herself up into the most confident pose she can manage on such a short notice, just as the door curtain slides apart, letting in a crowd of servants and nannies.

Nimeth's dark, tall figure in front draws the princess's eyes. The slave woman's face is impassive; her narrow Aethian dress glimmers with the silver trims at the neck and the hem. She stops a few paces away from the bed. Her long, slanting eyes measure the princess up and down.

"Good morning, Princess Gul'Agdar," she says coldly.

"Good morning, Nimeth." The princess forces her voice to sound calm and cheerful as she boldly meets the older woman's gaze. She wishes Hasan were by her side now to help her face the upcoming ordeal, but she forces the thought away. The decision to free him and forsake her duty has been her own. She can stand up to her mother.

"The sultaness wishes to see you, princess." Nimeth's anticipated words drop like a heavy stone between them. "After you eat your breakfast and"—she slides her eyes over the princess's outfit—"get properly dressed."

She bows, then turns and walks out of the chamber. Everyone in the room silently watches her go.

The wind travels farther over its endless realm, hissing through the sifting sound of sands.

"He must be captured back..."

"The one who freed him must be captured as well..."

"She must be contained..."

"... through love... through the power of tears..."

"Tears... of the Mother Goddess..."

"The djinn might find the answers... must not find the answers ... answers... in the Tower of Tearsssss..."

"Hey! Watch where you're going!"

A spear shaft hits Hasan on the shoulder. He hears a whip crack and opens his eyes just in time to dodge a lash.

Ouch!

He suppresses a smile. His shoulder, where the spear hit it, is actually *sore,* and the bruise spreading along the side of his body actually *hurts.* It was *pain* that awakened him from his trance, not a sense of something heavy moving in his direction, or of the terrified crowd parting all around him to avoid being whipped and trampled by hooves.

Pain.

He is human! He is no longer a djinn. He is free!

He lifts his head as the man on a huge, chestnut horse raises his whip again. The rider is wearing leather armor and a pointed helmet, and is carrying a short spear, currently tucked into a sheath at his stirrup. His narrow eyes from behind the steel plates of the helmet study Hasan with no emotion.

Hasan takes a deep breath. Ignoring the pain in his injured shoulder, he distances himself from the noise of the plaza, sending his thoughts into the guard's mind.

The guard sees a commoner in his way, a pilgrim too slow to clear the way for the Royal Guards of Avallahaim. The Plaza of Tears is always full of them. Except this commoner is unlike others. Instead of rushing away after being hit by a spear, he just stands there in front of the guard's horse. He shows no sign of fear. In fact, his expression as he looks at his bruised shoulder is that of surprise.

Something about this commoner draws the guard's eyes. He looks like no ordinary man. His muscular grace speaks of his familiarity with swords and sabers, not with pitchforks and rakes more appropriate for the simplicity of his dress. His calm gray eyes watch the guard without the fear of someone who has just been hit with a spear shaft and narrowly dodged a whiplash for getting in the way of none other but the honorary guard escorting Crown Prince Musa Jafar Avallahaim himself. Instead, the stranger's disquieting eyes study the guard with the calmness of a nobleman running into a servant while taking a walk in his own garden. Their look somehow makes the guard feel as if the stranger is wearing silk and gemstones, not a much-worn travel cloak over a simple white shirt and dark pants stained with dust, below which his feet are bare.

The guard's hand holding the whip lowers under the stranger's quiet gaze.

"I apologize, *taghit*," the stranger says, correctly naming the guard's rank.

Who is this stranger? The guard's mind races. *A former soldier? A mercenary? An imperial bodyguard?*

"I hope no offense is taken," the stranger continues, and saluting with his right hand at his shoulder, palm outward, he turns and disappears into the crowd.

How did he know our secret salute? the guard wonders. Palm outward, meaning: "all safe." He makes a mental note to talk to his soldiers about this strange man. But what would he say? That a stranger with gray eyes was not frightened by his raised whip? To make himself a laughingstock of the entire inner city? Not in a hundred lifetimes!

He searches the crowd for the stranger's head. It should be quite visible now, with his short brown hair and light-colored skin, with his height, taller than the average pilgrim on this plaza where they come from all over to see the Tower of Tears. Yet the stranger's head is nowhere to be seen. The *taghit* pauses, listening to the monotonous cry of the ceremonial guard.

"Make way for the great prince Musa Jafar Avallahaim, the heir to our beloved emperor, may the sun of his presence shine on us forever!"

It suddenly occurs to the *taghit* that he joined the royal train today disguised as a common guard, to be able to ride in front and be the first one to catch the crowd's mood, to be able to sense how loyal people are to their prince and what dangers one could expect for the young Musa Jafar. The emperor has personally dispatched him on this task, for it has troubled his majesty for a while that the crown prince with his feeble looks makes a questionable heir. The *taghit* has a sense that the emperor is considering naming his second son, Aram Bei, to take over from his older half-brother. But second-guessing the emperor is not his job today. His job is to leave behind all his signs of distinction, to ride at the head of the royal train as a common guard.

Which is exactly what he did.

How could the gray-eyed stranger have possibly guessed his rank? He might have recognized the *taghit*'s face, of course. But to do that he would have to be somebody from the inner city. He would have to have seen the *taghit* at least once in his life.

The *taghit* has an outstanding memory for faces. He is certain he has never seen the stranger before.

He stops his horse once more to peer into the crowd all the way to the roughly hewn walls of the ancient Tower of Tears.

As far as he can see, all the heads are properly bared and bent, black hair with various degrees of gray glistening in the beams of the morning sun. There is definitely no head among them with short brown hair and skin unusually light for an inhabitant of Avallahaim.

The stranger has disappeared without a trace.

An assassin, the *taghit* decides. *A good one, by the looks of it. I must find him at once!*

He directs his horse into the crowd and beckons to a man closest to him, a thin, ragged pilgrim with a foxy face and a greedy glint in his black, beady eyes.

An Old Legend

*H*asan presses his back against the stones of the tower wall and slides to a sitting position on the ground. The soft beams of the morning sun touch his cheek with warmth. Day is just dawning back in Dhagabad, but here, in Avallahaim, almost a thousand leagues east, the plaza is already full of people, and the young prince Musa Jafar is out for a morning ride.

He shifts against the stone wall and flinches at the pain in his injured shoulder.

This taghit is brutal, he thinks with a strange satisfaction. A mortal would probably be upset at being hurt this way. But a mortal could never fully appreciate how special it is to be able to *feel.*

He would never be able to thank the princess enough for the miracle of his freedom. By all the known laws of nature it should be impossible. And yet he is here, in Avallahaim, and he traveled here of his own free will, while the princess was still asleep.

She must be awake now and calling him. She must be worried that he left her without a word. But he had no choice. The vivid dream he had last night couldn't have been a coincidence. He hasn't heard the Voices in the Wind since the time of his imprisonment in the ancient desert. His freedom must have disturbed the ancient balance of powers. He must act quickly, before the Voices can reach out of the desert to fulfill their threat to contain him and the princess.

Before it is too late.

The Voices mentioned tears and the Mother Goddess. They also mentioned answers that he might, and should not be allowed to, find in the Tower of Tears. Which is exactly why he had to jump out of bed early and rush here, to the Plaza of Tears in Avallahaim, to take a look at the ancient stone tower.

How could they use tears to contain anyone? he wonders. *What secrets does the tower hide?*

He is sure there must be many secrets, for as far as he knows, the tower is older than anything else in this world. But how does one question these ancient stones?

He inhales a full breath of city air, complete with its smells of dust and rot, the stench of horse manure, and the mold of the damp stones composing the tower walls. No matter how hot and dry the deserts are around here, the stones of the tower always hold moisture. They also emanate a subtle smell of salt—just as they should, if they are really made of tears like the legend says. But he is not aware of any magic in the world that could turn tears to stone, to stay around for thousands of years.

Another sting of pain brings him back to reality. He raises his right palm to summon his power, feeling it rush through his body in a surge that makes his hair stand on end. Force flows out through his fingertips and hits his bruised skin, penetrating beyond to the crushed muscle and cracked bone, mending them with the tingling sensation of flesh coming back to life. The mending itself hurts, and Hasan allows himself a moment to savor his pain.

Leaning against the tower wall, he focuses his thoughts on the arrangement of its stones. This tower is over five thousand years old. Along with the Temple of the Great Goddess in Aeth, this is the oldest standing building in the world—built thousands of years before Hasan's birth. Apart from its incredible age, there may be some significance in the fact that this building, like the other one, is devoted to the goddess, the oldest deity worshipped by humankind. Maybe there is a link between the goddess worship and the riddle of the

Voices?

He closes his eyes, once more letting his mind float out of his body and enter the inner passages of the ancient stones. Legend has it that the tower was built from the actual tears shed by the goddess in grief for her lost son. Everyone knows, of course, that no tears could turn to stone and stand here unharmed for over five thousand years. But the Voices have definitely mentioned tears turned to stone. This legend must have a meaning that is connected to the very existence of this world...

He wakes with a start as something heavy hits him from above. Hasan opens his eyes, glad that he took time to heal his injury before venturing on another spiritual journey. Such a blow, on top of a cracked rib, would have felt like a nightmare.

"Sorry, mate," says a voice beside him. "Ye looked kinda dead. Had to make sure, ye know."

Hasan pushes aside the sack he was hit with, looking from the ragged pilgrim in front of him to the five looming figures at the man's back. Five riders, all dressed like plain guards. His friend, the *taghit*, in the middle, looks down on him with triumph.

"I knew we'd find you," he says. "News travels fast on this plaza. And some pilgrims are extremely observant and quick to understand our needs."

Hasan glances again at the ragged pilgrim with the foxy face, who is putting away a bag of coins. The man is grinning, obviously pleased with himself.

"No offense, eh?" he says. "You do look kinda suspicious, mate, what with short hair, light skin 'n' all. I only wants to do a service for my emperor, nothing personal, ye understan'."

"Get up!" the *taghit* commands, and the all-familiar spear shaft darts in Hasan's direction. Hasan lightly leans out of its way and springs to his feet.

"I mean no harm," he says to the *taghit*. "Please let me go."

"We have special people whose job is to decide whether you mean any harm or not. Move!"

What should I do with him? Hasan thinks.

He briefly considers sending the man off to his proper place in the royal guard, but decides against it. He doesn't want to attract unnecessary attention. Instead, he takes a step forward, fixing his eyes on the *taghit*.

I mean no harm. I am just a pilgrim here to see the Tower of Tears. You will let me go.

He walks all the way to the man's horse and takes hold of its reins, gently striking the animal's neck. He lets his gaze wander around, from one guard to another.

You don't know what you are doing here. You don't know this pilgrim. You don't need him. In your eagerness to protect the prince you must have strayed off the royal path.

"Sir?" one of the guards says doubtfully.

"What are you doing here, idiots?" the *taghit* barks. "The prince is over there, you morons! Move! Now!"

The guards, with puzzled looks on their faces, send their horses into gallops and disappear from view. The *taghit* takes a deep breath, looking straight through Hasan, who gently lets go of the horse's reins. He shakes his head and turns the horse to follow his soldiers.

The beggar-pilgrim stirs at Hasan's side.

"Are you some kinda wizard, mate?" he asks. "Blimey, I - didn't know! Here, take this!" He tries to push the bag of coins into Hasan's hand.

"Keep it," Hasan says absently, turning his attention back to the tower. He needs to study it better. But here he seems to be constantly interrupted. He needs to take the tower to a quieter place.

He knows of several places where he will be unlikely to get interrupted, but only one place where he feels entirely safe.

At least, for now.

The princess impatiently submits to the hands of the nannies and servants who are helping her to wash and dress and are serving her breakfast—freshly baked bread, and goat milk spiced with rosemary and mint. She must talk to Hasan before she goes to her mother, but her time is running out.

Where could he possibly be?

She peers through the open window into the intertwined branches of the garden, hoping against hope that Hasan is waiting for her outside, but the garden glade beyond her window is empty. She sighs.

As she looks farther into the garden, she notices something strange among the tall trees in the distance between the central and southern alleys, in the very heart of the wild greenery. She seems to catch a glimpse of a stone wall that she is sure was never there before.

A wall in the garden?

Still unable to believe her eyes, afraid that this strange vision will disappear before she has a chance to take a closer look, the princess gulps down her milk and, ignoring the nannies' protests, rushes out of her quarters. Did she just imagine it? Most likely, because she was walking in the garden only yesterday and nothing like a wall was there. But she saw it so clearly just now!

She knows her mother is waiting, and she cannot afford to delay too long, but surely a few minutes wouldn't matter, would they?

A wave of rich spring smells of magnolia blossoms, jasmine, and freshly cut grass sweeps over her as she steps out into the sunlit garden. She hurries through the meshwork of paths and alleys, straight to her favorite glade, and stops, unable to believe her eyes.

Instead of a glade, she is staring at a stone tower, its roughly hewn gray stones rising as high as the crowns of the tallest garden trees. The tower looms over her with its eerie shadow, emanating cold and dampness, making her forget for a moment that there are such things in the world as laughter and sunshine. The princess shivers.

"Good morning, princess," Hasan's cheerful voice says from behind.

She slowly turns around to look into his gray eyes, warm with laughter, and resists the impulse to throw herself into his arms. She is so relieved to see him. Has he been here all the time? Where did this stone tower come from?

"Hasan," she breathes out. "I am so glad to see you! You weren't there when I woke up, and I thought—" She cuts herself off, noticing something different about him. His guarded look suddenly reminds her of the old pain that used to dominate his feelings back at the time when she first released him from the ancient bronze bottle.

"Is something wrong?" she asks. "What is this—?" She pauses, hesitating how to name this strange building.

"It is the Avallahaim Tower of Tears," Hasan says. "I borrowed it for a short time."

"What do you mean, 'borrowed'? It isn't the actual tower, is it? It just looks like one, right?"

"Of course it *is* the tower itself," he says, proud as a child who has done something difficult and forbidden and is now boasting to his playmate.

"You took it away from Avallahaim? Why?" The princess has never heard of the Tower of Tears, but the name itself suggests mystery, an ancient, sad, legend that has to go well with these big, rough stones, with the damp chill they emanate, with the faint smell of salt that really makes her think of tears. At the back of her mind she also feels mischievous joy, akin to the one she saw in Hasan's eyes—that of a child sharing a forbidden game.

"Why is it called the Tower of Tears?" she asks, too curious to wait for a response to her previous questions.

"The legend says that the tower was made from the tears of the goddess Aygelle when she grieved for her son, Garran, whom she believed to be lost forever in the underworld," Hasan says. "The goddess cried so hard that her tears turned into stones as they fell. That's why they say in Avallahaim that there is nothing heavier than the tears of a mother grieving for her child. Anyway, the people of Avallahaim built this tower from Aygelle's tears to honor their goddess's grief."

"What a sad legend." The princess runs her gaze up the roughly hewn wall again. Something about this tower continues to disturb her. Maybe it has to do with the legend Hasan just told her? Something about tears and the mother goddess? Tears... She suddenly feels an itch under her eyelids

13

that usually comes from crying for a long time. Why is the feeling so clear, as if it has just happened to her? She cannot recall crying recently.

The opening at the tower base beckons her in a strange, eerie way—like a cliff may beckon one to jump to his death. She shivers, peering into the darkness beyond the gaping doorway.

"Can we go inside, Hasan?" she asks.

Why did I say that? Do I really want to go inside? Do I really want to be caught in this desperate feeling that the tower seems to emanate?

"It might be dangerous, princess."

"Dangerous? Why?"

"I don't really know," he confesses. "There is something important about this tower. That's why I brought it here. I needed a quiet place to study it, and in Avallahaim I kept being interrupted."

There are too many questions to ask, but the princess holds them back. She feels a strong urge to enter the tower. The gaping doorway is drawing her in, and she cannot resist it anymore.

"Let's go in, Hasan, please," she begs. Again, it seems as if this wish, these words, didn't come from her. She is reluctant to go in. On the other hand it seems urgent, as if her survival depends on entering this tower. But why?

"All right, princess."

His voice is filled with anxiety, but the princess ignores it as she steps into the chilly dark opening at the tower's base. The air here is damp, and a salty smell dominates the air. It vaguely reminds her of a boiling cauldron, when the cook throws salt into the water before adding rice to it. She used to observe this ritual regularly during her visits to one of the cooks, Naina, who always had a sweet ready for her favorite girl. Except that here, inside the tower, the salty smell comes from something cold, not hot. This coldness makes the familiar smell seem unpleasant, alien.

The dark space inside the tower is depressing. As the princess advances deeper and deeper, walking itself becomes hard, as if her thoughts alone could press on her shoulders with a physical weight. The staircase is lit only by occasional slits in the stone walls, too narrow to be called windows. Struggling up the stairs becomes so unbearable that the princess cannot possibly take it anymore. The cold dampness seems to be drawing strength from her. She stops, leaning against a wall, feeling a familiar burning under her eyelids. She feels so hopeless that she is ready to give up completely and sit here in the stone darkness of the tower until she dies of cold and fatigue. Tears roll down her cheeks, but she is too tired to care...

Hasan appears by her side even before she has time to think about it. He gently takes her hand, and in a blink of an eye she finds them standing on the top of the tower, in a square space surrounded by a solid stone banister.

"I am sorry, princess," Hasan says. "I shouldn't have let you do this."

"I am all right, Hasan." She sniffles, feeling the tears dry on her cheeks in the warm breeze above the treetops. She is so shaken that she cannot quite stand straight, and leans weakly on Hasan. She doesn't know what happened, except that she absolutely had to enter the tower and then had no strength to leave it. Even now, out in the open air, she feels a longing to get back inside, to sit on a stone step, to cry her eyes out, grieving for something she can never have.

"Is it really made of tears, Hasan?" she asks.

"I don't think anybody in this world knows, princess," he says thoughtfully. "Besides the temple of the Great Goddess, this is the oldest existing structure, much older than me or any of my teachers."

Why did he mention the temple of the Great Goddess? The memory of an elegant stone building buried inside an Aethian pyramid rises in the princess's mind. The memory is disturbing. It also seems connected not only to the stone tower, but to her dream of the little girl tied up on a riverbank as well.

"Are you sure you are all right?" Hasan asks.

"I am, really." She forces a smile.

What is the matter with me? It is such a beautiful morning, I am standing here with Hasan, and I shouldn't have a single care in the world. Why can't I get over this eerie feeling?

She leans over the banister and looks around. A magnificent sight opens to her from the tower top. Just below, the green semicircle of the garden, crossed by three radiating alleys with a network of little paths and glades in between, clings to the back of the royal palace. The palace itself spreads beyond in all its glamour—the huge central dome, covering the great ceremonial hall, the array of kitchen buildings behind it, the cascading roofs of the four palace wings, descending down the four sides of the palace. Her own wing, south, is the closest; the north wing with the sultan's quarters and the audience chamber lies across from it, almost obscuring from view the farthest of all, the west wing. She also sees the elegant white building of the sultan's harem with its seven courtyards, just beyond the north wing. Afraid to appear immodest even from this distance, the princess hastily looks away.

Farther away, across the palace plaza, she sees the domes and minarets of the al-Gulsulim mosque and, beyond that, in the distant haze of moisture from the recent rains, the meshwork of streets and plazas of the lower city of Dhagabad. And there, in the heart of it, where the river Hayyat el Bakr, coiling through the city, becomes much wider, she guesses more than sees the colorful turmoil of the port and the Dhagabad bazaar.

A sudden thought strikes her and she gasps, forgetting for a moment the tower, the magical view in front of her, and even the closeness of Hasan.

"Oh, no!" she exclaims. "I completely forgot! My mother is waiting for me!"

She dearly wishes to stay here with Hasan just a little longer, but her belated sense of duty urges her to obey, to rush to the sultaness's quarters and accept the punishment for being late.

"Do you want my help, princess?" Hasan asks.

"Yes," she says gratefully. "Can you please send me to my mother's quarters?"

"Certainly, princess," he says, just as easily as in the old times.

As he watches the princess's shimmering form disappear from the tower top at the command of his magic, Hasan allows himself a moment of indulgence, taking a deep breath, inhaling all the scents and odors of the garden. He savors them all: the overwhelming aroma of jasmine, the gentle fragrance of magnolia, sharp smells of cut grass and fresh earth. He inhales the more distant, mouthwatering odors of garlic and roast lamb from the kitchen, and even the faintest stenches of manure and stale hay all the way from the palace stables.

It is obvious to him that the princess has sensed something in the Tower of Tears, something that he couldn't catch. This fact alone makes him cold with worry, giving new weight to his dream and the warning he heard from the Voices. What if there really is something about tears and the power of the goddess that could capture the princess into the bonds of the ancient desert? What if the foretelling of the ancient scroll he saw ages ago cannot be avoided, even by someone with his powers? What if, as a result of her freeing him from slavery, she is now destined to become a djinn?

He can't possibly allow it to happen. He will do whatever is in his power to stop it. But what?

He shouldn't have let the princess enter the tower. He shouldn't have brought it here at all. And now, while she is talking to her mother, he should take the tower away as quickly as he can.

He looks over the stone banister down to the distant ground, barely visible through the leaves of the tree crowns, and summons a fraction of the tingling force from his fingertips to move in a breathtaking leap all the way to the bottom. The fall feels as wonderful as a splash of cold water on a hot day, and Hasan almost laughs out loud. Ever since he became a wizard, he has always enjoyed these rapid leaps in space— a normal way for a wizard to move around that always looks to mere mortals as if he has disappeared from one place and instantly reappeared in another. He wishes that someday he could share this feeling with the princess. Of all the people he knows she should enjoy it so much.

Extending his hands toward the tower, he summons more force into his palms. Drawing energy from the inexhaustible spot within the calm center of his body, he weaves its tingling net around the stone walls to embrace them in its invisible cocoon until the entire structure appears to his inner eye to be encased in light. He slightly shifts his hands to feel the tower rock back and forth, then lifts it off the ground to float in front of him. He resists the temptation to throw it in the air and catch it like a toy. After all, this tower is very old and he should treat it with respect.

He raises his face to the sky and closes his eyes, sensing the exact direction he needs to take and the amount of obstacles he may need to pass through on his way. And he lets out a mischievous laugh as he lifts his foot up to make the breathtaking step all the way to the distant city of Avallahaim, carrying a stone tower in his hands as carefully as if he were carrying a newborn child.

Sense of Duty

*T*he sight of the sultaness's quarters confirms the princess's worst fears. Her mother, sitting on the pillows at the head of the room, is dressed as if for an official audience. The sultaness's dark, graying hair is fully braided and covered with a shawl. Her full, round face is serious. She sits straight and formal, as if receiving a sultan's messenger and not her only daughter. Used to nothing but warmth and kindness from her mother, the princess feels her heart sink as she notices how the sultaness's eyes are avoiding hers.

Nimeth, a few paces behind her mistress, is still like a dark statue, her face impenetrable, her eyes cold.

The sultaness holds the pause for what seems an unbearably long time before finally opening her mouth to speak.

"Princess," she says. "My daughter, Gul'Agdar. I have asked you to come here so that we can have a serious talk."

"Yes, mother," the princess says. The solemnity of this reception left no doubt about that. She couldn't have possibly hoped that, after everything that happened during the last week, the thunderstorm would pass her by.

"I summoned you here today to remind you of your duty, princess," the sultaness says. "I am told that during the past week you have been quite indulgent in your pastime. I understand that you are euphoric after freeing Hasan from his slavery. But however wonderful it is for you and, undoubtedly, for Hasan that he is no longer a djinn, it doesn't change who you are."

The princess looks at her mother in disbelief. By freeing Hasan she has publicly declared to the citizens of Dhagabad that she refuses her role as the heiress to the throne and chooses to marry her slave instead. As far as she knows, her act has changed everything about who she is. After what she has done, no one would expect her to continue with her duties, which essentially come down to marrying a prince who will one day rule in her father's place and bearing children to secure the royal succession in Dhagabad.

Why does the sultaness say these things? What duty does she speak of?

"As a woman and your own mother I can understand you to some extent," the sultaness continues. "But I was hoping you would consider the consequences of your actions yourself. I don't know how far you went in forgetting yourself, and I will not press you into telling me that. What we need to think of is how to correct the damage."

"But, mother!" The princess feels blood rush to her face. Forgetting herself? Correcting the damage? How could her mother talk to her like this? "Hasan is my betrothed," she says. "I am going to marry him, and I will never, ever part with him again!"

The sultaness studies her for a moment with impenetrable eyes.

"I know that you enjoy Hasan's company, princess," she says. "We have been indulging you in that quite long, if you noticed. But the main thing you must have learned through all your training is unchanged. You are the princess of Dhagabad, and Hasan, with all his powers, is still a freed slave. Marrying him, for someone of your station, is completely out of the question."

The princess stares at her mother, at a loss for words. She had thought all this was over and behind them. How can her mother even suggest that she should abandon Hasan and go back to her duty, now that she and Hasan can finally be together?

On the other hand, a nasty little voice at the back of her mind tells her that they could have been together very well when Hasan was her slave, and now that he is free, nobody knows if he really wants to stay with her. After all, he is an ancient, all-powerful wizard, and she is only a girl, who knows nothing about his true powers.

She angrily forces the voice to shut up.

"I am going to marry Hasan, mother," she says.

The sultaness studies her for another moment.

"You are a grown-up, princess," she says. "Yet you speak like a child. We all understand his desire to share your company for the last few days, since pleasures of such kind have been out of his reach for too long. But did he really speak to you of marriage?"

The princess gasps. It feels as if her mother has slapped her. Angry tears spring to her eyes. She wants to yell at the top of her lungs. She wants to hurt everybody around her. She has never been violent before, but now she suddenly wants to hit something, to break something valuable that will make her mother cry.

She takes a deep breath and orders herself to calm down. She shouldn't give her mother the satisfaction of seeing that those words have hit the spot.

She *will not* cry!

She had expected to be scolded. She had expected to be told that she is a wicked, ungrateful daughter and a failure as the royal princess. She had expected her mother to be angry.

She had thought she had come here prepared for the worst.

She hadn't expected *this*.

"What would you have me do, mother?" she asks. She tries to be calm, but through the mist in her ears she is aware how forced her voice sounds.

"Your duty, princess," the sultaness tells her. "I would never have you do anything but."

"My duty," the princess says, "has been to marry a prince. But Prince Amir won't have me anymore. We have rejected all the other suitors. And I have announced to our people that I will marry Hasan."

"Your duty," the sultaness intones, "is *not* to marry whoever you announced to be your betrothed. This decision is not up to you. Your duty is to marry whoever your father chooses for you to marry."

The princess raises her eyes to meet her mother's gaze.

"Who?" she asks.

The sultaness shrugs.

"Your father is doing all he can to correct the damage you caused," she says. "An embassy is being sent to Veridue with gifts and our apologies. Perhaps things can still be set right. And if not Prince Amir, there are other rulers whose sons are still unwed."

"But—," the princess begins, then falls into hopeless silence. Her ears ring with restrained rage. Through the ringing, a nasty voice at the back of her mind, the one she has always forced into silence, becomes bolder. *What if your mother is right?* it says. The princess has only known Hasan for five years, and she cannot possibly hope to comprehend all the millennia of his life and wisdom. Of course, he promised her that he will belong to her forever, but it was done at the moment when he was overjoyed by his sudden freedom. If he comes to regret these hasty words later on, will she really hold him to his fleeting promise? Will she want him to be unhappy with her, when he can get anything in the world he wants?

Does she love him enough to give him up?

The sultaness clears her throat and speaks again.

"Your father wished me to remind you of your duty and to inform you that your wedding must occur within the next few months, well before your next birthday. You must prepare yourself accordingly, princess. Which includes decent behavior, as appropriate for a maiden and a royal princess."

The sultaness's voice wavers. Suddenly the princess realizes how hard it must be for her mother to keep this stern tone.

She is doing it for my own good, the princess thinks. *At least, she believes she is.*

"But mother," the princess says and stops. How can she explain to her mother that nothing really happened between her and Hasan, at least not in the way her mother implies? How can she explain that although she longs to be with Hasan, he would never take advantage of her that way, even if she secretly wishes he would?

How *dare* her mother suggest that Hasan would use her simply to satisfy his urges after the long imprisonment?

How could her mother ever think Gul'Agdar could marry somebody else?

On her way back from her mother's quarters, the princess feels so shaken that it is difficult to find her way through the familiar palace corridors. She is half-blind with rage. How *dare* her mother suggest all these things: that Hasan doesn't really love her, that she must marry the haughty, self-important Prince Amir, or another man, even worse than that?

How can mother put such poison into her daughter's head?

She doesn't care where she is going, as long as it's *away*—away from her mother's quarters, away from this hateful palace that chokes her with her sense of royal duty. Her feet carry her out into the garden, through a network of paths, through an opening between the jasmine bushes, back to the familiar glade.

The glade is empty. It bears no trace of the tall stone tower, as if all that happened here earlier today was a dream.

Exhausted, she sinks to the ground, leaning against the magnolia tree at the edge of the glade, sinking into the fragrant shade of its leathery leaves. The ground is hard and uneven. The ringing in her ears becomes louder, the bright spring day fading into a damp haze of mists floating low over the water. The jasmine aroma gives way to the sharp smell of wet earth, mixed with a faint fragrance of lotus.

She can almost hear the river splashing beyond the reeds in its turbid flow as she sinks into a deep sleep.

She dreams.

The Temple in the Reeds

*T*hea awakens to the sound of voices around her. Women's voices.

Mother? She opens her eyes with a happy smile. She almost cries out in relief to see a tall silhouette of a woman with thick, braided hair, outlined against the bright beams of the rising sun. Mother came back for her! All of her suffering is over!

Her smile fades as more silhouettes come to view. Three women, and none of them are familiar to Thea.

She sits up, trying to see against the blinding morning light. It must be at least an hour since the sunrise. She really slept long, after all the horrors of last night.

The women are studying her as if she is a strange animal.

"Do we need her?" says one of them. Her voice is young and high, and has an unpleasant shrill note.

"Well, Sobek didn't take her," says another one, her voice softer, not remarkable in any way.

"But she is too old to be trained!" the first one protests. "She must be at least nine!"

Thea opens her mouth to say she is actually eight, but at the same moment the shrill voice speaks again:

"Look, sister. Her family obviously didn't want her. Sobek didn't want her. What good is she to us?"

"I don't know," the plain voice reasons. "But the goddess doesn't protect girls from Sobek for no purpose. Maybe she

24

can still be trained. I am sure she can at least be a servant. You know it isn't up to us to decide."

They both turn their heads to look at the third woman, who has been silent up to now. Thea can now see their dark profiles, bathed in the stream of sunlight.

"We will let the Mistresses test her," the woman says in a deep, soft voice that sends shivers along Thea's spine. That voice seems to hold more power than she has ever heard before.

"But," the shrill voice protests, "you can't really mean to *test* her! She is too old! She is too wretched! Her family obviously can't even afford to feed her! Maybe she can be a servant, but tested?"

"It is not up to us to question the ways of the goddess, Eilea," the deep voice says. "If she was of no importance, Sobek would have taken her by now. We will let her be tested like everybody else."

"As you say, Ganne," the shrill-voiced Eilea says, bending her head.

"Untie her," the one called Ganne orders.

A dark silhouette bends over to Thea, a face finally emerging from the stream of blinding sunlight. The girl, Eilea, is unexpectedly, strikingly pretty, her upward slanting, merry eyes contrasted by a downright-bending line of her scornful mouth, a divergence of lines that makes her face fascinating to watch. Thea gapes as the girl holds out a narrow knife and cuts through the rope on her wrist in a single, practiced move.

Thea sits back on her heels, nursing her blistered skin, and studies her unexpected company.

The pretty, shrill-voiced Eilea and the girl with the plain voice seem to be no older than Thea's eldest sister Leota— about fifteen, not quite ready to be called women yet. They are dressed in white, knee-length tunics, with black leather belts that hold scabbards for their long, narrow knives. The third one, Ganne, is dressed differently. Her white tunic reaches down to her ankles. In addition to the belt she also has a silver necklace, shaped like a snake coiling into a strange figure of two ovals side by side, the snake's tail and head meeting in the middle of the figure where the two ovals touch. She watches Thea with her narrow, ebony-black eyes as she nods for the girl to follow.

Thea trails after the group along the thin path through the reeds, from where she came with her mother only yesterday. Thinking of her mother, she feels a sting of a tear running down her cheek. She angrily sweeps it away. She will not let these women see her cry.

At the end of the reeds, they turn away from the main path that goes into town and, eventually, to Thea's home, and the last of the girl's hope fades away. These women are not going to take her back to her mother. They are taking her to the mysterious Mistresses, who are going to *test* her to decide her fate. Thea shivers.

Ahead of them, at the border of the greenery and the yellow sands of the desert, looms a square building of smoothly hewn dark stone surrounded by a simple row of columns. Unlike the ornamental temples and palaces Thea is used to seeing across the river in the great city of Aeth, where she often goes with her mother to sell pottery, this building is simple—and this simplicity is so harmonious and elegant that it seems to shame all the elaborate ornaments Thea has ever seen.

She knows this building well. Every season her mother brings all of her seven daughters—of whom Thea is the youngest—to the flat space just east of the main entrance to pray, and to leave a basket of fruit as an offering. Yes, she can recognize this building even in her sleep.

The temple of the Great Goddess.

Thea doesn't know much about the temple, except that it is mostly women who come here to pray, and she has never seen anyone but women walk in and out of its doors. She has heard her mother say that the goddess aids all women and they must cherish her above all else, but Thea has always feared the strange temple and its mysterious women-priestesses. It is rumored that they serve the goddess by dance, and that this dance is more beautiful than any mortal has ever seen. It is also known that once a year the chosen priestesses take a barge across the river to the Temple of the Sun, to be joined in some holy rituals with the male priests of the Sun God. Thea doesn't know much about any of those rituals, but the thought of being taken to this mysterious, forbidden temple, makes her feel an unpleasant chill in the pit of her stomach.

Thea shivers as the cold shade of the temple falls over her. She stops, unable to force her legs to carry her forward through the dark opening of the door, where the white figure of Ganne steps through and disappears into the shadows.

A sharp push on the shoulder makes her stumble.

"Move, girl!" Eilea says from behind. "Do you think we have all day to waste?"

Another push forces Thea through the door. She stumbles forward and falls on the smooth, polished floor, feeling the endless shadows close around her.

The princess awakens to the sound of someone calling her. *Hasan.*

Struggling through the bonds of her dream, she feels his hand touch her arm, helping her to sit upright against the tree trunk. She feels his barely perceptible juniper smell that sends a pleasant shiver through her body, forcing away her sleepiness.

She looks into his eyes, feeling the warmth of his closeness slowly bringing her back from the faraway land of her dream. *So real.*

"Are you all right, princess?" He sounds concerned.

"I think so," she says uncertainly. "Why?"

"This seems like an awfully uncomfortable place to fall asleep."

Only now does the princess realize where she is. She can barely remember how, or why, she ended up in this glade, slouched so awkwardly against the magnolia trunk. As she sits up, her stiff body screams in protest. It must be because she didn't have a good rest at night, she thinks. Or because she was so exhausted by the conversation with her mother.

Then it all comes back to her. Not only the unpleasant thoughts of her future and her duty, but also both of her dreams about the girl named Thea. She now realizes why the riverbank where Thea was tied up has seemed so eerily familiar. It is the same riverbank where she stayed with Hasan after the incident in the temple of the Great Goddess, when they almost got killed by Hasan's former apprentice, the wicked Abdulla. The very same temple where Thea was brought by the three priestesses. And yet the surroundings of the temple looked different in her dream from what she remembers them to be. In her dream the temple itself was not inside the pyramid tomb, but outside in the open air. There were other differences too. The thicket of reeds on the riverbank seemed much wider, extending almost all the way to the foot of the temple. The desert lay farther away, and there was no sight of the pyramid tombs around. Did her dream twist her real memories, as dreams tend to do? Or is it that in her dreams she was seeing the temple as it really used to be, thousands of years ago, before King Amenankhor of the Eighth Dynasty ordered it buried inside a pyramid tomb?

This dream was much too real. She has to tell Hasan about it. But there are so many things she needs to tell him. It seems as if a lifetime has passed since she last saw him, before she fell asleep.

"I missed you, Hasan," she says.

He reaches out to take her hand. His touch, the hardness of his palm, the warmth of his slightly rough skin, makes her shiver. When he was a djinn, his touch never felt so human, so physical. She feels her skin tingle with pleasure.

"I am sorry, princess," he says. "I had to put the tower back before anyone noticed its absence."

She looks at him, enjoying his closeness, the feeling of calm strength that makes her worries seem fleeting in comparison to the force he emanates. Now that he is free, he seems even more powerful than before. It is difficult, with her meager abilities, even to begin to comprehend his true power.

Is her mother right? Is she really only fooling herself that such a perfect being as Hasan would ever want to share his life with her?

He looks into her eyes with concern. "Are you really all right? What happened?"

I had a conversation with mother, she wants to say. But she stops herself. She will not poison his ears with all the outrageous things she heard today. She knows he can read thoughts. Sooner or later, he'll know what's on her mind. And she doesn't want him to learn all the horrible things she heard in her mother's chambers. It is better if she tells him about her dream instead.

"I had a strange dream, Hasan," she says. "Or, rather, two dreams that seemed to continue one another."

"What dreams?"

"I was a little girl named Thea, in Aeth. It seemed to be happening a long time ago. And it was *so* real."

"Thea?"

"She was tied to a pole by her mother and left on the bank of the Great River, near the temple of the Great Goddess. And the most strange thing, Hasan, is that the place where she was tied seems so similar to the place where we sat once, remember?" Her voice falters at the memory of that time, over two years ago, when Hasan almost died at the hand of his former apprentice and the princess was caught in the blast trying to save him. Back then, Hasan couldn't lift a finger without her orders. He was still her slave. And now—

Hasan sits back, his expression thoughtful.

"This name, Thea, reminds me of something," he says.

"Thea's mother never came back for her." The princess's voice trembles. "But she was rescued by two apprentices and a priestess of the Great Goddess from the Temple of the Dance. They took her in to be tested by some Mistresses."

"Their head priestesses were called Mistresses," Hasan says. "They tested all the newcomers to determine whether they could be taught the Dance. They only kept the best ones; the rest were returned to their families or made servants in the temple. It was a great honor for a girl to be chosen to learn the Dance."

"Yes, they said so in my dream, too. They didn't want to

29

take her. But an older priestess called Ganne told them that since Sobek didn't take her, she must be tested. Who is Sobek, by the way?"

"In ancient Aeth they had a religion that worshipped animal gods. Sobek was the crocodile, a reincarnation of the Sun God who was believed to accept human sacrifices for the sun. Those that Sobek didn't take belonged to the Great Goddess."

"Yes, I somehow knew he was the crocodile... Something Thea felt... Anyway, one of the younger priestesses really objected to taking Thea to the temple. Her name was Eilea. But they did take Thea in the end."

"And?"

"I woke up when they brought her in through the temple door. She—I—seemed to be unwilling to go. In my dream, I felt so scared!"

He shakes his head. "Unfortunately, I don't know much about the cult. It was only served by women, and the only one of them who is still alive is Shogat, the slave of Caliph Agabei of Megina."

Shogat. A djinn. The princess's heart quivers at the mention of the name. She remembers very well the caliph of Megina, Abu Alim Agabei, a short man with an enormous mustache and a dangerous gleam in his small beady eyes. She also remembers the caliph's powerful, mysterious slave woman, Shogat. Back in the weeks before the princess's wedding, Shogat had nearly enslaved her with magic at the command of her master, who for some reason badly wanted to be the one to marry the princess. Only Hasan's interference saved her then from being completely bewitched into following the caliph to the ends of the world.

Shogat, a dancer so skillful she was called by admirers the Goddess of Dance, used to be a priestess in the Temple of the Dance and managed to become an all-powerful djinn—not like Hasan, by learning from books to seek out all the knowledge in the world, but by serving the goddess through dance that she perfected her whole life into immortality, and finally, into absolute power.

"Maybe we can ask her, Hasan," she says with uncertainty.

She is not willing to face Shogat again. But this dream may be important. It seemed so real. Besides, with Hasan by her side, what harm could Shogat possibly do to her?

Nevertheless, she feels relieved when Hasan shakes his head in response. And it feels strangely reassuring to hear him say, "I don't think it is wise to try to talk to her, princess. At least not while she serves Caliph Agabei. Maybe not even if she didn't."

The princess nods. "I hope these dreams don't come back, Hasan," she says quietly. "They are so real, they are frightening."

He meets her eyes. She sees concern flicker in their gray depths and melt away, replaced by the expression of tenderness that makes her heart leap and her body weaken. He leans against the tree by her side, his body only inches from hers. The draw is so strong it is hard to resist. Her body responds on its own accord as she edges up to him, resting her head on his shoulder, and relaxes against his side. He puts his arm around her, and his touch makes her head swim. Immersing in the contact, she doesn't want to think of her troubles anymore. She doesn't want to talk about the future. All she wants is to sit here, next to Hasan, and enjoy his closeness as long as she can.

The State Council

Suppressing the tremor in his hand, so unseemly for the ruling sultan of Dhagabad, Chamar Ali reaches for the letter respectfully held out to him by his grand vizier Shamil. The royal seal of Veridue, an imprint of the rising sun pressed deep into a splotch of red wax, seems to burn right through the paper.

Keeping his face free of emotion and his hands in control, Chamar breaks the seal and unfolds the paper with deliberate slowness.

> *"To the noble ruler of the fair land of Dhagabad, the honorable sultan Chamar Ali—the blessed one in the light of the gods' everlasting favor—we send our greetings."*

Chamar pauses to cast a glance around the room, where everybody is waiting in silence. The room emanates so much tension that it seems ready to burst. The sages of the State Council of Dhagabad, sitting still in a semicircle facing him, are fixing him with unblinking stares. Shamil, frozen in his respectful semi-bow, seems too intent on learning the contents of the letter to straighten up and step aside, as the protocol dictates. Large beads of sweat glisten on the bald spot at the top of his head, and Chamar feels his own forehead start to sweat just by looking at the older man. At the back of the room stands a small group of ambassadors that just returned from Veridue, led by a court sage and the princess's teacher, Haib al-Mutassim. His long white beard and mustache conceal his expression, but the sultan reads the tension in the set of the sage's shoulders, in the stiffness of his lean, tall figure. Even Chamar's beloved concubine, his beautiful Albiorita who does not leave his side even in the room of the State Council, is sitting straight and rigid, her face covered with a veil up to the eyes, her belly already starting to show the swelling of Chamar's unborn child.

Chamar searches her face for a reassuring glance and feels an inflow of warmth as her turquoise-blue eyes meet his. She gives him a slight nod, and he senses her encouraging smile under the veil. *If only she could give me a son,* Chamar thinks, *all of this would be unnecessary.* His daughter by the sultaness, the willful and disobedient princess Gul'Agdar, would not need to become the heiress to the throne, and Chamar would not have to place himself at the sultan of Veridue's mercy.

With a sigh Chamar returns to the letter.

> *"We desire nothing more than to see the beautiful lands of Dhagabad and Veridue mutually prosper and flourish, enriched by the union of our noble heir, Prince Amir, and the heiress to the sultan of Dhagabad. However, to give this union our everlasting blessings, we must first be ascertained that your majesty's eldest daughter, Princess Gul'Agdar, although undoubtedly blessed by unmatched beauty, possesses enough wisdom and other qualities necessary for a future sultaness and the wife to a ruler of both of our lands."*

Chamar's heart sinks. That is exactly what he was afraid of, and he had given his ambassadors strict instructions to that effect. What could have gone wrong? He glances at the sage Haib al-Mutassim, but the sage's expression is still unreadable. With a sigh, Chamar lowers his gaze back to the letter.

"More than that, we are deeply concerned about our son's happiness. He has been brought up in the proper rules and traditions of our ancestors, who proclaimed that a wife should fear and respect her husband and to see her duty, above all, in obeying her husband's wishes. Princess Gul'Agdar has deeply hurt our son's feelings and wounded his pure heart that has not known treason before."

Chamar pauses again. This letter is beginning to sound insulting. Does the sultan of Veridue forget what power the sultan of Dhagabad holds in his hands? Is he possessed by some unknown demon?

Resisting the temptation to explode and take out his anxiety on his voiceless servants, Chamar turns back to the letter, determined this time to read it all the way to the end.

"Your ambassador, the wise and learned sage Haib al-Mutassim, has opened our eyes to the reasons of this unfortunate incident. He has informed us that your young and inexperienced daughter was bewitched by her slave, a vile and treacherous djinn. We do indeed know from the sad experience of our forefathers that djinns are extremely dangerous and can bring nothing but peril to their masters. We understand that your daughter's repulsive slave must have somehow known that her reckless act on her wedding day would set him free of the ancient magic that bound his powers, and that he managed to use his evil magic to force her to act the way she did. We offer our condolences to you and your daughter for suffering such grave offense from the evil wizard, and rejoice at the news that he is no longer bound to be her slave, and thus she is free of his vile influence.

We hope that your daughter has begun her recovery from the much-too-long closeness to the demon, who used her so mercilessly for his own treacherous purposes. After she completes her recovery, we would be *willing to resume our negotiations about the marriage arrangement between her and our beloved son, Prince Amir.*

To make such negotiations possible, we would naturally require that the evil wizard is banished from your majesty's palace. We expect that your majesty has already done so, but we must make certain that your daughter's fragile mind is not influenced in any way by the powers that proved so destructive in the past. After the monster is safely out of the Dhagabad palace and your majesty can make all the necessary arrangements, it will be our pleasure to receive the fair princess Gul'Agdar as a new bride to our son and heir.

Signed: the ruler of the fair and prosperous land of Veridue, the honorable sultan Eljahed ibn Falh."

With a sigh Chamar lowers the letter in his trembling hand. He feels the roots of his dark, thick hair moisten with sweat. Over the bent head of his grand vizier Shamil, he meets Haib al-Mutassim's quiet gaze and beckons for the old sage to come closer.

"How did he seem, Haib?" the sultan asks.

"He seemed quite... agreeable, your majesty," Haib says with a slight pause as he searches for the right word, "after we explained to him the reason for the princess's sudden change of heart."

"And the prince?"

"His highness is young and impatient, your majesty. Besides"—a smile crawls over the sage's lips and disappears within the depths of his beard—"I believe it is the first time in the prince's life when a girl's choice was not in his favor. But he seemed willing enough to accept the explanation."

It had been Haib's idea to explain away the princess's improper behavior by the influence of Hasan's magic over her, and the council was especially pleased by it. During the days since the embassy went off to Veridue, Chamar had almost come to believe in it himself. After all, what else but magic could have driven his obedient daughter to forsake her duty?

"He asks me to banish Hasan," Chamar says, looking at nobody in particular. He pauses, offering them a chance to come forward with advice, but the room remains quiet, heavy silence almost palpable in the thick, dusty air.

Angry at having to ask for advice where he thinks it isn't right, Chamar directs his gaze at Shamil, whose sheepish manner makes him the usual target for the sultan's displeasure.

"Does my grand vizier have nothing to say to this?" he asks, raising his voice just a fraction. "Is he to convince me that a grand vizier's role in the State Council is merely for decoration?"

"Your majesty," Shamil's voice, cracked with age, trembles, making him indeed sound somewhat like a sheep. "I am not sure we can really banish Hasan from the palace. We do not have anybody with enough power to enforce it. Personally, I would advise against angering the dj—" His voice dies out as this inappropriate word is about to escape his lips. Hasan is no longer a djinn, in the sense of being enslaved by his bottle. He is, however, as powerful as a djinn would be, and that makes the very idea of confronting him dangerous, to say the least.

Such a cautious statement from his vizier angers Chamar even more.

"Wizard or not, he is presently our guest, and it is within our powers to let him know his presence here is no longer welcome."

"I am merely trying to caution your majesty." Shamil's voice sinks to a near whisper. A bead of sweat rolls off his bent head and down his neck. Taking pity on the old man, Chamar draws a breath and forces himself to calm down.

"I really see no purpose in Hasan's continued presence in the palace," he says. "He swore no loyalty to us, and therefore we cannot rely on his protection, or on his help in the matters of state. For the same reason we cannot even be sure he doesn't wish us any harm. And as far as the princess is concerned, I find myself agreeing with the sultan of Veridue. I am told she has been much too close to Hasan lately. His presence only confuses her. No matter what his powers are, our heiress can never marry a freed slave. All the neighboring lands will turn away from us if she does. And I believe everyone here agrees with me that as long as he remains by her side, she can only get more confused and less obedient. True, she may not be pleased if we deprive her of her teacher and companion, but she will get over it. In no time, she will become just like a proper princess should be."

"The princess is very delicate and sensitive, your majesty," Haib points out carefully. "And she really seems to believe her union with Hasan is possible. She may need more time."

"She had all the time she needed," Chamar interrupts impatiently. "Much more time than anybody else would have given her to spend with a man she is not betrothed to. She will do as I say. After all, if I command the land, do you think I won't be able to command my own daughter?"

Haib silently bows his head, and Chamar chooses to take it as agreement with his words. He continues after a short pause.

"Did the sultaness talk to the princess as we instructed her to?"

"Yes, your majesty. Under the circumstances, the princess took it rather well."

"Good," Chamar says. "She will be ready, then. I wish to talk to the princess first. Then I will talk to Hasan."

He moves his gaze around the room, satisfied to see heads bent in the proper response to the final words of their ruler. He summons more anger to silence the gnawing feeling at the back of his mind, telling him that he may not be doing everything right. Finally he turns to Albiorita, once again meeting the deep turquoise of her eyes and feeling her gaze soothe him like warm water.

If only she bears a son for me, Chamar thinks. *If only this son could live.*

A Voice from the Shadows

$\mathcal{T}$he caliph's palace in Megina is located in the very heart of the city, adjoining the main plaza and the bazaar. From his balcony in the east tower Caliph Abu Alim Agabei can hear not only the beehive hum of the street noise, but also some phrases, shouted at the top of people's lungs. Having grown up in this very palace, he enjoys this feeling of presence among his people, if only from the top of the palace tower. Not only does it give him the sense of never being alone, careful listening has more than once proven useful in determining the attitude of the people toward his rule, and given him chances to take the necessary steps. It is difficult for people in the street bustle to be careful about what they say. And the caliph never forgets a voice once he hears it.

Agabei could never understand how the rulers in other cities, like Dhagabad and Dimeshq, managed to maintain control of the people's loyalties from the distance of the upper city. There was never such a thing as upper and lower city in Megina. Its heart, in the very center of the bazaar, has always been the caliph's palace, reaching with its white towers straight up to the sun, shining with its golden domes high in the sky, looming over the people of Megina with its protective shadow. The walls and towers of the palace, rising up to the height of five to seven floors, seem even taller amid the two- or three-story buildings of the rest of the city, which is built on a plain that runs straight into the endless sands of the Dimeshquian desert. Among the flatness of the terrain, void of mountains, or even hills, the caliph's palace rises like a tall, golden-haired Baskarian beauty among the short, dark-skinned concubines, shining like a proud gem amid a barren field of gravel.

True, Megina has never been as prosperous as Dhagabad or Veridue, but it has its advantages, being the connecting point for the caravans that travel from Halaby and Dimeshq all the way to the distant Avallahaim and back, bringing goods from the busy port of Dhagabad on the river Hayyat el Bakr. The city of Megina is strategically placed right at the point where the caravans start on their long way across the desert to trade with the weapon masters of Dimeshq and the rug merchants of Baskary. It offers the travelers shelter and supplies for the road, as well as many other comforts they might long for. It is the biggest trade city in the known world, which makes it a prosperous place, even though the lands of Megina are not fit to grow too many crops.

Agabei looks down from the balcony, trying to catch a phrase floating up, interrupted by the buzz of voices all around it.

"The caliph... grip... all of... land!" a man is shouting. "Marriage... at hand!"

Silently cursing the loudmouths surrounding the subject of his interest, Agabei strains his ears to hear more, but the conversation is over. *No matter*, Agabei thinks. He will hear this voice again; he is certain of it. People who concern themselves with the caliph's private life can never keep away from the palace. Perhaps one of these days Agabei will go out again, dressed as a commoner, to personally meet some of the troublemakers whose voices are securely stored away in his mind. He will do anything to ensure his people's loyalty.

Stepping away from the stone banister, he turns to the balcony entrance, peering into the gloom of his chamber beyond. He doesn't hear any sounds from inside, but his magic allows him to sense a powerful presence that wasn't there just a moment ago.

"Shogat?" he calls out softly.

"Yes, master."

She steps out of the shadows. Although Agabei knows exactly where she stood, he is still startled by the suddenness of her appearance. Her dark skin and a plain gray tunic make her blend perfectly with the darkness of the chamber, and only her hair, pulled into a smooth knot at the back of her head, glistens in the light of a single lantern.

"You are wearing that robe again, Shogat," he says, pursing his lips to show displeasure. "Where is the outfit I like? I want you to put it on!"

"Yes, master." Her low, deep voice sinks into a half-whisper. She bows her head even as her tunic shifts shape and color in a blink of an eye. She is now dressed in a pants outfit of soft, semi-transparent cloth with a dark sheen. A shawl wraps her shoulders and breasts, leaving her flat, muscular stomach bare above the low waistline. The metal bracelets on her wrists glisten like silver in the dim light of the chamber. She stands motionlessly, her head lowered, as appropriate for a slave awaiting orders. Agabei can see that the muscles under her dark skin are tense, but her childlike face is impassive, and her huge eyes are cast down to look at the floor in front of her. He lets it be. He could never read her expressions anyway.

"What have you found, Shogat?" he asks.

"Not much, master." She speaks without emotion, her voice level. "I was unable to understand the source of the girl's power. From all I know it shouldn't be possible for anyone to free a djinn."

"Surely you could do better than that, Shogat," Agabei says impatiently. "I am not stupid. We both read the ancient text of the one who frees a djinn. More than that, we both actually saw her do it, right in front of our eyes, on the palace plaza in Dhagabad, with half the city as witnesses! I do still trust my own eyes!"

"Yes, master," Shogat says quietly.

He knows she doesn't necessarily believe everything the ancient texts have to say. Not as much as he does. But she also agrees with him that a power to free a djinn cannot be ignored easily. He recalls the exact words of the ancient parchment, faded with time, written in the hieroglyphic language Agrit that the high mages of old seemed to favor above all other languages for common use. Agabei had Shogat's help translating it, but he memorized it word for word:

> *The djinns will be slaves for all time, slaves to the ancient sands, and to those mortal and immortal ones who dare to challenge the power of the sands to command an all-powerful slave. Never can one wizard, mortal or immortal, command more than one djinn. Never can a djinn do any magic of his own accord. If, however, a person can find a way to free a djinn, such a person will become a threat to the existence of this world. If this person learns magic and gains absolute power, it can become the most powerful djinn ever, and the wizard who commands this djinn can rule the world. If this person remains free, it will destroy the world.*

This text was not complete, and not altogether clear to Agabei. Also, according to Shogat, it suffered a lot in translation—for instance, the usage of "it" instead of "he or she." Shogat said that there was a special word in Agrit to refer to a person without naming the gender, which was completely lost in all the languages known to Caliph Agabei. Similarly, there were two meanings of the word "slave"—a person owned by somebody, and a person obeying somebody's orders—which were two separate words in Agrit, and which, translated as one, roughened certain subtleties of the original. But Agabei was never really particular about literary styles. One thing is clear: they have found the one person who managed to free a djinn—Gul'Agdar, the princess of Dhagabad. It would definitely be wrong to allow her to remain free and destroy the world, assuming that an ignorant seventeen-year-old girl could really do such a horrible thing. Whatever the case, it would be much better to teach her magic and make her a slave to Agabei. If the ancient text is true, she will give him the power to rule the world. If the text is false, at least Agabei will get a beautiful concubine with magic powers on top of that. He has never really cared for such fragile beauties as the princess. But there is something about the combination of her white skin, dark blue eyes, and black hair, that is quite compelling. She could bring true pleasures to a man, if trained properly.

Agabei comes back from his thoughts and sees Shogat's dark eyes fixed on him. Her intent gaze burns.

"Please continue, Shogat," he says. "For surely you didn't come merely to me to tell me of your failure."

"No, master." A shadow moves over Shogat's face. "I sensed in the princess a great ability to learn. She is very receptive to the female side of magic. It seems to me that, taught at an earlier age, she could have become a dancer to the Great Goddess."

The caliph waves this away. He was never interested in Shogat's extinct, all-female cult.

"Was the djinn there when you visited the princess?" he asks. "Did he see you?"

"No, master," Shogat says calmly. "His presence could have ruined everything. Fortunately, he does not seem to share her bed."

Agabei shakes his head. "The girl's a fool. She owns a handsome, experienced man for over five years, and she doesn't use his skills for the pleasure of her body."

Another shadow runs over Shogat's face.

"She no longer owns him, master," she says.

"Even more surprising," Agabei insists. "She is quite a beauty, in her own way. In fact, she should seem quite desirable to a man who has been deprived of such pleasures for two thousand years. And she obviously cares for him. Girls at this age can be easily bent to a man's will. Perhaps, after his imprisonment, he lost his manhood? Or perhaps male djinns are not as capable as they look?"

Shogat's face remains impassive as she meets the caliph's gaze.

"If he was there, your plan wouldn't have worked, master," she says.

He nods. "You are right, Shogat. If they choose to be foolish, or incapable, all the best for our plan. Tell me, what did you do to her?"

"I opened her dreams to the powers that can teach her magic the way I was taught. For someone with the kind of talent she has, it should be the fastest way to achieve absolute power. If she is good enough to do it."

The caliph smiles. Dreams offer a powerful way to influence someone, catching people unawares at their most vulnerable moments. Back in Dhagabad, when he failed to be selected as the princess's future husband, he and Shogat were able to confront the princess in the dream world and almost pull her to his side. What Shogat did now was even more ingenious. Having the princess dream freely, open to magic without Hasan's interference, could indeed achieve a lot in her training. It could turn the princess, with her meek strength, completely over to Agabei, without Hasan ever suspecting a thing. And even if Hasan does guess that something is wrong, how could he possibly interfere?

"Well done, Shogat," Agabei says, looking at her in the semidarkness of the chamber.

He admires the frightening grace of her figure, powerful even in her submissive pose. His heart beats faster at the sight of her smooth hair, glistening in the light of a lantern, her long eyelashes, the curve of her wide nose, her full, sensual mouth that makes her face look like that of an innocent but seductive child. He longs to touch her dark skin, and the rippling muscles that betray hidden tension. Unlike Princess Gul'Agdar, the caliph knows the full use of a beautiful slave. But Shogat still has more to say, and Agabei holds back his passion.

"What of the other thing that I ordered you to do, Shogat?" he asks. "Were you able to find out more about Hasan?"

"I was able to find three people who knew Hasan in his former life, before—" Shogat pauses. Agabei watches her chest rise and fall in a deep, soundless breath before she continues in a quiet voice, "—before he became a djinn."

"Three people?" Agabei echoes. This sounds promising. Considering that Hasan is close to twenty-five hundred years old and that he has been imprisoned for the last two thousand of them, give or take a century or two, it is a wonder that Shogat managed to find anybody at all who still knew him before his transformation into a djinn.

"Three, master. At least two of them may be convinced to cooperate."

"Which two?" Agabei urges.

"One is the sultan of Dimeshq. He and Hasan were both wizards in Dimeshq a long time ago. The sultan has no reason to like Hasan. In fact, he may have reasons to hate him and wish him harm."

"Good. And the other?"

"The other one is also a wizard in Dimeshq, Hasan's former apprentice, who never followed the proper ways. From what I heard, he has become quite powerful over the time. His name is Abdulla."

"Just Abdulla?"

"Abdulla the Wizard, master." A smile crawls over Shogat's lips before her face resumes its impassive expression. Agabei knows that she finds vanity amusing, even if she has learned, as a slave, to properly respect his own ambitions. Of course, as a woman, all-powerful or not, she could never truly understand how ambitious a man can be. After all, the way she acquired her absolute powers, unlike some male djinns, had nothing, or almost nothing, to do with vanity.

"Very well," he says, pretending not to notice the flicker on her face. "Who is the third one you found?"

"The fey Zobeide," Shogat says.

"The head priestess of the Elements? What does she have to do with Hasan?"

"At one time they were... close, master," Shogat says, not letting him miss the tiny pause that holds so much meaning in itself. "She may turn out to be much more valuable than the other two. If she cooperates."

Agabei flinches with the effort to absorb the information. She is right, of course. Hasan's former love, a high priestess and a powerful sorceress, could be an invaluable ally, much more so than the other two. She would also be the hardest to persuade.

"Can't we force her to cooperate, Shogat?" he asks.

"If she cooperates unwillingly, she will not be of so much use, master," Shogat says. "It may be better if you try to charm her. She is quite lonely on that island."

"I heard she has women-priestesses to keep her company. Are you sure it is me and not you who needs to charm her?"

A distant smile creases Shogat's lips. She is still avoiding his eyes.

"I believe you will do just fine, master," she says. "Just make sure to present your motives in an attractive way. You know."

She silently raises her eyes to meet his gaze. He does know what she means. Aside from charming her with his manly qualities, Agabei may have a chance to play on Zobeide's feelings for Hasan—that is, if those feelings are still alive after two thousand years. Having seen Hasan, Agabei has his doubts. Judging by his apparent lack of interest in the princess, Hasan may have lost his taste for women. Surely such an experienced woman as the fey Zobeide would find the skillful and passionate Agabei more attractive. And if she is still so stupid as to hold on to her ancient love affair, she will surely do anything to rid Hasan of the company of the young and annoying princess Gul'Agdar.

He glances at Shogat, still tense, but in a different way. Over their two hundred years together he has learned to read her expressions, or rather, the lack of them. He knows that she is finished with what she has to say and they can now get down to the best part. At least, for him.

He steps closer to her, feeling the warmth of her breath and a barely perceptible smell of myrrh emanating from her skin. She is taller than him, as are most women he fancies, and as he stands next to her, he can see a little cleft at the base of her throat, right between the two smooth lines of her collarbones. He can feel her breath quicken as he draws her closer, brushing his lips against this cleft that he finds so exciting. No other woman has such a perfect cleft at the base of her throat, and that is part of the reason he wants her to wear this revealing outfit.

He puts a hand on her stomach and feels the muscles tense up and slowly relax, giving in to his touch. He never knows whether she is willing to submit to him, but her looks, the smooth feeling of her skin under his hands, her natural smell of myrrh, make him forget himself so completely that he - doesn't really care. After all, she is not only his slave, but one who has reasons to be eternally grateful to him for rescuing her from the unbearable torture of the ancient desert.

He cups her head in his hands, searching for the pin that holds her hair together, drawing her even closer as he buries himself in her incredible myrrh scent. He feels her hair come loose, enfolding him in its silky waves. The hairpin rings gently as it hits the floor.

"Shogat," Agabei whispers.

"Yes, master."

"You really think I know how to charm a woman?"

He feels her muscles quiver under his hands as he moves to undo the knot that holds together the top of her outfit.

"Of course, master," she whispers back. Her voice seems to falter slightly, and Agabei chooses to take it for the response to his caress of her small, firm breasts. He slides his fingers down her arm, feeling the cold of the metal bracelet on her wrist, and catches her hand, putting it on his shoulder. He finds her lack of response alluring for a start, but he does prefer a willing concubine in the end.

"I never had a woman better than you," he whispers as he moves his lips down her throat to stop at her breast. The feel of it momentarily takes his breath away. He blesses his magic for being able to find a djinn who is also a beautiful woman. Back then, in the ancient desert, he did well.

Agabei does have a harem, like a man of his station should, and he goes there from time to time to enjoy the attention of his numerous concubines. Any of them, hearing such a compliment, would burst into bashful smiles and mumbled praise to the caliph himself for his exceptional manly qualities.

Shogat never does anything like that. And yet, Agabei enjoys saying it to her more than to any other woman. It even crosses his mind that in her case it just might be true. He could never imagine a better lover than Shogat, despite her indifference, despite her unusual looks, despite her boyish figure that lacks some of the most appealing feminine curves.

"Take us to my bed, Shogat," he mumbles between kisses.

"Yes, master," she says quietly.

He realizes the change of surroundings only by the sudden abundance of light streaming into his bedroom through a large window, open wide to the clear afternoon sky. He lowers her on the bed and draws away to remove the rest of her garments—and his own, to enjoy the contact of his palms with her smooth skin and the overwhelming sight of her naked body.

Her skin burns his fingers. He can feel her muscles quiver as his hand traces over them.

"Shogat," he whispers as he draws her closer, drunk with her myrrh scent. "I wish for you to touch me. I wish for you to give yourself to me."

He feels her arms move to embrace him, to caress his back—her metal bracelets now warm from his closeness and smooth against his skin. Her lips open in what could have been her usual response of an obedient slave, but he covers her mouth with his, drowning out the words with his tongue as he charges in to the ultimate closeness.

"You have done well today, Shogat," he manages to whisper just before he finally lets go, sinking into the abyss of infinite bliss.

Tears of the Goddess

*T*he wind coils and snakes as it approaches the ancient stone temple that reigns over the desert. The voices grow clearer and clearer among the rustles and whispers of ever-shifting sands.

"The djinn has found the tower..."
"He must not find the answers..."
"She who freed him must be contained..."
"Through love..."
"Through tears..."
"Through knowledge..."
"She must not remain a maiden..."
"They must not remain..."
"... together..."

"But, father!" the princess exclaims, tears filling her eyes. The grand room of the State Council, with its slender ornate columns, blue-and-white mosaic, and vaulted ceiling momentarily becomes a blur, and then clears again as the tear rolls down her cheek. She hates to let her father and all the sages of the Council see her cry, but she cannot help it. She came here thinking she knew what it was all about—she expected to be reminded of her duty. She was prepared not to argue, to be gracious and obedient, like a proper daughter.

She wanted to buy time. But to learn that Hasan would be banished from the palace this very afternoon came as a blow that left her breathless and unable to control herself.

The presence of a pregnant woman with turquoise-blue eyes, the rest of her face covered with a heavy veil, makes it no better. The princess feels anger rising in her chest at the sight of the compassion in the woman's eyes.

"You can't do that, father!" she protests. "Hasan is so powerful! He can be so useful here!"

"Hasan is free now, princess," the sultan says sternly. "He doesn't belong to you anymore, and you cannot command him as you will. It is no longer your decision whether he leaves or stays."

The princess bends her head and lets her nannies Airagad and Fatima lead her out of the room. She can barely feel her way. Fatigue makes her head swim and her limbs tremble, so that she stumbles on the smooth stones of the floor.

This is the end, she thinks. *This is how we are finally going to part.* Hasan—to enjoy the wonders of the world and the power of his magic. The princess—to marry the haughty, dominating, and handsome prince, to become his shadow, his humble servant, and the mother of his children. She was born to such a fate. What did she expect?

She feels the nannies gently guide her through the turns of the corridor into her quarters and lower her on the sitting pillows. She feels other servants fuss over her, covering her with a blanket, putting another pillow under her back. Voices whispering. Concerned, fuzzy faces coming into view.

And then, she comes out of her trance with a snap.

"Hasan!" she exclaims. "I need to see Hasan!"

"But, princess," the nannies' voices protest around her.

"I need to talk to him. Find him and bring him here!"

"He is with the sultan," Nanny Airagad says reluctantly. "Your father sent for him as soon as you left."

With the sultan. Being banished from the palace this very minute. Being banished from her life.

"Leave me," the princess says in a hoarse voice.

"But, princess..."

"I command everyone in the room to leave right this instant," she says at the top of her lungs.

Through the veil of tears, she watches her nannies and servants bow and stream out of the room. Perhaps she will be able to think straight, if only she can stop this flood of tears that pours out of her eyes uncontrollably, leaving her empty of anything but raw grief. Or, perhaps, her tears will turn to stone as soon as they hit the floor, for her grief must surely be strong enough for that...

Thea starts as the door opens without a sound, letting in a streak of reddish light. She blinks against its unexpected brightness after all the time she spent in the dark. She has always been afraid of the dark, and when the shrill-voiced Eilea locked her in this empty room without windows, she cried until her eyes dried off on their own accord. During her night on the riverbank and the unknown period of time in the temple, Thea must have used up whatever tears she had, and now, no matter how much she tries, her itching eyes feel as if they cannot possibly shed tears again.

The door opens wider, and a silhouette appears in its frame: a woman in an ankle-long white tunic, holding an oil lamp in her hand. In the uneven flicker of the reddish light Thea recognizes Ganne—the oldest of the three priestesses who brought her to the temple. The one who ordered her locked in this room.

Thea shrinks away, but there is nowhere to hide. The square room has nothing but bare walls and the smooth stone floor.

Ganne steps into the room and kneels on the floor in front of Thea, peering into her eyes. Thea takes a closer look at the older woman's face—its perfect oval crossed with the narrow lines of her ebony eyes and a straight, full mouth. Her nose, wide and flattened, and her skin, the color of a ripening olive, tells of the priestess's Ghullian origin.

"I see you have cried," Ganne says in her deep, hypnotizing voice. "Good. You have made your first offering to the goddess."

She moves a hand across the floor, as if sweeping something off its smooth surface, and holds up her palm. Thea gasps.

The priestess is holding a handful of small oval stones, slightly grayish in color, resembling a handful of dark river pearls.

Thea could have sworn there was nothing on this floor just a moment ago. At least, she didn't notice anything when she was feeling around it in the dark.

"These are your tears," Ganne says in response to her puzzled expression. "Your grief was sincere, so your tears turned to stone. This is the first offering to the goddess you must make if you wish to serve her."

Thea doesn't wish to serve the goddess, or to give her an offering of tears, but this hardly seems like a time to bring it up. She cannot draw her eyes away from the tiny glistening pile in the woman's hand.

"You locked me here to cry?" she whispers.

"Yes. Let's go."

Ganne springs to her feet in a single flowing movement, so fast and graceful that Thea opens her mouth in awe. She has never seen anyone move with such frightening grace—almost like a snake. She glances at the one coiling into a strange symbol on the woman's necklace.

"Come. Get up," Ganne beckons; her voice is friendly, as if nothing happened between them. As if she hadn't been the one to order Thea locked in this room for the sole reason of making her cry.

Thea scrambles to her feet and hurries after the woman, afraid to be left in the darkness again. As she steps out into the corridor, the door behind her closes by itself with a barely perceptible click.

They walk back toward the temple entrance, and Thea's heart leaps with joy. They are going to let her go! That was the Mistresses' test—locking her up in that dark room. She was tested, and now they will release her to go back to her mother!

But instead of walking through the entrance into the sunlight outside, Ganne turns left, through another door Thea hadn't noticed before.

Thea stops in indecision. She could just rush through the temple entrance and be off—she knows the way from the temple to her home, and it is no more than an hour's walk. She could probably run the distance to her mother and sisters, to the smells of homemade bread and warm milk, to her mother's soft hands. The memory of those hands makes Thea ache with longing. But another thought rushes in like a splash of cold water. It was her mother who took her to the riverbank and tied her to a pole. It was her mother, with her wonderful hands, who left Thea for the night at Sobek's mercy. She never came back for Thea. She doesn't want her youngest daughter anymore.

Once again Thea's eyes sting, but no tears come. She has none left, having offered them all to the Great Goddess, down to the last glistening drop.

"Don't just stand there! Hurry up!" Ganne calls from the depths of the hall.

Sighing, Thea turns to follow the priestess. At least somebody wants her, she thinks, taking a decisive step through the little side door.

She finds herself in the most amazing room she has ever seen.

It doesn't look like a room, or even like an indoor space, for that matter. Both the floor and the ceiling are hewn so smoothly that they look like two giant mirrors, reflecting each other in their endless depths. The lines covering the ceiling in a spiral pattern reflect in the mirror of the floor, creating an impression of the inside of a sphere, whose smooth borders seem to twist the space itself into a single harmonious shape. It seems to Thea that she has suddenly stepped into the air and is floating between earth and sky.

"Come," Ganne's voice beckons, sounding even deeper and more surreal in the hollow space of the hall. "The Mistresses are waiting."

As she crosses the room in careful steps, Thea's eyes are drawn to the figure of a woman in the center, moving in a slow dance, so beautiful that it takes Thea's breath away. The woman's dark, slim body is naked save for a silver snake-shaped necklace similar to the one that Ganne wears. Her movements flow into one another so effortlessly that her body seems to acquire a new, fluid quality, like water flowing over smooth river stones. There is something frightening in the woman's movements, something resembling the snake of her necklace, coiling into the loops of the endless figure—two ovals side by side.

Thea also hears a slow rhythm—beaten on a strange, deeply sounding instrument—but she cannot take her eyes off the dancing figure.

She doesn't know how long she stands in the endless hall, breathless, her eyes filled with tears of wonder, watching the smooth, flowing movements of this dance, more beautiful than life. She loses all awareness of time, all memory of where she is, everything except an aching desire for the dance never to stop. When at last the beating of the slow rhythm ceases and the figure freezes motionlessly in the middle of the hall, Thea comes to her senses and draws a deep breath of the myrrh-smelling air that she somehow forgot to inhale before. *Did it only last a moment?* she thinks. Or was it an eternity that just aged her countless centuries into the future?

"Come here, girl," comes a voice from the shadows. With a start, Thea realizes that the room is not empty. There are at least ten women in gray, ankle-length tunics sitting on the floor in a semicircle. The one who has just finished her dance joins them, pulling a similar gray tunic over her head. This woman is dark and strongly built, her hair streaming down her back in a mass of braids.

Ganne pushes Thea forward and hisses into her ear, "Mistress Tamione calls you! Go!"

Thea takes several uneven steps toward the woman who called her.

Mistress Tamione looks very unusual compared to all the

other people Thea has ever seen. Although her facial features—slanting eyes, wide nose, and full mouth—are common in Aeth and Ghull, her skin and hair are almost white, and her eyes are light blue, in sharp contrast with the dark coloring of all the women around her. Her intense gaze sends shivers down Thea's spine—and yet, something keeps the girl from lowering her eyes before the Mistress. Perhaps the memory of the dance she just witnessed has made her stronger, giving her a sense of life worth living in the world, where such things as this beautiful dance exist.

"Do you like to dance?" Tamione asks.

"Yes, Mistress," Thea answers hesitantly.

"Did you like watching Mistress Ngara dance just now?"

Thea blushes, feeling all the eyes fixed on her. But she does want to answer this! And she does want to answer truthfully!

"I loved it, Mistress," she says. "It was the most beautiful thing I ever saw."

A whisper rustles through the row of sitting priestesses. She sees smiles pass over a couple of faces. Then they all fall silent again, as if waiting for something.

"Take off your clothes," Mistress Tamione suddenly says. Her voice is quiet, but Thea feels that she has been given a direct order, disobeying which would be unthinkable. And yet ... To take off her clothes? To make herself naked in a room full of people? To do something that would cover her in shame. Her mother has taught her better than that!

Thea crosses her arms tightly over her chest, backing away from the Mistress.

A hand firmly squeezes her shoulder, and Ganne's voice says distinctly into her ear, "If you disobey a Mistress again, girl, you will regret it for the rest of your life."

The tone of her voice, as well as the threat, are so terrifying that Thea feels weak and helpless; she cannot possibly resist any longer. She feels as if she is being forced to give up the core of her upbringing—her decency, which her mother taught her to value above all. With trembling hands she starts to unfasten the strings of her dress, her unseeing eyes filled with dry tears. She has no water to give to the Goddess anymore, but her tears are still there, hard and dry as stone. As she slowly pulls off her dress, she seems to feel the tiny stones painfully pour out of her eyes and hit the floor with a dry rustle.

She stands naked, helpless and alone, in front of the semicircle of Mistresses in their dark tunics.

"Dance for us," Tamione says.

Thea hears the beat of the unusual instrument and automatically starts to move to its slow measured rhythm. She would never think of disobeying a Mistress. She doesn't want to regret anything for the rest of her life as much as she regrets what has already happened to her on this day, the most horrible one in her life.

Thea has always liked to dance. She never does it when anybody is watching, of course. But she has always enjoyed imagining herself a peri, dancing on the smooth surface of a mountain lake, just like in the stories her mother used to tell. And now, dancing in the giant hall, naked under the eyes of a dozen strange women, she suddenly feels easy and free. She dances for Mistress Tamione, and Ganne, and the other nameless Mistresses staring at her with unblinking eyes. She dances for the tall, dark priestess who has just shown Thea what a dance can really be. But in some special way she doesn't even feel their presence here, in the temple of the Goddess. She dances for herself, for her inner freedom, for her new life. She is a peri, a spirit of the air, and the floor in the hall is as smooth as the still surface of a mountain lake...

The beat stops, and Thea slowly comes back to her senses. She looks at the faces of the Mistresses, motionless around her, suddenly feeling very small and defenseless. She shivers and looks around for her dress, lying some way off on the floor.

Mistress Tamione gets up from her place in a smooth movement that resembles a leap of a panther onto its victim. She steps toward Thea, and the girl feels goose bumps of terror rise on her skin under the gaze of the priestess's aquamarine eyes.

She backs away from the approaching woman.

"I will examine you now," Mistress Tamione says, reaching out toward Thea.

Remembering Ganne's warning, Thea forces herself to stay still. Her mind is screaming for her to run away. But she cannot hope to escape in this huge open room.

She had thought the dance was the test. She had hoped she had already gone through the worst, by giving her tears to the goddess and then having to undress in front of strangers. What now?

Tamione's strong fingers grab Thea and run along the girl's body so shamelessly that Thea starts to whimper. Even her mother never reached into places Tamione is examining, and Thea closes her eyes, actually thinking whether it is better to resist the Mistress now and regret it for the rest of her life, or to silently submit to this terrible procedure. But what good can resistance possibly do? This woman is so much stronger than Thea!

Mistress Tamione squeezes Thea's arm and pulls it up and back in a single sharp tug. The pain is so sudden that Thea shrieks, feeling her eyes itch from the tears she cannot shed anymore. Her vision blurs anyway. She is sure her shoulder must be broken, and her arm will now freely come off, in the same way that the arms of the clay dolls her mother makes crack off in the kiln if there were air pockets in the clay.

She has no time to recover when Tamione pulls up her other arm, then her legs, with the same sharp tugs. Unable to stand or to feel her limbs, Thea collapses on the floor.

She feels more hands on her, and through her blurred vision she recognizes Mistress Ngara. Deft fingers are now massaging Thea; the pain eases and goes away, leaving a slight tingling in her hands and feet. Through the mist in her head, she hears the women talking to each other.

"She is a natural dancer," Tamione says. "She can learn."

"But she is too stiff," Ngara objects. "Not flexible enough. Besides, she's too old. Even the naturals lose their ability by her age. You will be wasting your time teaching her."

"She may not make a great dancer, but she will serve the goddess well," Tamione answers firmly. "I say we take her."

Thea hears the indistinct chatter of other voices as she continues to lie on the floor, staring into one spot. She doesn't care what they decide. She lost all she had today. It cannot possibly be any worse.

She slowly comes to her senses, as she seems to hear a voice calling her name. *Mother?*

Thea sits up sharply. All the pain in her body is gone. She half expects to be awake from her nightmare, to see the familiar room in their small house, and her mother cooking rice cakes. Instead, she sees the endless hall, figures in long gray tunics crowded over her. She starts when the colorless face of Mistress Tamione emerges right next to her.

"Get up, girl," Tamione says.

"What happened?" Thea asks weakly. "Did you call me? How do you know my name?"

"I don't know your name," Tamione says. "I just called you back from where you were. What is your name, by the way?"

"Thea."

"Listen, Thea," Tamione says, handing Thea her dress. "We all enjoyed watching you dance for us. We can see that you like to dance, and we can teach you to dance even better. Would you like to learn to dance like Mistress Ngara?"

Once again Thea remembers the breathtaking sight of Mistress Ngara's slow, flowing movements. To dance like that ...

"Yes, I would, very much," she breathes out, all horror forgotten, unable to believe this offer is being made to her.

"Then you must know one thing," Tamione continues. "Learning to dance like this takes many years. You must completely abandon your former life and stay here, in the temple. You must work hard every day and obey your seniors. As a reward, you will become a great dancer and will serve our goddess as we do. Do you want to do it?"

"Yes, I do," Thea says firmly. To learn to dance like Mistress Ngara. That would be something. Maybe one day, seeing her dance, her mother will come to regret abandoning her and will take Thea back into their cozy little house? Thea is not afraid of hard work—they always had to work at home to help mother, and Thea's load was never easier for being the youngest. As for abandoning her former life—that life itself seems to have abandoned Thea first, casting her out into the hands of these women.

"Put your dress on," Tamione says.

Thea hurries to follow this order. She hastily scrambles to her feet, pulling on the dress at the same time, and turns to face the semicircle of priestesses.

"You have made your offering of tears to the goddess, and now you are ready to pledge yourself to her," Tamione says solemnly. "Repeat after me: I pledge myself to you, Great Goddess, the source and protector of life. I pledge my body and my soul, to serve you to the end of my days."

Thea slowly repeats these words, echoing in every corner of the giant hall. Their grave solemnity weighs on her heavily with a feeling of her life changed forever.

The princess wakes up with a feeling of dry itch in her eyes, as if she, just like Thea in her dream, has exhausted all her ability to shed tears. It seems that her tears have turned into stones that are scattered all over her pillow like dry grains of sand, making the pillow rough to the touch. She sits up in bed with the strange words from her dream still echoing in her head:

You have made your offering of tears to the Great Goddess and thus are ready to pledge yourself to her.

She tries to remember the exact words of the pledge, and unwittingly whispers them out loud:

"I pledge myself to you, Great Goddess, the source and protector of life. I pledge my body and my soul, to serve you to the end of my days."

The Foretelling

A tap on the door brings the princess back to reality. "Princess?" Hasan's voice calls out.

The loud voice of Nanny Zulfia booms next to him. "She told everyone to leave and not to bother her. Perhaps it is better if you come back another time."

"Hasan!" the princess exclaims, a little hoarsely after her sleep and all the tears she has shed. She hastily jumps out of bed, thinking of how terrifying she must look now, her face swollen from crying, her hair in disorder. But she really *needs* Hasan, now more than ever.

She runs over to the door and pulls the curtain open to reveal a large group of people gathered near the entrance. All four of her nannies are here, as well as some of her slave women and servants. But she only has eyes for Hasan, standing in front with an easygoing smile that makes the tight grip on her heart loosen, so that she can now breathe easier again. She smiles back, forgetting her tears and feeling the bonds of her haunting dream ease their hold.

"Come in, Hasan." She beckons him.

"But you cannot be alone with him, princess," Nanny Zulfia protests.

The princess regards her for a moment.

"I will permit you to come in as well," she says finally, "if you promise to stay at the other end of the room and not interfere in our conversation."

The pause that follows this uncharacteristic order from the princess, who is surely growing much too independent of late, seems to last forever. Finally, the nannies bow.

"As you wish, your highness," Nanny Zulfia says, stretching out the official form of address none of them would normally use with the princess.

The princess chooses to ignore the nanny's tone and beckons Hasan to follow her. She wishes with all her heart that this could be just one of their times together, one of their easy conversations. She also cannot stop thinking that if she had kept in pace with reality before, instead of trying to lose herself in her wonderful time with Hasan with no regards for the possible consequences, she might not be in such a desperate situation now. But, on the other hand, what could she have possibly changed?

"Hasan," she begins, and stops, unable to go on. The gentleness in his gaze melts her heart. She simply cannot *bear* to lose him! She bites her trembling lip, feeling the dry itch in her eyes that reminds her of her dream and all the tears she shed before she fell asleep. *Tears turned to stone.*

Can't she just forget everything and leave the palace with him?

"I am coming with you!" she breathes out, looking searchingly into his eyes. "I want to learn magic and stay with you, wherever you go."

Her heart falls as, instead of the joy she hoped for, she senses resistance in his gaze. And something else—an emptiness, a reflection of old pain that makes her heart quiver and stand still.

He does not share her wholehearted wish to be together.

He doesn't want her.

Was her mother right all along?

"I am sorry, princess," Hasan says, and she sinks into his voice like a stone into a whirlpool. "I can't take you with me, not now. Especially not to learn magic. It would make me very happy if this were possible, but it isn't—not yet."

"Why?" she whispers, raising her eyes again to submerge into the fire of his bottomless gaze. She feels an almost palpa-

ble link of flame, connecting their eyes, their souls, into a single entity that threatens to consume her, to draw her into its
burning depth. Then, as it becomes intense to the point of
being unbearable, she feels him sever the contact between
them. She struggles against the emptiness it leaves in her
heart.

"By freeing me, princess, you have disturbed the ancient
balance of powers that was there since the beginning of time.
Our very existence is now in great danger. I have reasons to
believe that if we remain together—and especially if you learn
any magic at all—it could make things worse."

"Worse? How?" She tries hard, but she cannot possibly
imagine anything worse than being away from Hasan.

"I don't know," Hasan says. "I've spent a lot of time lately
trying to find out, but I have not been successful. Not yet."

"But you must know *something*, Hasan," she insists.

Again there is a flicker of reluctance in his eyes before he
says, "There are certain texts that tell of the one who frees a
djinn. The texts are not exact, because freeing a djinn is something that has never been done before. But these texts come
from the times—and languages—not to be ignored."

"But you yourself said once that written information cannot be trusted."

"Ordinarily, yes," Hasan agrees. "But these particular writ-
ings can all be traced back to one origin, and this doesn't happen often. They are all translations of a very ancient text,
written in the highest magical language. At some point in my
life, I have actually seen the original itself. Only at that time I
didn't pay much attention to it."

"Why did you think it was so different?" the princess asks.

"Mostly because of its language, princess. The language of
the original can only be read and understood by the highest
mages, very few of whom exist in this world. Texts of that
kind are rumored to come from the time of creation itself,
written by those who existed before our world took its present shape. They are called the original foretellings. Some believe that these texts have to do with the forces that created
djinns, the forces that rule in the ancient desert—the one that

imprisoned me a long time ago."

He stops, but it seems to the princess that echoes of his voice keep wandering around the room, creating a hollow feeling of strange powers broken loose.

"And this text, this foretelling, has something to say about us?" she asks finally.

"Yes, princess. It is an original foretelling of the one who frees a djinn."

"What did it say?" she whispers, suddenly so afraid that she can barely make her lips move.

"I have seen it a long time ago," Hasan says, staring into space. "I believe it was destroyed, or it somehow disappeared from this world during the two thousand years when I was... imprisoned." He stops.

"You mean, you don't remember what it said?" the princess insists, trying not to make her voice sound too urgent.

"I do, but not word for word. And the exact words sometimes make all the difference. I read translations of it later on. The last one, written in Agrit, was in the Dimeshquian library until just a few years ago. I don't know what has become of it."

"Can you at least tell me what that translation said, Hasan?"

"Among other things, it said that the one who frees a djinn should not learn any magic. I really wish I could see the original scroll again. When I found it, I was still young and arrogant. I didn't believe in any foretellings at all. I didn't think it was important, much less that it had anything to do with me."

"So what can we do about it, Hasan?"

"Before we do anything, I really need to learn more, princess," Hasan says quietly. "I need more time."

She stares at the floor for a while with unseeing eyes. Time. That is something she doesn't have much of. Not with the wedding looming over her. Not with the fate of her land at stake.

"But," she says, trying to suppress the trembling in her voice, "if you leave the palace now, and I am forced to marry Prince Amir—"

"I'll find some answers before then," Hasan says. "Soon, I

promise. I really wish I could do something right now, but the forces of the desert are beyond my power. What I am afraid of most is that my presence here may be the very thing that is endangering you. In fact, I have reasons to believe that you will be much safer without me around." He holds her gaze, and a wave of emptiness sweeps over her. His decision to leave seems to be final. She might as well accept it. And yet she cannot escape the feeling that there is something he is not telling her.

"Where are you going to go?" she asks.

"I will stay in Dhagabad, princess. I'll visit you whenever you wish. Even if I am away from Dhagabad and you summon me, I'll hear it."

She sniffles, feeling so worn out that she cannot even think straight anymore. All this talk of the ancient powers that somehow endanger her existence, of the original foretelling of the one who frees a djinn, seem to go too far beyond her comprehension. She has freed Hasan because she *loves* him. If, for reasons she doesn't completely understand, she cannot be with him, she is willing for now to be content with his promise to visit her whenever she wishes. If only she could learn *some* magic, so that she could measure up to him at least in *some* ways. If only she could be just a little bit more certain about her future.

She suddenly feels her ears go blank to any sound, filling with deep ringing beats of strange, vaguely familiar music. She goes pale and sways in her seat, and only Hasan's firm hand keeps her from falling.

"Princess?" She hears his voice as if coming from a great distance. She grabs his arm, as if drowning, feeling its familiar warm safety even as the ringing in her ears slowly subsides, giving way to the usual rustle of the afternoon wind and the chirping of birds in the garden.

"I am sorry, Hasan," she says weakly. "I must be tired."

"Can I offer you something to eat?" he says, concern half-hidden by an encouraging smile.

He waves his arm, and a low table appears between them. Wonderful smells of meat and spices fill the air.

She looks at the magnificently laid table, feeling as if she has suddenly been transferred from the harsh reality into a fairy tale. Eating together is one of the joys of spending time with Hasan that had been denied to her earlier, when he was a spirit without flesh or any mortal needs. She enjoys seeing him taste the food as if for the first time, reveling in every bite with his newly acquired senses. She never realized before that being a spirit deprived him of so many normal things, such as the senses of taste, smell, and touch, and seeing his reaction to them, she seems to realize anew how strong and wonderful these senses can be.

The table has all the necessary components of a royal meal, complete with a large dish of lamb in spicy plum sauce and smaller plates of saffron-yellow rice, warm bread, mint sauce, olives, *sankajat*, darkly glistening grapes, and glowing orange persimmons. A whole feast, just for the two of them.

She feels fatigue and worry step away to leave room for a simple human hunger, the feeling always welcome in one sitting in front of a fully laid table. Even the sinking feeling that has been grasping her heart eases off, making place for hope and anticipation. Hasan did say that he will be near her, after all. He even said that it would make him happy if he could teach her. He'll find a way to solve their problems, so that they can be together. He will, because he is all-powerful and wise. All she has to do is wait and cope with her sense of uncertainty, all the while playing her not-too-demanding role of the princess in her father's palace. And enjoy the pleasures of life, such as this wonderful dinner with Hasan.

After all, if he stays in Dhagabad and visits her whenever she wishes, it will not be too different from them staying in the same palace.

She settles across the table from him on the sitting pillows and puts a piece of lamb into her mouth. The aromas of spices and herbs make her head spin with the richness of the sensation. She sips her favorite pomegranate cider and looks into his smiling eyes, and she enjoys every bite of the meal, until she feels she cannot possibly eat any more. After the meal, Hasan clears the table with a sweep of a hand, exchanging all the dishes for a steaming teapot, two cups, and a plate of sweet apricot cakes. The princess smiles as the pot rises into the air of its own accord to fill their cups with the finest green tea, and then settles comfortably in its cozy nest of a towel, just like a mother hen settles over her eggs.

"It must be fun to command magic so easily, Hasan," she says thoughtfully.

"Sometimes." Hasan smiles. "Some magic is really fun. Some can be frightening."

"Such as?"

"Such as, for instance, seeing possible futures."

"You mean prophecy?"

"Prophecy as such is not possible," Hasan says. "What one can sometimes see is a possible future that may or may not come to pass. Usually one doesn't know what to do to avoid or ensure the future revealed this way. So it leaves a sense of predetermination that can be frightening. Some people simply cannot handle the knowledge of a terrible fate that awaits them, or their loved ones, without knowing how to change it. They start doing foolish things that in themselves bring the vision to pass."

"What about these texts you spoke about, the original foretellings?"

"In a way they are a form of prophecy too, princess. But nobody knows much about them—that's why they are feared so much. Those few that came to pass were surprisingly accurate."

The princess suppresses a shiver, forcing away the frightening thoughts. The light in the room fades as the sky outside the window slowly acquires the deep purple shades of the evening. The princess remembers that they are not alone only when she sees the flickers of flame in the depths of the room and realizes that the nannies are moving around lighting lamps.

"Where are you going to go, Hasan?" she asks.

An eager smile lights up his face. "I think I'll rent a room in the lower city, as close as possible to the Dhagabad library. Of course, I should also find some work."

"Work?" She looks at him in utmost surprise.

"To earn a living, you know." He grins. "To pay for my food and a roof over my head—to be just like a mortal!"

The princess has been a mortal all her life, but such possibilities have never crossed her mind. She doesn't even know exactly what one can do to earn a living. It makes her wonder if leaving the palace and learning magic has more to it than she thinks.

"So what are you going to do?" she asks cautiously, not to reveal too much of her ignorance.

"The possibilities seem endless," Hasan says dreamily. "I can just make good use of my muscle and become a worker in the Dhagabad port. Or I can become an errand-boy in one of the shops, and stay there for room and board—the life is a bit better, and rich customers sometimes pay handsomely for delivery of their precious goods. I could also do something closer to the actual books—become a guardian in the library, or an assistant to the keeper, or even a scribe... Or"—his eyes light up with mischief—"I could offer my services as a bodyguard to some rich emir, and enjoy leisurely life—and lots of gold—in exchange for my willingness to die in his service!"

"Die?" The princess shudders.

He laughs. "More likely get a bruise or two in some street squabble. It rarely comes to more with rich emirs, even if they often like to think of themselves as the centers of all the deadly intrigues. Besides, I don't think there is any mortal danger that can possibly affect me in any way."

"Well, this seems like a lot of possibilities, Hasan," the princess agrees uncertainly. She is trying to imagine what it would be like for her if she suddenly found herself alone in Dhagabad and had to earn her living. What could she possibly do? What was she really trained in, except history, horseback riding, and some limited needlework? Could she really support herself with those meager talents, or would she have to starve as a beggar because she spent the first seventeen years of her life in other people's care? Maybe she really *is* fit only for one thing—to marry a prince and bear his children, serving as a decoration at the palace ceremonies?

"But you don't really need to earn money, Hasan, do you?" she asks. "I mean, you can get your food and shelter just by magic, can't you?"

"I can," he admits. "But for one thing, such use of magic draws on resources. If I were to create, say, a piece of bread, I have to use up some materials bread is made of. Which means that potentially, if the limit is reached, somebody else would have to go without bread."

The princess frowns, trying to understand. She never gave much thought to where the things Hasan created with his magic came from. But for that matter, she never really thought much about where other things she used came from, either.

"You mean, when you create something, you don't really create it, but transport it from somewhere else?"

"No, but I do use the same materials that nature—or people—use to create the same object. I just do it faster."

"I am not sure I understand."

"Well, princess, imagine I have to light this candle. Which means that I have to make it very hot very fast. Right?"

"Right."

"This action takes energy—something that surrounds us all the time, but in a very unfocused form. For instance, in order to move around, your body takes energy from the food you eat. A tree takes energy from the earth and sun to grow—" He stops, seeing a puzzled look on her face.

"All right, princess, let's make it simpler. Let's go back to the candle. What I need to do in order to light it is to take some energy and focus it into a tiny spot on the candle tip. Right?"

"Right."

"I can focus this energy with a tool. For instance, I can use a crystal ball to focus a beam of the sun. Or, I can do it by magic."

The princess suddenly remembers how, when she was eight years old and was playing with her friend Alamid in the garden with tiny balls of colored crystal, a sunbeam focused through her favorite pink ball had burned her skin. She vividly remembers a sudden sharp pain and a bright red dot on her skin that took days to heal.

"I understand, Hasan," she exclaims. "You focus the energy of the sun to light a candle!"

"In a way, yes," he says, staring at the tip of the candle that suddenly bursts to life with a tiny flame.

"But there is no sun now," the princess protests helplessly, realizing how stupid she must sound. What a terrible student of magic she would make! If she were ever to learn magic, that is.

"There is a lot of sun energy in the air that stays even after the sun goes down," Hasan explains. "It is not as visible as a sunbeam, for instance, but it is still there. Also, there is energy from other sources. Such as, every living being, every creature, and every plant emanates energy as it lives. I can focus your energy to light a candle just as easily. Or mine. But then you, or I, might feel that part of our energy is gone. Not if I just light a candle, of course. You won't feel anything. But if you had to, say, set the whole palace on fire, you would definitely feel exhausted. In fact, you may not have enough energy to do it."

"It looks so simple when you do it, Hasan," she says.

"Actually, focusing energy is second-level magic, princess. An apprentice of magic first needs to learn to see the essence of things."

"Like when you showed me the essence of a stone," she whispers, remembering how, years ago, Hasan showed her a sleeping lizard inside an ordinary piece of gravel.

"Yes." Hasan smiles, and suddenly she feels she is not doing so badly after all. She makes a silent, wholehearted wish that someday she can learn magic and become a powerful sorceress who could be a match to Hasan's powers.

"And that is why you want to work, Hasan?" she asks. "Not to waste energy? But if you make, say, a piece of bread the normal way, it still uses the same energy, doesn't it?"

If only she could have the vaguest idea about how bread is made. Or even what exactly scribes do in the Dhagabad library.

Hasan's smile widens. "Yes, it does, as a matter of fact. You are a very good student, princess!"

She flushes, pleased with herself.

"So, why work, then?" she insists, feeling bolder from the compliment.

"Because it uses energy in a much more balanced way," Hasan explains. "And because it is so much fun to earn a living for a change!"

The room is so dark now that she can barely see his face in the flickering light of the candle he lit with his gaze. In the distant depths of the room the lamps lit by the nannies cast shadows that wander around like giant winged monsters. She stifles a yawn, suddenly feeling so exhausted she can barely sit upright.

"It is past your bedtime, princess," Hasan observes.

"Thank you for reminding me, nanny." She smiles wearily.

"I should get going," he says. "And you should go to sleep."

"I slept so much today, Hasan. I don't understand why I am so sleepy again. I saw three parts of that strange dream already. As if I am reliving the life of that little girl, Thea, in very fast motion."

"What was the last part about?" Hasan asks, suddenly serious.

"She pledged herself to the goddess. But first she cried, until her tears turned to stone."

The princess pauses, seeing Hasan's eyes widen on his suddenly frozen face. His expression looks too much like fear. She snaps back to alertness, forgetting how sleepy she was.

"What is it, Hasan?"

"Tears turned to stone," Hasan says slowly. "How did it happen in your dream?"

"It seemed like some kind of a ritual. The priestesses locked Thea in a dark room to cry. She cried her eyes out, until she - couldn't shed any more tears. And then this priestess, Ganne, came in and scooped her tears off the floor. They looked just like a handful of stones. Ganne told Thea this was an offering to the goddess."

"Go on," he urges. "What happened afterward?"

"They took her to this large ceremonial hall. I think it was the same one where you took me before"—she pauses to take a breath—"except there were no murals of the dancing figures on the walls."

"And?"

The priestesses—the Mistresses—made Thea undress and dance for them. And then they made her say the pledge. I still remember it, word for word. And you know, when I woke up this afternoon, just before you came, it felt as if my tears had turned to stone too. They felt like sand on the pillow. And the words of the pledge were echoing in my head."

"You didn't say it, did you?" Hasan asks sharply.

"Say what?"

"The pledge."

"Well, I might have *pronounced* it—I mean, it was echoing in my ears, and I felt that if I said it out loud it might go away. And it did. Why?"

She almost catches it now—the abyss that opened for a moment at the back of his eyes. It holds despair. But when he looks at her a moment later, it is all gone.

"I think it is important that you sleep now, princess," Hasan says. "I will make sure you don't dream tonight. And that you wake up strong and refreshed tomorrow. I will come to see you as soon as you call me."

"But—," she starts to protest. She has slept enough today. She really wants him to stay just a little bit longer. To have another cup of tea, maybe? To explain why it is that the story of her dreams has affected him so much? To inhale his faint, intoxicating juniper scent that makes her head swim. To look into his calm face and feel reassured. Except that right now his face doesn't seem all that calm.

"Is anything wrong, Hasan?" she asks sleepily.

"Nothing, princess." He reaches over and puts his palm on her head, his fingers embracing her forehead, so that his hand becomes like a cup of energy focused around her face. She feels all worries drain from her mind. Her thoughts spin in a slow, lazy circle, a whirlpool of darkness, as the blanket of quietness falls over her ears. She hears a distant beat of a strange, deeply sounding instrument, a slow rhythm that grows fainter and fainter and finally disappears.

The Foretelling

The wind sweeps over the waves of the dunes. Its long, smooth gusts coil through the desert. They pass over the ghostly garden, along its barely visible paths and tinkling brooks. They stir the transparent branches of the tree crowns, making them momentarily substantial with the grains of sand they pour over the surface of the leaves. The wind moves toward the ancient temple reigning over the sands and pauses at the foot of the roughly hewn staircase.

As the wind approaches the temple, the voices become even more distinct against the rough, cold stone. Anyone listening to its slow, lazy gusts would clearly hear its human tones, which separate themselves in every sweep of dry sand grains. One could almost start to count the voices that seem to endlessly converse with each other in their eternal movement over the desert.

"She is trapped."

"She said the words."

"But she still needs to learn."

"He must leave her."

"They must not stay together."

"Together..."

"Together..."

But the desert is still empty of life, except for those immortal souls trapped in the dunes. There is no one to listen to what the voices of the wind say to each other at the foot of the temple in the heart of the ancient desert.

II

The Temple

Blood Ties

*T*hea lowers to her knees in a slow, smooth movement, like a snake coiling down from a tree branch. The movement continues as she sets a clay dish full of milk and honey on a low stone pedestal. Not a single ripple disturbs the opalescent surface of the liquid.

Slowly relaxing her muscles, Thea looks up toward the rising sun. It is exactly twenty measured breaths until the first sunbeam hits the thick liquid in the cup, lighting it up with a milky, golden glow. It has always been twenty breaths between the time when the chosen apprentice of the temple lowers the cup to the ground and the moment when the goddess smiles on the offering by letting the Sun God touch it with his first sunbeam.

Not anymore. Now it takes twenty-three breaths and one full inhale before the sun hits the cup. Three and a half breaths longer before the goddess smiles on her first daily offering. Three and a half breaths farther from the goddess's favor.

Thea's gaze settles over the slanting surface of the pyramid wall, a dark outline against the gold of the clear eastern sky. The pyramid is not finished yet. Its wall, hewn stepwise, is ending about halfway up toward where its tip should be when it's finished, to rise taller than the temple of the goddess itself. A pyramid tomb to the ruling king, Horankhtot, a monument to his death rising higher than the goddess's temple dedicated to life.

The Mistresses of the temple did everything in their power to prevent this building project. The choice piece of land near the water, across from the great city of Aeth, seems to be too good for a mere burial site, even for a king as great as Horankhtot. For centuries the kings of Aeth have been building their pyramid tombs down the river in the City of the Dead, which now has over two dozen of the great mounds, silently rising their four-sided tips toward the desert sky. Thea cannot help wondering whether the decision to choose a new burial site for the first king of the Eighth Dynasty right next to the temple of the Great Goddess is meant to diminish the temple's growing power before the rulers of the land of Aeth.

Thea has heard rumors that the powerful female priestesses of the Cult of Dance are becoming too much of a force for the male-dominated society of Aeth. The display of power King Horankhtot has shown by taking land from their temple seems to have gained him a lot of popularity among the crowds. People rejoice in diminishing the standing of the goddess's cult. It is even rumored that the priestesses of the goddess who go to the Temple of the Sun to join with its male priests in a holy ritual are not treated as respectfully as before. Eilea—the pretty, shrill-voiced girl who found Thea in the reeds almost ten years ago—came from her last trip to the Temple of the Sun in tears and spent two weeks in seclusion, attended only by the healers, among the horrified gossip of the young apprentices. And now this pyramid, the monument to the decline of the ancient female cult, is rising in steady steps eastward, depriving them of the first sunbeams of the goddess's favor.

Thea's breast slowly rises and falls in steady, measured breaths. Sixteen... Seventeen... Eighteen...

She hears a stir behind her, and as she lets out the air of her twentieth breath, her ears fill with the deep sound of the *tama domga*. The sun may be coming late to the temple, but no earthly deeds of the Aethian kings can make them change the ritual they have been following for many centuries, ever since the Cult of the Dance was born. The goddess smiles on her offerings, with or without the sun.

Thea gets up from the stone beside the cup and joins her sisters in Dance.

A row of bodies in knee-length white tunics moves in a single flow as the sun slowly rises above the half-finished pyramid and lights up the temple of the goddess in its soft golden haze. All of the apprentices are wearing *tadras*—wrist- and ankle-bands covered with bells—and yet no sound comes as their slim bodies move in perfect synchrony under the sunbeams. For years their training has been to learn to move so smoothly that none of the bells in the *tadras* make a sound. Only when this art is perfected can the apprentice priestesses join the morning ritual of the rising sun. To be the one to put out the offering cup is the highest honor of all, and Thea is glowing with pride at having achieved it today, for the first time.

The only sound on the stone platform in front of the temple is the deeply ringing beat of the *tama domga* in the hands of another apprentice, Riomi, the daughter of the temple. Each of them takes turns with the *tama domga* as they become advanced enough to play it, but Thea has never been the one to play *tama domga* yet. Her calling has always been for the Dance.

Absorbed in the flow of the Dance—her smooth, practiced movements blending together perfectly—Thea is still aware of people watching them from the respectful distance of the reed thicket. City folk and villagers, regardless of their views on the cult and its priestesses, gather here every morning to admire the beauty of the Dance. These observers are the reason why they are wearing tunics and not performing the dance naked, as they would in the great hall of the temple. The naked beauty of the goddess's dancers is too much for unprepared strangers to behold.

Thea doesn't care about the observers. She is absorbed in the Dance, in the way each of the movements follows the previous one, fitting into a sequence powerful enough to defy time and space in its flowing rhythm. As she dances, her mind wanders over a great distance. It leaves her body and soars, able to see their small group dancing in front of the temple from above. She dreams that one day her mind might fly off to visit wondrous, faraway places, to show her the great mysteries of the world. She is learning through dance, becoming wiser than she could ever imagine with each step.

As her body senses the vibration of the final beat on the *tama domga*, she freezes along with the other apprentices, now still, like a row of statues.

"Well done," says a deep voice behind her.

Thea turns to look into the narrow ebony eyes of Mistress Ganne, the priestess who took her into the temple. Ganne became a Mistress last year, at an unusually young age that speaks of her incredible talent. Her praise means a lot to any apprentice, and especially to Thea, who has felt a special bond to Ganne since the day she was first brought to the temple.

"Thank you, Mistress Ganne," Thea says, lowering her eyes, as appropriate when talking to a senior.

"Are you going somewhere?" Ganne asks.

The hour after the morning ritual, before breakfast, is usually free. In that hour priestesses and apprentices often go down to the river for a swim and check the sacrifice spot, to see if there is a girl tied up there whom the goddess might want—as a servant to the temple, or, perhaps, as an apprentice, like Thea.

"Riomi and I were going down to the river, Mistress Ganne," Thea says, her eyes still lowered.

"There is a woman over there who wants to talk to you," Ganne says. "She is waiting on the east platform. We gave her permission to see you. You may take off your *tadras* before you go."

"Should I see her, Mistress?" Thea asks. She has no one outside the temple whom she might want to see.

"I do not command you to go, Thea," Ganne answers levelly. "But I think you should."

Thea keeps her eyes down to suppress both her curiosity at who her unknown visitor might be and her disappointment at not going with Riomi and the other girls to take a morning swim and to walk by the sacrifice spot. It is always an event to bring a new girl from the river, especially if she is good enough to become an apprentice. Besides, Thea has grown very fond of Riomi, a quiet girl born in the temple to one of the priestesses after the Ritual of the Sun.

As the other apprentices disappear through the temple door to change for the swim, Thea carefully unfastens the laces on her *tadras* and slips them off her wrists and ankles. By habit she is not making any sound with them—hearing a bell of a *tadra* has become such a taboo that she cannot ever think of letting go of her guard to the point of making one of the tiny bells ring. It has been a large part of her early training to learn to move, dance, and perform other duties with her *tadras* completely mute. Now the absence of their weight on her arms and legs makes her feel light and empty.

As she walks down the path toward the east platform, half-hidden from the temple entrance by a row of cypress trees, she makes out a whole group of waiting women. She can count five younger women and an older one in the middle, all of them dressed poorly and bearing some likeness to each other. As she approaches the group, they start to seem vaguely familiar. But nothing really stirs in her soul. Who could she possibly know, or care for, in the outside world?

She stops in front of the older woman, careful to keep her face set into a calm mask of a trained apprentice, no thoughts or feelings betrayed.

"Thea?" the old woman says in a cracked voice. She steps closer to peer into Thea's face. A tear rolls down her cheek and disappears in the cracks of her withered skin. Thea is startled to see that the woman is actually not that old, but she looks a lot older from the permanent imprint of worry etched into her face. Her skin looks like a dry parchment, damaged by the constant work of the elements. Only her hair, grayish but still dark, braided into a snakelike mass, is familiar.

Ten years ago this woman was Thea's mother.

"Thea, my girl." The woman throws her bony arms around Thea's motionless form and buries her head on Thea's shoulder, her body shaking with sobs.

Over the woman's head Thea impassively studies the

group of five young women who are watching the scene with various degrees of concern.

They must be Thea's sisters. Only Thea remembers to have had six. There are only five of them standing here now. Quite possibly Thea could even recall their names. But why would she want to bother?

The sobbing woman seems to realize that there is no response to her embrace. She steps away, looking searchingly into Thea's eyes.

"Thea, my little one! Don't you remember me? I am your mother!"

Thea takes a step back, rippling her muscles to shake off the woman's hands, which still clutch her elbows.

"There is no mortal who dares to call herself my mother, old woman," she says levelly, keeping her voice free of emotion as she learned from the older priestesses in the temple. "I am the daughter of the Great Goddess. You would do well to remember that before putting your hands on me again."

The woman clasps her hands to her mouth to stifle what sounds half like a sob and half like a gasp for air. One of the girls reaches out to help steady her as she sways on her feet.

"What have they done to you, my little girl?" the woman says pleadingly. "Remember us? These are your sisters. They all grew up to be very pretty, just like you! Except little Ishana—she drowned in the Great River six years ago." The woman pauses to brush away a tear and looks into Thea's face with so much plea it could quite possibly melt a stone. "We are your family!" The woman's voice rises into a wail. "Don't you remember us at all?"

"My sisters are in the temple," Thea says coldly. "If you want something, you should talk to one of the priestesses, old woman."

She turns to leave and pauses as the bony hands catch her from behind. She suppresses a shudder of revolt that would have surely rung her *tadras* if she was wearing them right now.

"Wait!" the old woman pleads. "You don't have to talk to me, just don't go! Let me just look at you, at my sweet little girl! I missed you so much! You grew up to be such a beauty! We all missed you! We were so happy to learn that Sobek spared your life and the temple is training you as an apprentice! If only I didn't have to leave you back then, but we were starving, and everyone said I should abandon the youngest girl because she was too little to work! If only I could make you understand—and forgive me! The house was so empty after you were gone..." The woman's voice drowns in sobs that shake her feeble body, as if somebody is dropping stones onto her sagging shoulders. Thea pauses, uncertain of what to do.

"Please don't go!" the oldest of the sisters joins in, mistaking Thea's hesitation for a glimpse of feeling. "It was so hard to get permission to see you! Mother has been talking about this for a whole month!"

Thea stands still, without turning. She knows the name of the woman who just spoke to her. Leota, the oldest sister.

Once again she sends a complex wave through her body to shake off the bony grip of the feeble hands of the woman she once called her mother. She walks away toward the temple without turning, to the rising wail of voices behind her back.

"Fine!" a younger, angrier voice yells behind her. *Sister Betanat,* Thea recalls. "If you are too proud to know your family—fine! Go away! One day you'll find what it is like to be alone! You'll beg mother to forgive you yet!"

Thea doesn't stop. In smooth, steady strides she walks up the path and disappears through the temple door.

The princess pauses as one of the bells on her left arm gives a gentle ring. She waits for the echoes of the tiny bell, painfully loud in the dead quiet of her room, to die out before resuming the slow movement of the *tadra* exercise. Ten more catlike paces to the left. Sixteen to the right. Two more sets, slowly raising her arms above her head and lowering them back to her sides. Not much at all, if one didn't have to worry about the tiny bells covering the *tadra*s on the wrists and ankles.

The Goddess of Dance

The princess made the *tadra*s herself, with the help from Zulbagad, a skillful seamstress and her teacher in needlework. In her dreams the princess has participated in *tadra* practices through Thea so many times that her body has been increasingly missing doing it in her waking life. She felt an almost physical urge to make the *tadra*s and set aside a regular practice time. Of course she also misses the incredible feeling of being able to move with *tadra*s completely silent on her limbs, but she is definitely not as good as Thea—not yet. In the past months Thea in her dreams has aged ten years while the princess is still seventeen, waiting for her fate to be decided.

The last movements of the exercise leave her exhausted, all her muscles aching, her forehead covered with sweat. At the beginning it took her hours to finish the novice exercise set. Later she learned, with Thea's help, that the secret of moving without disturbing the *tadra*s too much lies in keeping all the muscles tight. The first attempts to do it right caused terrible muscle cramps, but those efforts seem to have been well rewarded. It now takes her only a little bit over an hour. She still cannot quite reach the next difficulty level, but even with her current skill she is much more fit than she was three months ago, and she has even gotten some approving comments from her riding teacher about it.

All finished, she takes several deep breaths before slowly taking off the *tadra*s, trying not to disturb them even though the exercise is over. The absence of their weight on her limbs makes her feel light as a feather, filled with energy despite her tiredness. Soon, when her *tadra* skills improve, she can begin to learn the Dance. Not the same, of course, with no one to observe her progress and make comments about what to improve on. But important nevertheless.

She really wants to learn to beat the slow, complicated rhythm of the Dance on the *tama domga*, but there is no way she can ever lay her hands on that rare and unusual instrument, which seems to have completely disappeared from the world after the decease of the Cult of the Dance. She knows very well what a *tama domga* looks like—an oval drum, with strings attached behind the surface, so that every beat echoes with a deep musical sound. She has tried many times to re-produce it on a regular drum, borrowed from the palace entertainers, but it definitely lacks a whole spectrum of sounds that make her version of the beat of the Dance almost unrecognizable.

Of course, she could ask Hasan to make her a *tama domga*. But something unclear even to her keeps her from telling Hasan the details of her dreams, and even the fact that she now practices with *tadra*s. She is telling herself that she wants to learn the Dance as a surprise, to demonstrate it to him one day. Of course, the real Dance is done naked, and *that* makes the idea of dancing in his presence unthinkable.

She submerges into the cooling water of the bath, allowing herself a moment of relaxation before getting up and dressing for her afternoon meal. A quick one. Because then, afterward, she can wander off into a distant corner of the garden and summon Hasan.

During the past three months, since Hasan was banished from the palace, they have been seeing each other every day without failure, meeting at the princess's favorite glade in the far end of the garden. As Hasan appears, answering her summons, he always makes himself invisible to everybody except her, and this way they can talk as long as they like without the fear of being discovered. To the princess's watchful wardens it appears as if she has taken to lonely walks in the garden—quite understandable, with the natural melancholy of a new bride-to-be. It also seems quite understandable that she is spending so much time in her favorite garden glade—after all, she is about to leave this place forever. And if one of her overzealous guards were to wander too close to the princess's refuge, the most they could hear is her talking to herself, which, if strange in itself, doesn't seem to be all that surprising considering all the other strangeness of the princess's behavior. She has received far too much education for an eligible bride. She has to get over most of it by the time she is given away to her new husband.

As the princess slowly puts her clothes on, enjoying the pleasant warmth in her exercised body, she hears noise outside. Feet running back and forth in the corridor. Muffled voices, shouting with excitement.

"Princess!" Nanny Airagad calls outside the door.

"Come in, nanny!" the princess exclaims.

This new procedure, established by the princess after withstanding a lot of pursed lips and side glances, seems to work perfectly. Nobody can walk into her room now without her permission, and after lots of initial resentment, it does seem to have become the most natural arrangement. After all, everyone has to ask the sultaness's permission to enter her room, except perhaps for the faithful Nimeth. The princess will become a sultaness herself in due time. It seems only proper that she should be treated with the same kind of respect. It also comes in quite handy with all her new activities that the nannies don't have to know about, such as *tadra* and drum practices.

As usual when she is excited about something, Nanny Airagad bursts into the room like a sandstorm, upsetting even the heavy door curtain in her powerful gust. She is closely followed by Sadie, a new slave girl from Veridue, sent over as a gift to the princess from her future husband. A plain, shy girl, with big watery eyes, she seems to be regarded by everybody in the palace as a natural addition to the furniture in the princess's quarters rather than as a living person. The princess feels sorry for the girl, who must be terribly lonely in her new surroundings, but there seems to be nothing she can do about it. She could, perhaps, make Sadie her new companion, but the princess feels far too preoccupied with her own problems right now, and definitely not up to sharing her time with a stranger. As a result, the new Veriduan girl remains a shadow in her presence, always there when allowed, never the focus of anyone's attention. The princess cannot help thinking that such a position at her side gives Sadie a unique opportunity to report on her every move to some interested ears, but the slave girl is so young and innocent-looking that such thoughts about her seem almost shameful. After all, Sadie never even talks to anyone except her pet bird, a sparrow hawk that she reportedly keeps in her room and lets hunt freely outside of the city. The princess often thinks that perhaps she should at least learn more about her new servant, likely to remain with her for a long time, but she keeps putting it off.

She slides an uninterested glance over Sadie and turns to Nanny Airagad, who seems ready to burst with excitement.

"What is it, nanny?" the princess asks patiently, giving the woman time to catch her breath.

"The sultan—the sultan—has a son!" Airagad stops, helplessly waving her arms that seem to be far ahead of the limits of her breath. *She must have run all the way from the central palace*, the princess thinks.

"What do you mean?" she asks sharply. She is now old enough to know, like everybody else, that the sultan seems to be unable to father a healthy boy, and thus she, his oldest daughter, has to bear the responsibility to be his heiress. She knows that the sultaness and many concubines have given birth to the sultan's sons, but that the babies invariably died at birth or very soon after. Surely the birth of another son cannot be such big news. And yet, there is something different in the way Nanny Airagad is talking about it now. Although young and excitable, Airagad is not known to favor running the long corridors between the palace wings without a good reason.

The nanny takes a deep breath and finally starts talking in a more or less normal voice.

"Albiorita had a son last night! He is still alive today, and Doctor Rashid says there is no sign that the boy is unhealthy. The sultan is beside himself with joy! He is talking about preparing the biggest feast ever as soon as Albiorita is well enough. He is treating her almost like a—a *wife*!"

The touch of disgust in Airagad's voice is obvious. No one in the palace approves of the way the sultan took Albiorita, his favorite concubine, out of the harem to live with him in the palace. A sultan is supposed to have only one wife, the sultaness. All his other women should be hidden away from men's eyes. Although Albiorita never appears in public without covering her face, the palace moralists, among whom the sultaness's and the princess's servants are the first, sneer at her presence whenever they can.

Of course, now everything might change. If Albiorita has managed to be the one to fulfill the sultan's dream and bear him a healthy son, her rank in the palace will fly up to immeasurable heights. She may even threaten the sultaness's place one day.

The princess sighs. If this had happened earlier, it might have relieved her of her role as heiress to the throne. Her marriage might not have been so important to the kingdom. She might not have needed to be betrothed to Prince Amir. Maybe now, when the birth of a brother puts her rank in question, Prince Amir will refuse to marry her? No, this seems to be too much to hope for.

"Is Doctor Rashid certain this child is different?" she asks.

"He seems to be," Airagad says. "I overheard him talking to the grand vizier. He said it was a big and healthy boy, very active for a newborn."

"If only Hasan could see him!" the princess exclaims. "He would know!"

"I don't think the sultan will let Hasan, or anyone with that kind of power, near his son. I heard that he is really beside himself with joy and concern. I only wish the kingdom could bear such strong emotions from its ruler," Airagad observes practically.

"Well, I think we should at least be happy for my father," the princess says. "He wanted a son so much!"

She remembers very well the sultan's empty eyes after one of his sons in the harem was born dead. She has seen the glances full of hope that he has been throwing at the pregnant Albiorita during the past few months. And she has heard a great deal of gossip, some of it related to her own destiny as the heiress to the throne.

She really does feel glad that the sultan's wholehearted wish to have a son has come to pass. And she hopes that whatever change this major news brings into her life, it will be a positive one.

The Wizards of Dimeshq

*T*he faint light of a single lantern is almost lost in the giant dark room. As before, Caliph Agabei feels strangely unnerved by this preference for darkness that his new allies seem to have. Of course, he could just tell them that he likes to have more light in the room; his wish, as that of a guest, is very likely to be honored. But it is too important for him to get full cooperation from the sultan of Dimeshq and his court mage, Abdulla the Wizard. He cannot afford to risk angering them in any way.

Agabei's eyes more guess than see a movement of the heavy door curtain. A dark shape noiselessly slides across the soft Baskarian rug toward the low sofa where the caliph is patiently awaiting, for the second time, his audience with the sultan of Dimeshq. The first time, after keeping Agabei in the dark room for quite a while, his majesty finally felt too busy to see his fellow ruler from the trade land of Megina. *No matter*, Agabei thinks. *If the sultan is such a fool that he cannot tell an enemy from an ally, it gives me all the more power.* Fools are easy to manipulate. This simple rule has never yet failed Agabei.

Of course there is an unnerving possibility that the sultan of Dimeshq is no fool. At least his court mage, Abdulla, doesn't seem to be one. But Agabei prefers not to think about that possibility too much.

He watches the court mage approach him in catlike steps.

At first glance Abdulla the Wizard seems very young, no more than a boy with a lively face and black, dryly sparkling eyes. As one looks longer, however, one can notice an ageless quality about the mage, a sort of glaze covering his features as if to distance him from everyone else in a cold, remote shell. It is unnerving to think that this strange man is one of the oldest beings Agabei has ever seen, save for Shogat and Hasan. He is also extremely powerful, as Agabei has to constantly remind himself. It is so easy to forget all that, looking at the thin, impatient youth, too slim for his wizard's robes, approaching him from the dark depths of the Dimeshquian palace.

"Greetings, O mighty one," Agabei murmurs, rising from his seat and folding his body into one of the most respectful bows he knows, short of kneeling on the floor.

Abdulla pauses in his steps and returns the bow with an air of impatience of one who never cared for formalities. Agabei knows it not to be true, but he takes special care to keep his thoughts to himself.

"His majesty sends his apologies," Abdulla says in his dry, ringing voice that sends shivers through Agabei's spine. "He won't be able to join us. However, he did permit me to discuss our plans with you."

"I am deeply gratified," Agabei says, suppressing his displeasure. He is willing to go along with the sultan's game, but only to a certain point. If the sultan thinks that Agabei needs permission to discuss his plans with Abdulla, he is missing the point of their interactions.

"His majesty and I came up with a plan that could make Hasan... indisposed," Abdulla continues, ignoring the deep undertones in the caliph's voice. "For the past centuries we have been searching for all sources of information about the djinns. I—we—have some personal interest in it."

This quick mistake and the quick recovery don't escape Agabei's ears. He is beginning to wonder how much power the sultan of Dimeshq really has over his court mage. Perhaps the reason for the sultan's indisposition lies not in his own wishes, but in Abdulla's orders?

"I am listening, O wise Abdulla," he says carefully, not to

reveal any of his doubts.

"As you surely know, Hasan's freedom changes everything we know about the djinns," Abdulla says levelly. "It creates an imbalance of powers that is, for certain reasons... inconvenient. We also learned that in exchange for... containing him again, we may obtain a piece of information, invaluable to the great sultan of Dimeshq and his meek servant." Abdulla folds his hands on his chest and lowers his eyes in a humble gesture. It looks so unnatural in the court mage that Agabei cannot suppress a shiver.

What a disturbing man, he thinks. *I hope I didn't get myself into a worse trouble by dealing with him.*

"The powers to contain an all-powerful wizard," Abdulla continues, "lie in the ancient desert outside this world. That is, of course, if he is still all-powerful."

"I am not sure I understand," Agabei says slowly. "Do you have reason to doubt his powers?"

"Perhaps I am complicating matters too much by tiring our guest's ears with too many details," Abdulla says ceremoniously. "Let me merely say that we feel we need extra precautions in dealing with a wizard of such power as we believe Hasan commands. We also feel we may have found a way to make him enter the desert and trigger the same power that imprisoned him originally to contain him again."

"Make him a djinn once more, you mean?" Agabei's heart leaps with hope. If only they could imprison the meddling djinn again, it would make all the difference. Princess Gul'Agdar doesn't even own Hasan anymore. Imprisoned, Hasan won't be able to do anything at all to interfere with Agabei's plans for her.

"Yes," Abdulla says, with a dark flicker in his eyes that makes Agabei shiver again.

"That would be brilliant, O mighty Abdulla!" Agabei exclaims. "If there is anything in my power I can do to help..."

A gleam in Abdulla's eyes makes him pause and momentarily regret his hasty offer. There are many things in his power that he is not willing to do to help this mysterious wizard and his more than mysterious master. He finds himself wondering exactly how powerful Abdulla the Wizard is. He looks at Abdulla's wrists, searching for the metal bracelets marking the djinn, and doesn't find any. Their absence, however, doesn't reassure him one bit.

"We heard that you possess a djinn, caliph?" Abdulla says conversationally.

Agabei's heart sinks.

"Yes, I do," he says, not daring to deny it for the fear of planting distrust in his powerful ally's mind. He doubts there is much room for trust in the dark labyrinths of Abdulla's mind, anyway.

"May I talk to him?" Abdulla asks in a tone that doesn't leave room for refusal.

With reluctance Agabei pulls out an elegant lamp of smooth, dark bronze. He sets it on the table in front of him and, under Abdulla's freezing gaze, softly caresses it with his hand.

"Shogat," he whispers. "I wish for you to appear in here."

As the smoke coils out of the lamp's opening, he silently prays that she doesn't respect his usual wish to appear before him scantily clad, that she will have the sense to wear her gray tunic he normally resents so much. He cannot bear to think of Abdulla's cold eyes falling on her breathtakingly bare stomach.

He notices Abdulla watching him from the corner of his eye, as if enjoying his obvious discomfort.

"This is Shogat," Agabei says, pointing nervously at the cloud of gray mist, quickly taking the shape of a motionless woman, her head bent. Thankfully, she must have heard his prayer. She is wearing her long gray tunic and the necklace with a snake pattern. The priestess's outfit from the Temple of the Dance.

As Shogat materializes fully and Abdulla takes in all her features, his eyes widen in awe.

"A Mistress of the Dance?" he whispers. "How did you manage to come by such a treasure, caliph?"

"I found her in the ancient desert," Agabei says reluctantly.

"Quite impressive," Abdulla observes darkly. His eyes

seem to eat Shogat alive. Even Agabei shrinks from his gaze. It is quite reassuring for his plans to see that Hasan has such a powerful enemy, but does the caliph truly want such a dangerous ally after all?

"What is she worth to you?" Abdulla asks. "If your plan works, and Princess Gul'Agdar becomes a djinn, you won't be able to command both of them, you know."

"I know," Agabei says, his mouth dry. He cannot bear to think of parting with Shogat. Is he really plotting something that will make such a thing likely?

"We need a djinn to help us capture Hasan," Abdulla goes on. "We need you to leave your djinn with us for a while."

"If she stays, I'll stay too." Agabei's lips become cold. He - didn't mean to oppose this frightening wizard. He was prepared to do anything he asked. But leaving Shogat in his hands? The thought itself makes his heart sink. He never knew he was so attached to Shogat before, and the strength of his response surprises him.

Of course, with Shogat's help, he can probably defeat both Abdulla and the elusive sultan of Dimeshq. But it doesn't seem like a good idea to fight them. They know too much of his plans. They might even decide to capture Princess Gul'Agdar themselves. Besides, who knows what else Abdulla the Wizard has up his sleeve?

Abdulla's cold gaze slides over Agabei and stops on Shogat again.

"Tell her to perform the Sacred Dance for me," he says in a tone that sounds more than a bit like an order. "I haven't seen the real Dance of the Goddess for two thousand years!"

"Do what he asks, Shogat," Agabei says, his lips stiff with effort. His whole being screams against it. But is he really prepared to defy this frightening man for such a seemingly innocent request?

"She must be a great lover," Abdulla observes as if to himself, as he watches Shogat pull off her tunic in the precise, practiced move of one who has done it too many times to perform the Dance before.

The caliph rolls his eyes in frustration. Of course the Sacred Dance is done naked. He hasn't asked Shogat to dance it for a long time, so he forgot. He never cared for her temple habits anyway.

He raises his gaze to the ceiling, blind with fury, as he hears the beat of the unseen instrument. The light in the room suddenly shines much brighter than before. Undoubtedly Abdulla must have summoned it to help him see the Dance better. He raises his eyes through the pounding of blood in his temples that makes him feel hot and burning, blurring his vision and hearing. And he moves his lips in a silent promise that he, with all his heart, intends to keep:

You'll pay for this, Abdulla the Wizard.

You move to the beat of the tama domga *you summoned from the depths of your past, your body shifting into the long-forgotten shapes of the Sacred Dance. Just like back then, you feel your mind fly free, free of your imprisonment, free of your absolute power, free of anything except the Dance. You feel all your knowledge, all your spiritual perception that allows you to simultaneously sense everything that is happening in the world enfold you, as if setting you free from the bonds of your slavery, from the command of your willful master who puts you so freely at his every use. You feel once again almost alive, the Dancer, the priestess to the goddess, the Mistress of the temple, and the little frightened girl who once pledged herself to the goddess till the end of her days.*

You wish bitterly that the dance, the real Dance, could set you free by the mercy of an unknown force that imprisoned you because you were too good, because through your dance you were able to learn everything there is to know in this world.

Hasan quickly moves his eyes along the endless shelves, summoning his inner vision to see through the dusty book covers. The books are talking to him, filling his mind with excitement. He welcomes the familiar sense of joyful peace, the very feeling that made him spend so much of his life in the company of books. He is eager to find the information he wants, but even his hurry cannot possibly deprive him of that special moment of stepping into a library full of books.

He needs to find the information about the ancient desert quickly. He doesn't have much time to find answers to the questions that may be critical to the survival of the world. His existence, his freedom, for all he knows, is impossible. He needs to learn what happened to him, and what is likely to come out of it. He needs to know the limits of his powers, if there indeed are any, and what will happen if he attempts to push those limits by learning even more than he already knows and by attempting to extend his knowledge into the other world that lies beyond the powers of the djinns. He needs to discover the source of the prophecy that foretold many centuries ago that the one who frees a djinn may become a threat to the entire existence of the world.

For a thousandth time he brings to mind the details of the scroll long lost, the original foretelling that seems to have disappeared from the world as finally as if it were swept away by the ancient desert itself. A magic scroll so powerful that merely touching it required summoning great power, and written in a language of which a mere word pronounced aloud could stop a bird in its flight. A scroll whose title contained the strange word familiar to him from the Agritian scroll, a word whose meaning he didn't quite comprehend back then and which later defined his existence for two thousand years. *Djinn.*

Although the exact words of the scroll, untranslatable to any of the ordinary languages, are vague in his memory, Hasan remembers its meaning very well. It said that if someone finds a way to free a djinn, such a one will also cause a great imbalance of powers that will lead to the destruction of the existing world. The two possible escapes from such destiny are either to isolate such a person from the use of any magic at all, or to train him as quickly as possible, so that he can in turn become a djinn. The scroll told that since the one who can free a djinn is bound to possess magic already, the only real possibility is to contain him as a djinn. Only the containment of this unique power and its bearer can save the world and its order, the scroll said.

Hasan is placing great faith in the alternative mentioned in the scroll. True, the one who frees a djinn is expected to possess enormous magical powers. But as it turns out, the princess, the one who actually did it, knows no magic at all. Perhaps they can avoid the horrifying possibilities mentioned in the scroll by isolating the princess from learning any magic. This may leave some hope for her to follow the first alternative and lead a normal life, unaffected by the ancient powers that tortured Hasan so cruelly for two millennia.

Later on Hasan encountered many translations of this text, or rather its retellings into the more common languages. The latest one he saw was an Agritian scroll in the Dimeshquian library that he noticed in passing when he was here with the princess's grandmother, twenty or so years ago. He recently tried to find it again and failed. The text seems to have disappeared without a trace, along with the old library keeper, now replaced by a new one, thin and nervous, completely unwilling to cooperate with any customer who would even suggest the existence of such a useless piece of parchment.

Hasan slowly moves along the row of shelves that stretches all the way to the distant skylights of the dome. He could spend months going through the contents of these volumes, much of it familiar to him, rewritten or retold by scribes and storytellers of the past two millennia, sometimes to the point of being completely unrecognizable. Some of them are new, and his probing mind notes them with interest to return to later. He would have loved to stay here and read, just read without the urge to discover something that bears direct consequence to his fate. But he has no time to spare. It has been six months since he was set free by the princess, and he has not yet succeeded in his search.

He pauses, extending his inner vision to the farther shelves, near the hidden entrance to the labyrinth, where he remembers last seeing the scroll. Something is not right here. It is as if somebody has deliberately swept through this library and removed all the evidence of the ancient desert and the djinns.

Hasan stops, trying to catch the fleeting impression of something that gave him that thought. A trace in the air, a magic signature that seems vaguely familiar to him.

Perhaps I am going about this the wrong way, he thinks. *If these books contained what I am looking for, I would have found it already. Perhaps instead of thinking of what I need to find, I have to think of who else might want to find the same information.*

There are not many wizards in this world who are not djinns and yet are powerful enough to identify the necessary information and make use of it. Hasan is sure he knows most, if not all, of them. Of course, there are also those who are not quite powerful enough but who possess djinns and thus are capable of using powerful help to learn anything they want. One might question how wise it would be to show your djinn any information that could possibly lead him to discover a way to his own freedom. But not all the djinn owners are wise. And, after all, before Hasan's case, it was considered absolutely impossible to free a djinn.

Hasan pauses again. Whoever left the trace he just detected in the air must have been aware that some wizards, at least the very powerful ones, might be able to sense it. In fact, the owner of the trace might even have expected that a wizard of extreme powers would eventually end up in the Dimeshquian library, and left the trace deliberately to attract such a wizard's attention. Something like that would, of course, require a lot of power. And a lot of wit. But is it impossible?

Hasan searches his mind for wizards who, he knows, are still alive and at the same time are capable of such a trick. The most powerful wizard he knows of is the old sage Al Haggat from one of the Stiktian tribes. As far as Hasan knows, the sage still lives with his tribesmen in the heights of the Halabean Range, practicing the Cult of Release and quite content with his simple ways of life. The sage has students and followers scattered throughout the lands, but as far as Hasan knows neither the sage, nor those who choose to follow his ways, have any interest in djinn-making. *They will be, as soon as the first of them achieves absolute power*, Hasan thinks. *But not yet.*

He can sense that the trace in the dusty air of the library doesn't belong to a djinn. There is an inhuman quality to the traces the djinns leave that has become so painfully familiar to Hasan that he can now sense it almost as naturally as breathing. The trace definitely doesn't have that quality. It belongs to a human, even if a human possessing outstanding powers.

Hasan suddenly realizes that he doesn't know that many wizards capable of leaving such a trace. Zobeide could have done something like that in the times of her youth, but she is now secluded to her Island of the Elements and is not into tricks anymore. If she wanted to achieve absolute power and become a djinn, she has had many chances to do that. Hasan is fairly certain Zobeide would be above such things now. That only leaves a few other possibilities. The caliph of Megina, Abu Alim Agabei, a wizard of considerable powers and possessing a djinn on top of that, is one. However if this was the caliph's work, his djinn would have left a trace here too—or at least the djinn's trace would have surely made this display much more impressive. The court mage of Avallahaim, sage Zor Ag Gad, even more powerful than the caliph, and definitely ambitious enough to wish for more power, is another. However, there seems to be no need for him to leave a trace of his presence here, so far away from Avallahaim; even one as ambitious as Zor Ag Gad would not wish to extend his influence over the mages in such distant lands. Perhaps, Abdulla, Hasan's former student?

As far as Hasan knows, Abdulla is still here, in Dimeshq, and over the years he has gained an incredible amount of power. In their recent encounter in the Temple of the Dance Abdulla came close to killing Hasan, and only the princess's interference saved Hasan from a deadly blow. Yes, Abdulla could have removed all the relevant texts from the library and left this trace in the air to warn the others who might come after him. Or, could he?

Hasan pauses for a second, trying to picture Abdulla. However likely it may seem, he has real trouble imagining

Abdulla doing something so carefully plotted, so calculated for many steps ahead. Abdulla has always been one of those who strike quickly, with lots of force, not caring much about the consequences. At least, that was the way of Abdulla the Apprentice back in the old days, and that seemed to be the way of Abdulla the Wizard last time Hasan encountered him in the temple. If Hasan were to bet, he would say this is not Abdulla's work. But if not Abdulla, then who?

Hasan extends his senses toward the magic trace. It seems long and thin like a wisp, leading somewhere into the darkness behind the last bookcase, past the invisible entrance to the labyrinth, through the library wall. As Hasan removes the substance from his body to be able to freely follow the trace, and steps face-first into the cool, gray stone, he senses the trace become larger, stronger, as if the library and the proximity of the labyrinth have shielded its full power.

Although the trace is stronger outside, it is much harder to follow it in the open air, with wind sweeping through the Plaza of Mages and along the narrow city streets. Focused on not losing it, Hasan comes to his senses only when he starts to hear screams and gasps all around him and realizes that he has been walking straight through the people in the noisy plaza, busy with activity. He smiles apologetically to an elderly woman who is backing off from him as fast as the crowd allows, hears a scream in his ear as he accidentally walks through a little girl under his feet, and at that moment loses the trace he was following.

He stops, not caring about the crowd anymore. The trace was here just a moment ago; he is sure of that. Now it is completely gone, as if he simply imagined it before.

Returning substance to his body, he retraces his steps into the library, ignoring the stare of the library keeper who saw him walk through the very same door half an hour ago and never come out again. He stretches all his feelings, trying to catch the same trace again, but it is simply not there at all.

Hasan relaxes, suddenly feeling very tired. This is much more serious than he thought. A wizard who can simply leave a trace is one thing. A wizard who can later remove the trace on command is a completely different matter. This is not to be taken lightly at all. And it considerably narrows Hasan's list of possible people who could do it, a list that wasn't very big to start with.

Perhaps he should pay a visit to his former apprentice, Abdulla, and try to find out who is behind all this? Yes, that does seem like a good idea.

Once again he leaves the library through the wall, in the exact place he passed a short time ago, which now bears no sign of the strange trace. Searching with his feelings for the available sources of magic in the vicinity, he separates one of them and sets out on his way to what he believes to be Abdulla's house.

The Lady of the Island

*A*gabei is gloomily watching the water splash around the boat. He hates sailing. And the boat Shogat summoned feels far too tiny to brave the Veriduan Sea.

"Isn't there any other way, Shogat?" he asks. "couldn't you have carried me straight to the island instead?"

"Nobody can approach the Island of the Elements in any way except by boat," Shogat answers impassively, shifting the sail to catch more wind.

"couldn't you have at least brought us closer to it?" Agabei asks, studying what looks like a dim bluish shadow on the horizon.

"This is the boundary of the island's magic," Shogat replies.

"I thought you were all-powerful," Agabei grumbles, settling deeper into the boat to avoid watching the greedy splashes of white-crested waves. They look like little animals, trying to eat him alive and rocking the boat to make their prey more accessible. He hates to think of what lies beneath, down in the depths of this turquoise-blue water. What if the monsters lurking in there come up this minute to swallow them and their boat?

"Is your magic ineffective here, Shogat?" he asks uneasily.

"It is effective, master. I just cannot use it to reach the island."

"Doesn't make sense to me," Agabei says. "Why would the

Elements want their followers to become sailors as well?"

"Water and Air are Elements, and they don't like to be conquered by magic, master. They have a right to restrict people from doing it near their sanctuary."

"I suppose so," Agabei agrees grumpily. While this information doesn't make him enjoy sailing any more, it does make sense. It also makes him uneasily aware that such an arrangement conveniently puts the Elements in complete control of who can reach their island at all. If there suddenly was a storm, for instance, it is not at all obvious whether Shogat could do anything to save them. They would never reach the island, for sure.

The island actually seems to be approaching much faster than Agabei thought. He can already make out a mountain off to one side that makes it look like a giant animal lying in the water. He can also make out the narrow opening of a bay, and jagged reefs marked by white blobs of angrily boiling foam.

"Are we going into that bay?" he asks nervously.

"Yes, master."

Shogat's voice sounds calm, but Agabei imagines a note of sarcasm in it. Perhaps she is right to be sarcastic about a grown man, over three hundred years old, desperately afraid of water. But Agabei never learned to swim, and he is not positive that Shogat's loyalty to him is strong enough to rush to his rescue if he doesn't have a chance to ask her for it. Besides, she is probably angry at him for not letting her stay with Abdulla in Dimeshq. She did seem quite eager to perform that naked dance of hers for the court mage. Maybe she and Abdulla made some kind of arrangement behind Agabei's back?

"Shogat," he calls out gloomily.

"Master?"

"Did you enjoy dancing for *him*?"

"I assume you mean Abdulla the Wizard, master?"

"Yes, him."

"I always enjoy fulfilling my master's wishes," Shogat replies, and turns her attention to the sail.

Agabei clenches his teeth. Now he has no doubt Shogat is

mocking him. But he also has no way of restraining her. Not now, when he is completely at her mercy and at the mercy of this tiny sailboat.

The jagged teeth of the reefs appear all around them so suddenly that the caliph's heart jumps in terror. The boat dangerously rocks under his weight.

"couldn't you at least put up some protection against these reefs?" he demands.

"The reefs are part of the element Earth," comes the reply. "They don't like to be conquered either."

Agabei tries to shut his eyes, but the sharp turns and tugs of the boat just make it worse. He notices that Shogat has put away the sail and is now maneuvering with a short, wide oar. In her strong hands the oar seems to turn the boat almost in place.

To take his mind off it, Agabei directs his gaze toward the perfect oval of the bay, bordered on the far end by a white band of coral sand. Beyond the sand stretches the wild greenery of the jungle.

Everything appears empty.

"How do we find this fey Zobeide?" he asks impatiently as Shogat guides the boat between the last two reefs into the still waters of the bay.

"It won't be hard, master," Shogat replies. "And I believe she can hear us right now."

Agabei bites his tongue. He has almost let his irritation threaten his chances with Zobeide. He needs to be more careful, no matter how annoying Shogat chooses to be at the moment.

The boat gently hits the sand. Shogat lightly jumps into the water and, with an impassive face, offers a hand to Agabei.

"It is not deep, master," she says, her expression a mask of devilishly calm sarcasm.

Ignoring her hand, Agabei heavily drops overboard. The warm water comes up to his knees, but the splash makes him wet all over.

He curses under his breath. It is not clear why Shogat - didn't carry him ashore. Surely if her magic works here, she could have done that easily. Agabei feels the strong presence of his own magic, even if overshadowed by the magic of this island. If Agabei still has his powers, so should Shogat.

"Where to?" he asks, avoiding her gaze.

"Up these stairs." She points into the depths of the greenery beyond the sand, and Agabei sees a marble staircase leading into the infinite shade of intertwining branches.

He hates walking in the sand. His wet shoes and pants immediately become full of it, and even the flaps of his long robe, heavy with water, start shimmering with tiny bits of coral after just a few paces. The caliph stops.

"Shogat," he says. "Explain to me exactly how magic works here."

"It is best to use it as little as possible, master. The Elements don't like interference."

"But you can still use it, can't you?"

"Yes, I can, master."

"In that case I wish for you to make me dry and clean of sand this instant!" Agabei hisses, letting all the restrained fury out through his teeth.

"But, master..."

"Do it!"

"Your wish is my command, master." Shogat bows her head, and the caliph feels the blissful release from the weight of water and sand that was tugging down on his legs just a moment ago. He makes the last few steps into the shade of the trees and stops to catch his breath on the marble stairs.

"Thank you, Shogat," he says, studying her bent head with smoothly glistening hair, and the curve of her slender neck. Something did change in her after the encounter with Abdulla. Maybe it was the Dance that she hadn't performed in centuries and that must have filled her with memories of her distant past. Or perhaps the unknown powers of the Dimeshquian wizard have awoken something else that Agabei doesn't quite understand. Whatever it is, he just cannot feel angry with her. Not when she stands so open in front of him, her muscular stomach bare to his greedy eyes.

He feels a strong longing, an urge to touch her smooth

skin, to inhale her myrrh scent, but he cannot afford to do anything of the kind when the woman he came to see can watch him with the aid of the Elements she serves.

"You are welcome, master," Shogat says, her voice soft, her eyes cast down. She is not going to help him much, that's obvious. But he can still command her as he pleases.

"Where do I find her, Shogat?" he asks, searching in the folds of his robe until he feels a familiar touch of cold metal under his fingers.

"Up these stairs, a path will lead you through the forest into a marble palace, master. Go all the way through, to the hall at the end. It has a basin filled from underground streams. Priestess Zobeide is waiting for you there."

He nods, pulling the lamp out of his pocket. He sees Shogat swallow hard as her eyes follow the glistening object in his hands. He knows she must resent going in there, after being imprisoned by these tiny walls and tortured in the desert for countless centuries. But apart from being necessary right now, it should also serve her right, for giving him such a hard time before.

She never meets his gaze as he opens the delicate lid and holds the lamp out to her. Her body slowly loses substance, turns into a wisp of myrrh smoke, and coils into the narrow opening of the lamp.

Agabei steadily follows the path through the ancient forest, inhaling the smells of earth and leaves, so rich in this out-of-the-world place that they make his head swim. Shogat's instructions seem clear. He finds the marble palace and the hall at the end quite easily.

His heart quivers in anticipation as he steps over the threshold of the giant hall in the jungle palace, and stops in awe.

Rumors of the past two millennia have described the fey Zobeide—a well-known sorceress and the head priestess of the Elements—as a lady of unsurpassable beauty and magic powers. For the immeasurable centuries she has been a woman of legends and songs that praised her golden hair made of pure elemental fire and her eyes, green and shiny like two emeralds, holding in their depths the ancient wisdom of creation itself. Rumors said that anyone who encountered the Lady of the Island lost his heart to her forever.

Rumors didn't do her justice.

Standing in awe in front of her, Agabei, a connoisseur of women's beauty, senses infinitely more in the fey Zobeide than any legend or song could possibly describe. She is not merely a beauty of legends and songs. She is also a woman of flesh, in the most ancient and overpowering sense of the word.

He suddenly feels helpless in front of her. Is he, with his meager charms of a skillful seducer, arrogant enough to think that he might tempt this woman to follow his ways? Can he possibly believe that it was Hasan, a wizard of youthful looks and questionable powers, who left this magnificent woman for a silly mortal girl, and not Zobeide, who discarded Hasan like an unnecessary toy after having all the fun she wanted with him?

Agabei opens his mouth, but words fail him. The shifting shadows in the depths of her narrow emerald eyes make it impossible for him to utter a single word.

Yes, she would make an invaluable ally. To win her trust would mean everything to him. But now, standing in the green marble hall, he feels like no more than a helpless little boy trying to win the trust of an adult in his childish game of deception.

Smile shimmers in her ever-shifting eyes as she steps away from him and gestures toward a pair of deep, comfortable chairs at the side of the marble pond. Agabei gasps at the perfection of her movements. She turns to him and smiles again, this time with her lips. Her eyes seem to pierce him through.

"Welcome, Caliph Abu Alim Agabei of Megina," she says.

As if in a dream, Agabei moves to the indicated chair and sits down opposite her.

"How may I be of service to you?" she continues in her

deep voice that makes his skin rise in goose bumps. Perhaps Agabei is a little too susceptible to women's beauty. This could surely become his downfall.

"I am charmed, Lady Zobeide," he finally manages, his voice strained by a lump in his throat. "I came to seek your wisdom, but I never thought..." His voice falters and dies, but the admiration in his eyes speaks for itself.

Zobeide laughs in a deep, clearly ringing voice that sounds like the music of an ancient instrument.

"I heard that the caliph of Megina is an eloquent man," she says.

"You flatter me, lady, for no eloquence in the world can measure up to your wisdom and beauty."

"I am sure you didn't come here to talk of my beauty, caliph," she says, the deep emerald of her eyes becoming darker.

"Alas, no," Agabei says, forcing himself to concentrate. He really can't afford to be overwhelmed by her beauty to the point of losing perspective. He feels lost anyway. He also realizes that he cannot lie to this woman, as he initially planned. He has to be upfront with her about his motives; otherwise he will get thrown out of here and the most he can hope for is to be allowed to collect his boat on the way.

"I came," he begins, taking a deep breath, "to talk to you about Hasan and Princess Gul'Agdar."

He pauses, expecting an outburst. But if the mention of these names causes Zobeide any discomfort, there is no sign of it in her face. She continues to study the caliph with what he takes to be mild amusement.

He doesn't like it one bit. Apart from hating to be laughed at, he needs her to have some interest in the matter. He cannot possibly hope to raise her interest and secure her help if she continues to find him amusing.

"What about them?" Zobeide says levelly.

Agabei's heart leaps. That is what he was looking for. That unnatural levelness of her voice at the mention of her old acquaintance. She cares, after all.

"I heard, O mighty lady, that you knew Hasan back in his

... his wizard days, and that you even used to call him your friend."

"That is no secret, caliph," she says with a dry smile. "We were both studying magic in Dimeshq. It was a great city of wizards back then..." She rolls up her eyes, smiling to some distant memories.

After what he judges to be a decent pause, Agabei dares to continue.

"Perhaps you heard, wise lady, that until recently Hasan used to be a slave of this girl, Princess Gul'Agdar of Dhagabad," he says cautiously, feeling that he is treading on very uneven ground.

"And of her grandmother before that," Zobeide continues with just a touch of impatience. "So what?"

"I am certain, my lady, that you also know that recently the girl somehow managed to set Hasan free."

Zobeide shifts in her chair.

"I am much more informed of events here on this island than you may think, caliph. While I appreciate you coming all this way to tell me about the fate of my old friend, I am afraid this trip was hardly necessary."

She makes a movement to stand up, but Agabei stops her with a pleading gesture.

"Please, my lady Zobeide. With your permission, I haven't finished yet. I have information that the act of freeing a djinn might have triggered a chain of events that could be a serious threat to Hasan, and to all of us. To the whole world, as a matter of fact."

With relief he watches Zobeide sink back into her chair, her eyes fixed on him intently.

"What makes you think so?" she asks.

The caliph lets out a tiny sigh. He suppresses the urge to wipe his forehead and clenches his hands together to hide their tremor. Getting her attention was all he hoped for, and despite the obstacles of coming to this island, despite having to wait for almost three months to have all the signs right for the trip, despite their immense difference in age, the caliph has finally managed to get just that. The emerald eyes fixed on his face have in them all the attention he needs.

"I have encountered a scroll," he says. "An ancient scroll written in Agrit. A scroll which I believe to be a translation from a magical language so powerful that somebody with my meager talents cannot even hope to touch it."

"What makes you think it was a translation?"

Agabei stops. He doesn't want to introduce Shogat into the conversation, although Zobeide must certainly feel Shogat's presence, even if the djinn is safely contained in her lamp.

"I had... help identifying it. Help from an extremely powerful sorcerer whose name is not relevant here."

She nods. Intent on hearing more, she seems to be willing to accept the explanation, at least for now.

"The scroll contained a prophecy. Not a real prophecy, I mean," he adds hastily, seeing her frown. He knows how reluctant the higher mages are to admit even a possibility of a prophecy being accurate. They are too much into probabilities and possible futures. But everybody admits that there could be some things foretold about the future, and that the more magic the author of the prophecy possesses, the higher the chances for it to turn out true. "It was a foretelling," he continues, "of the one who frees a djinn. At the time I first encountered it, it seemed a preposterous suggestion that such a thing was possible. Nevertheless, I studied the scroll with great care. My... sorcerer friend helped me to trace the origins of the text to the very beginning of time."

"An original foretelling," Zobeide says thoughtfully. "To my knowledge there are only three or four of them in existence. I have never seen one myself. What did it say?"

"It said that freeing a djinn is nearly impossible, but if one does free a djinn, such a one will destroy the world. The only way to avoid this is to teach this one magic and contain it as a djinn."

"Was there anything more specific?"

"I have memorized it, word for word. Allow me to recite it for you, my lady."

Agabei slowly speaks the words of the Agritian scroll,

pausing to make sure every one of his words sinks deep into her mind.

The silence that follows seems to last forever. It feels as if the words of the scroll possess magic of their own, even spoken in the most common language, and they leave a trail in the air that hangs heavily over the marble hall.

"Where is the scroll now?" Zobeide finally asks.

"I—when I came back to the Dimeshquian library recently, I couldn't find it anymore," Agabei lies. "Somebody must have found it and took possession of it."

He is certain the current library keeper in Dimeshq, the one who succeeded the unfortunate keeper of the scroll, would rather die under torture than identify Agabei as the one who took the scroll. Just to make sure, Agabei also asked Shogat to wipe the man's mind, replacing the memory of the event with uncontrollable fear.

"I wonder about the original one," Zobeide says slowly.

So does Agabei. He desperately wonders where the original scroll is kept, but he is also aware that his strong but still limited magical powers won't allow him to do much with it even if he finds it. At most he will see the writing as a number of intertwining lines.

He starts, suddenly aware of a pair of emerald eyes fixed on his face.

"Why did you really come to me, caliph?" she asks.

He takes a deep breath.

"I believe, lady, it is our duty to the world to make sure that Princess Gul'Agdar learns magic as quickly as possible and follows her destined path. If she fails to do so and becomes, in some unknown way, a threat to the world, I don't even want to think of the possible consequences."

"I still fail to see the connection to me, caliph," Zobeide says, the undertones of impatience back in her voice. "-shouldn't you be talking to Hasan instead?"

"I have learned, Lady Zobeide, that Hasan is deliberately preventing the princess from learning magic. I know that you must have more influence over him than any other living being. I came to beg you, on behalf of all the creatures in this world, to interfere and make sure things take their natural course."

He pauses like an actor at the end of an inspired monologue. He has just invented this last bit on the spot, and he is especially proud of it.

"I am sure Hasan has his own reasons," Zobeide protests, but there is not much conviction in her voice. Agabei knows his words have hit the spot, and he sits back, waiting for her thoughts to unravel.

"I suppose I could let the princess be tested by the Elements," Zobeide says after a lengthy pause. "The Elements are a force that existed since the beginning of time. They can initiate her into her natural magic and let the events take their course. I suppose there should be no harm in that."

"I heard that the Path of the Elements is treacherous," the caliph puts in gently. "An incapable one might die in the test."

"She won't die if she is ready," Zobeide says lightly. She obviously doesn't believe in harm coming from the Elements. But if the princess dies, it may ruin all the caliph's plans.

"What if she is not?" he insists.

"She must be. Otherwise she wouldn't have been able to free a djinn. Besides, if you have heard so much about the dangers of the Path, you may have also heard that the degree of danger depends on the gateway one takes to set on the Path."

"The gateway?" Agabei has heard something about the gateways, but his knowledge on the subject is not deep enough. He should have asked Shogat more about it!

"There are several gateways in this palace and the forest that surrounds it," Zobeide explains. "The most treacherous, the most dangerous one, lies through this basin." She gestures toward the marble pond in the center of the hall, its turmoiled water rising in boiling domes to the greenish surface. "But there are others."

"What is the least treacherous one?" the caliph asks, nervously licking his dry lips. Was it really wise to come here seeking this woman's help?

Zobeide smiles.

"The least treacherous gateway also lies in this room, caliph. Its location, however, is a secret known only to the priestesses. We don't want anyone to choose an easier Path than the one appropriate for them. The Elements placed us here to direct the ones wishing to walk the Path to the most appropriate gateway."

"Your help in this matter is invaluable, Lady Zobeide," Agabei says weakly. "But I must beg you to direct Princess Gul'Agdar to the least treacherous Path. Her survival is too vital for this world."

"I don't recall the scroll saying anything about that," Zobeide says dryly.

"It is vital... for me," Agabei confesses.

"Ah." Zobeide's eyes light up with a strange fire. "That brings me to my next question, caliph. What is your interest in all this? And please spare me the speech about saving the world. You don't strike me as the kind."

"I bow before your wisdom, Lady Zobeide," he says with an uneasy smile. "I will gladly tell you my secret. I know it will be safe with you. My interests lie in the part of the text that tells about the one who frees a djinn becoming the most powerful djinn ever. If I could take possession of the djinn Princess Gul'Agdar will become, I will feel myself rewarded for eternity."

"So, you plan on ruling the world?" Zobeide's eyes flicker. "A dangerous path, caliph. Not the wisest choice for someone of your stature."

"One can always dream," he says, spreading his arms in a gesture of a man trying to embrace eternity. "You can do what you think right, Lady Zobeide. But you cannot deny me my dreams."

"It seems that I can, in this particular case," she says, the strange glow still in her eyes. "But don't worry, caliph," she adds in response to his pleading gaze. "I have no personal interest in the matter. I will direct Princess Gul'Agdar toward the least treacherous gateway. You have my word, caliph— she will not die."

"Thank you, Lady Zobeide," the caliph exclaims earnestly.

"I will always praise my stars for having such a wise and powerful ally."

He exhales with relief. He has gotten what he came for. She will help the princess to learn magic while guiding her through the safest Path of the Elements. She will use her influence on Hasan to keep him out of the way. And then the caliph will finally get what he wants.

Somewhat shakily, he rises to his feet and bows to her. This conversation has not been easy.

"Farewell, lady," he says.

She doesn't rise to see him off. Instead, she measures him with a glance that makes him feel naked and vulnerable. Then she points toward the gaping doorway, her gesture so commanging that Agabei's feet carry him out of the room even before he has time to think.

"Keep dreaming, caliph!" she calls out as he is already walking away along the marble halls, down the forest path, all the way to the beach, on his way searching for Shogat's lamp in the folds of his robe.

The Challenge

*T*he princess slowly exhales and lays down her *tadra*s. Today's exercise, although tiring as usual, went much better than the earlier ones. At times she could almost feel the silence of the *tadra*s the way Thea in her dreams does—the silence that reverberates with a special calm feeling in the center of her body and passes a detached stillness on to her mind. At times she almost felt her mind leave her body and soar, seeing her own helplessly naked figure slowly moving across her chamber down below.

The princess sinks to the floor and leans against her bed, enjoying the short rest. She is sweating and her limbs are trembling. And yet, at the same time, she feels strong, energy filling her with a lightness that makes her feel as if she is about to fly.

She reaches under the bed to put the *tadra*s away into their box until the next day. And freezes, her hand in midair.

There is a shimmer in the air in front of her. A shimmer usually produced by Hasan right before he appears in front of her. A shimmer she has been able to see much more clearly after her *tadra* practices started to open up her inner vision.

Hasan? Here? Now?

She cannot possibly let him see her as she is now, naked, *tadra*s in her hand, sweat glistening on her unbathed skin.

She drops the *tadra*s into their box with a jingle that makes her wince, and jumps up, heading for the only cover she can reach in time—a light bath sheet on top of her bed.

In a movement so swift and precise it would have frightened her if she could see it, the princess leaps to the bed and pulls the sheet around herself even as the shimmering silhouette becomes clearer.

A woman. Definitely not Hasan.

Hastily wrapping into her improvised garment, the princess peers into the airy outline, which is becoming more substantial by the moment. She sees a long, glittering dress that reflects any color it faces without having a color of its own; flame-red hair falling in fiery tongues all the way to the floor; a perfect face that seems to be carved out of marble, crowned by a wide golden band on the woman's brow.

Zobeide. The head priestess of the Elements. Hasan's special friend from his distant past.

"Zobeide?" the princess asks uncertainly. She is still shaken by the suddenness of the priestess's appearance. *What could Zobeide want with me?*

A frightening possibility springs to mind, and the princess exclaims before she has time to think, "Is Hasan all right?"

"I would imagine so," Zobeide says in her deep voice that betrays no emotion. "You should know it better than me, girl. I haven't seen him in a while."

Something in her tone makes the princess shiver and regret her hasty words. Who is she to worry about Hasan, an all-powerful wizard? Who is she to think that Zobeide will come to her if Hasan is in trouble?

A smile curves Zobeide's shapely mouth. She speaks. "I came to see you, Princess Gul'Agdar."

"Me?"

The green eyes fix her with a calm, steady gaze. A shadow passing through them suddenly reminds the princess of a sea monster lurking in the emerald depths of the ocean. She shivers.

Relax, she orders herself. Zobeide is a friend of Hasan. That makes her the princess's friend, however frightening this woman may be. She mustn't forget her manners. It is an honor to be visited by such a powerful sorceress, who normally stays on her island to be visited by kings at the time of their need.

"Would you sit down, Zobeide?" the princess asks, pointing to an armchair, the best one in her chamber, even if worn out a bit. This armchair is usually occupied by old Nanny Zeinab, and the princess trusts it to be comfortable. "I am sorry for this outfit." She throws an awkward glance down, trying in vain to see what she looks like, wrapped in a sheet. "I was—"

"—practicing with your *tadra*s. I know." Zobeide walks to the indicated chair and settles in it with the easy air of one who feels at home almost everywhere.

The princess stares.

"How did you know about the *tadra*s? I didn't even tell—"

"—Hasan. I know that as well. And a wise decision it was too, princess. His feelings for you really cloud his judgment."

His feelings for you... These words make the princess's heart melt, so that she forgets all caution in front of the older woman. Zobeide seems to know everything, so she cannot possibly be wrong about this. Hasan does have feelings for her, feelings strong enough to cloud his judgment in something that makes perfect sense to everyone else.

The room suddenly seems brighter, as if the sun has smiled in right through the magnolia-shaded window. The princess becomes aware of the special sweetness of the garden smells and the singing of birds, now even more musical than before. She absently smiles to Zobeide, who is still fixing her with a gem-hard stare.

"I came to make you an offer, Princess Gul'Agdar," Zobeide says. "I saw you practice with the *tadra*s—an ancient way to learn magic from the woman's side. While your efforts are admirable, your progress without the proper guidance seems to be slow. How long ago did you start?"

"About three months," the princess says, holding her breath in hope. Learning magic? Is that what she is doing with the *tadra*s? Is that why something in her mind cautioned her against telling Hasan? Because *his feelings for her* may cloud his judgment against what is right?

The Challenge

"I know that you are capable of more," Zobeide continues. "After all, you were able to free a djinn—a deed of great power, which all of the highest mages thought impossible. That proves you can become a great sorceress, if trained properly."

The princess's heart fills with joy. Becoming a great sorceress is all she could dream of. To learn magic, utilizing the great power she apparently has, hidden inside her. To become immortal, like Hasan. To become, sometime in the future, his match...

What is happening now can only happen in books, she thinks. *A great sorceress coming to tell you that you have a special power inside you and that with proper training you can become a great sorceress yourself. None other than the fey Zobeide herself offering to train you—what could possibly be better?*

And yet, a nagging thought at the back of her mind forces her to speak up, to voice something that her loyalty to Hasan doesn't allow her to forget.

"Hasan said he saw a text telling that it may be extremely dangerous for me to learn any magic at all."

"I thought that Hasan might have seen it," Zobeide says calmly. "That is why I mentioned clouded judgment. This text merely tells of possibilities. All of the possibilities I have heard of so far confirm that the one who frees a djinn must be properly trained to follow a certain path. There are dangers involved, of course. That is why Hasan is reluctant to let you do it. His feelings for you really get in the way, don't they?"

That warm wave again, soothing the princess's troubled heart. *His feelings for you*—how wonderful it sounds! Could she really believe Zobeide knows what she is talking about?

"What dangers?" she asks nevertheless.

"Magic is a dangerous thing, princess. It is dangerous for anyone to step on the path of learning magic. Some people even die from not using magic correctly. But let me put it this way. You learned horseback riding and you enjoy it a lot, right?"

"Right."

"You know that some people fall off a horse and break their

neck. Some people hurt themselves and become crippled for the rest of their lives. Horses are large and dangerous beasts that need to be controlled. Did it stop you from learning?"

"No..."

"Exactly. Magic is a dangerous beast that needs to be controlled. Sometimes we must learn not just when and how to use magic, but when and how *not* to use it. Surely Hasan must have told you that?"

"Something like that, yes."

"In preventing you from learning, Hasan is acting like an overprotective father who cannot bear the thought of harm coming to his child and thus prevents her from learning the necessary things. This is why I came here with an offer to you."

"You will train me to learn magic?" the princess asks, holding her breath so that the words won't jump too forcefully out of her mouth.

"No."

The princess's heart sinks. Of course, how foolish of her to suggest that. This is not a story in a book, after all. This is real life. But if not, what is Zobeide here for?

"Even I cannot take something like that upon myself, princess," Zobeide continues, seemingly undisturbed. "I am offering you to go through the Path of the Elements."

"The Path of the Elements?"

"The path to be walked by anyone who wants to be initiated into the magic of the Elements. You will face challenges on this path, of course. If you pass them, the Elements will open your senses to magic, so that you can be guided in your studies. How far along are you?"

"Far along in what?"

"In your training." There is a touch of impatience in Zobeide's voice. "Who was it that initiated you into the cult of the Dance?"

"My dreams," the princess says absently, her thoughts focused on what Zobeide's told her about the magic of the Elements and what hidden dangers the priestess's offer might hold. Maybe when Zobeide realizes the princess is not going through any real training she will lose interest?

Zobeide's sharp voice snaps her back to reality.

"Your dreams?" It sounds as if the woman is startled by something. But what?

"One day I just started having these dreams," the princess explains obligingly. "About a girl named Thea who was left on a riverbank by her mother, and then was picked up by priestesses from the Temple of the Dance. In my dreams I seem to be reliving her life. I simply follow what they teach Thea in the Temple. Only... I am not nearly as good."

"Thea," Zobeide says slowly. "It means 'Dancer' in the ancient Ghullian tongue. Something about it sounds familiar. I am not sure what, or from where. Now, tell me, princess, when did you start having these dreams?"

"About six months ago."

"Did you start learning the Dance as well?"

"Not yet. I am not ready. But I am learning the beat. Only, I have to use a regular drum. I wish I had a real *tama domga!*"

"Show me," Zobeide says. It doesn't really sound like an order, but disobeying it seems to be unthinkable to the princess.

Moving awkwardly in her improvised outfit, the princess reaches under the bed and pulls out a drum. It does look a bit like a *tama domga*, less oval, perhaps, and a bit too tall. The palace craftsmen even attached a handle to its back, so that the princess could hold it vertically, like a real *tama domga* player.

She sits down on a pillow and holds up the instrument in her left hand, resting its tip on the floor and leaning it against her knee. Then she slowly starts beating the complex, sixty-four-step rhythm of the Sacred Dance. *Tum-tumm... Tum-tumm-tumm... Two pairs into four. Two fours into eight. Two eights into sixteen. Two sixteens into thirty-two. Two thirty-twos into sixty-four. Tum-tumm-tum-tumm-tumm-tam... Tum-ta-ta-tamm-tum-tum-tamm... And again, a similar beat with slightly different undertones for the second step of the dance. Two pairs into four...*

Sixty-four beats of the step. Sixty-four steps of the cycle. Sixty-four cycles of the Dance.

She closes her eyes, trying to imagine the deep sound of the real *tama domga*. The drum seems much too blunt, its sound lacking the depth, the music of the hidden strings, whose ringing force could easily fill the giant hall of the Temple with a low, deep sound. As it is, the drum in her hands sounds as light as a street dancer's, but the captivating rhythm of the Dance is entrancing nevertheless.

The princess stops and raises her eyes to Zobeide. To her surprise, the priestess of the Elements is looking at her with an intent, somewhat dreamy expression.

"Your calling is for the music, princess, not for the Dance," she says. "You can still learn the Dance and become quite good at it with time. But the music is your special talent. I'd say, if you could get a real *tama domga*, your studies would go much faster."

"Where could I get one?" the princess asks hopefully.

"I am not sure if one still exists. But if you are meant to have it, you will. What of my offer?"

"What would I need to do to be initiated by the Elements?"

"You would have to go with me back to the island and walk through the forest. You will face the challenges of all the four Elements, and if you pass, they will accept you."

"What if I don't?"

"Then you will be rejected," Zobeide says simply.

"Rejected?"

"You will not receive aid from the Elements. It will make your becoming a sorceress significantly less likely."

The princess pauses, considering it. There seem to be no real downsides. If she succeeds, she will get help and guidance from the most powerful source she knows. She will get a chance at greatness, rarely offered to any mortal. If she fails—well, she will just go on as she is, practicing her *tadras*, hoping one day to break through to the next level of magic, with or without help from the powerful beings surrounding her. Only—she doesn't want to fail.

"Is there any way I can prepare for the challenges?" she asks.

"There is no way to prepare," Zobeide says. "There is not

even any way to tell what the challenges will be. They are different for everyone."

"But isn't it true that to become a priestess of the Elements one must learn for centuries!"

Zobeide straightens up in her chair.

"Nobody is offering you to become a priestess, girl," she says. "But I am offering you a chance some people would die for. Take it or leave it. What will it be, Princess Gul'Agdar?"

"I want to do it," the princess breathes out, words coming forth from her mouth almost before she has a chance to think.

"Let's go, then," Zobeide says, standing up.

"But I—"

A strong sea breeze catches the princess's voice and blows it back into her mouth. She barely has time to grab her bath sheet and pull it around herself before the wind tries to sweep it away and leave her naked and helpless in the middle of the sea.

They are standing on a raft, or, rather, a wooden platform floating right on the surface of the ocean. The platform is absolutely flat. There is nothing to protect it from the waves, rising high all around them on the storming sea. But the water seems to be calming down right at the edge of the flat wooden boards bearing their weight. Not even a splash touches the princess's bare feet, so close to the rippling, salty crests outside the platform's tiny space.

She also notices that, among the random gusts of wind, there is a steady breeze that blows from the back and carries their platform forward with unbelievable speed. The misty shape of the Island of the Elements approaches so fast that no sailboat could have possibly outrun them. In no time they reach the treacherous reefs surrounding the island, and the platform maneuvers seemingly on its own accord straight into the bay.

"How did you do it, Zobeide?" the princess whispers.

"I didn't do anything, princess. The Elements guided us through."

The platform runs aground, digging its front into the white coral sand. They walk off without even moistening their feet.

Only now the princess remembers what she was going to say.

"I didn't have time to bathe and change, Zobeide. I really don't think this outfit is appropriate."

"Where you are going, you don't need any clothes, princess. Don't worry."

Somehow this reassurance worries the princess even more. But she seems to have no choice, or say, in the matter.

Zobeide walks over to the stairs in long strides, and the princess hurries along, partly out of the desire not to fall behind, partly because the white coral sand burns her feet. All the time she keeps wondering what it really is she has gotten herself into, and what Hasan would say if she were to ask his advice.

Hasan, she calls out inwardly. *I know I am going against what you told me, but I am doing this for you! Forgive me if you can!*

Hasan stops to take one last look at Abdulla's house. He is not surprised that his former apprentice is nowhere to be found, and that the housekeeper, a thin man with a malicious gleam in his eye and an unmistakable aura of magic around him, won't tell him anything about Abdulla's whereabouts. It is only to be expected, with all the things going on in Dimeshq. He is not worried either that the man is likely to tell Abdulla all about his visit. Hasan has too much power to go around unnoticed to people like Abdulla. In fact, certain magic signatures in Abdulla's house make him suspect that his former apprentice knows all about the trace in the library and that he has expected Hasan to show up at his house sooner or later.

What disturbs him most is the complete absence of other leads. If Abdulla wanted Hasan to find his house, he would have left a trace for Hasan to follow further. If Hasan is walking into a trap prepared by Abdulla, he cannot be allowed to lose his way. Unless, of course, the trap is not ready yet. Which makes it vitally important to find it before his would-be attackers expect him to.

The Challenge

He stops, for the hundredth time probing the air in every direction. Nothing. What if...

A sudden image of the princess flashes into his mind. He vividly sees her face, frowning, bearing a concerned expression. She is whispering his name, lips only. She is surrounded by trees he has never seen around the Dhagabad palace.

The image is so sharp it shakes him almost like pain. She is in trouble, and she needs him. But where?

Nobody except Hasan is aware of this strange link that has been established between them ever since she set him free. It is almost like a trace of their old link, when she was his mistress and her every wish made him come to her whatever he was doing at the moment. Now that he is free, he doesn't have to come to her every time she needs him, but he is nevertheless acutely aware of her thoughts of him. In his present image the princess isn't trying to summon him. But her emotions, when thinking of him, are so strong they shake him like a jolt of power. And she is obviously in grave danger, although she doesn't seem to realize it.

He has to find her right now. But he cannot pinpoint where she is. These strange trees... There is an aura of magic surrounding the place, an aura that doesn't let him see the location clearly as he would for any other place.

Hasan sighs. There seem to be a bit too many magic auras around him lately. It is to be expected, of course, since the forces that imprisoned him before must be after him again. He has to act quickly. But first, he needs to help the princess.

Once again he tries to penetrate the aura and identify the strange trees. The aura is too strong. It seems to be bouncing his own efforts back at him. Frustrated, he directs his senses away from the trees to the aura itself.

A silent thunder goes off in his mind, momentarily throwing him off balance. Shaken, he withdraws. Whatever the place is, it seems to be extremely resistant to the outside magic.

Think. Forget your magic. Just think.

There is only one power he knows that does not tolerate any touch of magic applied against it.

The power of the Elements.

Suddenly it all comes to his mind in a flash. The strange trees surrounding the princess. The only place they grow is at the Island of the Elements, right around the marble palace. But how in the world could the princess—?

Zobeide.

But why would she—?

I must go there. Now.

The only way to the island is by boat. Half an hour at least, with calm sea.

He summons his magic, measuring his way, a single step all the way from Dimeshq into the middle of the Veriduan Sea. Picking up a boat on the way. Praying for the sea to be calm and for his way to the island to be smooth. Praying that he is not too late.

The Path of the Elements

"Take off your clothes," Zobeide commands.

The princess throws an uneasy glance around the marble hall. They seem to be alone. But to take off her clothes and be naked? That is unthinkable.

She suddenly remembers Thea's feelings when they told her to undress and dance on the day she was brought to the temple. She remembers the girl's fear and confusion, so similar to her own. But she is almost ten years older than Thea was then. She should be smarter than that! She agreed to go with Zobeide, and now the priestess of the Elements is merely telling her what to do. Nothing to worry about. At least, she hopes there isn't.

With shaky hands she unfastens the knots of her sheet and slips it off.

"Good." Zobeide's green eyes seem to measure her up. The princess feels uneasy under her gaze.

"Now, get into the basin," Zobeide says. "This water is the beginning of the path."

"But... it doesn't seem to lead anywhere," the princess says in half protest, backing away from the turbulent water. "It is just a pond of water."

"Well," Zobeide's eyes light up with a dry flicker. "If it is just a pond of water, no harm in getting inside, right? You wanted to take a bath, didn't you?"

"I suppose so," the princess says with uncertainty, and takes a cautious step into the basin.

The water is cool and slightly tingles the skin. She also feels a pull of the underwater currents tugging at her feet.

"Is there anything helpful you can tell me about the challenges, Zobeide?" she asks, taking another step. As the water touches her body, it evaporates off her skin, rising above the basin in a cloud of mist. The water is now reaching above her knees, and in the mist she can barely see herself or where she is walking. She can still clearly see Zobeide, standing motionlessly on the side of the pond.

"You will be challenged in turn by the four Elements: Water, Earth, Fire, and Air," Zobeide tells her. "In some cases the answer will be logical; in others it may be quite physical. It is impossible to say what these challenges will be and how to solve them. It is completely up to you."

"How will I get back?" the princess asks, raising her voice over the mist that now reaches up to her face. The image of Zobeide is beginning to fade. The air becomes warm and damp, with a slight smell of pine.

"The Elements will guide you," Zobeide says, her voice muffled by the blanket of mist.

The princess takes one last step in, the water reaching up to her breasts. Milky waves of mist enclose her, hiding everything from view. The marble floor of the basin under her feet gives way and disappears as the strong current pulls her down into the cool, tingling water.

At the side of the basin Zobeide watches the white turmoil below with calm satisfaction, like a cook watching her brew steam and boil in its cauldron. She doesn't know if she will ever see this girl again. Probably not, for even the accomplished mages can die very easily entering the Path through this marble basin, the most treacherous gateway. The girl certainly seems a disappointment, for all the fuss around her, for all the prophecies and all the powerful wizards trying to win her over. Zobeide doesn't really know what Hasan finds in common with this child, except gratitude for freeing him from his imprisonment.

She throws another glance into the mist, which swirls to form a likeness of a mirror in its milky depths. She sees Hasan, guiding a small boat through the sea around the island with a frown on his face, and smiles.

She has had enough time to get rid of the girl. It is safe for him to come now.

Zobeide curls up like a cat in her favorite chair near the water, and settles down to wait.

The turmoil around her makes the princess completely disoriented. The water pulls her in deeper and deeper. She forces her eyes open, but all she sees is the turbid green glow. A terrible thought strikes her. Maybe Zobeide didn't really want to help her? Maybe she tricked her to come here and drown?

Her lungs are burning for air. If not for her training of the past months, she would have already drowned. Even as it is, she cannot last much longer.

Think, she tells herself. *Look around and think.*

The green color around her is uneven. She can see that one side of it is lighter than the other.

Kicking as hard as she can, she manages to turn her body around in the whirling water. She struggles with all her might to pull toward the light. Her lungs are burning. Her vision is starting to blur. The water is pulling her downward with such force that changing directions seems impossible.

Push, she tells herself. *There is nothing impossible here. This is only water. You know how to swim. Just push harder.*

She doesn't want to die. She pushes with all her might, kicking against the strong current, against the turbid green glow, against her blurring vision, against her constricting lungs that seem to weigh her down heavier than stone.

Just as she finally feels ready to give in and take a full breath of tingling greenish water, her head suddenly cuts through the surface. She inhales, coughs, and inhales again.

And keeps being pulled down by the strong current.

In fact, with her head in the air, it feels very much like

falling.

She opens her eyes again and manages to see, far below, a pond of water surrounded by jagged rocks.

She is being carried down in a waterfall, rushing its tons of greenish water down to the rocks below.

The challenge of the Water.

The princess measures the distance as well as she can. She is about halfway down. That gives her some time to act. But not much.

Taking a deep breath, she dives back into the waterfall. She struggles with all her might to cut through the wall of water, which, as she now knows, must have limited thickness on both sides. The waterfall always has a wall behind it. A rock face, along which the water runs down. Unless, of course, it is falling off a ledge.

She forces her eyes to stay open as she pops her head out on the other side of the water. No rock face. Just as well, perhaps, because at her speed she would have hit herself very hard against it. But—something. Something to hold on to.

Thick cables of vines, growing down off the ledge of the waterfall, hang on the edge of the water. The princess grabs them with both hands.

The cables are slippery. Her hands slide off them, pulled by the force of the water.

She can clearly see the jagged rocks below, with a particularly sharp tip sticking out right underneath her. She forcefully shuts off the vision of what her body would look like, skewered on the sharp tip of that rock.

She grabs the slippery cables again and pushes with all her strength until her body pops out of the falling wall of water. Her hands are still slipping, but she grabs on as hard as she can. There is no water to pull her down now, only the weight of her own body that feels so wet and heavy that the mere strength of her hands shouldn't be enough to keep it from falling.

She clenches her hands so tightly that she feels the burning pain as the skin blisters off from the friction of the vines. The ground is still approaching fast. The roar of the falling water is deafening.

With all her remaining strength, the princess sways her body to cling to the bundle of vines with her arms and legs. Her skin burns as the friction slows down her fall, her feet touching the ground slowly, almost gently. Her legs give way and she falls into a pool of mud behind the roaring waterfall, which is shaking the ground with its sheer force. A cold shower of muddy splashes is hitting her from all sides.

She has never imagined a waterfall this big.

Hasan lets the boat run into the sand and jumps out even before it stops moving. The sense of danger, of being too late for something important, urges him to rush, to run up the stairs, along the forest path, through the marble corridors and halls. To the room with the marble basin in the center.

The princess can't possibly be here, he tells himself. It was just a vision. All he is here for is to be reassured. She could never have found her way here without help. And Zobeide— what could Zobeide possibly want with the princess?

He runs into the hall and stops. His first feeling is relief. The princess is not here. It is just Zobeide, alone, curled up in her favorite chair. He was wrong, just as he thought. No harm done; he'll just spend some time with his good friend and leave.

Hasan's eyes fall on the water of the basin. It is boiling more than usual, the remains of white mist quivering above its surface.

His heart sinks as he turns to face Zobeide. It *is* true. But how? Why?

"Zobeide..." He looks up to meet her impenetrable gaze. "Did you bring the princess here and send her on the Path?"

She doesn't say anything, but he sees the answer in her eyes nevertheless. His heart sinks. He looks again at the fading mist and struggles against the feeling of terror seizing his heart.

"You didn't send her—in there, did you?" His voice falters

as he meets her eyes with a plea.

The emerald eyes smile at him. Shadows are flickering in their depths, but their surface is calm.

"Of course not, Hasan," she says. Her voice is soothing, like music. "This Path is certain death. I sent her through the easiest gateway." She glances over to the window at the end of the hall, open widely into the forest beyond. Following her gaze with relief, Hasan sees white mist floating outside the window as well.

Through the window, not through the pond. Through an easy gateway, not through the hard one.

Of course, it doesn't mean the princess is safe. The Path of the Elements is treacherous and rough no matter what gateway one takes. It also makes his plan of isolating the princess from learning any magic highly unlikely. But if she does have a chance to come out alive and well, it is there, through that gateway beyond the window.

"Sit down, Hasan," Zobeide invites him. "She is beyond our reach now. You'll have to wait for her here. Finally, after two thousand years, we can sit down and talk once more."

He obeys her gesture and settles into a cozy armchair opposite hers. It is true, they haven't had a chance to talk for quite a while. But why did she do this to the princess? How could she interfere with his plans so brutally?

She doesn't know what she is meddling with. She couldn't have seen the original foretelling. Perhaps she only wanted to help, knowing how the princess has been longing to learn magic.

He sighs, forcing himself to relax. There is nothing he can do now anyway, except enjoy the company of an old friend.

"It is good to see you, Zobeide," he says.

"Likewise." She smiles and studies his face for a while. "I missed you, you know. I was so happy to learn that you are free. Why didn't you come to see me earlier?"

"I was very busy, Zobeide. I am not sure whether my freedom can last. I was looking for information to help me."

"Did you find anything?"

"Not really," he says with caution. "But I haven't given up yet."

Zobeide smiles and stretches out her palm. A dish appears in her hand full of glistening oval shapes, deep purple in color. A sweet and slightly tart smell fills the air.

"I heard that since you are free you can enjoy food once again," she says. "Try these *alzahar* fruits. They don't grow anywhere else but here."

Hasan absently reaches out, picks up a cool, slightly moist fruit and takes a bite. Fresh, sweet taste fills his mouth. He suddenly remembers he hasn't eaten anything since early morning and, finishing the *alzahar* fruit, helps himself to another one.

"I am so glad you are here, Hasan," Zobeide says. "Even if it seems that I have to thank the princess for that. You really care about her, don't you?"

"I do care about her, Zobeide," he says. "But there is a lot more at stake than just caring. I wish you hadn't sent her on the Path. She really shouldn't be learning any magic at all."

"Why?" Zobeide gives him an innocent look. "She is so eager to learn!"

"I know, Zobeide. But learning magic puts her in great danger."

A shadow rises in Zobeide's green eyes, but Hasan, absorbed in his thoughts, doesn't notice it.

The princess forces herself to get up and move. She is so cold and wet that her teeth are rattling and all her body is covered in goose bumps. She wishes she at least had her bath sheet here. But a wet bath sheet wouldn't help much, and there is so much water around there is no hope of getting anything dry enough to actually make a difference against the cold.

Move, she tells herself. *You have to get out of here.*

She looks around her temporary shelter. In front, the ground-shaking wall of water is pounding down from the immeasurable heights of what she takes to be the island cliffs. Behind her is a shallow cave made of wet earth, with roots and vines, similar to those that saved her life, hanging down in a likeness of a curtain.

The obvious exit from this place lies on the other side of the waterfall. But getting under this pillar of water, pounding down from the sky with unbelievable force, seems like suicide. The princess remembers the jagged rocks she saw from above and shivers. There must be another way out.

She turns her attention to the wall behind her. It seems that only parts of it are made of rock. The spaces in between are filled with earth. The same earth that serves as a foundation for the vines that saved her life.

The princess glances at her bleeding palms. A small price to pay for her life. And yet, such an inconvenience now, when she has to dig the ground with her bare hands.

She looks again at the bundles of vines hanging down from above. As expected in this damp place, the water is dripping down each of them in small streams. That's what made them so slippery in the first place, she thinks. But now this water may actually come in handy. If only there was more of it.

In spite of her desperate situation, she cannot help smiling. Who would have thought that standing here, wet to the bone, trapped by a waterfall after being almost drowned in it, she would be actually wishing for more water?

She collects as many hanging ends of the vines as she can reach and pulls them together, winding them into a likeness of a rope. Its end, combining all the water dripping down the individual vines, becomes the source of a considerably sized stream of water. Even better than that, the princess can now direct this stream by pulling just one vine.

She points her improvised water hose at the wall of earth in front. The earth resists it for a while, and then a big slab of it comes off, almost hitting the princess.

Holding on to her bundle of vines, she climbs off to the side, continuing to wash off pieces of the mountain. In the semidarkness of the cave, lit only with whatever light finds its way through the wall of water in front, she cannot even see her progress very well. Chunks and slabs of earth come off the rocks and slide under the waterfall, their crashed remains disappearing down the river that she presumes exists somewhere beyond.

She cannot really hear anything above the roaring water, but she finally realizes that something has changed by the change of pressure on her bundle of vines. In fact, she can almost imagine a hollow sound of water inside the cleft between two rocks she has washed clear of earth. The princess lets go of the vines and cautiously approaches the hole she has made. It is dark inside. Worse than that, the earth above the entrance seems to be loose. She can vividly imagine walking under this newly made vault and being trapped inside by falling earth.

She grabs the vines again and directs their stream of water inside. Nothing. She will just have to get in and find out for herself.

The walls on the sides of the passage feel smooth and solid to the touch. It is the ceiling she cannot see, the ceiling that is worrying her. She creeps deeper into what she hopes to be a tunnel, feeling like a mole creeping into its self-made hole in the ground. She cannot see a thing in front of her. The light from behind is so dim that it doesn't help much.

She reaches out to feel the walls with her hands. Here is the place where the rock ends, giving way to wet earth under her hands. There is also a wall of earth in front, too deep for her stream of water to reach. How naïve of her to think she could really wash her way through the mountain!

Something pounces onto her shoulders from above. The sharp smell of freshly dug earth becomes more prominent as the ceiling of her cave streams down on her with force. She sinks to her knees under its weight, but the earth keeps falling until it buries her completely in its damp, soft mound. The princess only has time to cover her face with her arms before everything around her sinks into complete darkness.

"Can you sense something, Hasan?" Zobeide asks intently. "You froze, just a moment ago."

"She is in terrible danger, Zobeide," Hasan says. "I wish there was a way to get her out of there!"

"You know the Path cannot be reached from the outside," Zobeide says. "It is up to the Elements now."

"I know." Through his link with the princess, Hasan can sense her agony. But he is powerless to do anything to help her.

"Why can she not learn magic, Hasan?" Zobeide asks with an innocent expression that, against her intentions, makes Hasan very alert.

I should tell her, he thinks. *It doesn't make any difference now, but she might think of something I missed. Maybe we can still do something.*

"There is an original foretelling about the one who frees a djinn," he says.

Zobeide regards him for a second, her face bearing an impenetrable expression.

"Funny you should mention that," she says. "The other day there was a caliph here who kept babbling about the same foretelling. He kept calling it 'prophecy.'"

"Caliph Agabei?"

"You know him?"

"He was trying very hard to marry the princess some time ago. He has a djinn, you know."

"I didn't know that. But I did sense a strong magical aura around him. I assumed it was his own. Of course, now that I think of it, I realize it was much too strong."

"He must have kept her contained."

"Her?"

"The djinn Agabei owns is a former Mistress of the Dance."

A light inside Zobeide's eyes flashes brighter. Her face twitches as she turns away from Hasan.

"What did the caliph want?" Hasan asks, trying in vain to catch a glimpse of her expression. "What was he here for?"

"He wanted my help to initiate the princess into magic. I assume he saw the foretelling too. The caliph seems to believe she can become a djinn so powerful that owning her will help him rule the world."

"What a fool," Hasan says forcefully.

"Oh?"

"Agabei doesn't understand the powers he is meddling with. He is like a child who wants a toy and will stop at nothing to get it. I bet he didn't even see the original scroll. He must have quoted you some Agritian translation or something."

"Actually he quoted me a translation into common speech. But he did mention Agrit."

"I believe he is not nearly powerful enough to read the original."

"Did you read it, Hasan?"

"Of course I did," he says impatiently. "Otherwise I wouldn't be so worried. To the caliph the foretelling is just words. He doesn't even know what powers he is trying to wake."

"I guess I should have talked to you before coming to the princess," Zobeide says. "I thought I was doing her a favor. She seemed so eager to learn any magic at all."

"You should have definitely talked to me, Zobeide. You don't know how dangerous this Path is for her."

The same cold flicker lights up the depths of Zobeide's narrow, emerald eyes. But this time she turns away faster than before, not to let Hasan see it.

The River of Fire

*T*he princess tries to move. The fall of earth has stopped—
or, perhaps, it has simply become so distant that she cannot
feel it. Maybe the whole mountain is now on top of her! *This
is what it feels like to be buried alive,* she thinks. She orders herself to calm down. *This is just a test,* she tells herself. *This is all
part of your training.* As she knows from Thea, the most important part of any training is to remain calm at all times.

The weight of earth on her back is considerable, but not
unbearable. Which means that the earth fall has stopped and
that she is not buried too deep under it. At most, as deep as
the height of her cave.

She tries to move her legs. After a lot of initial effort she finally finds herself able to push back with one foot, then the
other. Not bad, really.

She tries to remember in which direction she was going before the fall started. All the sides seem to be mixed in here, in
her freshly made grave. She doesn't even remember which
side is up and which is down. How can she get out if she
doesn't even remember where *out* is?

Calm down, she tells herself. *Calm down and think.*

She is, after all, much better off now than a short time ago
when she was falling down and only had seconds to figure
out a way to escape. That is, assuming that she can get out of
here. Otherwise, a fast death might have been better than a

slow one, buried alive under a mound of earth.

You are alive and you can move, she reminds herself. *You can get out of here. Think.*

Before the earth fall started she was walking forward into the cave. The first slab of earth to hit her was pretty heavy. She sank to her knees. Was she still facing the cave then? Yes, she thinks so.

She tries to remember what happened afterward. She had covered her face and head with her arms. And here they are, raised above her head in a protective gesture, a bit numb from being in that position for a while under a considerable weight of earth. Can she move them? Yes.

Assuming she fell forward and not backward, and she is now lying facedown and not faceup, her head and arms should be facing the tunnel she made, and her legs should be pointing back to the waterfall. If she digs in the right direction, she can get out of here. Now, which way should she go?

There is no way to tell what awaits her inside the mountain. More rocks and wet earth, most likely. No air to breathe. Even now, though there is some air in the space between her arms and her face, it is getting staler by the minute. She will soon run out of air, and then it won't matter anymore.

She should go back to the waterfall, she decides. Maybe she can use the vines to force her way through the wall of water. In fact, right now it seems to be a really good idea. Why didn't she think of it before walking so stupidly into this tunnel?

She tries to kick her legs backward, to turn around. It is not easy, with all the weight of earth keeping her down. She kicks with all her strength and finally pushes herself forward a couple of inches. Forward. Away from the waterfall.

This won't do, the princess thinks. *I have to turn around.*

The struggle of the next several minutes brings her even deeper into the mountain. There seems to be no way for her to turn and go back. She is trapped, forced to move forward, bringing herself farther and farther away from the little cave behind the waterfall that now feels almost like a haven of safety.

She stops, panting. The air has a stale aftertaste and doesn't seem to be satisfying her desire to breathe anymore. Should she stop, to save some air? To live, perhaps, several minutes longer?

No, she decides. *If I must die here, I will die struggling. I will not lie, buried, and wait for my end! Thea would never have done that. Hasan would never have done that. I will struggle while even a single breath is left in my body.*

She doesn't care anymore in which direction the waterfall is. Maybe she was wrong and it is really in front of her? Maybe she fell backward and not forward when the earth hit her from above? Maybe she should just stop thinking and fight, moving in the only direction that seems possible, digging like a worm, deeper and deeper into the side of the mountain?

Her hand pops out of the wall of earth into emptiness so suddenly that she feels as if she is losing balance and grabs on to the inside of her tomb with the other hand. Of course, she is in no danger to fall anywhere. She is safely embedded in earth. But there seems to be empty space in front! Just a foot ahead she will finally be able to take a breath.

Move, she urges herself. *Move.*

Her head is spinning, her lungs burning from the lack of air. The breathing movements her chest is making out of habit don't seem to be bringing any relief. She is suffocating in this mound of earth, and by struggling just a little bit she may finally find a *real* open space, to take in a full breath of *real* air.

The thought makes her nauseated. She has no breath left to struggle. She cannot make it through these last few inches. Let her hand breathe for her out there.

Move, a voice at the back of her mind tells her insistently. *Kick. You are almost there.*

Just a moment of rest, she pleads, not sure anymore who is it she is trying to talk to. *My hand can breathe for me. I can feel it take the fresh air in through the skin. If I move now, I will disturb it.*

Her body seems to move by itself in what seems more like convulsions than a real effort, but she does manage to push her head a little bit forward. To pop her face, finally, into the empty space in front.

The wave of air hits her nose and mouth just as she feels that the breath of the air substitute around her will be her last. There is so much air around her now that she feels she can burst with its sudden inflow. Her lungs unfold to catch its wonderful, fragrant flow that might have seemed stale to her in her former life, but now seems fresher than any air she has ever breathed. She lies there for a while, breathing, enjoying her rest and the abundance of space around her, as if she has just been born again.

The space she has popped into seems to be huge, much bigger than the little cave beyond the waterfall. She feels wind on her face, tinged with a slightly medicinal smell of sulfur and fungus. As she pushes herself completely free of the earth mound and looks around, she sees a distant reddish glow off to her right.

She tries to sit up. She is still trembling from the effort. Every part of her body and hair seems to be full of earth. She finds herself wishing she could get some water to wash off, and smiles inwardly. Just a short while ago she had all the water she needed and was anxious to get away from it.

She pauses to reflect on what has happened to her so far. Zobeide told her that if she failed a challenge she would simply be rejected by the Elements, but it certainly doesn't look that way. The princess has never been in a life-threatening situation before, except, perhaps, during her and Hasan's encounter with Abdulla in the Temple of the Dance. But this time it feels unbelievably real. In fact, she is fairly certain that if she failed any one of the challenges she would have died. Maybe this is all an illusion? Maybe she is still swimming in Zobeide's basin and this is all just a test in her mind?

She clenches her hand into a fist. The skin, torn by the vines in the waterfall, stuffed with earth from all the digging, hurts so much that her eyes fill with tears. Her fingernails are broken. Her feet sting as she steps onto the fine, sharp gravel of the cave floor. It all feels much too real to be a part of her imagination.

She read that if in doubt whether you are dreaming or

awake, you should pinch yourself and see whether you feel any pain. You cannot feel any pain induced in a dream unless it is part of your real-life sore. But before getting into Zobeide's basin, she was very healthy. And every step on that gravel feels too painful to have any doubts of this kind.

This is real, she decides. *Maybe Zobeide just wanted to kill me, not test me, but I am not going to die. I am going to find a way out of here!*

Assuming, of course, there is a way out.

She scrambles up to her feet; still shaky on her legs, she reaches out into the darkness to find some support, but her hands search the emptiness in vain. There seem to be no walls here. The cave around her has no visible boundaries, cool wind wandering through it freely, soothing her burning skin.

Fixing her eyes on the distant red glow, she starts to walk slowly toward it, carefully feeling her way on the sharp gravel floor. She is not used to walking barefoot. But she doesn't seem to have any choice.

This is just pain, she tells herself. *And it is not that unbearable. You can stand it. Think of the pain Thea had to endure when the priestesses whipped her for any misdeed. Your pain is nothing compared to that.*

She suddenly realizes that in her dream about the temple she seems to feel all the pain Thea is feeling. Following her own logic, this means that the dreams about Thea are not dreams, but another reality.

She doesn't know what is real anymore.

Real or not, it doesn't matter, she finally decides. *There is only one way out of here—forward, toward that reddish glow. Walk!*

The gravel under her feet forms the start of a path, bordered by bigger rocks on the sides. This winding path is steadily descending into the heart of the mountain. The air becomes much warmer. The reddish glow is getting so bright that she can now see quite far into the depths of the cave. With its giant open space, with grotesque shapes of columns growing from the floor and ceiling, throwing monstrous shadows, the cave resembles the underground Stiktian temple she visited with Hasan such a long time ago.

She follows the path around a giant boulder that marks the entrance into the next chamber of the giant cave, and stops in awe.

The space in front of her is even bigger than the one she just left. The entire center of it is occupied by a chasm, running in a wide, jagged line all the way across. A river of liquid fire flows along its bottom, emanating the red glow the princess has been following all the way from the beginning of the path.

Blazing heat hits her face, making the last bits of earth on her skin dry up and crumble off to the floor of the cave. Her face and body start glistening with sweat. The heat here is worse than anything she has felt before, worse than the hottest day of the dry season out in the open desert.

The river of fire majestically flows past her, from time to time sprouting tongues of flame from its surface. The path the princess has been following runs down to the nearest bank and up on the other side, winding upward into the darkness.

She stops in indecision. There seems to be no way to get to the other side of this lava river. If she comes any closer to it, she will burn for sure. On the other hand, nobody said she has to cross it at all. Maybe if she goes back the way she came and looks some more, she will be able to find another, easier way out?

Something inside her tells her this cannot be. This is no ordinary path through the mountain, after all. This is the Path of the Elements, here to present her with challenges. At least that is what Zobeide told her. But the same Zobeide also told her there is no risk in here except to be rejected by the Elements. She obviously lied about it. Why then assume that she didn't lie about everything else too?

The princess turns to go back where she came from. She just has to walk around this boulder. The heat is much more bearable back there, she remembers. She just has to walk away from the lava river and then she will have time to think.

A thunder rolls above her head. She feels the ground shake, and small rocks and sand pour from the ceiling like rain. The path under her feet erupts with small cracks, as if hit by a giant hammer. She barely has time to move when the huge boulder in front of her shakes and sinks right into the floor of the cave. A wide crevace opens in the place where the boulder just stood, and in a wave of heat she sees, far below, a pond of liquid fire.

Pillars growing out of the floor and ceiling of the cave start breaking off and sinking inward, into the new pools of lava opening here and there. The ground is shaking so hard that the princess barely keeps her balance. She has a hard time shifting out of the way of rocks that fall like rain all around her and hit the lava flow with tiny splashes of fire. She finds herself standing on what looks like a tiny island among the boiling flame, no longer connected to any solid piece of land. The island itself shifts and leans to the side as the fiery tongues lick its foundation like angry ocean waves.

The heat becomes almost unbearable. Every breath of air burns her mouth.

I am going to burn, the princess thinks. *I will fall and be consumed by the flames below any moment now. Good-bye, Hasan! Forgive me if you can!*

Hasan sits up sharply. The image of the princess's face once again springs vividly into his mind. It twitches in agony, her pain and fear so intense that they echo through his own body.

"Fire," he whispers. "She is burning, Zobeide."

"She will be all right, Hasan," Zobeide says lightly. "The Fire will challenge her, but she is in no real danger on the Path I sent her. What makes you think she is in trouble, anyway?"

"I just had a vision," Hasan says reluctantly. Something keeps him from telling Zobeide about the bond between him and the princess. It has nothing to do with trust, he tells himself. It is just something nobody really needs to know. A weakness, perhaps, that is always better to keep to yourself.

"You know you cannot really see her now," Zobeide says with a smile. "Nobody can penetrate the Path. Even with your powers."

"My powers," Hasan says slowly. "That's key to everything, isn't it, Zobeide?"

He turns to meet her gaze, aware of the sudden tension in her still shape.

"I know that since you became free nobody can tell what your powers really are," Zobeide says. "But you, Hasan, you must know, don't you? Do you feel any changes? Do you feel that you can do less than before?"

"I am not sure," Hasan says, almost truthfully. There is something he doesn't like about the sudden intensity of her gaze. *This is Zobeide,* he reminds himself. *She is your friend. She was your lover, a long time ago.*

Did he trust her then, millennia ago, when he found such intense happiness in her arms? Not quite. Almost, but not quite.

Nothing has changed after all, Hasan thinks. *I didn't quite trust her then, and I don't quite trust her now either. I will not tell her that my powers seem to be unaffected by my freedom. I don't know why, but I won't.*

"Come, Hasan." She laughs, but her eyes are serious, and shadows are playing in their narrow depths. "How can you not be sure? You must know what your powers are!"

"Really, Zobeide." He smiles in response and gives her one of his most innocent looks. "I would have told you if I knew, wouldn't I?"

"You always liked to play with me." She laughs again, her deep voice ringing like music. "And"—she looks straight into his eyes, the fire in her gaze flashing deeply into his soul— "you always used to drive me crazy by your games. Do you remember?"

"Yes, I do, Zobeide," he answers.

She is the one playing a game with him this time. It makes him very uncomfortable that he cannot figure out what her game is.

"I have been thinking about us for centuries, Hasan," she whispers. "And I kept asking myself: if Hasan were free, is it possible that he would come back to me? Is it possible for us to be together again?"

"Do you truly wish for that, Zobeide?" he asks quietly.

Her glance sends a sharp vibe straight into the depth of his being. He shivers at the intensity she emanates. He sees the answer he knows she cannot give him. Her eyes answer him without words.

She truly wishes for that, more than anything. But she knows, as he does, that it can never be.

The Palace of the Winds

*T*he island among the lava river is getting smaller and smaller, pieces crumbling off its sides as easily as if it were made of dry bread. The princess feels the rock under her feet shake and rise up, tilting like a horse rising on its hind legs to make a leap.

A leap.

There is another island off to her right, a bigger and steadier one. It is quite far, but if she leaps with all her might, if she judges the distance right, she might just land on top of it.

The heat is becoming unbearable. She feels her skin wither under it. She can smell burning hair. A leap would just prolong her agony. If she leaps, she would be better off jumping down into the lava below. A few moments of terrible pain and then—

Don't give up! Hasan was tortured in the desert for almost two thousand years and never gave up! How can you give up after just a few moments of pain?

The rock under her feet shakes and gives way. She takes a deep breath of burning air, and pushing off with all her might, she jumps, her arms out, aiming for the next island of rock. The breath she took burns from the inside. Despite the pain, it seems to give her new energy, to make her lighter, to float her like a balloon above the boiling lava.

She hits the rock and grabs on with all her limbs. A bit too far. Her head and shoulders are hanging down the other side. But most of her body is still on top.

It is so hot!

She frantically scrambles back, onto the safety of the flat top of the rock island. Shakily, she gets up to her feet. This island is not stable either. She needs to find another support.

Taking in very small breaths through clenched teeth, she turns to look around. There is another island, a bit closer, and seemingly off in what she thinks to be the right direction. Can she make another jump?

The ground under her feet starts shaking again. The island she is standing on might sink any moment.

Now! she tells herself, and leaps even before she has time to think.

It is easier this time. She lands almost right. Her left leg slides off, but she grabs on with the rest of her limbs and quickly pulls herself on top.

I cannot bear this heat anymore.

How many more jumps can she make? One? Two? It doesn't seem to matter now. It is either jump or stay to wait for certain death. She is not about to wait. She will *not* let anybody take her destiny into their hands anymore. Not her father. Not Zobeide. Not the elemental Fire, trying to eat her alive!

She clenches her teeth and jumps again. She doesn't need to think or prepare anymore. Her eyes identify the right spots, and her muscles summon the necessary amount of strength on their own accord. *To the left. Jump. Hold on, collect yourself, climb back on top. Forward. Jump. Collect yourself. Right and forward. Jump.*

Suddenly she cannot see any more lava in front of her. She seems to have reached solid land. One more jump and she is safe. It seems so far, though. Can her tired muscles make it?

As she pushes off into the air for her final leap, she realizes she has missed it this time. Not by much. Just half an inch short of the edge of the rock wall.

She lands with her stomach on the jagged wall descending into the chasm. She is so strained, so terrified, that she doesn't even feel any pain. She grabs on, her hands and feet searching for the tiniest cracks to hold on to, to stop her sliding, to pull herself up.

The edge is so close. From below she can see the beginning of the path where it picks up after crossing the chasm and runs upward, into the darkness, into safety. Only, she missed this time. She is going to die.

Her foot, sliding so close along the rock that its rough edges take off pieces of skin, suddenly finds a hold. A tiny crack, just enough to squeeze in her toe.

To stop sliding.

She pauses and catches her breath. She is not sliding anymore. She is hanging like a bat on the rock wall, holding on to it with a single toe.

There must be more cracks around here, she urges herself. *Move. Find them. Pull yourself up.*

Breathing hurts so much it brings tears to her eyes. Tears that dry immediately under the blazing heat. Her skin seems to be blistering. She imagines a smell of burning flesh. And a much stronger smell of burning hair.

She has never been so hurt before, never felt so much pain. Will she ever recover, even if she gets out of here alive?

Stop that, she tells herself. *No thoughts. Just move.*

Her searching fingers find a thin crack on her left, running diagonally up. She pushes her fingers in, forcing away the thoughts of what would happen if the earthquake continues and the crack closes down.

Pulling herself up with her left hand as far as she can stretch without losing her foothold, she reaches up with her right arm. She can almost reach the edge. Almost. If she pushes off with her foot, she might just be able to catch on.

A calmness suddenly comes over her mind. She imagines herself back in her room, practicing with the *tadras*. Pushing off with her foot to stretch up, smoothly, so that the *tadras* will stay absolutely silent.

The sounds around her cease. She is not hanging on a rock face. She is standing on one foot in a giant marble hall, reaching up with her right arm. She is wearing *tadras*, and her movements must be absolutely smooth, so that the bells do not ring.

She pushes off the floor and jumps up, reaching with her right hand, using the momentum of her jump to catch on to the ledge and pull herself up, all the way to safety.

Slowly, the princess becomes aware of things around her. She is lying facedown on the hot gravel, which runs forward and up in a winding path. Her short, labored breaths burn from the inside. Her raw skin throbs; it seems as if most of it is not even there anymore. She feels the intense, gagging smell of burning hair.

Get up and move.

Slowly, painfully, she pulls herself up to her feet and makes her shaky way upward, along the path. The sharp gravel digs into her feet, but she doesn't care anymore.

After what seems like ages of walking the princess suddenly realizes that the air around her has become quite a bit cooler, and the light, now coming from somewhere in front, is no longer reddish. It looks like genuine daylight. She has passed through the mountain to its other side.

The light blinds her as she steps out of the cave into the forest. She stays there for a moment, swaying, not sure where she is supposed to go now.

She hears a faint tinkling of a brook, and slowly turns her head to look. The movement makes her wince. In fact, any movement is painful beyond bearable.

Water... She needs water.

The brook, making its way around the moss-covered rocks, widens at the roots of a giant tree to form a pond. Not too large. Just big enough for one person to bathe in. The princess makes her painful way right into the water. A voice at the back of her mind cautions her. This could be another challenge of the Element Water. What if this forest pond, like Zobeide's basin, leads straight into a waterfall?

She doesn't care anymore. She has no strength left. If the Elements want to drown her now, let them.

The water is cool and at least waist-deep. It is transparent and has a soothing, amber color. The princess sinks into it, letting it close over her head, feeling all of her skin absorb it and heal, spreading back to life—like a dry, withered leaf gets new life when soaked in the water. She feels the heavy waves of her hair unfold behind her back. So she didn't lose it after all. Not all of it, anyway.

She opens her eyes and mouth, letting the water flow freely through, drinking in its slightly bitter, medicinal taste, washing away the burns of fire she was forced to breathe for so long. Then she turns over to her back and floats, face up, opening her healed eyes to the soothing greenery of the tree crowns, feeling her aching muscles relax and her sores go away.

After a while she finds the strength to sit up and wash herself, water covering her up to her chin. Her body doesn't feel sore anymore. She can feel no pain in her wounded hands.

She pulls a hand out of the water and stares in amazement.

The skin on her palm is white and smooth like always, as if she has never left the Dhagabad palace at all. As if none of the terrors she just lived through ever happened.

Why, then, does she still feel so tired?

The amber water of the stream soothes and caresses her back to life. It must possess healing powers. Or maybe the Element Water took pity on her for calling upon it for help so many times today?

The princess slowly gets out of the water and makes her first, unsteady steps toward the path, curving happily through the forest undergrowth. In front, through the trunks of majestic trees, she can see the greenish walls of the marble palace. Zobeide's palace.

Is this all, then? she thinks. *Am I supposed to go back now?*

She walks toward the palace, her steps steadier and steadier as she leaves the horrible mountain behind. Looking back, she can still see its forested slopes, ascending to crown the top of this island, like the back of a giant sea beast sticking out of the ocean. Now she knows what this beast holds inside.

As the princess reaches the palace, she pauses. This is not the door she used before. This seems to be some kind of a back door, standing ajar. Beyond it the princess can see a marble passage running off, with two more openings to the sides.

She briefly considers wandering through the forest to find the front door of the palace. But the forest undergrowth seems to be especially thick here. Who knows what perils might be hidden inside? Although completely healed, she doesn't want to hurt herself again by treading through the forest without a path.

She carefully steps over the threshold onto the cool marble floor.

The passage in front of her is leading forward, curving out of sight in about twenty paces. There are two openings on the sides. In the depths of the palace she hears echoes, as if wind is sweeping through, whistling in the empty marble corridors. This part of the palace certainly doesn't look like the one she has seen before.

She hears a thud from behind. Spinning around, she finds herself facing a blind wall. The door she has just walked through is not there anymore.

Horrified, the princess runs her fingers along the marble surface. No trace of a door. As if this passage she is standing in just ends abruptly with a wall.

Feeling the hairs at the back of her neck rise, the princess remembers the Dimeshquian Labyrinth—a test for the highest mages, shown to her once by Hasan. Once anyone finds a way in there, there is no way out except by finding its center. The entrance door closes without a trace behind the one who walks in. Could it be that she has just found herself in a similar labyrinth? But to walk through the labyrinth in Dimeshq one has to possess considerable magical powers. Last time she had Hasan to guide her through. This time she is all by herself. How can she possibly find a way out?

Panicked, she looks around. There are three possible passages she could take. Is she supposed to summon her inner vision to see a magic arrow pointing to the right one? How could she do it? And what is she supposed to see? This is not the Dimeshquian Labyrinth, after all. It may have a different key.

The wind is whistling off in the distance, making her feel

cold and uncomfortable. As if there is rough weather some-where nearby and she has to face it naked.

What is the key to this labyrinth? she thinks. *There has to be a key!*

She remembers reading a tale about a hero who used a ball of thread to find his way through a labyrinth. That hero had one advantage, though. All he had to do was to go inside the labyrinth and return. A thread can be very handy if one needs to retrace one's steps. In this case, however, she has to do something different. She has to find her way... where? Some-where. Out of here. She doesn't even know what she is searching for.

Maybe this is not a labyrinth, she tells herself. *Maybe all I need to do is walk forward and I will find Zobeide and the marble hall. It seemed quite easy to find the way through the palace before.*

Of course, she always had a guide, like Hasan or Zobeide. Now she is on her own. If only she knew where she was sup-posed to go. She is not sure she wants to see Zobeide again. But there seems to be no other choice.

Determined, she walks forward along the curving corri-dor. She quickly realizes her mistake. The corridor loops back-ward, sprouting more side passages, until it rolls back on itself and ends in a wall.

She retraces her steps and takes a passage on the left. Very soon she comes to a fork. She takes the left passage again, the whistling of the wind becoming more distant, making her feel more comfortable. Left. Left again. She has read of this strat-egy, to always choose one side when exploring a labyrinth. Only she has never bothered to work out exactly how it would help.

The passage in front ends in a wall. She cannot hear the wind anymore. Luckily, there seems to be enough light in here. Although there are no windows, or lanterns, or any other apparent light source, the corridors are lit with what seems very much like daylight. She retraces her steps to the nearest fork. Right, then left, left again, and left. Into a wall. Retracing the steps...

She doesn't realize she is lost until her hand, running

along the wall, hits a familiar crack. She has been here before. Her eyes don't remember, for all of these passages look alike, but her hand remembers for sure. This is the place where she turned left the second time. No, the third time, after taking two right passages. Or was it the fifth time? She is not quite sure. How could she make a loop like that? She was following the instructions of always walking along one wall. Perhaps she should have stopped and worked it out first...

She has no idea where she has come from and which passages she has already explored. Her legs are sore from walking. She is feeling tired and weak. All the passages seem a blur. She cannot even recall in which direction she was walking before stopping to look at this treacherous crack on the wall. Maybe it is not even the same one?

Tired, she sinks to the floor. She will just take a little rest and then go on. Where? Can she find the place she started? Probably not. And even if she did, what good would it be?

She feels terror seize her again. This is very different from hanging over a fiery abyss or pushing your way through a mound of earth. There is nothing that urges her to act, and this absence of urge in itself creates such emptiness that it is very hard to keep on fighting. What makes it even worse is the empty howling of the wind, barely audible in the distance.

She buries her face in her hands. She can't do it anymore! She should have died back there in the waterfall! Now there is no quick and easy way to die anymore. She will have to die slowly, of hunger and thirst, maybe turning into a ghost to haunt this place with its hollow passages. Like this horribly wailing wind.

She pauses.

The wind.

All the passages in this place seem alike. There is only one difference between them. *The sound of the wind.*

The wind must be the answer. She needs to follow the sound until she finds it source. It has to be the exit from the labyrinth. And if not, at least it will be something *different* from these maddeningly similar passages.

She quickly gets back to her feet and follows the passage

backward, where the sound of the wind seems to be louder. At times she almost can't hear it. What a fool she has been! The wind was so loud near the place she entered this labyrinth! All this time she has been walking away from her goal, guided by some stupid, animal desire to keep warmer.

She runs into a wall at the end of the passage and stops, listening to the distant wail. It seems to have been a little bit louder back there, before that turn. Was there a passage leading off at that place?

She walks back to the nearest passage, off to the right. Yes, the sound seems to be stronger here.

She comes across another place that somehow seems familiar. The wind is getting louder, so that she doesn't need to catch her breath anymore to hear its distant sounds. When did she see this place before?

She runs into a wall again and turns back. And then it hits her. A curving passage in front, and two openings off to the sides.

The wall behind her used to be the door that let her in. She turns to the wall and once again runs her desperate fingers along smooth marble. Nothing. No cracks, not even a hollow sound when she knocks on it. Just the pain in her knuckles hitting solid stone.

After all this time all she has done was return to the place where she started!

Despair seizes her again with its cold hand. She fights the strong urge to give up, to sit here on the floor and wait for the end. Maybe someone else will come along the same path she did, and then the door in the wall will open once more? *If* the next one along the path even makes it this far, past the challenges of Water, Earth, and Fire, straight into the challenge of the Wind.

She breathes deeply and takes a few decisive steps forward, to the fork where the three passages run off to different sides. She just came from the left one. The one forward, as she knows, ends nowhere.

She takes the right passage.

After a few turns it starts to feel as if the maze of the marble corridors is becoming much denser. There are many openings in the walls on her sides. It becomes harder to choose which passage to take. The wind seems to be coming almost equally from many of them, as if wandering in the pipes and tubes of a giant organ.

The princess stops. She has just taken two wrong turns, having to retrace her steps after hitting the wall. And the sounds seem to be fainter than before.

She closes her eyes. Her head is swimming and her legs are so tired she is afraid they will give way any moment. But she cannot give up now! Not after coming this far!

Not until she finds out where the wind is coming from.

Eyes still closed, she feels her way along the wall. It seems that the sounds are stronger on her left. Right around here there should be an opening of a side passage.

Her left hand tracing the wall sinks into emptiness. Here it is.

She turns left without opening her eyes. This time the sounds seem to be stronger in front. She can hear an additional tone to the wind's howling somewhere deep in the labyrinth: a barely audible high-pitched whistle she couldn't hear before. Somehow it makes the wind sound friendlier. More like the winds sound in the open spaces she has been used to all her life.

The change in the sound feels so encouraging it makes her forget her tiredness for a while. She rushes forward with new strength.

After a while she loses count of the turns and passages. She doesn't want to open her eyes anymore for the fear of seeing the same blank maze. And it seems that in the absence of vision her hearing sharpens to the point where she can unmistakably detect the sound of the wind getting stronger.

She hasn't run into any more walls since she started to rely entirely on her hearing.

The sounds are now so loud that they are almost deafening. Enhanced by the narrow passages, the wind now sounds like a symphony played by some strange orchestra. As she turns into the last corridor, she suddenly feels a wave of wind sweep over her, hitting her face and blowing back her hair. She stops and slowly opens her eyes.

The Chosen of the Water

*T*he maze of passages has ended. The princess is standing in a huge, round hall with a skylight opening far above to the clear afternoon sky.

The hall is filled with wind. She can feel heavy waves of air coming in through the opening above, twirling in the giant, circular space with howling and wailing that echoes so far in the passages behind her.

On the other side of the hall she sees a large doorway leading off into what looks like another hall beyond. Through the door she seems to make out the glistening of greenish water in a marble pond. Is that Zobeide's hall?

She carefully sticks a hand out into the space in front of her. The wind hits it with such force that she barely has timie to pull back to avoid being swept into the twirl. The wind blows her long hair across her face. She steps back, pushing the annoying hair out of the way.

She has to make her way across this hall. But how?

She carefully puts out her fingers to touch the wall of wind rushing past her face. It has a definite direction, twirling toward the left and slightly upward. She has a suspicion its flow is directed toward the door on the opposite end. But how can she know for sure?

She lets a strand of her hair into the wind. It flies off to the left, almost horizontally, with such force that the pull actually hurts. She hastily draws back, afraid for the hair to be pulled off her head.

It seems that if she jumps into the stream of air, it will carry her almost directly to the door she needs to take.

It could also carry her past the door and smash her into one of the smooth walls of this marble cylinder.

Or, it could catch her in its endless twirl and carry her around the hall forever.

There is only one way to find out.

She pushes off the wall of the passageway and dives head-first into the stream of air. A powerful wave catches her and sweeps her off her feet. She sees a wall flying straight toward her, and the airflow turns at the last moment and sweeps her past. Her trailing hair hits the wall behind her.

It feels a lot like being caught in a stream of water. As in water, she feels an urge to close her eyes. But she cannot afford to do that. She has to look out for the doorway. She has to catch on to it.

The doorway sweeps past in a blink of an eye. She stretches out her hands, but it is too late. Her fingers brush the smooth wall without any way to hold on.

The stream of air has a slight upward pull. If she misses again on the next round, she will be carried out of reach of the passage altogether. She has to hold on this time.

Keeping her eyes open, she struggles against the air current trying to turn her over. Her feet take to trailing up behind her. It feels so unreal to be floating upward in the wind like this.

She forces her hands to track the wall, forces her head to stay clear, not to spin, to let her eyes keep a clear mark of the opening in the wall. Here is the first passage again, coming up. She has made a full circle. She is about halfway up the doorway. The current is still going upward, but she should have another chance to hold on as she reaches the opposite side.

The walls are going by too quickly, the patterns of the marble becoming a blur in her eyes. She feels numb and almost misses the moment when her fingers tracing the wall hit the opening.

The princess thrusts her hands inside the opening and grabs on with all her might.

The impact is so strong that she feels as if her arms are going to break off. She clenches her teeth, struggling against the air stream. Before, it was hard for her to even pull her hand back in. Now, she has to pull in her whole body against the force so strong that it easily keeps her afloat, legs dangling in the air behind her.

Her fingers are slipping. She won't be able to hold on.

This is my last chance, she thinks. *If I can't hold on, the air current will carry me toward the open skylight in the dome.*

Out into the sky.

Her slipping fingers suddenly find a support. A notch in the smooth marble that feels almost like a handle.

She holds on to it with all the strength of her failing arms.

The pull of air seems to be weakening.

Struggling with all her might, she manages to pull herself an inch toward the passage.

Her arms are getting numb. She cannot feel her fingers anymore.

She can't make it. She will have to let go.

She can't let go.

A strange force keeps her body struggling in spite of all. She *knows* she can't give up. She is so close. She has been through so much. She has to pull herself in.

Pull—herself—in...

The stream of air is slowly giving way. Her dangling feet find support on the smooth wall, and pushing against it, she finally manages to pull herself forward enough for her head to reach the opening.

She gets hold of it with her chin. She keeps struggling.

It becomes easier with her head inside the opening. The princess finally gives in to her body, which seems to be struggling entirely on its own. She concentrates instead on getting into the passage. Shoulders first. The marble corner presses painfully against her breasts, but she is past noticing such simple things as pain. Her torso, curving around the corner into safety. Her kicking legs.

The flow of wind is not supporting her anymore. She slides off and collapses on the marble floor.

A wave of fatigue overtakes the princess. It seems to take ages for her to be able to sit up, to struggle weakly up to her feet, to make a few uncertain steps onward along the corridor—

—into a huge, greenish room with a marble pond in the middle.

It looks almost exactly like Zobeide's hall. But it has no windows overlooking the forest and no other entrances except the one the princess came through.

The marble basin in the center looks different too. The water in it is not boiling in constant turmoil. It is mirror-still, and it emanates warmth, almost like a living being.

The princess stops. What is she supposed to do now?

She has a nasty feeling that whatever it is she needs has to do with this still, warm water.

Can I bring myself to step into a green marble pond again?

No. Anything, but not this. She cannot be pulled into the whole circle once more.

She won't survive it.

Slowly, uncertainly, she makes her way to the pond and carefully dips a hand in there.

She feels no pull on her hand this time. The water feels warm and soothing, beckoning. It is full of small bubbles that pleasantly tingle her skin.

She feels her body ache with desire to be embraced by this water. In fact, the thought of staying out of it any longer feels like torture.

Trembling with impatience, she lowers her feet over the edge and submerges into the receptive warmth of the pond. As the water tingles and caresses her, she moans slightly. It feels almost like many pairs of hands touching her with their soft, sensual fingers.

She closes her eyes, giving in to the ecstasy of a feeling she has never experienced before. It feels wonderful to the point of being terrifying. She doesn't want it to stop. She wants,

above all, to share it with someone. She longs for it so much
that her eyes fill with the tears of her desire for this person to
be here with her, right now.

Hasan.

She sees his face as vividly as if he were there, looking at
her intently with his deep, gray eyes.

"Hasan," she whispers, breathing out his name with such
strength that it seems as if her soul itself pours out with this
single breath of a word.

His lips move in response.

"Gul'Agdar," he says quietly.

Blowing her words back to her.

Blowing her soul right back into her body.

She wakes up with a start. The green marble room is gone.
She is lying on a platform in the middle of a room so white
that its blaze hurts her eyes.

Am I dead? She lies for a while, contemplating the possibility. She cannot feel anything. Is her body still there?

She tries to move. Fingers first, then toes. Then, very
slowly, her limbs.

She seems to be all there. Or most of her, anyway.

"She is awake," says a voice beside her. A woman's voice.

"Gul'Agdar?" calls another voice.

She doesn't recognize any of them. Where is she? Who are
they? What happened?

She tries to rise on her elbows, but she is too weak for that.

"Drink this, Gul'Agdar."

She feels warmth at her lips and automatically takes a sip.
Surprisingly, she feels no taste in her mouth. She doesn't even
feel as if she has swallowed any real substance. The drink
seems to consist almost equally of water, air, and fire that
makes her mouth tingle. It also tastes weakly of earth.

The drink of the Elements.

Is there such a thing?

She slowly inhales the white, blazing air. Can she move
her lips? Can she make her voice come if she summons it?

"Who are you?" she asks. The words come hoarsely, but
they seem to be quite audible. At least, she hopes they are au-

dible somewhere outside her head.

"She speaks," says a voice. "She is truly alive."

I am alive, the princess thinks. She cannot quite believe it, but she trusts the strange voice to know what it is talking about.

"She took the hard way and survived," says the first voice again. "She must be strong."

Am I?

"The last one seemed strong too," the other voices say. "But he never passed the Fire."

"I think a soul is out there wandering in the Palace of the Winds right now."

"Remember the one who made it all the way to us and died without waking up?"

"Lady Zobeide must have had great faith in this one if she sent her through the most treacherous gateway."

"Amazing, such a faith in one so young."

"We should mind this one."

"We should use her proper name."

There is a pause, and then the voices draw closer, as if their owners are leaning over her. The princess still cannot see a thing besides the blazing white. Is she really alive?

Two pairs of hands pull her up to a sitting position.

"Get up, Gul'Agdar," the voices say insistently. "You must go and receive your prize."

She blinks, and the room suddenly comes into view.

She finds herself surrounded by water. The platform she is lying on appears to be floating in the middle of a large pond that fills the entire space up to the walls. The walls themselves seem not entirely solid, as if the platform is floating in the middle of an ocean surrounded by mists.

The princess also sees the owners of the voices. Four women with long, flowing hair held by silver circlets on their brows, their dresses long and shimmering like Zobeide's but with a blue sheen to them. Their faces, beautiful and distant, are smiling at her.

"Come, Gul'Agdar." One of the women beckons.

"The Elements have initiated you," another one says. "You

are favored by Water."

"Go and receive your prize," the third one murmurs, her voice soothing like a breeze in a forest meadow. This one has a tiny mole on her cheek that makes her look different, almost substantial compared to the others. She smiles at the princess with the mischief of a child inviting her to play.

"Who are you?" the princess manages.

"We are the priestesses of the Elements," the first woman says.

"We are favored by Water."

"We are here to greet you."

The platform floats onward as they talk. They are now approaching a wall of mist. It emanates chill and moisture, just like a real mist would. The princess shivers and stands up to be level with the strange women. Still naked, she pulls her long hair around herself to cover up at least a bit.

She gasps as the platform enters the mist. It feels like going blind again. Then, just as suddenly, the platform hits solid ground, and the mists part with a soft popping noise.

She is standing in a small circular room. She is alone.

In front of her is a stone pedestal with something blue lying on top.

"Go and take your reward, Gul'Agdar," murmur the voices from the mist.

She steps closer to the pedestal and reaches out toward the blue—cloth?

It feels light and pleasantly silky. Soothing.

She picks it up and unfolds a robe of blue silk, a dress cut in the Dhagabad fashion. Something falls out of it as she pulls the dress up. A stone on an elegant silver chain. She bends forward to pick it up and admires its quiet, delicate beauty.

The opaque, watery stone is yellowish in color and almost transparent. Yet as she looks at how it catches the light, she sees a blue flame in its depths, sometimes glowing with a scattered light, sometimes shining as a single blue beam.

She has seen a stone like that only once before, in a ring on Zobeide's forefinger.

The Stone of the Elements.

The token that gives those initiated into the cult the aid of the Elemental powers.

She glances at the stone pedestal again and gasps, her newly acquired treasures falling out of her hands.

Right in front of her is the object that seems to have come straight out of her dreams. An oval drum with a handle sticking out of its upper end as it stands there, leaning against the marble pedestal. The strings attached to the handle run out of view behind the drum's surface.

A *tama domga.*

Dreamily, the princess reaches out to take the strange instrument into her hands. It feels unreal to touch its smooth, leathery surface and to hear the gentle ring of the disturbed strings. It feels just as if she has been magically carried back, thousands of years ago, into the temple on the distant bank of the Great River Ghull...

She leans the oval drum against her knee and begins to beat the slow, sixty-four-measure rhythm of the Sacred Dance.

Ancient Allies

"This is taking too long, Zobeide," Hasan says. "Something is wrong."

He turns to her almost in time to catch a glimpse of a smile that passes across her lips.

"Some of the challenges are difficult, Hasan," Zobeide says. "It takes a long time to overcome them."

Hasan gives her a searching look while keeping outwardly relaxed. Zobeide's eyes are fixed on the greenery outside the window, but he is certain she can feel his gaze.

What is she hiding from me? he wonders. *What is her game?*

"Tell me more about your powers, Hasan," Zobeide says absently.

She looks as if absorbed in the view outside, but this time he manages to catch something he missed before. A set of her neck, a slight groove of a tense muscle under her perfectly smooth skin. He notices that her gaze, seemingly fixed on the forest outside, is directed inward, through her eyes, through the side of her head, straight into his soul. *She wants to know how powerful I am. Why?*

"Where is the princess, Zobeide?" he asks. "What have you done?"

His voice is still calm, but something in his tone makes her turn sharply and give him a long, knowing stare.

"Why do you worry about her so much?" Zobeide whispers. "Why can't you let your thoughts away from her? You are free now! Free to do as you will!"

"I *am* free, Zobeide," he says quietly.

They look at each other for a long time. The room remains quiet except for the hissing and rumbling of the hidden streams in the marble basin.

The sound of an opening door echoes unnaturally loud in the quietness of the room. A figure standing in the doorway makes Hasan's heart jump. It is familiar to him all the way to the smallest curl of her dark hair. And yet...

She is wearing a silky blue robe, the deep sapphire blue that brings out the shine in her eyes the way a perfect setting brings out the deepest shine of a precious gem. A silver pendant with the Stone of the Elements set into it rests below the hollow of her throat, and the clear blue flame emanating from the stone adds to the overall glow that seems to surround her small figure. Her face is pale and drawn, and there is a quality to it that he has never seen before—a sharp determination of the kind that can only be brought about by considerable inner strength.

Gul'Agdar, the princess of Dhagabad, the apprentice of the Elements, and yet much more than that.

Her eyes meet his to share a long moment of silence. He searches for a trace of her old confusion and doesn't find it. Then he rises from his chair to meet her.

"Hasan." The way she speaks his name makes him feel singled out, distinguished from the rest of the world into a special inner world with her. He answers her the same way.

"Gul'Agdar."

She brings out an arm from behind her back, so that Hasan and Zobeide can see the object she was holding there, up to now hidden from view.

The drumlike musical instrument gives a low hum as its hidden strings get disturbed by the movement. Hasan hasn't seen one in centuries. In fact, these instruments had become rare even at the time when he was a simple wizard in Dimeshq, slowly but certainly moving on his way to absolute knowledge.

A *tama domga*.

With a smile that Hasan feels is intended only for him, the princess steps into the room. Then she turns to Zobeide, and Hasan feels an almost audible clash when their eyes meet.

"I passed the challenges, Zobeide," Gul'Agdar says, her voice cutting through the air like a knife. "I am now the Chosen of the Water."

Is Hasan imagining it, or did he just see Zobeide shiver under the princess's gaze?

"I see you received a *tama domga*," Zobeide observes. "The Elements have acknowledged your talent for music, Gul'Agdar."

They look at each other for another long moment and then break the contact. Hasan can sense actual power emanating from the princess, a presence that definitely wasn't there before. Or was it?

"Can you take me back, Hasan?" the princess asks, turning back to him. Her eyes are shining softly, the familiar warm glow back in them.

"Gladly, princess," Hasan says, rising.

He looks at Zobeide, now studying both of them with an expression he is unable to read.

"Good-bye, Zobeide," he says softly, searching her eyes for any sign of an emotion he could relate to.

"Good-bye, Hasan," she says with a smile, but her eyes, looking from him to the princess and back, are cold.

The wind curls up the steps, through the double row of columns, through the narrow entrance, and uncoils freely inside the giant, hollow space of the desert temple. The voices continue their whispering, now even more distinct than before.

"It is breaking us apart," the voices whisper. "It has to stop."

"The green-eyed one is helping us... ussss..."

The voices wander around inside the dome, conversing with each other, acquiring distinct notes that differentiate them from one an-

other.

"The green-eyed one is training the girl..." The voice that spoke trails off to a high, ringing pitch, almost female. "She is our ally."

"She wanted to kill the girl," another voice murmurs—a low, rumbling voice that could have been male if it didn't belong forever in this hollow world. "If the girl died, the danger would have ended."

"She should have died," a third voice agrees.

"If the girl died, a great power would be lost," a new voice whistles. It sounds like a draft caught in a narrow space, almost like a wail. "But she survived. She passed the test. She will now learn faster."

"The green-eyed one is our ally," the other voices join in. "She is helping us to contain the girl."

"The green-eyed one is powerful," the first, female-like voice whispers, coiling in the circular space of the dome. "Is she close to being contained?"

"We don't know... know... know... know..." The voices echo throughout the ancient temple and settle down in the depths of its hollow passages.

For the moment the wind rests before starting on its new tour of the endless desert.

As she watches Hasan and the princess go, Zobeide slowly shifts in her chair. Her eyes, following them, bear a hardened expression, a veil of steel temporarily shielding their emerald depths. Her pale face seems to be carved out of marble, as beautiful and as still as the faces of the ancient statues.

After what seems like a long time she stirs, turning her gaze back to the marble pond, the gateway the princess went through to face the Challenge of the Elements.

The mists rising from the pond's surface coil in front of her, forming an oval that hangs in the air. Tiny droplets of water swell and fuse, occupying more and more area, forming a single ball of water with a flattened surface in the middle, surrounded by mist. A mirror of water in a misty frame.

Zobeide's eyes search the depths of the mirror, waiting.

The Goddess of Dance

She remains stone-still, but some feeling breaks through the emerald steel of her eyes as she watches a face appear—a pale, handsome face whose black beard and curly black hair accent so well the fiery look of the haughty, dark eyes. A man who was her lover for many centuries, until their love-hate relationship drove her at last to this deserted island in the middle of nowhere. A man of her distant past, who challenged her so dramatically back on the pentagram plaza in Dimeshq over two thousand years ago. A man whose advantage over her was shattered so unexpectedly by the interference of a youthful-looking mage with quiet gray eyes, known to Dimeshq of the time by his unremarkable name, Hasan.

Galeot-din al Gaul, the former Dimeshquian court mage.

Galeot-din Ali, the current sultan of Dimeshq.

"Your majesty," Zobeide says, her mouth twitching. This title stands between them as a tribute to his vanity, a useless quality that is quite possibly preventing Galeot-din from gaining even more power. She knows that his equals, the great mages, use this title to remind him of his limits, and that he hates this constant reminder of his hard-earned position that serves both his pride and his shame. It gives her great pleasure to see him flinch, soothing her hurt pride and the heart wound inflicted by Hasan. She is not about to let her feelings about any man bother her, but it does feel soothing to cause another man displeasure.

"Is he gone, Zobeide?" Galeot-din asks stiffly.

"Hasan?" she asks, enjoying another flinch of his pale face. Galeot-din hates Hasan for many things, among which public victory over Galeot-din on the main plaza of Dimeshq ranks perhaps even higher than winning the affection of Zobeide, Galeot-din's woman, and becoming her lover for many years. She knows that Galeot-din has never forgiven Hasan for sparing his life back in that ancient duel. Because of Hasan, being alive in itself has become an embarrassment for Galeot-din, and she is not about to let him forget the humiliation.

"Yes," Galeot-din answers forcefully.

"He and the princess have just left. I believe they are sailing off the island right now."

"So, the princess survived?" Galeot-din asks. He doesn't care one way or the other, Zobeide knows. It may have been her own private plan to get rid of the girl, but her two allies, the sultan and the court mage of Dimeshq, didn't have room to think of these small matters. The focus of their interest has always been Hasan.

"I am not sure what went wrong," Zobeide admits. "I sent her through the most perilous gateway. And she is not that strong, or so I thought."

"She is much stronger now," Galeot-din points out, returning some of the sarcasm. "Perhaps the foretelling is right. Abdulla here seems to pay a great deal of attention to it."

In the shadows behind Galeot-din, Zobeide catches a glimpse of Abdulla's thin, nervous face. His darting eyes send shivers through her even across the distance of her watery mirror. She finds herself vaguely wondering what kind of a lover he would make, with such unpredictable fierceness burning so close under the surface, with so much fire in him that it shines through his eyes like an eternal torch. She knows that the court mage leads an ascetic life. She makes a mental note to look into it one day.

"Perhaps," she says, dismissing the subject to press on with the more important part of the conversation. "Let's talk about Hasan."

He really should stop flinching at the mention of Hasan's name, if he wants to join forces with me against Hasan, she thinks. It also reminds her how dangerous an enemy Galeot-din may turn out to be, should their interests happen to diverge. If he could hate someone because of a passing rivalry that ended over two thousand years ago, she should be more careful about insulting him now. On the other hand, their own relationship goes back so far that he is probably not going to change toward her no matter what she does.

"What did you find out, lady?" Abdulla asks.

"Hasan doesn't seem to know the limit of his own powers," Zobeide says. "But he seems to believe that his powers - didn't change after he gained his freedom."

"Could he have tricked you into thinking that? Do you think he trusted you?"

"I believe he trusted me at least until the last minute," Zobeide says, keeping her voice steady to overcome the sudden pain that seizes her chest. Trust... Did she just do something irreversible, to lose a dear friend? Or did she do it long ago, back when she first thought she had lost him forever?

"If we could only be sure that he is really all-powerful," Abdulla says thoughtfully. "The desert will not imprison him if his powers are not absolute."

"What makes you so worried, Abdulla?" Zobeide asks. "They should be absolute, if he himself believes so. And they will serve his ruin after he encounters the True Library. The magic there should be enough in the end to trap him for eternity."

"I don't deal in possibilities, lady," Abdulla says with a slight bow. "If his powers are not absolute, we need a backup plan."

"If his powers *are* absolute and he is free in this world, it gives us all hope," Galeot-din puts in.

Not for the first time Zobeide marvels at how well these two men get along, despite the enormousness of their egos, despite the way that Abdulla, probably the stronger of the two, has accepted the secondary role of the court mage and in return is treating his sultan like an overly spoiled child. *Common interests force people to make so many compromises,* she thinks. *I only hope this alliance will last for as long as necessary.*

"Do you think, if something goes wrong, that caliph of Megina can help us?" she asks. "I heard he has a djinn."

She catches a flicker go through Abdulla's face that for a moment sets it aglow with a new feeling, a passion so fearsome it makes the man look like a beast.

"Yes, he does have a djinn," Abdulla says. "A djinn he doesn't deserve. And yes, if Hasan's powers are not absolute, we might have to use her to eliminate him."

Her, Zobeide notes. *He knows. Perhaps, he may even have seen her, the mysterious priestess of the Dance? Perhaps that memory is what lights up his eyes with this animal glow. He should really make an interesting lover.*

"There is another thing I found," she says. "There seems to be some link between Hasan and the girl. She may prove to be a problem after all. It is very unfortunate that she survived my test."

"Yes," Galeot-din agrees. "We have to deal with that too. Do you know the nature of their link?"

"No." Zobeide shakes her head. If she didn't know Hasan well, she might have missed this link altogether. His sudden flashes of anxiety when Gul'Agdar must have been in grave danger—what was it he was feeling?

"I think Caliph Agabei might be helpful in that as well," Abdulla puts in. "He seems to be very keen on getting the girl into his service, one way or the other. And now that she has been initiated into magic, it seems to be going according to his wishes, doesn't it?"

"But I heard she is supposed to marry that boy, Amir or whatever, of Veridue," Galeot-din protests. "shouldn't we meddle with that arrangement, Abdulla?"

"We don't usually 'meddle,' your majesty," Abdulla says in an icy voice that holds as much mockery in pronouncing this title as Zobeide's own. "But we have, in fact, made arrangements to ensure that our ally, Caliph Agabei, gets her instead."

"Good."

Abdulla thinks he is much stronger, Zobeide observes. *And Galeot-din is accepting it. I should definitely explore more of the court mage's hidden qualities.* She holds Abdulla's gaze, giving him a long, promising look. She shifts in her chair to let the line of her dress emphasize more the shapely curve of her breast. Then, with a sensual smile, she turns her attention back to Galeot-din, making sure that each of the men believes this display was for his sake only.

"You know what to do next, Zobeide," Galeot-din says, taking his eyes away from her body with visible difficulty.

"Yes," she says, pitching her voice low to bring out its most seductive undertones. She lets her gaze slide past Galeot-din and once more meets the shining eyes of Abdulla as she speaks, letting each of them believe it is meant for him alone.

"Until later, then."

The mirror shivers and breaks into a cloud of mist that slowly settles back over the green marble pond.

The Joining Ritual

"*T*he barge is here! The barge is here!"

Riomi bursts into the room, flustered and breathless. Her soft, round face is crimson red, as always when Riomi is excited. Everyone in the room, gathered around Thea and the other apprentices being prepared for the journey, looks up at her with frowns. The barge was supposed to be here exactly at this hour. There is no reason to be all flustered over it.

Thea's heart races, but she is so involved in the solemn ritual of preparation for her journey across the river that she cannot possibly allow herself to show it. Besides, if she gets excited over the arrival of the barge, what will she do when she gets to the Temple of the Sun, where so many new things will happen to her all at once?

The first journey to the Temple of the Sun occurs when an apprentice completes her training and is ready to become a full priestess. Among the apprentices chosen for the journey this year, Thea is the youngest, which is an even bigger achievement since she started her training at least three years later than the others. Some of her older friends, including Riomi, are now fussing over her, rubbing ointments into her body and arranging her hair into a ceremonial knot. This smooth knot at the back of her head symbolizes the bond of her servitude to the goddess. It means that whatever happens in the Temple of the Sun will be for the higher cause, and it is

Thea's duty to submit to it.

"Are you ready?" a shrill voice says in front of her. She raises her eyes to see Eilea, the priestess's pretty face bearing everlasting scorn. For an unknown reason Eilea seems to have disliked Thea from the start, and now, at the sight of Eilea, Thea feels her stomach tighten.

"Don't get too warmed up for the kind of welcome you will get from the priests of the Sun, talented girl," Eilea says, her shapely mouth bending into a downturned crescent shape. "They are quite bored across the river, you know."

Thea holds a pause, waiting for Eilea to continue. But the priestess's upturned, ever-laughing eyes study her in silence.

"Would you tell me more, Eilea?" Thea asks carefully, not to show disrespect to her senior, and yet not quite able to keep the edge out of her voice.

Eilea's eyes laugh at her triumphantly, while her mouth releases its downward bend into the almost-straight line of her crooked smile.

"You think they want to see you dance? You have been practicing for weeks, I heard. Well, girl, let me tell you something. They will not even let you finish the first segment of the Dance! They will rush on you like a pack of hyenas! And there will be many more of them than you'll ever want! If I were you, I would practice my tolerance to pain instead."

"That is enough, Eilea!" says a stern voice from behind.

Eilea bows her head and steps aside to let three Mistresses, Tamione in the lead, approach Thea, now fully dressed in her white tunic, fragrant with myrrh, her hair in a knot so smooth it glistens in the flickering light of torches.

The three Mistresses make a stunning combination in looks. Mistress Ngara, on the right, is tall, dark, and heavily built, her face bearing a grave expression of Fate. Mistress Ganne, on the left, resembles an elegantly carved statuette of olive-colored jade, her narrow eyes bearing a distant look of the Future in their ebony depths. Mistress Tamione, in the middle—with her pale skin, ivory-white hair, and light aquamarine eyes—looks at Thea as if through the remote depths of the Water.

The Joining Ritual

"Don't listen to anyone, Thea," Tamione says in her soft, caressing voice, whose deep undertones reverberate through Thea's spine. "This is a great day, and we are all proud of you. What the goddess sends to you today is a test, yours only to endure. All you need is your faith and your skill."

She bends forward and gives Thea a light kiss on the forehead. Thea has a momentary vision of sands and hot wind sweeping through the desert.

"Whatever happens to you today," says Ngara in her low, deep voice, whose tones resemble the low beat of the *tama domga*, "you must remember that your soul is pledged to the goddess and that the significance of this ancient joining ritual with the priests of the Sun goes far beyond whatever form it takes."

She also gives Thea a kiss, and Thea feels as if she is suddenly surrounded by chilly stone walls, small under a giant dome running up to immeasurable heights over her head.

"Remember," says Ganne, whose melodious voice sounds so soothing after the heavy words of Ngara. "Whatever happens to your body, your core is untouched. Focus on the essence, not on the form, and your essence will emerge, pure and wholesome, from the bonds of the ritual."

In turn she bends to kiss Thea on the forehead, and as Thea is swept with her new vision—a garden full of fragrant flowers, tinkling brooks, and leaves rustling in the breeze—she hears Ganne's voice whisper into her ear:

"Bring us back a daughter to the goddess."

As the barge navigates through the meshwork of side streams and pools into the open water, Thea gasps in admiration. She hasn't seen the open part of the Great River since the almost forgotten time when she went with her mother and sisters to the city of Aeth to sell pots. Now, as the barge rocks on the waves of the powerful, turbid stream below her feet, she has a strange, sinking feeling in her stomach. It seems to her as if the tall chair she is sitting on will overturn and dump her into the water, spoiling her carefully prepared outfit.

To divert her thoughts, she moves her gaze over to the half-naked rowers, their dark bodies glistening with sweat as they pull long oars to direct the barge diagonally upstream. One has to row hard against the current, Thea realizes, to keep up with the mighty flow of the Great River Ghull and end up in the city of Aeth, instead of being carried downstream all the way to the City of the Dead.

Thea has never seen men so close. The sight of their muscular bodies is strangely disturbing. She feels a chill in her stomach and a weakness in the small of her back and hastily looks away to rest her eyes on the rolling waters of Ghull.

In the distance she sees Sobek—his lumpy, glistening back looks like a log half-submerged into the shallow waters near the shore—waiting for his prey. As the barge moves closer, Sobek's eyes and nostrils turn their way, studying the barge as it sweeps by his sacred spot. Or, perhaps, the god is away now and it is only his crocodile body that Thea sees swimming in the river.

All through the journey Thea carefully avoids looking at her traveling companions—four apprentices, new like her, and ten priestesses, on their second journey to the Temple of the Sun. Thea is dying to ask the older women what it is like in there. But all of them are strictly bound by the vow of silence. At least, until the ritual begins.

As the barge hits the shore, Thea sees a huge crowd in holiday garments meeting them at the pier. The tall men in white robes with wreaths of flowers on their heads are undoubtedly the priests of the Sun. They step forward, holding out white lily wreaths, and as each of the women from the barge sets her foot on the pier, they lay a wreath on top of her head. Each of the men then takes a priestess by the hand to lead her through the streets of the desert city of Aeth to the Temple of the Sun.

Thea's priest is very tall, with unusually light hair and liquid blue eyes that slide over her in a single icy glance. Thea shivers as she feels his huge hand close over hers. She follows him automatically, looking through the parting crowd with unseeing eyes. What is it that awaits her ahead? What will they do to her, those strange men whose closeness feels so alien to a girl who hasn't seen a man up close since she was eight? Will they hurt her, like Eilea said?

It can't be that bad, Thea tells herself. After all, some of the priestesses are here for the second time already, and they seem quite content with their fate. Besides, they are here to follow the will of the goddess they all pledged to serve to the end of their days.

Thea forces herself to stop thinking about the future, to forget the disturbing feeling of a man's hand holding hers, and to look around. She hasn't been to the city for over ten years. The last time she walked down this street was with her mother and her sister Ishana, now dead. She can see the tapered pyramid shape of the temple's main chamber at the end of the main street, its doors standing ajar to welcome the guests. She can also see the narrow side streets running away on both sides, curving to hide from view the busy city life. One of these streets is the one her mother used to take on the way to her pottery stand at the bazaar.

Although she can vaguely remember some of the buildings and streets, Thea doesn't really recognize the feeling of the city—as if everything here has changed in the past ten years so much that the city itself has become different. Despite the width of the main street, enough for at least six horsemen to ride abreast, and the grandeur of the buildings, some of them rising to the height of five floors above ground, the city seems smaller. It could be, of course, that the city looks different from the eye level of an eighteen-year-old girl, about to become a woman and a priestess, than that of an eight-year-old child. It is possible, but Thea finds it so hard to believe.

As they walk into the tapered shade of the temple, Thea feels the chill run through her body and once again becomes painfully aware of the warmth of the man's hand closed over hers. Her own palm begins to sweat, and she feels weakness in her stomach that suddenly makes her sandaled feet unsure of their footing.

What will they do to me? What sacrifice will the goddess ask me to make?

She suddenly becomes aware of the crowd all around them that must have followed them all the way from the pier. She hears the singing of many voices. At first, she cannot make out the song among their uneven choir. Then she recognizes the ancient Hymn of the Joining, telling of the union between the Great Goddess and the Sun God. Everyone around them is celebrating. People are cheering and singing to honor their arrival, oblivious to what will happen to them inside. Or, maybe, knowing exactly what will happen and cheering about it?

Thea suddenly realizes that all of them from across the river are nothing more than a bunch of helpless women in the power of big, strong male priests who are supported by the crowd, cheering them in what they are about to do. She throws a wild look around even as the hands lead her inside and the heavy doors of the temple shut behind them, blocking the sunlight.

They are standing in a huge stone hall, bigger than anything Thea has seen before. The tapered walls form a giant pyramid-shaped vault, supported by a thick column in the middle that enhances the feeling of grandeur without breaking the space inside the temple. Thea sees many small doors leading off to the sides, and a large stone table at the end of the room.

They were taught about this before their trip. The stone table is called the altar. The male priests make animal sacrifices on it. The dark, uneven color on and around the table is the color of dried blood. The faint, tart smell in the air is what blood smells like after being washed over the stone surface and drained through the holes in the floor.

These men kill in here. And now, the priestesses of the goddess, the Giver of Life, will dance on this dried blood to start the symbolic joining of the two cults to produce new life.

Thea suddenly realizes the new meaning of a line from the Hymn to the Goddess:

The Joining Ritual

From the old blood new life springs forth,
Life and death unite in a circle of rebirth.

The priests form a circle and sit down, cross-legged, on the bloodstained floor, illuminated by a mix of torches and slanting sunbeams falling through the narrow holes in the pyramid walls. In the deadly stillness, the priestesses lay down their lily wreaths and their robes. To the slow beat of the *tama domga* they start their synchronous movements of the sacred Dance.

Fifteen slender bodies move like one. Their measured heartbeats become the beats of the *tama domga*. There is nothing in the world around them. Nothing between them and the Dance. All the other movements in the world have stopped, and even the flow of time itself has slowed down to the measured beat of the Dance.

Thea's mind soars to the endless heights. She sees their bodies moving down below, and the rest of the world opens to her, the entire world no bigger than the palm of her hand. She is one with the goddess. She and her sisters are one. They are invincible.

And then, from the heights of her vision, she starts seeing other bodies moving among them. Strange, foreign bodies, so unlike the perfect, slim bodies of the priestesses. Animal bodies. Bodies of men.

With a start, Thea's mind snaps back into her own head. She sees a man right next to her, his naked body rippling with muscles, his breath hot on her cheek as he moves in closer to her. The sharp, metallic smell of blood hits her nostrils with new force, and she realizes that the other priestesses are separated from her by these strange, male bodies that have moved in to dance with them, to interrupt their ritual even before they have finished the first segment of the Sacred Dance.

The low beats of the *tama domga* accent the smell of blood and naked bodies, the warm rhythm of the breaths, the glistening sweat. Dark, animal powers rule this room now, making the sharp smell of blood rise and cloud the priestesses' heads like incense fumes. Thea feels a cup raised to her lips and automatically takes a sip of the thick liquid, sweet and sharp-smelling like blood. The liquid flows through her body with warmth and makes her head swim.

She sees a man right next to her, moving in closer. His arms are spread to the sides, and in his light gray eyes she sees the gleam of a beast closing in on its prey. She barely recognizes that he is the same priest who placed a lily wreath on her head and led her through the streets only a short time ago. Or, a long time. Who knows how much time they have spent in this room that seems to take away all that is human and leave only the animals, dancing naked in the fading evening light?

She hears moans and whispers around her. The bodies move into tighter groups, scattering through the giant pyramid hall. She feels something touch her bare hip, something both smooth and soft, like a baby's knee, and hardened underneath like iron. The priest next to her is slowly closing his arms around her, and she realizes with horror that it couldn't have been his hand that touched her hip. And it could not have been another priest, since the two of them are now standing alone, away from the others, near the stone altar.

Trembling, Thea lowers her eyes to the strange thing that is touching her, brushing against her skin. Seeing what it is, she produces a wild, inhuman scream.

The room becomes momentarily still. All eyes—clouded with lust, sharply alert, or misty with pain and tears—stare at her in silent reproach. How can she, a girl, disturb the ancient ritual? How dare she not submit to the normal course of events?

Thea, awakened by her own scream, looks around the room with rising terror. Everywhere on the floor she sees naked bodies, one priestess to two or three men, doing something that she cannot quite comprehend but that makes her shudder with disgust. She sees the face of the apprentice priestess Ohe—a loud, cheerful girl who was so excited about going to the Temple of the Sun just yesterday. Ohe's face is wet with tears; she is biting her lip, helplessly trying to push off two men whose huge bodies cover hers, hiding it from view. To the side Thea sees another apprentice, struggling without much conviction.

They all know they must submit, Thea thinks. *They are disgusted and frightened like me, but they don't dare to fight. This is the will of the goddess. And these men are not trying to make it any easier for us. It is just like Eilea warned me.* Or is it the will of the goddess too that we are all taken here, on this bloodstained floor, with such animal violence?

She feels strong hands catch her from behind, trying to force her down onto the floor. And then something snaps inside her in a blinding flash of anger. *Nobody dares to treat the priestesses of the Dance like that! This is wrong, and I will not submit to this! We are* not *going to lie helplessly on this floor, waiting to be sacrificed for the greater good. What are we, animals?*

"No!" she screams, tearing free of the hands holding her and hitting the man behind her with an elbow. The priest, not expecting this, stumbles back, releasing Thea. She jumps forward, over the bodies at her feet, and turns to face the whole room.

"Sisters!" she cries out. "Don't let these animals treat you like this! We must leave this instant!"

The room remains still for several moments. Thea waits for the women to stir, to break free, but nobody moves. Then two men leap up to their feet and start advancing on Thea. She backs off toward the side door.

"Come!" she shouts. "Save yourselves!"

"Nobody is going to hurt you, silly girl," the nearest priest says with a grin. He has a scar across his face that also takes off part of his hair, making him look more like a cutthroat than a servant of a god. He spreads his huge, hairy arms and in a snakelike leap plants himself between Thea and the door.

"I have her," he tells the priest closing in from the other side.

The women still make no attempt to escape. One of them, Daine, the older priestess, sits up from among the most disgusting bundle of bodies Thea can imagine and calls out to Thea in a soft voice. "Come back, Thea! This is the will of the goddess! You must go through with this, or you will never be a priestess!"

Thea feels her throat contract in a half-sob, half-gag as she imagines herself on the floor among this orgy. She hears the hairy priest pant as he approaches her, and the mere sound of it makes her hair stand on end. She can never be a part of this, even if this means never becoming a priestess.

With a yell she leaps into the air and kicks the man right in the middle, where, by her calculations, it should hurt the most. As he bends over with a gasp, she sweeps past him, through the little door, along a winding corridor, as far as possible from the horrible room. She hears screams of rage behind her, but she is running like the wind. No man can overtake the dancer of the goddess if she is flying for her life.

Sel

*T*hea runs deeper and deeper into the temple, throwing glances over her shoulder to watch out for the possible pursuit. The torches on the walls are scarce, and after a while she is forced to slow down to choose her way. She has been running through too many forks and turns of the endless corridors, and by now she feels so hopelessly lost and exhausted that she probably could never make it back.

No matter. She will never be a priestess now. She will be banished from the temple, the only place in the world she can call home. She will never again see her friend Riomi; or the Mistresses Ganne and Tamione, who took her in and guided her through her training; or the pretty and scornful Eilea. She failed. She doesn't deserve to live anymore.

Thea sinks to the stones of the corridor and buries her face in her hands. Horrible pictures she saw back in the hall make her shudder with terror. She feels dirty from the hands that were grabbing her, and especially from *that thing* that brushed against her hip. What happened to her? What has she done?

In desperation, she buries her face deeper into her hands as her body shakes with uncontrolled sobs. She bitterly wishes to be dead right now, struck by the angered goddess on this very spot. Why, oh why can't she die right now? She doesn't want to face her future existence, banished from all the life she ever wanted!

A hand touches her shoulder. She shrinks away from it in terror, not daring to look up. Has she been caught? Will they now do to her what they did to her sisters back in the hall?

"There, there," a voice says gently by her ear. "What happened to you, girl? Who hurt you?"

Thea slowly raises her tear-stained face to look into a pair of gentle, hazel-brown eyes. A man. A priest of the Sun, judging by his robes. Not one of those from the hall. This one looks older and definitely more caring than the others. He must be, oh, at least thirty-five. And he has a golden chain around his neck, unlike the other priests she saw today. A senior priest, most likely. *What do they call their seniors?* She tries to remember. *The Masters, by analogy with the Mistresses of the goddess? No, that doesn't seem right. What does it matter, anyway, for a girl who has forsaken her duty and doesn't deserve to live?*

Thea suddenly becomes painfully aware of being naked, and shrinks away even more, curling into a ball on the stone floor.

The priest steps away and unfastens a clasp on his shoulder to remove the cloak he is wearing on top of his robe. Bending down again, he holds his cloak out for Thea.

"Here," he says with a fatherly smile. "Take this. You must be cold."

Thea carefully reaches out to pull the cloak toward her and shrinks back, holding it in front as a shield.

"I won't hurt you," the priest says, a smile flickering in the corners of his mouth. "Get up. Put on the cloak. You'll be warmer."

Keeping a careful eye on him, Thea slowly rises to her feet and wraps the cloak around herself, careful to reveal as little as possible of her bare skin. She hasn't been shy of her nakedness for a long time. But after today she will never again feel comfortable under a man's gaze.

"There. That's better," the man says, a smile surfacing from behind his concerned expression. It seems to Thea as if the sun has suddenly come out from behind a cozy white cloud. She feels a strong urge to trust this man, who seems to be so unlike the other priests.

Sel

"You must be one of the priestesses from across the river," the man observes. "shouldn't you be in the main hall?"

"I—I ran away," Thea whispers, lowering her head. *He is going to take me back there,* she thinks. *And they will do to me all the horrible things they are doing right now to all the other priestesses. Probably they will also give me a beating for hurting one of the priests.*

"You seem too young for this," the man says gently, reaching out to touch her cheek and pausing as she shrinks away from him. "Maybe you came as a *tama domga* player?"

"No, I am an apprentice," Thea says, briefly resisting the temptation to avoid her fate by telling the man she is indeed a *tama domga* player. "I am—I was going to become a priestess today."

"You must be very talented to make a priestess so early," the man says, studying her with concern. "Still, I don't think you are ready to be here."

"Why aren't you in the main hall?" Thea dares, flashing her gaze up to him. "I thought all the priests are."

"All the young priests are," the man corrects her. "I took part in my fair share of rituals some years ago."

"You?" Thea asks in disbelief, trying in vain to picture this kind man among the beasts in the main hall. "You seem so... different."

"Older, you mean?" His eyes again light up with laughter. "I wasn't always old, you know."

"You are not old!" Thea objects, and flushes at the intensity of her words.

"Thank you," the man says with a mischievous grin. "And, by the way, these boys back in the hall, they are not really bad. They are just... insensitive. Too eager to get what they want. Young men are no longer taught respect these days."

Thea shudders again at the memory. Insensitive. Eager. That doesn't quite seem to sum it up for her.

"My name is Sel," the man says. "What's yours?"

"Thea," she whispers, not quite sure she should really tell her name to a stranger.

"Thea. A beautiful name. It means 'dancer' in the old Ghullian. Did you know that?"

"No." Thea's eyes fill with tears. Dancer. She was destined to be one. Until today.

"And it means that whatever happens to you, you are going to be a great dancer," Sel continues. "You already showed it by coming here so young."

"I will never be a dancer," she whispers. "I failed."

"Come with me, Thea," Sel says, holding out his hand. "You need to eat and to drink something warm. You'll feel better, I promise."

Thea hesitates for a mere second before taking his hand. She has nothing to lose. She can never even find her way out of this maze, anyway. And this Sel seems like such a nice man.

Sel leads her forward, away, as it seems, from the main hall. They go deeper and deeper into the labyrinth, until they emerge from one of the corridors into a wide space. Besides the passage they came through, there are about a dozen doors here. All of them seem to be locked.

"Where are we?" Thea asks as Sel lets go of her hand to fish out a key from the depths of his robes.

"We just passed through the central labyrinth to emerge at the senior priests' quarters. Most of the buildings in the Temple of the Sun can be accessed only through the labyrinth."

Thea looks around in fascination. The entire Temple of the Goddess has only one building, which fits the living quarters of the priestesses and servants, the classrooms, the kitchen area, and the great dance hall. She cannot even begin to imagine the size of the structure that has many buildings accessible only through the labyrinth, in addition to the giant hall she came from.

Sel pulls the door open and beckons her inside.

"This is my room," he says. "As it happens, I have some bread and wine saved for supper. I will be honored if you share it with me, Thea the Dancer."

Thea cautiously steps into the room after him. She has never been alone with a man before, and although Sel seems so trustworthy, she is not sure she should accept his invitation. On the other hand, what has she got to lose?

As Sel moves around lighting lanterns, the room's sparse furnishings come into full view—a low bed, a table, and a dark wooden chest against the opposite wall. Sel sits on the bed and gestures Thea to the chest.

In the light of the lantern between them, she finally has a chance to take a better look at her new acquaintance. He does look at least twice as old as she is, but he doesn't seem like an old man at all. There is something so youthful in the way his eyes glitter with hidden laughter, in the way the smile always stays in the corners of his mouth, that he seems at times to be no older than a little boy. His wide, sun-darkened face, crossed by a few deep lines, is lit with the glow of his sharp, brown eyes that seem to pierce her through. His straight, sun-bleached hair falls on his broad shoulders, set in a way more appropriate for a young athlete than a senior priest. And he is handsome, Thea thinks. Handsome in a rugged sort of way.

Sel reaches under the bed to pull out a basket and a large clay jug. He opens the basket, producing two mugs, a loaf of bread, a large piece of goat cheese, and a handful of long, amber-colored grapes. Thea suddenly realizes how hungry she is. She eagerly digs her teeth into the sweet, freshly baked bread topped with dry, salty cheese. It seems delicious. She never thought that such a simple meal could be so tasty.

Sel watches her, laughter dancing in his mischievous eyes. He holds out a cup of wine for her, and, thirsty from eating salty cheese, she drinks it in two gulps. He slowly drinks his own and pours more for both of them.

Thea's head starts to spin. Her body is warm and heavy from the wine. She feels easy and relaxed, as if all the terrors of today never happened. She looks into Sel's laughing eyes and feels that she can now forget all her worries. She can worry later. Now there is this wonderful food, this sweet wine, and this man, the first man in her life she has really talked to. He makes her feel easy, so that all her troubles go away.

"I am glad you feel better, Thea," Sel says. "I hope our boys didn't hurt you too much."

Thea darkens for a moment, but talking about it doesn't

seem to be painful anymore. On the contrary, she now feels like talking to somebody about it.

"They—they were grabbing me," she says. "They behaved like animals." She shudders at the thought of *that thing* touching her hip. "And then I saw what they were doing to the other priestesses. I couldn't—I just couldn't—"

She stops, unable to go on. She doesn't even really know what they were doing; it just felt so disgusting back then. Somehow, right now, in Sel's reassuring presence, it doesn't seem so bad anymore.

She suddenly wishes she could just sit close to him and cling to him, to feel his warmth, to let him hold her the way her mother used to hold her when she was a child, so tight that they almost felt like one. During her years in the temple she has never experienced physical closeness to anyone. She longs for it so much right now that all her thoughts and feelings focus on this longing. She glances at him sidelong, not daring to suggest it and yet so lightheaded it is hard to resist her desire. Of course, he is a man and she shouldn't really think of getting close to him. But her own seniors have sent her here today to do much worse things with men than a simple embrace.

"You can sit next to me if you want, Thea," Sel suddenly says, his mischievous eyes lighting up with a gentler glow.

She wants it so much she doesn't need to be told twice. She sweeps over to his side and buries her face in his shoulder, throwing her arms around him and feeling him, after a hesitation, gently embrace her. She clings to him as a drowning man clings to a lifesaving rope, inhaling his smells of sundried reeds and wild grass.

She feels the hardness of his muscle under the thick folds of his robe. This closeness, that she hasn't experienced since she was a child, suddenly awakens in her another kind of desire, a desire for more closeness, a desire to feel the warmth of his skin next to hers, to be even closer to him than she is now.

The strength of this desire scares her. She has never felt anything like this before. It overwhelms her so much she cannot possibly resist it anymore.

"Sel," she whispers, withdrawing from him just enough for him to hear. "I want you to take your robe off. I want to feel you next to me."

He moves his hands to hold her burning face between his palms and looks deep into her eyes.

"Are you sure you won't regret it, Thea the Dancer?" he asks. "I don't want to do anything to hurt you."

She tries to answer, to reassure him that she really wants what she asked, but her trembling lips fail to form into words. Instead, she draws his face close to hers, searching for his lips, surprised at her own actions and yet unable to stop herself. It feels as if somebody else is controlling her body, some animal instinct that suddenly broke loose from the bonds of her mind. Her body, a beast long asleep, has awakened. Unlike Thea— a confused girl who has never known the touch of a man—it knows exactly what to do.

His lips.

The kiss drowns her. Half-aware of her actions, she moves her hands along his body, feeling the hardness of the muscles tensing up to her touch. Her trembling fingers move to unfasten the clasp of his robe, or the cloak that she is wearing. She cannot tell anymore. She struggles with the heavy folds until he gently pulls her away to undo his own robe. He lets it slide off to reveal his muscular torso and then carefully helps her out of her cloak.

She sees admiration in his eyes as her body is revealed in all its naked perfection. She has never thought of herself as good-looking, or any particular-looking whatsoever, always focusing on the perfection of her dance. She knows that compared to some other apprentices her body is too flat, missing some of the more shapely curves. But now, seeing the admiration in Sel's eyes, Thea feels overwhelmed with excitement as she, in turn, admires the mature shape of his body, definitely not that of a young boy, but even better for the comparison.

Pushing aside the annoying and useless cloth, she reaches out to him, so overwhelmed that she feels weak. She shivers as his strong hands hold her up, almost lifting her off her seat, then gently lower her onto the bed, his burning skin touching hers, their bodies so close that they almost feel like one. But she still wants more.

"Sel," she whispers. "I want... to be closer. I want all of you. I want us to be one."

She is not quite sure what she is asking for, but she knows she really wants it now—and with him. She is certain that whatever it is, it will make them even closer, and she wants to be close—to be part of him—forever.

"Are you certain that is what you want, Thea?" he asks, searching for her eyes.

The tenderness in his gaze is overwhelming. Drunk with his smell of sun and reeds, she reaches out to him to pull him close.

So close.

"Yes," she whispers. *Yes. Yes.*

His hands stroke her with gentle firmness, leaving her breathless with desire. He plays her body like a *tama domga*, his touch evoking a response as strong as the deep ringing of its hidden strings. She lets out a moan she cannot hold in anymore, feeling that she may burst any moment from the bliss that fills her from the inside, seeking a way out. She loses herself in the sure movements of his hands. She is absorbed in his touch, in the way he plays her body, evoking a deep beat almost as pure, as perfect as the Dance. Her mind leaves her body and soars to the immeasurable heights. And yet, it also stays inside, to savor every moment of her ecstasy.

She vaguely feels him move in closer; she feels his weight against her, and a momentary pain there, down in the burning spot between her legs. And then, finally, when she no longer can tell their bodies or their senses apart, the ultimate bliss and the ultimate release.

The Royal Family

*T*he great ceremonial hall is shining so brightly with lanterns and decorations that the princess feels momentarily blind walking in. She is dressed in blue, and she briefly notices heads turn as the servants and courtiers stare at her unusual outfit. Since the day she turned twelve she has worn white, until the Elements presented her with this sapphire-blue garment.

She is not sure what prompted her to wear this blue garment today, to the ceremonial feast in honor of Albiorita and her newborn son, but she enjoys the startled look in her father's eyes. Moving through the parting crowd of courtiers with her small suite of nannies and slave women, the Veriduan girl Sadie among them, she approaches the royal canopy. She feels vulnerable in this crowd without the reassuring presence of Hasan, who was the first in her suite ever since the day she first let him out of his bottle. Her feeling of vulnerability seems even worse after the dream she had last night, the dream of Thea in the Temple of the Sun, which has not only deeply shaken her but made her longing for Hasan even stronger than before. This dream has penetrated to the very foundations of her sensuality, leaving her mind and body encased in a dreamy state of one who cannot quite wake up to real life. She needs all her strength merely to walk through the ceremonial hall to her place, among the rising whispers around her.

The royal canopy at the end seems different. It has been extended to accommodate a small canopy on the side, slightly lower than the sultan's and the sultaness's seat. And there, beside her parents, at the head of the feast, she sees a tall, slender shape clad in shimmering silk. A veiled woman holding a baby in her arms, her eyes raised lovingly to the sultan beside her.

Albiorita. The mother of the first healthy son born to Sultan Chamar Ali.

Sliding her gaze briefly over Chamar and his concubine, the princess turns to look at the sultaness in her usual place beside her royal husband. Even from this distance she can see the strain on her mother's pale face that now lacks some of its healthy, majestic glow—as if the mere presence of a successful competitor for her husband's favors, one honored so far above her station at this glamorous feast, robs the sultaness of her usual cheerful disposition.

As the princess walks up to her place under the canopy, she sees her mother's eyes fixed on her and gives her a reassuring smile. She bows to her parents before taking her seat to the right of her mother, under her own small canopy adjoining the main one. She cannot help noticing that her place, the way it is set, puts her in equal position to Albiorita on the sultan's left, under the canopy exactly symmetric to hers.

She doesn't care about such things. But as she looks at her mother, she sees the sultaness's pursed lips and the way she glances sideways at this canopy arrangement. The princess gives her mother another encouraging smile and notices a tear glistening in the corner of the sultaness's eye. She then turns to meet the eyes of Nimeth, sitting motionlessly behind her mistress. The Aethian woman looks at the princess in a strangely new way, with a calm respect that makes a startling change from Nimeth's earlier air of superiority.

The princess realizes that she must have changed a great deal in these past few months. She briefly wonders where this change will lead her with all her new training, with all the prophecies and foretellings associated with her.

The Royal Family

I wonder where Hasan is now? she thinks. *I must talk to him before all is over. Maybe now that my father has a new heir I finally have a chance to take my destiny into my own hands?*

Her gaze falls on the table in front of her, so full of exotic dishes that there hardly seems to be any free space. Her nose is hit simultaneously by the smells of clove, mint, and saffron, mixed with thousands of other, subtler but equally mouthwatering spices. *It must have taken the cooks days to prepare this feast,* she thinks.

The princess notices right in front of her dishes of quail in sour sesame sauce, sweet and spicy *sankajat*, and honeystewed walnuts. She smiles. Her friend from the kitchen, the cook Naina, must have ordered these dishes put in front of her, knowing that the princess has always liked them. Unfortunately, she doesn't feel in the least bit hungry right now.

She casts another glance at her mother. Abandoned in the middle of this glorious feast, the sultaness is sitting unnaturally stiff and straight under the canopy next to her husband. The plate in front of her is untouched. The princess focuses her thoughts, as she learned through Thea, to send her mother a feeling of calmness. She sits there, focused, until a side glance tells her that her mother is more relaxed now. Relieved, she sees the sultaness pick up a piece of *basturma*—a smoked, spicy meat—from her plate and absently chew on it.

Relax, mother, the princess is telling her silently. *This is all to the best. Let the sultan be happy.*

She knows this is not entirely true, at least for her mother. It may be best for the princess to lay down her role of the heiress to the throne, but her mother's position may suffer a lot more if the sultan names his newborn son an official heir. On the other hand, the princess also knows that she is not nearly powerful enough to transmit her actual thoughts to her mother. All she hopes for is that the sultaness senses her sympathy.

The sultaness does seem to sense something from her daughter, something that causes her to relax and to glance warmly at the princess.

She looks so different, the sultaness thinks, letting go of her bitter thoughts for a moment to admire her daughter's grace-ful posture, enhanced by her new, unusual blue outfit that comes from an unknown source. *She shouldn't have worn it here,* the sultaness thinks. *But she does look nice in it. Something about her has changed. She is so mature, so independent, so con-trolled. She would make a great sultaness in her time—if only my husband doesn't do something foolish to ruin her chances.*

She sighs, throwing a glance at the sultan, deep in conver-sation with Albiorita. *Why did this have to happen to us?* she thinks.

The sultaness's lips tremble, and she lowers her gaze to her plate. Why have the gods been so unfair to her? Why couldn't her husband give her a son and heir in due time, so that they wouldn't have to go through all these changes almost twenty years after their marriage?

Her flow of thought is interrupted by fanfares, followed by the sounds of hushing all around. Not that this hushing is necessary at the royal canopy. The only conversation here comes from the sultan, exchanging quiet words with his con-cubine. And the sultan is now silent, watching intently the master of ceremonies, who is rising from his seat and ad-dressing the hall in his clear, trained voice:

"Chamar Ali, the great sultan of Dhagabad"—he pauses, waiting for the ceremonial words "May he live forever!" to roll through the hall and die—"wishes to address his noble guests!"

A speech, the sultaness thinks. *We are going to hear more praise to that woman.*

She briefly looks away, wishing she had the courage to rise and walk away as she feels like doing, and meets the quiet look of her daughter's dark blue eyes. The princess is smiling at her, supporting her. *This beautiful, loving creature is the only one who* cares!

The sultaness's eyes fill with tears, and she raises an end of her silk scarf to her eyes to wipe them off, as well as to hide her face from the curious eyes.

"My beloved subjects," Chamar says next to her, standing up from his pillows and raising a full goblet in his hand. "We have gathered today to celebrate the most joyous occasion any ruler can hope for: the birth of my son, Chamari Hamed, the royal heir to the throne of Dhagabad!"

He raises his goblet to the loud cheers that fill the giant hall all the way to the dome.

He is mad, the sultaness thinks. *How can he announce his heir like that, in front of the whole court? What of his arrangements with Veridue? What will happen to the princess now? How will they receive her after learning that this marriage doesn't really give them access to the Dhagabad throne?*

She knows enough of the affairs of the state to realize all the dangers of such a turn of events. But she also knows her master and ruler enough to realize that this will not stop him from doing such a thing. He has wanted a son all his life. He is beside himself with joy.

The cheers rise in the hall, but the sultan still has his goblet raised. He wishes to continue, and seeing this sign, the hall once again sinks into silence.

"We have another joyous reason to celebrate today," the sultan continues. "Together with the honorable sages of the royal council, we have looked through the books of Dhagabad law in search of proper ways to name my son, Chamari Hamed, the official heir to the throne in the status of a prince."

The sultaness notes the pleasure with which the sultan rolls this name on his tongue. *Chamari* Hamed. Chamari, son of Chamar. Up to now all the sultan's children have been named Chamarat, daughters of Chamar. *It must be very special for him to pronounce this,* the sultaness thinks. *But a prince? How?*

"You all know," the sultan speaks, "that the laws of Dhagabad decree for the sultan to have only one wife, as opposed to his subjects who may take up to four wives according to the rules set by the gods and their holy prophets. This ancient law has been passed so that there is no question of the sultan's proper heir, so that his elder son by his only wife can become his rightful successor. However my wife, Sitt Chamar"—he gestures toward the sultaness, motionless on her pillows—"has failed to give me a son, and my country a proper heir."

Sitt Chamar. Wife of Chamar. He hasn't used my proper title, the sultaness thinks. *Gods, what is this man doing?*

Her devastation of earlier is now replaced by fear. Like a madman, the sultan is driven on to his own doom, to the doom of his country and his proper heiress. What is he up to?

"The sages of the royal council," the sultan continues, "have found the law that comes into effect when the sultan's wife is unable to bear a son. In this event, the sultan's concubine who has mothered the sultan's eldest son becomes his second wife, and her son becomes the crown prince and the heir to the throne. I gathered you today to announce my marriage to the beautiful Albiorita, my beloved concubine and the mother of my heir!"

Again the hall drowns in cheers as the sultan takes a sip from his cup and lowers it, waiting for his subjects to settle down.

They knew, the sultaness thinks. *They have been prepared for what was going to happen in this hall today. Otherwise, none of them would have cheered at this outrage. I am the only one who - didn't know.*

On the other hand, the courtiers of all times have always cheered at whatever their sultan says at the head of a feast with his goblet raised.

She exhales a breath that suddenly seems painful in her chest. *What is to become of me?* she thinks hopelessly. *What is to become of my daughter?*

"As a symbol of our marriage, I remove my bride's veil from her face, so that all of you can behold her unearthly beauty!" the sultan announces. To the continuous cheers he helps Albiorita up from her seat. The concubine hands her child over to a woman who appears by her side.

A free woman, the sultaness realizes, noticing the absence of metal bracelets on the woman's wrists. *A nanny for the little prince Hamed.*

As the sultan removes Albiorita's veil, the hall gasps in admiration, exaggerated by the necessity to be polite, but genuine to some extent. The sultaness herself has to admit that she has never seen a woman like that before. *Baskarian beauties are legendary for a reason,* she thinks. *Nobody in these parts has ever seen such white skin, blue eyes, and golden hair as Albiorita's. Nobody before has been brave enough to unveil such a perfection in front of everyone's eyes.*

"From now on," the sultan announces, "this woman will be known to you as Sitt Albiorita, the mother of the royal heir, the sultaness, and the second wife of your sultan Chamar Ali."

Second *wife. At least he had the decency to abide by the law to the end. He will not shame himself by casting me out like an unnecessary toy.*

Knowing her husband well, the sultaness also realizes that he would not cast her out even if he wanted to. He has always been fair, even if compulsive at times. He knows that she failed to give him a son through no fault of her own.

She briefly wonders whether Albiorita's son is really fathered by the sultan. The concubine—the second wife—has been enjoying too much freedom in the palace, outside the harem, being the focus of everyone's attention for the past two years. Who knows to what lengths she would have gone to fulfill the sultan's dear wish for an heir?

"You will refer to my second wife as 'your majesty' at all times!" Chamar announces. "I now wish for my family to welcome my new wife as their new sister and mother."

He gestures for the sultaness and the princess to rise, and leads Albiorita toward them. Under his heavy gaze, the sultaness embraces her new sister, secretly wishing she had enough strength to strangle her. Then, watching the princess in turn embrace her new mother, she wonders at herself. She cannot help feeling bitter, but there is really no need for such violent thoughts. It is all the gods' will. If the sultan is meant to have a male heir, who is she to wish otherwise?

The sultan gestures for the crowd to fall silent again. Two women step forward from behind Albiorita's canopy. One of them is holding the baby boy. The other one is leading by the hand a girl, a little bit over two years old.

"I present to you my family," the sultan says. "My elder wife, Sitt Hattieh, and her daughter, Princess Gul'Agdar. My younger wife, Sitt Albiorita, and her daughter, Princess

Eleida. My son and heir, Prince Hamed ibn Chamar!"

This time he raises his goblet and drains it all the way to the bottom, throwing it on the floor afterward to shatter it to a thousand pieces. Wild cheering drowns the hall. All the courtiers drain their goblets, shattering them on the floor afterward. The hall fills with movement, the courtiers hurrying up to the royal canopy to congratulate the happy family. Servants and slaves rush around, collecting broken glass and wiping the puddles of unfinished drinks. Among the turmoil, the sultaness turns to meet the eyes of her daughter, now officially named Princess Gul'Agdar, just like she, the sultaness, after twenty years has officially reclaimed her given name, Hattieh.

The princess's dark blue eyes are shining. *She is happy*, the sultaness thinks. *Why?*

She wonders at the amazing feeling of peace emanating from her daughter, at the sense of calm maturity that she has never noticed before. Under her daughter's gaze she feels her own tension, frustration, and fear give way to a similar feeling of calmness and inner peace.

We will live through it, she thinks. *Everything will be all right.*

Sparrow Hawk

*H*asan runs his gaze up the shelves of the Dimeshquian library. Today he is not here to read books. The magical trace is back. It is hanging in the air in about the same place, perhaps a touch clearer than before.

There are only two possibilities as to why the trace has returned: either the mage who left it visited the library again on some mysterious business while Hasan was away on the Island of the Elements; or, if this trace was a trap in the first place, somebody might have come in deliberately to reset it. Which means that the trap is ready for Hasan and somebody wants him to take the bait.

Hasan stops, briefly considering the alternatives. Forget the trace and leave? But he cannot possibly forget it, especially if it was left deliberately for him. He has a puzzle to solve, and any clue may prove to be invaluable. Follow the trace, right into a possible trap?

He has a feeling this must be a trap, but he doesn't really know it. Not for sure. Besides, what does he have to fear, being immortal and all-powerful? No wizard in the world can possibly be his match.

He takes a decisive step toward the trace, extending his senses to fully probe its shape, its strength, and the direction it leads off to. Through the wall, right beside the hidden entrance into the labyrinth.

This time, on his way out of the wall, he walks right through a beggar who is perched on the stairs of the library to get better access to the passing crowds. The beggar screams, making Hasan wince. He notices two women staring at him and realizes that, intent on following the trace, he must have made himself too insubstantial, and they must be able to see right through him.

"A ghost!" a woman screams. "By the prophets, this is a ghost!"

"He is a ghoul!" the other woman joins in. "A monster! He is going to drink our blood!"

I thought I looked more trustworthy than that, Hasan thinks, avoiding the woman's upraised fist and accidentally passing through a merchant's cart. *So many people here on the plaza! I'd better make myself invisible.*

He focuses on the trace, ignoring the screams of women who see him disappear in front of their eyes. Last time he lost the trace right about here. This time it still hangs in the air as clear as back in the library, beckoning for him to follow.

I wonder who is trying to catch me, and how exactly they are planning to do it, Hasan thinks, following the wisp coiling through the air. The crowd is especially thick here, right by the pentagram platform for magic duels, and Hasan tries to ignore having to pass through people every second.

He is relieved when the trace takes him onto the platform itself, along one of its diagonals, and off into a side street of Dimeshq. The flavor of the magic he is following is beginning to remind him of something. Or, rather, somebody from his distant past. *Could it be Galeot-din?* he wonders. *Could he possibly still be alive and around here?*

When Hasan encountered Galeot-din at this pentagram during their magic duel ages ago, the court mage of Dimeshq was not yet immortal. Powerful, yes. Possessing a lot of offensive magic. But by no means ready to take a bigger leap into eternity. It is quite easy to imagine that since then the court mage has achieved his immortality. It is also likely that he has never gone far enough to become an all-powerful djinn. After all, even such mages as Zobeide and Abdulla have never reached that end. Abdulla, for one, despite all his faults, seems to have a great potential in him. If he is not a djinn yet, he must be consciously holding himself back from becoming one.

The trace leads off into the upper city. Hasan follows the widening streets, past the blind walls of the rich villas, past the luxurious gardens of olive and orange trees, uphill, all the way to the sultan's palace. The streets here are empty. As in Dhagabad, the sultans in Dimeshq have chosen to place their residences among the rich nobility, away from the noisy crowds and narrow streets of the bazaar. From the height of the upper city, the sultan's palace—shining with its white, blue, and gold ornaments—proudly overlooks its realm, like an eagle nested on a cliff overlooks its hunting grounds down below.

The trace takes Hasan right through the locked palace gates, making the two guards on the sides of it twitch nervously at the unknown disturbance of air between them. They both seem not only aware of it, but quite comfortable with it, Hasan notices. Somebody in this palace must often make his entrance this way.

He follows the trace up the main stairs, through the audience hall, along the stairwells and corridors of the giant, ornate buildings—a whole city on the top of the hill, perhaps even bigger than the palace in Dhagabad. The trace takes him deeper into the palace, all the way through its wide and inhabited central part, into a lonely tower flanking the palace on the east side.

The passages around him become darker and emptier. Save for occasional guards, placed evenly throughout the corridors, he sees no courtiers or servants walking around here.

Private quarters, he guesses. *But whose quarters are they?*

By the luxury of their surroundings, the quarters might very well belong to the sultan himself. But why is it so lonely and dark in here?

He stops before a small door under an ornate, blue-and-white archway. The trace here suddenly becomes very strong. In fact it turns from a mere trace into a *presence*. He is certain that the wizard who carefully laid out the trace for him to follow is behind this door right now.

Waiting for him.

Hoping to trap him in some unimaginable way.

There is only one way to find out, Hasan decides.

He pushes the door open and enters the dark room beyond.

The sultan of Veridue, Eljahed ibn Falh, raises his eyes to watch his oldest son and heir Amir walk into the room. The prince's movements are deft and confident, his white-and-gold cloak flying behind him in time with his swift steps. The prince's handsome face bears a haughty expression, embedded into his features both by his noble origins and by his nineteen years of royal upbringing.

He will make a great sultan one day, Eljahed thinks as he often does when observing his son. *What a joy to his father's eyes.*

Aloud he merely says, "Come in, my son."

"You summoned me, father?" the prince asks, walking up toward the sultan's desk near the window. Despite his many advisors, the learned sages of the Royal Council, Eljahed prefers to use his own judgment in the affairs of the state. He spends many hours in his private study and often calls in his son Amir to explain various documents to him. But his heir notably prefers military exercises and swordplay to sitting in a dusty room behind a desk, and Eljahed doesn't blame him for that. The prince is, after all, very young. When Eljahed was Amir's age he couldn't quite appreciate the value of digging through piles of documents either.

Of course, if the prince showed at least *some* inclination toward reading, it would be even better. But he will, in time, the sultan hopes. He must. And if not, there are always the sages of the Royal Council to help.

He points toward a thin, crumpled piece of parchment unrolled on top of his desk and catches a look of boredom in his son's eyes. Prince Amir's gaze wanders away from the desk toward a cage with a sparrow hawk in it. The bird glances at him with its dry, black bead of an eye and clicks its beak before turning away toward the open window.

"I need to tell you something, my son," Eljahed says. "This parchment—"

"What are you doing with the sparrow hawk, father?" the prince interrupts.

Patience, the sultan thinks. *The boy is as impatient as this bird. If he continues to be this way, people will end up using him as their tool, just like they do with birds.*

"The sparrow hawk is my messenger," he tells his son patiently. "It just flew in from the palace in Dhagabad."

"Dhagabad?" The prince looks at the sultan sharply. They are expecting his bride, Princess Gul'Agdar, to arrive from there very soon. The palace of Veridue is now busy with the wedding preparations. At least this matter obviously holds the prince's interest, the sultan observes.

"Remember the slave girl, Sadie, that we sent as a gift to your bride, the princess of Dhagabad?"

"Yes," the prince says absently.

He doesn't remember, Eljahed thinks. *I should have emphasized it more back then.*

"I chose this particular slave girl because of her outstanding talent with birds," he says aloud.

"Birds, father?"

"Yes, my boy. Birds. Ravens and sparrow hawks. They make great messengers, you know. For example, a sparrow hawk can fly between Dhagabad and Veridue in less than one day. And it can even carry a small package along with it. Tied to its leg, for instance."

The prince looks again at the crumpled piece of parchment, and realization slowly dawns upon him.

"You sent the girl Sadie to spy on the princess?"

Good, Eljahed acknowledges. *Except for one thing.*

"As a future sultan you should learn to use strong words sparingly, my son," he says. "We in Veridue do not 'spy.' We merely like to be informed of things."

"Sorry, father," the prince says, bowing his head.

"This message is the third one I've received from Dhagabad since Sadie went there three months ago," the sultan continues. "The first report was quite satisfactory. She informed us that the djinn has left the palace as we requested and that the princess has taken to spending a lot of time alone."

"But father," the prince puts in, "I know that these demons, djinns, can appear anywhere if summoned. When you say 'alone,' do you mean she is secretly seeing her djinn?"

"Very clever, my son." The sultan nods with approval. "We made sure that Sadie checked what the princess was doing behind the closed doors of her chambers or in the distant corners of the garden. At all times checked she was indeed alone. When she was in her chambers, however, she seemed to be doing some strange physical exercises."

"Physical exercises, father?"

"Something resembling a dance. Performed... er... naked."

The prince flushes in embarrassment.

He is still so young, Eljahed thinks. *So innocent, my boy.*

"Do you think she is doing magic, father?" the prince asks, finally finding his voice.

"No. Sadie didn't notice any change in the princess's apparent inability to command magic."

"Does this girl, Sadie, know any magic herself, father?"

Once again Eljahed nods his head in approval. *The boy is quick*, he thinks. *Impatient but quick.*

"Yes, she does, my son. Not a whole lot, but enough to sense these things. Allow me to go on, however."

"I apologize for interrupting, father." Amir once again bows his head. "I won't do it again."

"Sadie's second report was a bit troubling," the sultan continues, "but it didn't really alarm me. She reported that Sultan Chamar Ali's favorite concubine bore him a healthy boy who could potentially become the sultan's heir. Rather late for an heir to be born, of course, but—"

"Does it mean that Princess Gul'Agdar doesn't carry the right to rule anymore?" Amir asks, forgetting his promise not to interrupt.

"It hasn't been quite clear, my son," Eljahed says, sighing

again at his heir's impatience. "Until the third report came in today."

He points toward the piece of parchment on his desk.

"Read it," he says. "Aloud."

Amir carefully picks up the parchment, so thin that it seems transparent, and so fragile that it crumples with any blow of air from the window. The bird in its cage, seeing the message that has been tied to its leg for a whole day, makes a clicking noise with its beak and steps closer to the prince.

"Go on," the sultan urges.

> *"To our honorable ruler and the sunshine of our land, the great sultan Eljahed ibn Falh, from a humble and unworthy slave Sadie, daughter of Ghar. Three days ago Princess Gul'Agdar mysteriously disappeared from her chambers, leaving behind all her clothes except for a bath sheet. She was missing for a day and a night and finally reappeared wearing a strange blue robe and a precious pendant with an unknown stone. She also brought back a musical instrument of a kind nobody has seen before. Meager powers allow your humble servant to sense that the princess now commands magic."*

Amir lowers the letter with a trembling hand.

"She went to see the djinn," he mutters, his words intense with fury. "Naked. She—she can't be my wife now, father! The vile demon has dared to touch the most sacred thing. He has spoiled her purity. She is... not suitable anymore. She is a *slut!*"

"Patience, my son!" the sultan commands, raising his hand. "These are all serious accusations. We don't know if any of them are true yet."

"But I—I can't marry her, father!" the prince protests. "After what she did back in Dhagabad? After the way she behaves now? She is a *whore*, not a princess!"

"I command you to read the letter to the end," the sultan says. "You may not want to marry her, and this can be one of the reasons, true. But not the main one."

"I may not?" the prince asks.

"Read!" *The boy could drive a holy prophet insane.*

*"Yesterday the sultan Chamar Ali held a feast in honor
of his newborn son and the concubine who bore him.
At the feast he announced that, in accordance with
Dhagabad law, he is taking the concubine as his second wife, and that his son, Prince Hamed, will now be
the official heir to the throne of Dhagabad."*

The prince lowers the letter, his face pale.

"So she is not the heiress anymore," he whispers.

"And not well-behaved enough to be your wife, my son,"
the sultan agrees.

"But how do we get rid of her, father?" Amir asks. "We cannot just tell the sultan of Dhagabad that we refuse, can we?"

"It is not advisable, my son," Eljahed agrees. "We in
Veridue always act with caution."

"What is your plan, father?"

"Let me just say that we can make other arrangements for
Princess Gul'Agdar that will conveniently get you out of this
wedding and at the same time serve our relationship with an
old ally."

"What ally? How?"

"Princess Gul'Agdar is leaving Dhagabad next month with
a wedding train that will include the people we send for her.
I plan to arrange it in such a way that she will never reach
Veridue."

"But—how?"

"The road from Dhagabad to Veridue is treacherous, my
son. Accidents happen all the time. Even the elite guard escorting your bride-to-be can be easily overpowered."

"You intend to kill her, father?"

"By the gods, no, my son! We don't want that on our con-
science. Princess Gul'Agdar has no value to anyone if she is
dead. On the other hand, if she is alive—"

"Value, father?"

"I did not mean literal value, son. We don't intend to sell

her or anything. Let us just say that there are people who wish to obtain the princess regardless of whether or not she bears any rights to the Dhagabad throne."

"Who?" the prince asks.

Should I tell him? Eljahed thinks. *Does he really need to know how this complex arrangement came about? After all, he is just a boy, idealistic and naïve. On the other hand, he is my heir and he needs to learn politics as early as possible.*

"For instance, our old friend Caliph Abu Alim Agabei," he says.

"The caliph of Megina?"

"Remember, he was in Dhagabad among the suitors on the princess's seventeenth birthday."

"Oh, yes, the princess was babbling to me about him trying to bewitch her or something." A shadow runs across Amir's face at the memory of how his pride was hurt back then, during his failed wedding.

"I doubt he would have tried to bewitch her," Eljahed says. "The caliph is our old friend, and he has let me know in no uncertain terms that he would be glad to marry the princess if our arrangement with the sultan of Dhagabad, for any reason, fell apart."

"You mean, you talked to him before, father?" Amir asks sharply. "But you learned only today that the princess is not a... desirable bride anymore."

"After I learned about the birth of the sultan's son, I started looking into possibilities. I didn't give any promise to the caliph. Yet."

They stare at each other for a long moment. Father and son, unmistakable in the likeness of their sharp features, dark eyes, haughty expressions. *One could almost see my face in his,* Eljahed thinks. *I only wish I could teach him all I know in time for his succession.*

"We'll find you another bride, my son," he says. "One worthy of you."

"Thank you, father." Amir's eyes rest on the cage with the sparrow hawk, now asleep on its perch. In passing, he notices a blank piece of thin parchment on his father's desk.

After I leave, he will write a reply to the girl Sadie, he thinks. He'll arrange everything. Perhaps I should offer to take part in these arrangements, but this is really not my style. My father is so much better at intrigues than I am. He believes the country can be ruled by paperwork alone. He doesn't realize that it is a noble image more than wisdom that makes people follow you. He certainly doesn't know some things, my father.

The prince lowers his eyes, bowing to the sultan, as if afraid that some of his disrespectful thoughts can escape through his eyes. Obeying his father's dismissal he leaves the dusty room, his thoughts already far away on the training field, where he knows his lieutenants are waiting for him to signal the start of the sword exercise.

The True Library

*T*he room is so dark that Hasan has to summon his inner vision to see clearly into its depths. He can only see one figure, sitting comfortably in the cozy-looking armchair with its back to the door. But he knows there are two people in here. Two wizards of enormous powers.

Although he cannot see their faces, he recognizes both of them at once, putting together the trace he was following and their now-familiar magic auras.

Galeot-din al Gaul, Hasan's ancient rival, the former court mage of Dimeshq. And Abdulla the Wizard, Hasan's former apprentice.

Only now Hasan realizes that the trace he has been following has been left by more than one wizard. That's why it has been so hard to identify. It bore no distinct signature of anyone he knew. But it did make him think of many possible candidates. Including, as it turns out, Abdulla and Galeot-din, the two wizards who left the trace together to lure him into their trap.

But what do they hope to do with him? Even though they are both incredibly strong, Hasan doubts they are strong enough to overpower him. Absolute power is not something to joke with.

"So, you really believe you are all-powerful, Hasan," Abdulla observes from the unseen depths of the room.

The Goddess of Dance

Zobeide, Hasan remembers. *She was trying to find out if I was all-powerful. Are the three of them working together against me? But why?*

"I know you are wondering why we lured you here, Hasan," Abdulla says, stepping out of the shadows to approach his seated accomplice. "It must have looked like a trap to you. And I believe you have reasons to suspect we are your enemies."

He puts a hand on Galeot-din's shoulder and squeezes it. Galeot-din's face turns even paler than before.

Abdulla is stronger, Hasan thinks. *He is definitely in charge here. And Galeot-din cannot quite control his anger.*

"As it turns out," Abdulla continues, "we would like to offer you an alliance, Hasan. You have something all of us want: an impossible combination of absolute power and freedom. You can understand that achieving these two things together is the desire of every wizard. We want you to help us both to become all-powerful and free."

"What makes you think I can help you?" Hasan asks, finally breaking his silence.

"Maybe you cannot. But we do believe there is something you can do that will help us considerably."

Something I can do. What is it you are afraid to break to me, Abdulla? What do you want me to do? Hasan can sense that Abdulla is waiting for him to ask the next question, and he decides for once to indulge his former apprentice.

"What makes you think I *will* help you?" he asks.

"We think that it may be in your own interests," Abdulla says. His face is still passive, but there is a triumphant flicker in his eyes.

Two thousand years haven't changed you much, Abdulla, Hasan thinks. This time he holds the pause to deliberately try to disquiet Abdulla, knowing that his old apprentice is wishing for him to ask the next question.

"We believe we know something that holds the key to your freedom," Abdulla says finally.

Again, Hasan holds the pause, waiting for Abdulla to continue. Galeot-din and Abdulla exchange glances of uncertainty.

What did you expect? Hasan thinks. *That I will rush at your offer with outstretched arms? That I will trust two men who still hate me after two thousand years?*

Finally, Abdulla stirs, acknowledging his failure to take control of the conversation.

"During the past two millennia," he says, "Galeot-din and I have done a lot of studies. Since we already know the sad experience of our fellow wizards"—he bows slightly toward Hasan—"we focused a great deal of attention on studying anything that has to do with the ancient desert. And we found something that may hold a key to djinn-making."

He stops, watching Hasan's face intently.

This certainly can be useful, Hasan thinks. *If there is something I could have done differently back in my wizard days, it is paying more attention to the ancient desert.*

"Have you ever wondered where the original foretellings come from, and why they disappear without a trace after staying for some time in this world?" Abdulla asks. His smirk tells Hasan how much interest Hasan's own face must be showing, but he doesn't care. If Abdulla and Galeot-din have information about the foretellings, it has been worth it to come here after all.

"There is a library," Abdulla says. "A library of foretellings, in the heart of the ancient desert that makes the djinns. It holds thousands of scrolls that disappeared from this world completely, and many thousands more that nobody in this world has ever seen."

"How do you know this?" Hasan asks slowly. He has to hold his breath not to sound too forceful. A library of foretellings! If there is one indeed, it could answer all his questions. It could tell him how to help the princess to avoid her foretold fate. It could tell him how one should go about being an all-powerful wizard without also becoming a djinn. True, it could be of enormous help to people like Abdulla and Galeot-din, who are afraid to reach out for absolute power because they don't want to become imprisoned. And Zobeide, he realizes. Zobeide must want it too. That is why she must have sided with them.

"We have used our combined powers to search the desert in our dreams," Abdulla says. "Together we were able not only to walk through the sands, but to enter the temple and reach its most distant chambers. That is where we have found the library. It holds more scrolls than you can imagine, in such languages that even touching them requires enormous power."

"How do you know there are original foretellings in there?" Hasan asks. "How can you tell that some of them have been in this world?"

"In the dream world we couldn't move any scrolls, of course," Abdulla says. "But there were several scrolls lying open, and we could see their contents. One of them was about the one who frees a djinn."

He pauses, and Hasan swallows a lump in his throat. *That one.* If he could only see it again! Even that will help him immensely in his quest. But is Abdulla telling the truth?

"I know you must be doubting my words, Hasan," Abdulla says. "You have always been the cautious one. I'll quote you the first phrase of the scroll—short enough not to disturb too many powers by the sound of its language."

He looks straight at Hasan, and his lips move in a combination of sounds that don't really seem like human words. The sounds shake the air like thunder as they leave his throat, ringing in the room with such force that the walls tremble and books slide off their shelves as if pushed by an invisible hand. A dark winged shape falls down from the depths of the vaulted ceiling and twitches on the floor in agony, finally going still.

A bat, killed by the magic of the words that should never be spoken out loud.

He didn't need to say so many words to make his point, Hasan thinks, swallowing a lump to restore his hearing.

Abdulla looks at Hasan with his dark, impenetrable eyes. Hasan knows Abdulla must be tired from summoning so much power to say the words. But he also knows that his former apprentice would rather die than show his weakness.

The True Library

"Are you convinced?" Galeot-din says from his chair. The shock makes his voice sound less dominating than he would have liked, perhaps.

"Yes," Hasan answers slowly, looking at Abdulla. "What is your offer?"

"We want you to go into the library through a portal and read the scrolls that may help us get the information on how to become all-powerful and free."

Hasan pauses, considering. He could do that. It would take enormous powers from him, but he could definitely do that. And he really needs to do it, now that he knows about the library. The only question is, why do they need him? Surely each one of them could enter the library with support from the other's power.

"Why do you want me to do it?" he asks. "Why not do it yourselves?"

"Two reasons," Abdulla says. "First, as you know, a portal requires a lot of energy. A portal into the library takes much more than an ordinary one, used simply to enter the desert and get a djinn. Galeot-din and I together barely have enough powers to maintain the portal itself."

"And second?"

"Second is that, on top of that, one needs power to touch the scrolls themselves. Of all wizards we know, you are the only one powerful enough to approach any scroll in there."

True, Hasan thinks. *Before becoming a djinn I couldn't have accomplished such a task. That is why the treasures of that library are safe from this world. One needs an all-powerful wizard to go to the library and read them.*

He also thinks that it was quite ingenious of Abdulla and Galeot-din to join their dreams to find the library in the first place. If only he knew of the importance of the desert back when he was approaching absolute power!

"Galeot-din and I will create a portal for you to go through without spending any of your power," Abdulla says. "This way you will have enough energy left to read all the necessary scrolls and come back when you are ready. Since you will depend on your own power to return, you will also not need to worry that we won't be able to bring you back."

Wise, Hasan thinks. *He means, I will not need to suspect that they purposely want to leave me behind, but he doesn't want to pronounce such words out loud. I don't have to trust them to do this. The question is, why do they trust me?*

"How do you know I will share the information I find in there?" he asks.

"We will go with you," Abdulla says. "After we help you through the portal, Galeot-din and I will enter the library through our dream link. This way we will be able to read what you read without spending the same energy as you."

I have to give him credit, Hasan thinks. *He has grown to become quite good. It took longer than necessary, perhaps, but he is soon going to be one of the strongest in existence. Especially if this plan succeeds.*

He briefly considers whether he really wants to give such dangerous people as Abdulla and Galeot-din a key to absolute power. But he seems to have no choice. He probably cannot get it all by himself, without Abdulla and Galeot-din helping him through the portal. He may not be able to preserve enough powers to go both ways on his own and also read the scrolls inside. And even if he refuses their offer now and tries to do it later on his own, they can still catch him there through their dream link. Knowing their need, he trusts they will do just that.

"Let's do it," he says.

Children of the Temple

*T*hea carefully feels her way along the dark street. The ferry has left her right in the middle of the town. It took half of the coins Sel gave her to convince the ferryman to take her across after dark and to bring her to the town, ignoring her priestess outfit. She has thrown the rest of the coins into the water. She doesn't want to keep anything of Sel's. It gives her too much pain to think of parting with him forever.

Thea throws a glance to her right, into the darkness upstream, toward the familiar reed thicket and the smooth stone building surrounded by columns that used to be her home until yesterday. Now, after she failed to go through the ritual and shared Sel's bed instead, she cannot go there anymore.

She has nowhere to go.

The night is cloudy and the moon—the only possible source of light on the dark town streets—is not visible. Thea carefully feels her way, thankful for the sandals that protect her feet from the rough cobblestones. She wishes she could get rid of her temple dress, a white, knee-length tunic of an apprentice. But she has no other clothes to wear. And she is thankful at least for the knife that hangs at her belt. You never know who you might meet on the dark town streets.

Thea stops at the corner, peering at a familiar low building with clay walls and a small, unevenly shaped window.

Many years ago, this used to be her home—the house

where she used to live with her mother and six sisters. In another life, she could have had a family waiting for her here. If only she hadn't turned them away so cruelly when they came to see her in the temple.

She stands on the dark street, looking at the familiar window—narrow at the top and wide at the bottom, almost a triangular shape. When she was little, she used to laugh at this shape so much, together with her sisters Ishana and Betanat. Ishana is now dead. And Betanat is the one who threw the last words at her, back at the temple: "One day you'll know what it's like to be alone!"

How was Thea to know that this day would come so soon?

Back to the river, she decides. *I will join Ishana, who drowned in the river six years ago. Perhaps Sobek will be merciful and take me quickly this time?*

She turns to go, and stops at the sound of familiar, warm laughter coming from the window. She recognizes the voice of Leota, her oldest sister. And children's voices, too.

Children? Could it be that her sisters have children now, so that this poor house can continue to be alive with laughter and happiness?

Tears roll down Thea's cheeks. She was cast out of here ten years ago, when her mother decided she couldn't afford to feed her youngest daughter. She then cast her family out, when they came this year to visit her at the temple.

Now she has lost both of the homes she ever had.

She suddenly recalls something else Betanat said to her. "You'll beg mother to forgive you yet!" Betanat had shouted, after Thea turned her back on them to return to the temple.

Beg forgiveness?

Priestesses of the goddess never beg. But she is not a priestess. She will never be one. She has no choice but to beg her mother to take her in.

Or, to throw herself into the river.

Thea feels so much longing for the warmth of the house beyond that window, the house lit with lanterns whose soft glow pours out onto the cobblestones of the street. The house warm with laughter.

She can beg to be forgiven by her mother. Maybe her mother will take her back. And if not—the river will always be there, rolling its heavy waters past its endless banks. The river will always lie waiting for her.

Shakily, Thea crosses the street and reaches over the garden gate to undo the latch. Her fingers know their way much better than her head. She has to search around for the latch, and remembers that she always had to stand on her toes to reach it before. Now, fully grown, she has no trouble reaching the latch that falls easily under her fingers. She pushes the squeaky wooden gate and lets herself into the yard.

The door of their brightly lit house is open. Inside she sees several women sitting around a table, and two little girls playing on the floor. The yard seems much better maintained than before. It is well swept, and the privy house in the far corner is not crooked anymore, but stands straight, its newly painted door fitting exactly into place. There is a new doorway at the end of the yard, leading off into the neighboring house, the one that used to be occupied by a noisy family of shoemakers with five sons who always played tricks on Thea and her sisters.

Somebody has built a row of shelves along the side wall, to accommodate her mother's pottery. Somebody has also planted a tree in the corner of the yard, a small peach tree covered with white, fragrant blossoms.

Somebody is obviously taking good care of the house these days.

As Thea approaches the open doorway on her shaky legs, she sees that the movement inside the house has stopped. Alerted by the noise of the creaky gate, the people inside are all watching a thin young girl with loose hair, dressed in a dirt-stained white tunic, approach them from the outside.

Thea stops in the doorway, blinking against the bright light.

Five women are sitting around the table, among the remains of an evening meal of rice cakes and sour milk pudding. Thea can easily name them all, from oldest to youngest: Leota, Alda, Ora, Betanat, and Galis. Three of them—Leota,

Ora, and Galis—look more like the father Thea never knew, with curly brown hair, wide faces, and narrow, slanted eyes. The others—Alda and Betanat, as well as Thea and the now-dead Ishana—bear more likeness to their mother, with huge eyes, almost straight black hair, and full, childlike mouths.

Her sisters. Her family. Her flesh and blood.

The women she renounced.

Leota slowly rises to her feet, looking Thea straight in the eyes. The two girls playing on the floor crawl under the table, eyeing Thea with fearful curiosity.

"Go away!" Leota says. She makes a shooing movement with her hands, as if Thea is a stray dog. "Do you think you can treat us the way you did, and then just come here, as simple as that? You are not welcome here anymore."

Thea lowers her head. She does not move. She has nowhere else to go.

"Where is mother?" she asks quietly, barely moving her lips. She hopes mother won't throw her out as quickly as her sisters. But they have every right to do it. How could Thea possibly think of coming here?

"Why, do you want to tell her once again that she is not your mother anymore?" Betanat asks, sarcasm oozing from her every pore. "Do you enjoy hurting her again and again?"

"Leave, Thea," Galis says quietly. "You know you are not welcome here."

Thea lowers her head even more, but she still doesn't move. Tears coming up from her throat threaten to choke her, but she doesn't want to let them into her eyes. She doesn't want her sisters to see her cry.

The thought that she herself brought on this kind of treatment makes it worse.

"Go!" Betanat demands. She gets up to her feet and, walking past Leota, grabs Thea by the shoulders and pushes her toward the open door.

Only the dancer's reflexes save Thea from falling. She stumbles across a bucket the two children left on the floor and knocks over a chair. The little girls giggle, crawling deeper under the table.

Children of the Temple

"What is the noise, girls?" comes the voice from the other room. "I told you not to disturb me!"

Mother.

Thea watches her mother appear in the doorway, wearing a nightdress, with a small candle in her hands. She stops, narrowing her eyes against the light, trying to see what is happening in the house.

"I told you, Leota, it is time for the girls to go to sleep. You should take them home before your husband gets back. And you, young ladies"—she turns her fond gaze to the children—"I thought I taught you better than leaving your toys around."

"It wasn't our fault, grandma," the older girl says. "It's her!"

She points a finger in the direction of the door. Following it with her gaze, Thea's mother freezes.

Her hand with the candle lowers, and hot, yellow wax drips onto the floor.

"Thea?" she whispers.

Moving like a sleepwalker, she slowly approaches her youngest daughter.

For a moment it seems to Thea that her mother is accepting her, that she can now, like so many years ago, fall into her mother's arms and forget all her worries. But the older woman stops several paces short, her face hardened.

"Did *they* send you here?" she asks sternly. "Your new family? Did they tell you to steal my granddaughters from me?"

She steps between Thea and the children, her eyes shining with anger.

"You are not welcome in this house," she says, raising her arm to point to the door. "Leave. Now."

Slowly, Thea turns toward the door. She feels numb from the shock and from the tears she still isn't allowing herself to shed. She feels so exhausted that she doesn't care anymore. *It's the river for me,* she thinks. *The Great River will accept me into its womb. The Great River will care for me, its stray daughter.*

She takes two steps toward the door and her knees give way. She sinks to the floor, curling up into a ball. Tears, released by this motion, pour out of her eyes with such force that Thea feels they might wash her eyes out of their sockets.

She senses the room behind her fall into dead silence.

Wiping her eyes with both hands, she shakily scrambles back to her feet. *Leave,* she tells herself. *They don't want you. You can cry somewhere else.*

The flood of tears slows. She stops in the doorway and turns to cast the last look at this place that used to be her home.

She looks at her mother's face and suddenly sees the old woman's lips tremble. Entranced, Thea steps back toward her and sinks to her knees at her mother's feet.

"Forgive me, mother," she mutters. "I'll leave, I promise, but first I want to beg your forgiveness."

"Thea," mother whispers, bending down to look into her eyes. "Why are you here? Why aren't you back at your temple?"

"It is not my temple anymore," Thea says, and these simple words, the truth, seem to cost her all her strength. She sinks into her mother's arms and sobs until she cannot cry anymore. She feels many hands help her up and lead her to a bed; she feels many arms embrace her. She also hears many voices around her, but she doesn't seem to make out the words. What she does hear doesn't make any sense.

"She is burning up," the voices are saying.

"She is ill. What have they done to her?"

"Take the children away, Leota. Can't you see she's sick?"

The world around her becomes darkness, and she sinks into a deep, deathlike sleep.

Thea wakes up, feeling the warmth of a sunbeam on her cheek. She blinks, unable to recognize where she is. The temple? But there is never any sun in the temple. There are no windows at all in the apprentice quarters.

Why does this room seem so familiar?

She looks around. Her vision is blurred. She is having difficulty turning her head. What is wrong with her?

She can see next to her several empty beds. She is not sure about their actual number, but they do seem to occupy most of the room. Where is she?

She forces away the numbness in her ears, forces back the memories of last night, of how she came here, to this room, assisted by many hands.

Hands of her mother and sisters. They have accepted her back!

She is home.

She also remembers the events from before that left her so worn out. The barge. The Joining Ritual she ran away from. The labyrinth underneath the Temple of the Sun. Sel.

Sel.

She longs to see him one more time, to touch his rough skin, to look into his laughing eyes. To cling to him, inhaling his smell of sun-dried reeds.

She will never see him again.

But she is home, with her mother and sisters, back to her old life.

She tries to sit up in bed, but her head feels so heavy she cannot move. Noise that doesn't seem to come from the outside fills her ears. She hears voices that she knows she left behind forever. A hum of many voices, dominated by the more distinct voices of Mistresses Tamione, Ganne, and Ngara. The shrill voice of Eilea. The soft voice of her friend Riomi.

All of them lost forever in her previous life.

As she tries to move, struggling through the pain in her burning body and the noise in her ears, the voices seem to approach, filling the room around her, along with fuzzy shapes, dressed in green and brown village garments, or in white and gray priestess's tunics. She hears phrases spoken by the people long lost, and some people lost more recently.

"She came here last night. She seems ill."

That is the voice of Ishana. No, Ishana is dead. Alda, then? Betanat?

"She was so exhausted."

"And dirty."

"She practically fell asleep in our arms."

"The man told us she took the ferry from the city of Aeth last night. He recognized her temple outfit. She seemed strange. He followed her all the way to this house."

Could it be Riomi speaking?

Thea tries in vain to make out the fuzzy shapes crowded around her bed. What's wrong with her? Why can't she see?

"By the gods, my little girl," an older voice says with concern. "I have never seen her so ill. What happened to her?"

Mother?

"Nerve exhaustion," a reasonable-sounding voice says.

Mistress Tamione, Thea thinks, giving up reason. If all of these voices from her past and present life, including her dead sister Ishana, insist on speaking to her all at once, why should she try to fight it?

"We received word from the Temple of the Sun early this morning," Riomi's voice explains. "She missed the returning barge. They tried to keep her in the temple until morning, but she ran out. They were concerned about her."

"We need to take her back with us," Mistress Ganne's voice says.

"But she says she has been cast out," Leota's voice protests.

"On the contrary," Tamione corrects. "She is a full priestess now. Incredible, for one so young. She went to the Temple of the Sun for her first Joining Ritual yesterday."

"Her joining was not like the others'," Ngara's deep voice says. "She is carrying the child of none other than Selquin Al Sohl'ad, the head priest of the Temple of the Sun. She must be taken care of."

"She is in no shape to travel," mother's voice protests. "Can't we care for her here?"

"She is right; it's dangerous," the shrill voice of Eilea joins in. "We don't want to lose the child."

"I have sent for a litter," Tamione's voice says. "It will be here any minute."

"What is the matter with her?" mother's voice says again. "Is it contagious? Are my grandchildren in danger?"

"Don't worry," Ganne's voice says. "It is not contagious. She was just too shaken up yesterday. Her joining was different from the others'. The goddess has granted her full awareness of the ritual."

"She will become a great priestess," Tamione's voice speaks again. "And the temple will have your family richly rewarded for your gift of such a unique girl."

The voices sink into an indistinct murmur, probably moving into another room. Or, perhaps, Thea's head has become clearer and she can now realize that these voices are not, cannot, be real. Selquin al Sohl'ad, the head priest? Her Sel? This just cannot be. He is the man she loves, and she has given herself to him willingly, of her own accord. Not as a part of some ritual. Because of that she is now an outcast, not a priestess. And how could they possibly know she is carrying a child when her joining—her affair with Sel—only happened last night?

Feeling dizzy from too many questions, she sinks into semi-sleep, struggling against the increasing rumble in her hurting ears. She feels hands touch her, lift her, carry her as she sways, floating on top of the heavy waters of the Great River, which majestically flows past its endless banks.

The wind sweeps over the ancient dunes, out in the open space of the endless desert. The voices, once again barely distinguishable among its dry gusts, keep on their conversation.

"The all-powerful one is now back under our control," the voices say. "He is in the library, in the heart of our desert. We can contain him once more if he is still all-powerful."

"Is he still all-powerful? Can we contain him now?"

"He is... he is... he is... we can... we can... we can..."

"... now..."

The wind wanders on, raising clouds of sand, here and there piercing the walls of a container embedded in a dune, listening to the sighs of anguish, barely audible in the crimson haze above the sands.

The wind sweeps on across its endless realm.

The Goddess of Dance

III

The Dance

The King's Messenger

*T*hea.

Yes, Ganne, Thea says in her mind, watching with her inner vision the Mistress approaching the doors of the great dance hall.

She stops, lowering her arms from the last figure of the Dance, and watches Ganne open the door and enter the hall.

You are upset, sister, she says in her mind, looking at Ganne's small, elegant figure becoming more and more clear of the surrounding shadows.

There is trouble outside, Ganne answers without words, approaching her.

Their eyes meet to share a long moment of silence.

"I'll go talk to them," Thea finally says, this time choosing to pronounce the words aloud. "The man who leads them is related to me, after all. Assemble the Mistresses, sister. We'll drive them away."

A light smile touches Ganne's lips as she nods to Thea and turns to leave.

Thea reaches out for her gray tunic and pulls it over her head, straightening the snake necklace over it. She doesn't bother to put on her sandals or to check if her hair, pulled into a smooth knot at the back of her head, is in order. Instead, she draws a deep breath as she sets on her way across the hall, toward the temple entrance, in long, gliding strides.

Near the door she runs across a young girl, an apprentice in a knee-long white tunic with *tadras* on her wrists and ankles. Thea slides her gaze over the girl, trying to recall her name.

"Aelana?"

"Yes, Mistress Thea." The girl lowers her eyes, as appropriate when talking to a senior.

"Call in the other apprentices. Have them meet me in the great hall."

"Yes, Mistress Thea," the girl whispers, and hurries off to the apprentice quarters.

So young, Thea thinks in passing, on her way to the outside. *What will she grow up to be?*

She takes another deep, calming breath and steps outside into the blinding sunlight. Pausing, she considers a view opened to her.

The entire space around the temple that used to be open all the way from the desert to the riverbanks is now occupied by stone pyramids. At least a dozen of them have been erected here during the last few centuries, an ugly tribute to the deaths of the Aethian kings. She looks at the tomb of King Horankhtot, the first king of the Eighth Dynasty, rising directly in front, in the path of the rising sun. To her left, a bit off, there is a pyramid being prepared for the ruling king Amenankhor, whenever he chooses to pass away into a better world. To Thea it looks just like a pile of stone, perhaps monumental enough to overshadow the other piles of stone around it, but no less ugly for the comparison. At its side, a smaller pyramid is rising up with its half-built walls. A tomb for the king's younger brother, Ptahankhtep.

A new rule, to build tombs not only for the king but for his family as well. Of course, since King Amenankhor has no heir, he probably believes that his younger brother will succeed him. *I hope it happens soon,* Thea thinks, and stops herself. A priestess of the goddess shouldn't allow herself these destructive thoughts. It is bad enough that the lands next to the goddess's temple have been turned into a burial site.

She turns her attention to the group of people gathered on

the east platform in front of the temple: a large group of men, with hammers and other stone-breaking tools. In the distance she can see more workers with loads of equipment on their heavy, horse-driven carriages. They look as if they came to take down one of these pyramids. But that would be too good to be true.

As her eyes fall on the man leading the group, her heart leaps, awakening a feeling that she has believed to be buried deep within her heart.

It cannot be, she tells herself. But it looks so real. The same laughing eyes, the same sun-bleached skin and long hair, falling on his broad, athletic shoulders.

Sel.

She knows that Sel, *her* Sel, the only man she ever loved, has been dead for many centuries. She also knows that this man, named Al Saddim, the advisor to the king, is a descendant of her and Sel's son, who was sent to be raised in the Temple of the Sun as soon as she gave birth to him after her first and only Joining Ritual.

Does this man know he is going to be talking to his ancient fore-mother?

She summons her concentration to detach herself from the look of this man's eyes, so similar to the eyes of his ancestor. It happened so many centuries ago, back when she was a confused young girl, silly enough to fall in love for the rest of her life with the first and only man who ever shared her bed. She is so different now. She doesn't even think of herself as Thea anymore. Everyone except her sisters calls her Dancer, the name that she also first heard from Sel. Her love for Sel is probably the only thing that remains of the old Thea, a girl long forgotten everywhere outside the temple walls.

As she walks down the stairs toward the group, a murmur comes through the east platform. They have obviously heard of her, the mysterious priestess, a spiritual leader of the Temple of the Dance. There is nobody in these parts who hasn't heard of Shaina, the name that means "Dancer" in the old Aethian tongue.

The man who looks like Sel steps forward. He is obviously

nervous, but he is doing a very good job of hiding it. A man of good lineage, led astray by excessive politics.

"Greetings," he says, carefully avoiding any form of address, and bows to Thea from the waist.

Not a very respectful bow, Thea observes. He was obviously instructed to diminish the priestesses in front of his workers.

She silently holds his gaze, causing the man to shift nervously from foot to foot. The group behind him backs off, abandoning their leader in the open space in front of this strange woman, who makes them shiver in spite of her slight build and youthful look.

"My name is Al Saddim, the advisor to the great king Amenankhor," the man continues. Noticing that Thea is not about to break the silence, he asks, "What should I call you, priestess?"

"You may call me Dancer," Thea says calmly, keeping her eyes fixed on his.

She hears gasps all around her from those who didn't recognize her up until now. *My reputation precedes me,* Thea thinks. *Otherwise they would have thought they were talking to a young girl. They probably still do.*

All of the immortal Mistresses—Tamione, Ganne, Ngara, the shrill-voiced Eilea, her friend Riomi, and others—look just like they did when they were in their twenties. Except for the eyes. It is hard to hide such knowledge as they all possess. It always comes out through the eyes.

"Well, Dancer," Al Saddim continues, his darting eyes betraying his nervousness, "the king sent me to talk to the priestesses of the temple."

"You may talk to me, Al Saddim," Thea says. "I am a priestess. What is it the king wants from us?"

"The king"—Al Saddim pauses to draw more air—"has outlawed the Cult of the Goddess. Since you haven't given an answer to any other of the king's messengers, he sent me here to deliver his final warning. It is the king's wish that your temple be destroyed. All of you are to leave this place and go back to your homes."

Our homes. Thea's home, along with her town, ceased to exist centuries ago. It is now replaced by a city with a name that Thea never bothered to remember. Her mother and sisters have been dead for at least four hundred years, as far as she can tell. But it is useless to tell it to this man, her direct descendant. They don't have a concept of immortality at the king's court.

Of course, the younger apprentices, like this girl Aelana, probably still have some kind of homes. The temple girls don't often come from noble families, but surely their parents are better off than Thea's were. They might still take the girls back. But who is this king to order such a thing?

"Go back to your king, Al Saddim," she says. "Tell him to concern himself with something that is his to command."

Amid the stunned silence that follows, she turns to go back to the temple.

"Wait, Dancer!" Al Saddim calls after her. "These men are here to begin the destruction of your temple. The king's orders are to take it down completely, and use its stones in the building of the new pyramid. He showed mercy by ordering me to come here first and give you this warning. You only have time to collect your things. This is not your place anymore."

Babbling, Thea thinks. *You should learn to control yourself better, king's advisor.*

She doesn't turn or slow down her steps.

"Let them try," she throws back over her shoulder, already halfway to the temple entrance.

Back inside the dance hall, she overlooks the rows of apprentices and priestesses, the gray figures of the Mistresses in front, all looking at her with questions in their eyes. She addresses all of them at once.

"Sisters," she says. "Daughters of the goddess. Let us join together in Dance to strengthen the walls and foundation of our temple. Let us move together, so that no man can do any harm to our sacred cause."

She signals to the *tama domga* players to start their low, synchronous beat. *Tum-tumm... Tum-tumm-tumm...* Two pairs into four. *Tum-tumm-tum-tumm-tumm-tam... Tum-ta-ta-tamm-tum-tum-tamm...*

Thea feels them all join into one with the movements of the Sacred Dance, all the bodies in this hall moving together, blending their minds and hearts into a single creature of the goddess. With the Mistresses at its core, this creature extends its senses to the stones of the temple itself, becoming one with the ancient, harmonious structure. Together with her sisters she feels the rough tools of Al Saddim's workers attack the walls, pounding on them, forcing with all their might the downfall of the ancient temple and its rebellious, all-female cult.

She knows that while the priestesses dance together in this hall, the workers won't be able to move a single stone in the smooth walls of this building, the priestesses's home for eternity. She smiles inwardly, sensing the men's confusion as they notice that all their stonecutting tools are not able to make even a scratch on the smooth stone surface. And finally, defeated, they lay down their tools and leave, in awe of the power of the goddess and her priestesses, of the ancient cult that cannot be defeated by kings.

Hasan, please come here, the princess calls in her mind.

She opens her eyes, hoping to see the instant shimmer of air that always precedes Hasan's appearance. But the air is clear and still, except for the gentle wind that strokes her face with its cool, impartial touch. From the balcony she can see over the greenery of the garden all the way to the bluish silhouettes of the distant mountains.

Hasan! she screams in her mind one last time.

Nothing happens. Something must be wrong. He promised he would be nearby to answer her call when she needed him. And she has never needed him more than now, when she must leave with her wedding train to go to Veridue, never to return back to this palace where she spent her entire life. She has been hoping beyond hope that he will find a way to get her out of this wedding. She has been trying to contact him without much success for the past month, ever since they parted after he brought her back from Zobeide's island. And now she must take this final step, to leave her home forever, without Hasan by her side.

"Princess. It's time." Nanny Airagad appears in the balcony doorway, her eyes lowered. Seeing the princess alone, she raises her head in surprise.

They expected me to see Hasan for the last time, the princess thinks. *She is surprised that he is not here. Oh, Hasan, what happened to you?*

A thought crosses her mind that Hasan may not want her anymore, that he simply decided to abandon her to her fate. She angrily forces the thought away. Only her feeling of vulnerability is possibly bringing about such a horrible thought. If Hasan is not here, hasn't come to see her for the entire month, it means he is held up somewhere else. He has things to do, more important than her problems.

He cannot be in danger, because he is all-powerful. Can he?

But what can be so important to him that he cannot even come and see her on the day when the princess is about to leave for Veridue to get married?

The princess angrily shakes off tears, too ready to spring into her eyes. She is no longer a girl! She is a mistress of her own fate! She will go to Veridue and tell Prince Amir that she doesn't wish to be married to him. She will then return to Dhagabad and accept whatever fate she is entitled to as an unmarried princess with no rights to the throne. Maybe she will even *work,* as Hasan once suggested he would.

"I am ready, nanny," she says to Airagad, still waiting with her head bowed.

Of her four nannies, only Airagad and Zulfia are going to accompany her to Veridue. Old Zeinab who has raised not only the princess, but Sultan Chamar before her, has decided to retire, feeling that the hardships of the trip and the change of environment are too much for her old age. The fragile and kind Nanny Fatima, to the sultaness's great resentment, has been assigned by Chamar to take care of the new princess Eleida, who has recently turned three.

The princess overlooks her room, where all the inhabitants of the south wing have gathered to say good-bye to her. She meets the eyes of her mother, red with tears. With the princess's departure, with the new wife Chamar has taken, there will be nothing much left for the sultaness in the palace, and she is crying as much for the princess's departure as for the disappearance of her old lifestyle.

The princess steps forward to hold the sultaness in a long embrace.

"I'll come visit, mother," she says. "And you can come to visit me. Veridue is not that far."

I'll come back soon to stay here forever, she thinks. But she cannot tell it to her mother.

She moves to embrace Nimeth, by her mother's side. Nimeth's dark eyes pierce her, and the princess wonders how many of her thoughts the strange woman is guessing.

"We'll miss you, princess," Nimeth whispers, pressing the princess tight against her bony chest. It almost seems to the princess that Nimeth will say "Come back soon," but these words never actually escape the older woman's lips.

The princess moves around the room to embrace old Nanny Zeinab, tears standing like pools in the deep lines on her face, and the sad and silent Nanny Fatima. She gives a slight hug to her childhood playmate Alamid, now married to the grand vizier's youngest son and pregnant with her first child. She hugs the women from the kitchens, the palace servants and slaves, the wives and daughters of the court noblemen who came to say good-bye to her.

Her new mother, Albiorita, is not here, and the princess is thankful for that.

Before finally leaving her quarters, the princess pulls a shawl over her head, lowering its end down to hide her face. As a bride, she cannot show her face when traveling in a litter across the lands of Dhagabad and Veridue. She has to keep even her eyes covered at all times, except when alone with her female servants.

This time she is grateful for such an arrangement. She doesn't want everybody to see the tears that so annoyingly stand in her eyes, about to escape any moment and roll down her cheeks. She is *leaving*. Leaving this place, the only home she has ever known. Leaving Hasan, who abandoned her for an unknown reason at the time of her great need. Going away to the people who resent her for having failed them before, to a haughty prince who doesn't care about her one single bit.

Of course, she is going to refuse to marry him and come back. But what if it doesn't work?

Hasan, why have you abandoned me? she whispers inaudibly as she is being helped up into her litter inside the palace courtyard. As the realization that he is really not coming sinks in, she feels so empty that nothing seems to matter anymore. She is alone, and the meaning of this word she has never truly known before hits her like a hammer. Alone. Hasan is gone. Her only true friend and the man she loves—gone.

She feels the litter sway as the mighty Ghullian slaves pick it up. Through a veil of tears she looks with unseeing eyes past the palace gates that open for her one last time, past the towers and minarets of the beautiful al-Gulsulim mosque, through the city streets that become more and more crowded as they approach the lower city and the port of Dhagabad, listening to the monotonous cries of the captain of her personal guard:

"Make way for Princess Gul'Agdar of Dhagabad!"

Absolute Power

*H*asan peers through the dusty, thick air of the library at the scroll lying on the floor in front of him. Yes, it is the same scroll he remembers. The original foretelling about the one who frees a djinn. He reads the complex lines of the highest magical language, absorbing, once again, the words of power that he first encountered so many centuries ago.

In the past two millennia the scroll hasn't changed, but seeing it again after having read so many translations, he can understand the urge of other mages to translate and memorize it, to preserve this knowledge through millennia. He can feel the energy flow out of him even as his mind perceives the meaning of the prophetic words.

He has plenty of power in him. Even though each scroll takes so much energy from him, he can still read many scrolls in this endless library, its walls of shelves running out of sight and disappearing into the vaulted depths of the ceiling. He can probably read hundreds of them before he needs to give any thought to saving his strength for the return to the other world. But there are thousands and thousands of scrolls in here. He cannot even begin to comprehend how many scrolls there are. He cannot possibly hope to read all of them. All he can hope for is to find the information he needs quickly, before he runs out of strength and gets trapped in here.

Suppressing a shudder, he reads the part of the scroll that

tells that the princess—the one who frees a djinn—is destined either to become the most powerful djinn ever, or, if she remains free, to destroy the world. He sends a silent curse to Caliph Agabei, who pushed Zobeide into initiating the princess into magic. Perhaps Zobeide deserves a curse, too, he thinks. But he will not curse an old friend, however much trouble she might have caused by her recklessness.

He scans through other scrolls scattered around the floor in front of him. Whoever was here last surely didn't bother to clean up after himself. At least a dozen of these priceless parchments, shimmering with their magical ornaments of text, are lying on the floor, open for him to read their mysterious contents.

Since he doesn't really know where to look for what he needs, he might as well start with these open scrolls. If nothing else, it will save him the energy of taking them off the shelves with no idea what is hidden inside.

Sensing the ghostly presence of Abdulla and Galeot-din at his back, he moves over to the next scroll lying on the floor. It is written in the same language, and seemingly in the same hand as the first one. It is not exactly an original foretelling. But it is close. It was definitely written by the same wizards, or the same entities that created these ancient texts, at the time the world he knows began its existence.

He reads the glowing intertwined lines of the scroll, and freezes.

It is definitely not an original foretelling. But it does hold vital information about the ancient desert and the absolute powers. And now that he is reading it he wishes bitterly that he either read it much earlier or never read it at all.

Only now it becomes clear to him why Abdulla and Galeot-din wanted *him* to go to the ancient desert. Why everybody has been trying so insistently to find out if his powers are indeed absolute.

It is all here, in the scroll in front of him—the scroll Abdulla and Galeot-din must have seen when they first found the library through their dream link—open for anyone wise enough to look before rushing through a portal into this god-forsaken place.

Hasan senses the nervousness of Abdulla and Galeot-din's shadows behind him as they realize what he is reading. But he doesn't bother with them anymore. He peers down at the scroll, trying and failing to find anything that might help him get out of trouble this time.

All the while the information from the scroll pours into his head, forming into more comprehensible words as he goes through it.

The ancient desert was created at the time of great need, to contain beings with absolute powers, the scroll says. If an all-powerful wizard enters the desert, he can never leave it again. He is doomed to stay there for eternity, slowly forgetting who he is, slowly becoming one with the unknown entities that rule the desert.

It can't be, Hasan tells himself, his mind racing. *I can't really be trapped here! I can do anything I want! Can't I?*

He tears his gaze away from the scroll and summons all his power to create a portal back into his own world. He throws so much energy at it that under ordinary circumstances it would have been enough to blast the damned temple down to its foundation.

Nothing happens.

Try again, he tells himself. *You needn't throw so much power into it. Just try. You can do it.*

But in the depths of his mind he knows that the scroll in front of him cannot lie, that he is trapped here for eternity, and there is no way out for him.

He laughs out grimly, thinking that in a way his former apprentice Abdulla has invented the most efficient way to ensure that Hasan finds everything he can in this library about how an all-powerful wizard can free himself once and for all from the bonds of the ancient desert. However much he wanted to find this information before, he now needs it infinitely more. It has now become his only hope.

If, indeed, there is any hope left.

The princess feels her litter rock and come to a halt. She sits up on her pillows, wondering whether she should pull her veil over her face and take a look outside the curtains, or spare herself the heat of the seemingly endless plain on the outskirts of the Veriduan lands.

Their last stop must have been only an hour ago. They shouldn't be stopping *again*. Otherwise they will never reach Veridue on time. After two full days of the journey, the princess is fed up with traveling.

She feels her litter being lowered to the ground. There are many voices outside, shouting.

I should take a look. Reluctantly she lowers the loathed veil over her face and pulls open the door curtain on her left, where the voices seem louder.

At first she cannot understand what's happening. The small group of her servants and slave women are crowded close to the litter, covering their faces with their hands. Her personal guards, most of them from Veridue, save for two soldiers and their captain whose name the princess never bothered to remember, are rushing about, waving weapons in a seemingly disorderly manner. The eight Ghullian slaves carrying the litter are crouching on the sand, obviously unwilling to take part in whatever is going on around them.

It takes a moment for the princess to realize there are other figures rushing around in a fight with her guards—figures in sand-colored robes that blend perfectly with the environment, their faces covered by masks. She sees her two Dhagabad soldiers and their captain fall to the ground, pierced by the curved sabers of the attackers.

An ambush?

Before she can think of anything to do, a masked man appears in front of her and bends down to her litter.

"Princess Gul'Agdar?" he asks, his voice muffled by the cloth over his face.

She sits up straight on her pillows.

"Who wants to know?" she demands.

"Good enough," the man says. "You will have to go with us, your highness. We'll take you to a safe place where you will await the arrival of your groom."

"Prince Amir? But—"

"Not anymore," the man says firmly. "Close the door curtains, your highness. My men will watch you at all times. If we catch you peeking, we'll have to tie you up and blindfold you. I suggest you give us no reason for that."

"How dare you?" she demands, all the generations of her royal ancestry unleashed in this outburst of anger. "I am a princess!"

"That's all I needed to know," the man says. He signals to the Ghullian slaves to pick up the litter and snaps together the door curtains right in front of her face.

"But what of my servants?" she calls out.

"They are no longer your concern, your highness," comes the reply.

She leans back on the pillows, her heart racing. She has been kidnapped! But by whom? Who could possibly want her, now that her rights to the throne are revoked? Perhaps somebody who hasn't heard about it? She knows that Veridue cannot be happy about her change of status, but it didn't prevent her wedding arrangements, did it? Who could have decided to kidnap her within the Veriduan borders on her way to her royal groom?

She tries to listen to the noises outside. Her kidnappers are using common speech, not the Veriduan dialect. Mercenaries, she decides, for hire by anyone who wishes to accomplish a deed of questionable decency. A perfect way to keep one's hands clean, paying these professional bandits to do the dirty work.

She can also hear the indistinct chatter of women, her slaves and servants following the litter in a tight group. She doesn't hear any voices of the Veriduan guards she grew to know during the past two days of her trip.

Did they kill everyone? she thinks. *Are all my two dozen guards dead to the last man?*

She forces herself not to think about it right now. Whatever happened to her guards, she is powerless to help them. On the other hand, if she manages to get out of this alive and unharmed, the servants who were captured with her may be spared too. If only she knew on whose behalf these men are acting and where they are taking her.

She thinks of Hasan again, hoping that whatever is holding him away from her is over and he can finally save her from her fate. But, as has become usual in the past month, she gets no response.

She sighs. During her journey to Veridue she has learned not to cry about it too much. After all, what can she possibly change, except learning to rely on nobody else but herself?

By the direction of the scarce sunlight finding its way through the heavy curtains of her litter she can determine that they have turned back and are now heading the way she came earlier today. This further confirms that her captors are not acting on behalf of Veridue. Not that she really thought for a moment that Prince Amir and Sultan Eljahed would be crazy enough to kidnap the prince's own bride. *They are probably taking me back to Bahdra,* she thinks.

Bahdra, located midway between Dhagabad and Veridue in the place where the River Hayyat el Bakr spreads into many branches before meeting the Veriduan sea, is one of the most colorful places she has ever seen. Formally independent from any rule, Bahdra is the biggest melting pot for merchants, cutthroats, and fortune-seekers on this side of the Dimeshquian desert. Her textbooks say that the source for both Bahdrian power and its independence lies in the city's strategic location at the exact point where the biggest trade ways between Dhagabad and Veridue, both by land and by water, cross.

Bahdra maintains its independence by paying tribute to both countries. It supports its wealth by charging a passage fee for crossing over, or under, the Great Hayyat Bridge.

Yesterday the princess spent a night in the biggest and most respectable tavern in the noisy city, specially prepared and secured for the visit of the royal bride. She left Bahdra after a luxurious breakfast only an hour ago. Now that they have turned back to Bahdra they should reach it very soon at the pace her kidnappers have set, which is quite a bit faster than her honorary guards were taking before.

If her kidnappers are headed for the same tavern where she spent the night, she can hope to get a word to its owner, who could then send an urgent message back to Dhagabad. Unless, of course, the man has been bought to assist the kidnappers. In which case—

She feels the litter make a sharp turn and suddenly becomes aware of a new hum of voices outside. She can also sense a whole bouquet of new smells that find their way through the curtains into the litter. Horses, sweat, jasmine oils, incense, roast lamb, and cheap brew simultaneously hit her sensitive nostrils in a wave that brings so many pictures to mind. She imagines herself out on that street, without a veil, pushing her way through the dense crowd of the bazaar that in Bahdra seems to occupy the entire city. She has always wanted to be able to do that one day.

The noises and smells fade as the litter turns again, probably entering one of the smaller side streets. The kidnappers are leading them through many turns and bends, probably making their way through the meshwork of the small alleys. After she finally loses count of turns, she senses the streets around them gradually become empty and quiet.

So much for the tavern, she thinks.

The tavern is located on the main street that runs all the way from the city gate on the Dhagabad side, across the Hayyat Bridge, over to the Veriduan gate and the main road beyond. It is easily the noisiest street in this noisy town. Up until now she didn't realize that Bahdra could have such streets as the one they seem to be on now, so quiet that even the feet of the Ghullian litter-bearers, shod in soft leather boots, echo hollowly against the stone walls.

The litter stops and sways as it is lowered to the ground. She hastily leans back on her pillows, not to appear as if she has been trying to take a peek outside. Although they seem to have reached their destination, she doesn't want to risk being tied up and blindfolded.

A hand pulls open the curtain, and a masked face looks inside.

"Get out, your highness," a muffled voice says. "We are

home."

Ignoring the offered hand, she climbs out of the litter, steadying herself on its side. Thankful for the veil that hides the direction of her eyes, she tries to take in as much of their surroundings as she can. But there is nothing of significance to see. The narrow, cobbled street curves out of sight in both directions, without betraying any street signs or anything else to indicate where they might be. Even if she knew Bahdra well, she probably wouldn't be able to tell where they are. She sees on her left a crowd of her women-servants with solemn faces and, farther away, the pack animals that hold the belongings they brought along from Dhagabad. The Veriduan guards are nowhere to be seen.

"We need to blindfold you now, princess," a man behind her says, and before she can say a word, thick cloth falls over her eyes. She feels deft fingers tie a secure knot on the back of her head.

"Move, your highness." The man urges her through what feels like a small door in the blind, windowless wall she remembers to be in front.

She steps in and holds out her hand, afraid to stumble and fall on the unknown floor. The air in here smells of a strange combination of mold and expensive perfume. Rough hands support her from behind, and she suppresses an urge to shake them off, knowing that they couldn't belong to anyone but her captors. But better to be supported by unfriendly hands than to fall down into the unknown blackness of a strange house.

The hands lead her into the depths of the building, up two flights of stairs, through many turns of a seemingly endless corridor. As she starts to feel panicked from being blind for so long, they suddenly turn her one last time and lead her into what seems, by the movement of air and the faint smells of food and manure finding their way from the street, to be a large room.

The hands pull the blindfold off, and she blinks against the suddenly bright daylight.

She is standing in a large, luxuriously furnished room with

a window opened wide to the incredible view over the city. Beyond the window, or, rather, a door, since it runs all the way to the floor, she sees a small balcony overlooking the uneven, clay roofs of the city itself and the grassy plains beyond, which are crossed by the blue ribbons of the many branches that sprout off from the River Hayyat el Bakr before it reaches the sea. She can even imagine she sees the sea itself, beyond all the greenery, but the bluish haze over the horizon might just as well come from the vapors that rise from all the river branches in the summer heat.

Off to her right, on the river's Dhagabad side, rise the low, yellow dunes of the desert that makes the lands between here and her home so unpopular with the travelers. A strange landscape that puts a desert so close to the river and the sea, right beside the grasslands. She herself has tasted the discomforts of these sands in her first day and a half of travel, and she now looks at them with a shudder. The only reason she keeps peering in that direction is because she knows that beyond the desert lies her home, and even if she travels on foot she can get back in only a couple of days.

"This will be your room, your highness," a man says behind her. Startled back from her thoughts, she turns to look at the three guards who brought her here, still masked. Having obviously accomplished their task, they are now moving back toward the door.

"Wait," she calls after them, trying to sound as royal as she possibly can. "If you are going to keep me here, I wish for my things to be brought in as well. And I need my servants to attend me."

"We'll send your things up," one of the men replies, pausing to look back at her. "As for the servants—we'll see about that."

He steps through the door and closes it behind him with a thud.

Alone, the princess stands still for several minutes, listening to the sounds outside. Her music-trained ears, even more sensitive after her *tadra* and *tama domga* practice, clearly hear two men settle on watch right outside her door and the third man walk off in the direction they came from. She guesses the third man to be the one who spoke to her, most likely the leader of her kidnappers.

Moving quietly, not to miss any sounds that can possibly tell her more about her situation, she moves around the room, searching every corner for possible means to escape. The low, luxurious bed in the center, laid with many rugs, pillows, and silky sheets, seems to hold no secrets in it. The sheets could be used later to make ropes, she notes. Maybe at night, when the guards leave her alone to rest and sleep, she can do that. Especially if they send at least some of her servants to tend to her.

Besides the bed there is a water jug and a small silver basin that seems much too ornate for a bandit lair on the outskirts of the city. This room was obviously prepared for her visit. Which means that they probably knew in advance she was going to pass this way. That certainly makes more unlikely the possibility that her kidnappers are ordinary ransom seekers who saw her passing through the city yesterday and decided to earn some money by abducting her. Unless, of course, they have a steady business of this kind and keep this room constantly ready for their chance guests.

She walks out to the balcony. As expected, it overlooks a large courtyard with high walls rising on all sides, and at least five armed men in sand-colored robes standing guard at its different exits. *So much for climbing down the rope from the balcony,* she thinks. *That will not get me very far.*

She hears a thud of the door behind her and moves back into the room, not wanting to appear too alert or suspicious to her captors. *Let them think I am as helpless and unfit as a proper princess should be,* she thinks.

She forces away the thoughts of how helpless she really is against these armed men, who overpowered her guards in a blink of an eye. Watching three masked men bring her luggage and set it in the depths of the room, she also does her best to force away the thoughts of Hasan, who, if he were to appear in here right now, could make all her troubles disappear in an instant. He knows where she is and what has happened to her. He always knows these things. There is no way he could have been ignorant to her pleas of help. If he chooses not to come to her aid, it merely means she will have to figure this one out on her own.

"What of my servants?" she asks when the men set down all her things and move toward the door. But the men simply bow to her and leave without answering.

Alone, she thinks. *I am alone.*

She walks over to the pile of boxes and packages and fishes out the *tama domga* in its soft leather carrying bag.

During the past month, since Hasan stopped visiting her, she has been spending long hours playing her *tama domga*. She has found out that the low, deep sound of the instrument has the ability to calm her mind and force the unpleasant thoughts away. It also has helped her greatly to concentrate and decide what she wants to do with her life. Gradually, she has come to depend on this personal form of meditation. Now, alone and in trouble, she feels it necessary to use her favorite instrument to calm down and concentrate on ways to escape.

She pulls the *tama domga* out of its case and settles it on the floor against her knee. Sinking into a familiar, comfortable position, she begins the slow, deep beat of the Sacred Dance.

Sadie

"I think I need to hear this again, Shogat," Agabei says, trying not to sound desperate. "From the beginning."

Honestly, when these immortals plan things, they don't bother to make it simple. At times Agabei almost forgets that he is, at least technically, one of them.

"In response to the interest you expressed in Princess Gul'Agdar, master," Shogat says, as calmly and indifferently as before, "the sultan of Veridue has hired mercenaries to kidnap her on the way to the Veriduan palace. She is now being kept in Bahdra, awaiting your arrival."

"My arrival."

"Yes, master. To claim her as a bride."

There is only one way out of this, Agabei thinks. *And that would be forward.*

"Why did the sultan of Veridue suddenly decide to do such a thing, Shogat?" he asks carefully. "And spare me the bit about his respect for me. I read enough of it in his letter. I want the real reason."

"He has learned that the sultan of Dhagabad now has a son and heir, master," Shogat says in a tone that suggests that it should now all become clear to Agabei.

Agabei sighs. Under other circumstances he would have found her manner irritating. But now he is so lost he doesn't even care.

"A son and heir?" he asks, after waiting in vain for her to continue. "So what?"

"It means," Shogat says with the same indifference, "that Princess Gul'Agdar is not an heiress to the throne anymore, and therefore she is not the most desirable bride for Prince Amir."

"All right," Agabei says with a premature sigh of relief. "I think I understand now. Veridue doesn't want the princess anymore, and so Eljahed decided to do me a favor and grant the wish I expressed earlier to be the one to marry the princess in the place of Prince Amir."

"Just like this letter says, master." Shogat points to the Veriduan letter on the table, written in Sultan Eljahed's spidery handwriting. It does say exactly what Shogat explained, except for the part about Sultan Chamar Ali's son. But Agabei cannot get rid of a troublesome feeling that there is more here than meets the eye.

"Isn't it true that Sultan Chamar Ali of Dhagabad is incapable of fathering a son, Shogat?" he asks.

"Yes, master. But his new Baskarian concubine—I mean, wife—"

"I said he was incapable of *fathering* a son," Agabei repeats. "I know something of his condition. It does not depend on who the mother is."

"Well, master." Shogat stops and raises her eyes to him. "She had help."

"From whom?" Agabei holds his breath, scandalized. An unfaithful concubine! A sultan who can't keep his women in check! That is surely a signal to the downfall of a kingdom.

"Let me just say that this was arranged by Abdulla the Wizard."

"*Abdulla and the sultan's concubine?*"

Shogat's lips twitch with a quick smile. "Not this way, master. Abdulla has used his magic powers to make sure that the child she was carrying—the sultan's child—was a boy, to be born healthy."

"A magically cured child," Agabei says thoughtfully. He is relieved that nothing has happened in Dhagabad to shake the foundations of its sultanate. Deep inside he also feels a slight disappointment that the juicy piece of gossip he was hoping to hear has turned out to be something else. And yet—this boy is not really the sultan's son. He is not even supposed to be alive. Is Abdulla the Wizard powerful enough to interfere with human lives? Isn't it just possible that this time the court mage of Dimeshq has gone a little bit too far?

"Will the boy live, Shogat?" he asks slowly.

"After the princess's fate is arranged, it really doesn't matter, master," Shogat says calmly.

It doesn't matter to her, Agabei realizes. *Perhaps it also doesn't matter to Abdulla, who has gone too far this time; perhaps the problem is that I dare not reach far enough in my hopes and ambitions. Perhaps all the truly powerful wizards think there is no problem in meddling with people's lives to ensure their success.*

"I suppose not, Shogat," he says. "I suppose not."

He pauses, considering everything he has heard so far. Abdulla, a wizard of enormous powers, has interfered with the princess's fate in a subtle and quite ingenious way. Nobody could trace this sudden change of Prince Amir's heart to Abdulla or Agabei. And if anything goes wrong, the one to blame would be Sultan Eljahed. It may well turn into a war between Dhagabad and Veridue, but he, Agabei, will be unaffected in any way. Except that if something goes wrong, he might miss this perfect chance to get the princess into his power.

"Can we pick up the princess now, Shogat?" he asks.

"We need to wait, master," comes the reply. "The only thing you need to do right now is send a message to Sultan Eljahed, expressing your gratitude and telling him that you and your suite are leaving for Bahdra today."

Again, she is a little bit too fast for him.

"Leaving for Bahdra?" he asks. "But we don't need to actually travel there in order to get the princess. You can just use your powers to bring her here."

She raises her head and gives him a calm, quiet look.

"Sultan Eljahed doesn't need to concern himself with the way we bring her to Megina, master. If you write that you are leaving for Bahdra with your suite, it doesn't mean you are really going to do that. It is just an appropriate formality."

"All right," Agabei agrees. "I'll write a letter right away. Can we get her then?"

"In several days, master," she says.

Agabei raises his head.

"Several days? Why?"

"We need to give the sultan of Veridue time to notify Dhagabad that the princess has been kidnapped by the desert raiders. Then, after the panic rises in the Dhagabad palace, you can come forward and rescue the princess, with the appropriate story of how you happened to be in the area. This will make you her savior, while Prince Amir will naturally assume the role of an unworthy suitor who didn't manage to keep what belonged to him. At the same time it will probably come out that the princess is not the heiress anymore, and Veridue will have a legitimate reason to refuse to take her as a bride. Perhaps we could also throw in a bit of gossip that the princess has been abused by her captors in more than one way and has lost at least some of her purity. Sultan Chamar Ali will be desperate to marry his daughter off and will gladly accept your proposal."

Agabei takes a moment to run all this information through in his head.

"Doesn't it sound too complicated for someone of your powers, Shogat?" he says. "We can just take the girl and be done with it."

This time Shogat looks at him with an actual expression in her eyes. In fact, it looks more than anything like pity. *Pity for my slowness,* Agabei thinks, feeling resentment similar to that of a neglected child facing his overzealous teacher.

"Your life as a ruler," Shogat says in a tone that suddenly reminds him of his politics lessons back in his young days, "will be much better if you maintain peace with the neighboring lands. If you take the princess now, you will look like a kidnapper who has arranged this transfer of ownership through hiring desert bandits. If you wait several days, you will have a chance to look like a hero who saved her from a fate worse than death. It is even possible that the princess herself will look at you this way and accept you as her husband without resentment. Isn't it worth the wait?"

"I suppose so, Shogat," Agabei says slowly. In all the excitement he never gave a thought to the princess's feelings. She is not like any other woman he wants to take. He has *plans* for her. It would indeed be helpful if she cooperates. And yet—things could happen in several days that will ruin all his plans. Someone else might rescue the princess. Or—

He freezes in terror, realizing that he has just overlooked something so simple and obvious, something that can, and probably will, ruin his plans in an instant. Something that has been gnawing him all through this conversation before he finally recalled the name for it.

Hasan.

"What about Hasan?" he asks. "As soon as Hasan learns about this, he will rush to her rescue. If, of course, he didn't do it already."

"Hasan is currently... indisposed, master," Shogat says, and her eyes light up with an expression that Agabei cannot quite read.

"Indisposed? How?" he asks sharply, his mind racing. If only his so-called allies could keep him better informed! Abdulla did say once that he and Sultan Galeot-din Ali had found a way to contain Hasan. But Agabei expected it to happen with quite a bit of a noise. He didn't think that Hasan would disappear so quietly, leaving no trace behind.

"Abdulla and Galeot-din have found a way to make Hasan return to the ancient desert, master," Shogat says. "Since he is all-powerful, that action has trapped him there for eternity." Her eyelashes quiver and drop, just in time to hide a twitch of pain in the depths of her huge, dark eyes.

Is she sorry for him? Agabei wonders briefly, deeply intrigued by what he is hearing.

"But Hasan is all-powerful, Shogat," he presses on. "How could he have fallen for such a trick?"

Again he seems to see pain momentarily transform Shogat's impassive face.

"Abdulla and Galeot-din have found an alliance with the powers that cannot be named, master," she says levelly. "These powers, the very same powers that created the ancient desert itself, want Hasan to be captured. They are there to watch that no all-powerful wizard remains free. While Abdulla and Galeot-din are no real match for Hasan, these powers are far greater than any of them."

"And they want to side with Abdulla and Galeot-din to capture Hasan?"

"For the time being, master," she says, leaving the end of the phrase trailing in the air with a dangerous ring to it. Agabei shivers. There are too many things in this world he doesn't know. Quite a few of those things he doesn't even wish to know. The powers that trap the all-powerful wizards for eternity, the powers that can make a man as frightening as Abdulla obey their bidding, are far beyond what Agabei ever wants to comprehend. It is much better to command a djinn, who can take care of all this for you.

"Is there really no way for him to come back, Shogat?" he asks.

"Very little is known about the powers of the desert, master," she says, her voice so level that it sounds unnatural. "But Abdulla's knowledge comes from a source that has never failed before."

She lowers her head in a movement that would have looked like mourning if her face hadn't been so calm. Agabei watches her for a while, her bent head, her hair gathered into its usual knot at the back. Priestess hairstyle. He has never been able to break her habit of wearing it in such a boring way. *She should let it loose more often,* he thinks. *She has such beautiful hair.*

"I'll write a letter to Sultan Eljahed, Shogat," he says. "You may go now."

"Yes, master." She bows and fades into thin air until only a slight shimmer remains on the spot where she stood just a moment ago. As Agabei steps over to his desk, he finds himself wondering whether he is really doing the right thing, trying to get Princess Gul'Agdar into his service. Will he lose

Shogat if he does that? After all, if he believes everything the prophetic scroll has to say, it has mentioned that one master can never command two djinns at once. But what is he going to do without Shogat? And what will happen to her, a djinn, if her master obtains himself another djinn in her place?

The princess stirs as she hears the door behind her open and close with a thud. She steps away from the railing of the balcony and peers into the depths of the room, trying to see who is there. Her captors didn't bother to give her any lanterns or candles, and now, as the light outside slowly sinks into transparent desert dusk, she can barely see from the balcony into her room.

Her stomach muscles tighten as the unknown figure, visible only by its movement, slowly approaches the balcony door. She tenses up, preparing for a struggle. Although she cannot do much to defend herself, she is not about to give up easily!

As the approaching figure finally reaches the balcony, she slowly exhales, allowing her muscles to relax into their previous state of passive alertness. She calmly studies the girl, who has large, watery eyes and a plain face, with thin lips pursed into a passive expression of obedience.

Sadie. The Veriduan slave girl. The quiet, mousy girl whose only company has always been her pet sparrow hawk.

In all her troubles, the princess almost forgot the Veriduan slave girl among her suite. Now she gives it another thought. *Poor Sadie*, she thinks. *She might have known some of the Veriduan guards who were sent to accompany me. Even if she didn't, she might be taking it very hard that her countrymen have been slain, trying to defend me from the bandits.*

The princess feels a special bond to Sadie, now that they are both captives in this unknown place and their fates seem to depend on each other. She feels the need to comfort this quiet slave girl, who must have been picked by her captors out of her suite to tend to the princess exactly because of her innocent, plain looks.

The princess steps forward and gently touches Sadie on the cheek.

"Sadie, I am so glad to see you!" she says, meaning it. "Where are the others?"

"Princess," Sadie says in her usual half-murmur. "They sent me to serve you. They wouldn't let anybody else come."

"But is everybody all right? My nannies, my servants, my slave girls?"

"Yes, they are all fine, princess. They placed them in the room at the other end of the hall. It is not as big as this one." Sadie gazes around the semi-dark room. "But it is"—she pauses—"convenient."

"Good," the princess breathes out. At least this is out of her immediate concern now. "What of—?" She pauses, hesitant to ask the question. "What of my guards?"

Sadie's eyelashes quiver, and she lowers her head.

"Some of them were killed, princess," she murmurs. "The others—some of them—escaped."

Escaped. That sounds better than what she thought. Maybe at least some of her guards survived. Then they should have raised the alarm by now. They might have organized the search already. Surely there must be enough people in Bahdra loyal to Dhagabad and Veridue who will rise to defend their princess and the bride to the royal heir.

"Do you have any idea who our kidnappers are, Sadie?" the princess asks.

"No, princess. But I heard that there are a lot of bandits in this area. They catch noble people and hold them for ransom. I am sure that's what they want. Ransom."

This thought had already occurred to the princess earlier, but she is not sure it is entirely true. She welcomes this chance to discuss it with somebody, hoping that another opinion, as well as a chance to talk this through, will help her find the most likely explanation. It might be helpful to know what awaits her to form an escape plan. And she does believe she needs an escape plan. She is not going to sit here and wait for whatever it is they have planned for her.

"But they knew my name," she says. "When they attacked us, they knew exactly who I was."

"I am sure the news of your passage through Bahdra must have spread through the city when we stayed there last night, princess," Sadie says. "That's why they must have followed us. They are probably hoping to get richly rewarded by your father, or your husband-to-be."

"I suppose you are right," the princess agrees. Something in the way Sadie has readily explained her kidnapping bothers the princess, but she cannot quite put a hand to it.

They walk back into the room that has by now become very dark.

"I wish they would give us some light," the princess says.

"Would you like me to go ask them, princess?"

"Not now. Maybe later." The princess is not sure why she has dismissed the offer. Something in the Veriduan girl's manner that she cannot quite catch—as if Sadie is waiting for something—is bothering her. The princess feels it very important to keep the conversation going.

They sit down on the pillows opposite each other, barely visible in the dusk. From here the outline of the balcony door, the only source of light, seems much brighter than it really is.

"What were you doing on the balcony, princess?" Sadie asks. Something in her voice sounds almost alert, as if the reason for asking the question is more important than the mere necessity to pass time together with nothing else to do.

New suspicions arise in the princess, and in reply she pitches her voice low, making it sound lazy and relaxed, as appropriate for a princess who spent all day in boredom.

"I was just looking at the view, Sadie," she says, stretching the words as someone who has too much time on her hands. "It seemed much too dark inside. And the view from my balcony is so pretty."

She tries to catch Sadie's expression, but all she sees in the dusk is the white oval of the girl's face, turned toward her in an alert, intense way.

She begins to feel very uncomfortable in the company of her new slave girl. Something here is so wrong. *Why did they choose Sadie to attend to me?* she thinks. *Maybe they were trying to send somebody I am the least familiar with, just to make me feel more uncomfortable? Well, in that case they succeeded. But why does she make me feel so strange? Could it have been her own idea to come here, instead of Nanny Airagad, or Zulfia, whose cheerfulness and pure physical strength might have proven to be so useful in finding a way to escape? At least they are the people I could* trust, she thinks. *I can trust almost any of my servants. Except Sadie. I simply don't know her enough. And this strange feeling she emanates...*

Her thoughts are interrupted by a sudden movement from Sadie, who raises her head and straightens up on her pillows so quickly that it becomes immediately obvious to the princess why the Veriduan girl looked so strange before—she has been tense. All this time she was like a tight coil ready to spring. And what triggered it was—

A sound from the balcony.

It doesn't sound like anything alarming to the princess. It resembles—yes, the flapping of wings. A bird.

Sadie jumps up and runs to the balcony with amazing speed. Intrigued, the princess rushes to follow. She sees a reluctant look Sadie throws at her. The girl obviously doesn't want to be followed. *But since we are locked in here together, she will just have to bear with it,* the princess thinks. *Too bad for her if she doesn't want it.*

As she runs to the opening of the balcony, she sees Sadie stand outside by the railing. A slender, grayish bird is nestling on the curve of Sadie's arm, leaning its head affectionately to its mistress. A sparrow hawk. It must have flown away during the attack and found its way back here. *What a smart bird,* the princess thinks.

Then she notices something that Sadie is obviously trying to hide from her. Something small tied up to the bird's leg. A small package, its size no more than that of a large almond. And yet it looks so bulky on the tiny bird's leg.

A letter.

The princess raises her eyes and meets Sadie's watery gaze.

"Give me that, Sadie," she says.

Sadie

Sadie doesn't move. Her eyes staring at the princess have a heavy, frightening look in them. She reaches out without looking and takes the package off the bird's leg in a deft, practiced move. Then she releases the bird into the dusky evening sky.

"I want to see that," the princess says firmly. "Give it to me."

"No," Sadie says, clutching the parchment tightly in her hand.

"You are my slave," the princess says, raising her voice just a fraction higher. "I order you to give it to me."

"Or what?" Sadie asks, her murmuring voice acquiring a new, steel quality to it.

The princess suddenly feels very strange. As if a new being has suddenly awakened within her. As if somebody else, much older and wiser, has taken over her mind when she had no idea how to handle it, and is now giving orders to her.

"Or I will take it from you," she says quietly.

This sounds so uncharacteristic that it surprises even the princess herself. The effect on Sadie is much more dramatic. She goes pale and presses tighter against the railing, clutching the note in her hand.

She is afraid of me, the princess realizes. *Do I really look that frightening right now?*

Her body seems to act on its own. She reaches out and grabs Sadie's wrist with her left hand. The fingers on her right hand move in to find a spot, close to the hand, where, as she knows from Thea's lessons, the muscles that control the fingers come together in a single cord. She holds Sadie's wrist even tighter and presses on this spot with her thumb.

She is vaguely aware of the girl struggling to break free, and she is sure that if she was in complete control of her own mind she would have let Sadie go. But this new being awakened in her doesn't let her pay attention to such minor details. She hears Sadie scream as her palm opens under the pressure of the princess's fingers and the tightly folded piece of parchment falls out into the princess's outstretched hand.

Ignoring the girl's attempts to get the letter back, the

princess pushes her away and quickly unrolls the parchment. She is aware of the voices outside and the sound of running feet. *The men in the yard must have heard Sadie scream,* she thinks. *They are going to come any minute. But a minute is all I need.*

Holding off Sadie at the distance of her outstretched arm, she quickly scans the lines written in an unknown, spidery hand. *"To our loyal servant Sadie,"* it says. *"It is our wish to make sure that Princess Gul'Agdar remains safely captured and out of trouble until the caliph of Megina, Abu Alim Agabei, her new groom we have arranged for her, arrives to pick her up. We are grateful to you for helping us to arrange this kidnapping and wish for you to remain by the princess's side until further notice and immediately report to us any suspicious activity her highness happens to engage herself in. Signed this day in the royal palace of Veridue by the Sultan Eljahed ibn Falh."*

The princess raises her eyes. She is so shaken that she forgets all about her struggle with Sadie and lets the girl snatch the letter back from her. Sultan Eljahed. The caliph of Megina. How in the world did they come to such an odd arrangement, which seems to go against Veridue's best interests and their agreement with Dhagabad? What are they planning for her now? Why is Caliph Agabei so keen on marrying her in Prince Amir's place?

Her thoughts are interrupted by a loud thud as the guards throw the door open and burst into the room. They are carrying torches that instantly flood the dark chamber with their thick, reddish light.

"Princess?" asks one of them, a tall man with a neatly trimmed beard. "We heard screams. Is everything all right?"

In her new alert state the princess doesn't fail to notice that the guard's eyes are directed not at her but at Sadie by her side, and that he visibly relaxes after Sadie gives him a barely perceptible nod.

Sadie is their ally, the princess thinks. *And now she has given them an all-clear sign, which means that she is not going to tell them what happened. Unless, of course, I do. But why would I do such a stupid thing?*

Sadie

"It is very dark in here," she says in her best royal tone. "Very hard to see our way around the room. Can you bring us some lanterns?"

"Certainly, your highness," the man says, with another quick glance at Sadie. This time the princess doesn't bother to look. She knows they will bring the light. And that is all she needs.

The man signals to somebody outside the room, and two men walk in with burning lanterns, which they fix into the wall-mounted holders. The room immediately becomes brighter and friendlier, almost cozy.

Too bad I am leaving soon, the princess thinks. *This seems to be such a comfortable place to spend the night.*

She briefly wonders at this new line of thought that seems so foreign to the Gul'Agdar of old. Her dreams and her initiation by the Elements have changed her completely and finally. She is never going to let anyone else decide her fate.

She watches the guards leave and lock the door behind them. Then she turns back to Sadie.

The Veriduan Dress

*T*he fear in Sadie's eyes is hypnotizing. As she advances on the Veriduan girl, the princess feels the strange creature inside her arise with devilish joy at the sight of the fear it awakens. The princess herself doesn't feel any joy in causing fear. But she does feel blissfully and securely *in control.*

"Take off your clothes, Sadie," she orders.

"But, princess," Sadie says, backing off and throwing hopeful glances at the door. "I—"

"*Now,*" the princess commands. She raises her voice just a fraction, but the words, enhanced by the creature that controls her, come out so powerful that Sadie cowers in the corner.

Then the princess feels a tingle of power that comes from the Veriduan girl and resists her own. The creature inside her pauses in the first sign of hesitation.

Magic. The girl obviously knows magic. And she is now trying to summon it, to resist the princess's attempts to overpower her.

Sadie rises up from her crouched position and meets the princess's eyes.

"Get back, your highness," she says with terrifying quietness. "Or I'll call the guards and tell them to tie you up."

She will, the princess thinks in a sudden uprush of panic. *She knows magic. And I—I do seem to possess* some *power, but I have no idea how to use it against her.*

She sees Sadie's eyes flicker in triumph as the slave girl notices the momentary hesitation in the princess's commanding pose.

She is winning, the princess thinks. *But if I let her win now, I will be a prisoner for the rest of my life. I cannot let her win.*

She takes a deep breath, calling back the creature inside her, welcoming its renewed presence in her body and mind taking over the actions she is not sure how to perform on her own. She feels the Stone of the Elements on her neck start to pulse, filling her body with new energy and confidence.

She advances on Sadie. The girl backs off, opening her mouth to scream, but a short glance from the princess freezes the sound in her throat. She goes pale and presses her back against the wall.

"Your clothes," the princess says again. "Now."

She extends her hand in a commanding gesture, and this time Sadie begins to unfasten the clasps of her Veriduan robe with trembling hands. Moving clumsily, as if the remains of her power are still urging her to resist, she lays down her dress and pants and begins to unfasten the strings of her undergarments.

"Enough," the princess says. "Just give me your head shawl."

She and Sadie are about the same height, and their hair is wrapped similarly around their heads. Of course, Sadie's skin is several shades darker than the princess's, and her plain features cannot be confused with the vivid lines on the princess's face, but in the dark, wearing Sadie's Veriduan dress and head shawl, the princess can impersonate her for a little bit. Just enough to get out of here.

The obvious difference between Dhagabad and Veriduan clothes should make it easier. Unlike the Dhagabad-style short blouse and wide pants, the Veriduan women wear a kind of a long coat divided in front, and narrow pants underneath. They also have a completely different manner of wrapping their head shawls—not in a hood-like Dhagabad manner, with the face open and most of the shawl hanging over the shoulders and back, but square on their heads, tied with a band across the forehead, so that the flaps hang almost straight over the face, making it even easier to disguise oneself as someone else.

The princess reaches into one of her travel bags and pulls out a handful of long silk scarves—a piece of luggage that she considered to be the most useless one, which has unexpectedly turned out to be handy.

If I ever travel like this again, she thinks. *I will make sure to bring along lots and lots of useless things.*

"Come here, Sadie," she says. "Lie on the bed."

The girl reluctantly obeys, throwing dark glances at her mistress. The princess ignores her. She waits for the girl to settle down on the bed and ties up her arms and legs with silk scarves. Her hands seem to move on their own. Besides her needlework lessons and Thea's adventures in her dreams, she has never tied serious knots before. She has definitely never seen a real person being tied up on a bed, and never even dreamed of doing it herself.

She doesn't like doing it now. But there is too much at stake. Besides, the creature inside her makes it so much easier for her to ignore any kind of doubts.

She pulls another scarf from her bag and, folding it down to a neat little ball, stuffs it into Sadie's mouth, securing it in place with a hair ribbon. Finally, she covers the Veriduan girl with a blanket up to her eyes and steps back to look at her work with a mixture of horror and satisfaction.

It looks just like someone curled up in bed to sleep. In the semidarkness of the chamber, under a blanket, it is impossible to see the gag in the girl's mouth or her tied hands and feet.

What is the matter with me? the princess thinks. *What possessed me to do such a horrible thing?*

She walks away from the bed, faintly aware of Sadie's muffled attempts to break free. *Just an hour,* she thinks. *Give me an hour and I will disappear without a trace.*

She vaguely realizes that this thought cannot possibly have come from her. It seems to be coming from the same strange creature that has settled inside her so securely that it now seems to have a mind of its own.

The princess quickly undresses down to her undergarments and puts on the Veriduan clothes. She tries her best to fix the head shawl in the way she saw Sadie do it, leaving the front flaps to hang as low as possible, hiding her face from view.

"Sorry, Sadie," she whispers. "I have no choice."

Her eyes fall on the *tama domga*, perched against a sitting pillow beside the bed. The instrument is easily the most precious possession she has. She cannot possibly leave it behind! But, on the other hand, how can she bring it with her? She will be immediately noticed with its bulky shape on her back.

I'll come back for it, she decides. *Later, at the head of an army that will search the city of Bahdra from top to bottom and eliminate this nest of bandits!*

She suppresses a shudder at the violence of the thought that shouldn't, couldn't have possibly come from her. Then she decisively walks toward the door and knocks on it. As an afterthought, she blows out the lamp closest to the door, so that no light at all can possibly fall on her face. The remaining lamp is now shining on her from behind, making her resemblance to Sadie as good as it will ever be.

After a painfully long pause she hears the scraping of a key in the lock, and the door opens a little bit.

"What?" the guard asks from the outside in a sleepy voice.

"The princess is asleep," she whispers. "I need to go out for a bit."

"Right," the man says, and opens the door just a bit wider to let her slip through. In the semidarkness of the passage he doesn't even give her a full look, locking the door behind her and turning back to his fellow guard sitting on the floor by the wall.

They are playing cards, the princess notices. *They don't want to be interrupted. Good.*

She pauses to recall the direction from which she was brought in blindfolded this morning and sets off along the passage.

"Hey! Wait!" the guard calls after her.

She freezes without turning. If she turns now, the torchlight will fall directly on her face. She will be discovered.

Shall I run? she thinks, her heart racing.

"Tell Abdoul to bring us some brew!" the man calls out. "I know those bastards are drinking down there! And remind him that he needs to replace us in an hour."

"Sure!" the princess says over her shoulder, hoping that her voice doesn't sound too stilted with relief, and rushes off to the staircase.

Treading as lightly as she can, she descends down the two flights of stairs. She is not sure this is the way she was brought in. She wishes she had been braver this morning and dared to take a look from under her blindfold. But how could she possibly have done that?

At the bottom of the last staircase she sees three passages leading off in different directions. She tries to remember anything about the way she was brought in, but she cannot tell the difference between the passages.

I survived the Palace of the Winds, the princess thinks. *I can find my way out of here!*

As far as she remembers, on her way in she didn't turn before ascending the first flight of stairs. Therefore she should choose the passage running off straight into the darkness in front. Unlike the other two passages, there even seems to be another light at the end of this one.

Half-running, she reaches the light, hoping to find—

Yes! A door.

The door yields with a creak, and a wave of dry, horse-smelling wind hits her face. She steps through the opening and finds herself in a large, moonlit yard.

This is the same yard she has seen from her balcony. The yard full of guards.

How could she have taken a wrong passage? After all she has done for her escape, how could she have blindly walked out here before peeking out to make sure this is the right exit?

She turns back to the door, hoping to slip back through before she gets noticed. But it is too late.

"Hey! Who is there?" a voice shouts from a distance.

"Don't move!" another voice joins in.

Heavy boots echo through the yard as at least three men run up to her from behind.

She turns slowly, hoping that the evening shadows and the overhangs of her head shawl will make her unrecognizable, and pitches her voice low to imitate Sadie's murmuring voice.

"It is me, Sadie," she says.

The guards stop several paces short, peering at her face. She shifts from foot to foot, keeping her head bowed in a manner that she saw in Sadie, a manner that also conveniently allows her to keep her face hidden. She is thankful for the long sleeves of her dress that hide the absence of the metal bracelets on her wrists.

"I thought you were supposed to be with the princess," one of the men says uncertainly.

"I—" The princess stumbles, momentarily overtaken by panic. Any moment now they will discover her trick and take her back upstairs, shamed and quite likely tied up as well. She takes a deep breath. She cannot afford to let her panic loose! She has to appear calm.

"The princess is asleep," she says. "I came down to look for my bird."

"Your bird?"

"My sparrow hawk. The princess was getting suspicious and I let it loose just before dark. I have to find it before nightfall."

"Yeah," a man calls from across the yard. "I saw the two of you on the balcony just before dusk. There was a scream and the bird flew off."

"It was dark in the room. Her highness tried to follow me to the balcony and stumbled. She screamed and scared off the bird," the princess lies, frantic to come up with a believable story on the spot. She hadn't thought of having to give explanations. She hadn't really thought her disguise would hold if she was forced to talk to the guards up close. All she was thinking of was getting out into the street and running away. Will they believe her now? Or has she just ruined everything?

She waits out one of the most painful pauses she has ever experienced while the guards exchange looks.

"Well, go on, find your bird," the guard next to her says. "But I got to tell you—we ain't seen no bird here. You might have to go all the way to the city to look for the blugger."

To the city! That is exactly where she wants to go! Can it be that they will just let her through this door now? Can it be that the story she made up on the spot will work even better than she hoped?

"I have to find the bird before nightfall," she says again. "Otherwise it might lose its way and come to harm."

"All right, but be quick about it," the guard says. "If you are not back in an hour, we'll lock up and you will have to stay on the street until morning."

He gestures toward the small door leading out of the courtyard. Still unable to believe her luck, the princess walks over to it on stiff legs. She pulls the door open with a creak and slips through into a dark, empty street.

She pauses, deciding where to go. Now that she seems to have gotten away, she feels, most of all, weak and shaky. She is half-expecting to hear the door behind her creak again, to hear the guards' voices telling her to stop and come back. She is not safe yet.

Trying not to appear in too much of a hurry, she sets off down the street in the direction where, as she saw from her balcony, lies the city center and the Dhagabad desert beyond.

The streets in this part of the city are small and curved. Every now and then she sees suspicious people walking by or crowded in small groups in front of dirty-looking inns. She hurries past them, her head lowered. Luckily, her simple Veriduan dress makes her look like an ordinary serving girl off on an errand for her mistress. To feel safer, she pulls the head shawl lower over her face, so that nobody will notice her unusually white skin or catch a facial expression inappropriate for a servant.

Her plan is to find the tavern she stayed in before. At least the owner knows who she is. He is also rich enough to provide her with means of returning to Dhagabad. If nothing else, he can give her a fast horse. With all her riding lessons, she can expect to be able to withstand the journey to Dhagabad, which shouldn't take more than a day.

That is, if the bandits don't pick up her trail.

The streets around her are becoming more and more crowded. Even at this late hour the shops are still open and there are lots of people outdoors, on their way to and from the numerous taverns, or passing through the city in search of food and shelter. She sees serving girls like herself rushing around alone or with an escort of silent slaves, obviously brought along to help carry the goods for their masters. She sees horses and camels tied to the posts in front of the tavern doors. Occasionally a donkey loaded with packages makes its way through the crowds. The mixed smells of stable, food, and perfumed oils become overwhelmingly intense.

She has always dreamed of finding herself in the middle of a bazaar without a litter and a veil. She even dared to dream that she will also walk there alone, without any escort, just like an ordinary citizen could. Now that it has actually happened to her, she cannot find room for excitement anymore. All she wants now is to get out of here. To be *safe*.

She is not sure she will ever feel safe again. Not without Hasan by her side.

She waves away the painful thought and stops, trying to pick up the right direction. What was the name of that tavern? Oh, yes. "The Oasis." What else could it be, for the most famous tavern in a desert town?

She looks around in search of somebody to ask for directions and notices a broad, motherly woman accompanied by a huge Ghullian slave. The woman is strolling around with no visible goal, gaping at the people in the bazaar with an expression of deep belief that everyone around exists entirely for her entertainment.

She seems nice enough, the princess thinks. *It should be safe to ask directions from her.*

She walks up to the woman, keeping her head down, in a manner she believes appropriate for a servant approaching a noble woman.

"Excuse me, mistress?" she asks, putting on a humble look. "I am looking for a tavern called the Oasis. Can you tell me how to get there?"

The woman turns to study her with interest. Up close the princess can see the woman's double chin, sparsely covered with coarse, black hair, and an ugly-looking wart sticking out on the side of her nose. She hastily lowers her eyes.

"New around here, eh?" the woman says thoughtfully. Daring another glance, the princess sees a strange sparkle in the woman's beady eyes and a meaningful look she gives to her Ghullian slave.

"My mistress is just passing through town," she says quickly. "She has sent me on an errand. I need to hurry, otherwise she will be very angry."

"And who is your mistress, girl?" the woman asks, moving closer. Her skin has an unpleasant, medicinal smell. The princess back off. Why is the woman studying her like this? What does she want with the princess? What is the new trouble she is getting herself into?

"My—my mistress wishes to travel incognito," she stumbles. "She is on her way to Dhagabad."

"Incognito..." The woman reaches out toward her, and the princess subconsciously shifts out of the way.

"Come, girl," the woman says, the folds of her fat face rearranging themselves into a fake smile. "It is not safe here for a girl like you. Let me and my faithful Odo walk you to the Oasis."

"No, thank you very much," the princess says, backing off from the woman. "I have to run."

"Hey!" she hears from behind as she mixes into the crowd, speeding away from the strange woman and her slave. Her heart is racing. She is not sure what the woman wanted from her, but her inner senses tell her she has just narrowly escaped with her life.

Hasan was right, she thinks. *Bazaars are not safe places at all.*

Hasan. Oh, Hasan, where are you? Why have you abandoned me? She clenches her teeth and pushes her way through the crowd.

On the street corner she sees a blind old man with an outstretched hand, settled firmly against the wall. *He doesn't look too dangerous*, she thinks. *At least he is blind. I can ask him without the risk of being chased.*

She steps up to the man and says, "Excuse me, can you please tell me how to get to the Oasis?"

The man turns to her, and she suddenly sees that he is not blind at all. Through a tear in the old cloth covering his eyes she catches a glimpse of his alert, dark eye. She backs off, terrified.

"Alms for the poor," the old man wails.

"I just want to know the way," she says, uneasy under the concealed, dark look.

"Help me, girl, and I will help you," the man says. He adds quietly, in a completely different tone, "No money, no information."

Money. She doesn't have any money with her. She turns away from the man and determinedly pushes her way through the crowd, hearing the resumed wails behind her back:

"Alms for the poor! Alms—"

The crowd on the streets is thinning. Night is approaching, and the bazaar is slowly settling down to sleep. All around the princess merchants are shutting the windows to their shops, street peddlers are covering up their carts, and the remaining passers by dive into the shelters of their houses or nearby taverns. The streets will get empty soon. With the kind of people she knows to be lurking out here, she cannot possibly afford to stay outdoors alone.

She has to find the Oasis. But how?

She walks into a side street, emptier than the one she just left, and suddenly notices a shadow behind her. As she turns to look, the shadow freezes by the wall, but her senses, sharpened by fear and her recent training in magic, allow her to make out the shape of a huge, dark-skinned man.

He looks exactly like Odo, the fat woman's Ghullian slave.

Ride through the Dunes

*T*he princess feels the skin on her back rise in goose bumps. It can't be Odo. This doesn't make any sense. But if it really is Odo, what does he want with her?

She remembers the strange look in the woman's beady eyes and decides she doesn't really want to find out. She resumes her walk, heading for the nearest tavern, which is easily recognizable by the row of horses and camels tied to the posts in front, patiently waiting for their masters to get their dose of food, brew, and gossip. Luckily, there seems to be no lack of taverns here in Bahdra.

The princess calls forth all her skills acquired in *tadra* practices, allowing her to glide across the ground very fast without appearing to be in a hurry. The shadow falls behind. Whoever is following her doesn't seem to realize how fast she is moving. Or, maybe he is not following her at all?

She approaches the horses, then pauses. Her heart is beating so fast that she is afraid of it actually making sounds outside her chest, betraying to her pursuer—her *possible* pursuer—what she is up to. Just as she manages to convince herself that she is just being paranoid, she sees the shadow leave the niche where it was hiding and creep along the street toward her.

She swallows the terror that threatens to encase her body in a paralyzing stupor and approaches a tall chestnut horse at the end of the row with a saddle still on. Its master has obviously just arrived, and the servants from the tavern are going to come out any minute to unsaddle and clean it for the night. She has to hurry up.

With trembling fingers she unfastens the reins, tied loosely over a post. Then she pauses, listening.

No sound. Even the shadow crawling along the wall seems to have disappeared.

She takes a moment to consider her situation. Is she doing the right thing? If she steals this horse and gets caught, they will cut off her hand for theft. Even if she reveals herself, which is extremely dangerous in her situation, these people might not believe her. But what else can she do? She cannot just walk into this tavern and ask for help. She has no money or escort. And women without money and escort are not usually welcome in taverns, unless they have services to offer. Of course, she can merely ask them for the directions to the Oasis. But how can she find the courage to go back outside, with this shadow lurking about, with the danger of being caught by the bandits, who surely must have discovered her absence by now?

She seems to have no other choice. All she needs to do is make sure she doesn't get caught.

She throws the reins back over the horse's neck and swings into the saddle with a smooth, trained move.

A shadow appears right in front of her. A huge, dark-skinned man, trying to grab the reins.

"Get her, Odo!" shouts the voice from down the street.

The fat woman and her Ghullian slave! They are chasing me. Why?

The horse, frightened by the sudden movement, leaps aside, kicking the next horse in line. Then it rears, its flailing hooves hitting Odo square in the chest. The giant man grunts and falls backward, landing flat on the stones of the street. The other horses start kicking and neighing, trying to break free and raising a terrible ruckus. Only the princess's skill with horses allows her to stay in the saddle, to take control of the reins, to direct the chestnut along the street away from the tavern.

"Thief! Stop thief!" the fat woman screams behind her.

The princess throws the horse into a gallop and disappears beyond the bend of the street. Only after the screams behind her fade into the darkness, swallowed by the sound of galloping hooves, does she allow herself a small sigh of relief. At least for the moment she seems to be safe.

Why was Odo chasing me? Forcing the thought out of her head, she throws the horse into gallop. The horse seems to know its way. It carries the princess down the emptying streets, through a meshwork of dark alleys, toward a straight and wide street that the princess can finally recognize.

The main street of Bahdra! The one that runs from Dhagabad, across the bridge, past the Oasis, all the way to the Veriduan lands.

She slows the horse to a trot, and looks around. To her right, the arch of the Great Hayyat Bridge rises over the river. She knows the Oasis to be somewhere to her left, deeper into the city of Bahdra. Going to the Oasis now would mean turning back toward the possible pursuit. On the other hand, if she just rides across the bridge, she can start in the direction of Dhagabad right now. With luck, if she rides all night, she can reach it by the next afternoon. She can reach the lands of Dhagabad much sooner, and then she can hope to find shelter and help from people who are loyal to her father and not busy organizing ambushes to kidnap her.

She turns to the right. At the bridge she slows her horse to a walk, listening to the old boards creak dangerously under the hooves. She knows the bridge to be sturdy enough to hold at least two dozen riders at a time, but she still feels uneasy as she watches the slow, thick waters of Hayyat el Bakr from the height of the horse's back.

As she finally reaches the other side, she exhales the breath she didn't know she was holding. She is now approaching the far outskirts of Bahdra, on the Dhagabad side of the river. Just knowing this makes her feel better.

"Halt!" a man calls from ahead. Her heart immediately leaps again. Has she been discovered? Do they want her now for horse theft?

Peering into the darkness, she makes out the outline of a gate and men with spears walking toward her.

It is just a guard post, she tells herself. *Relax.*

Guards come up to her, holding their long spears at attention and glaring at her through the darkness. Seeing that she is a woman, they start chuckling and winking to each other.

"Where are you off to at such a late hour, sweetie?" one of them asks.

"I—I am on an errand for my mistress, Princess Gul'Agdar of Dhagabad," the princess spurts out, not finding anything better to say. *Next time I escape from bandits I am going to think all these explanations through in advance.*

"The princess of Dhagabad passed here almost a day ago," the man says. "She must be in Veridue by now."

"Why don't you stay here with us, my pretty?" another man joins in. "I am sure your princess doesn't really need you until morning."

All the guards burst into heavy laughter, obviously thinking their comrade to be very witty. The princess clenches the reins tighter in her hand, ready to send her horse into a gallop at the first sign of trouble.

"The princess was... delayed," she says. "She found out that I forgot to bring her... her grandmother's wedding shawl. She sent me back for it as a punishment, because it was my fault."

"Wedding shawl?" the man asks with a chuckle. "But you are a Veriduan girl. Why would you serve the princess of Dhagabad?"

"Her groom, Prince Amir, gave me to the princess as part of a wedding gift," she explains, shifting nervously in the saddle. Why can't they just let her pass?

"How do we know you are telling the truth?" the man asks her darkly.

The princess sighs. Her anxiety has become so unbearable that she cannot hold herself anymore. She starts talking even before she has time to think whether it is wise to speak her mind.

"I am just a girl," she says. "What harm could I possibly

do? I don't see any trouble for you in letting me pass."

She pauses, expecting an outburst. But the guards merely nod to each other.

"I guess she is right," another guard says. "No harm in letting a girl through. Besides, what she just told us sounds so stupid that no one in their right mind could have made up such a story."

So much for my storytelling skills, the princess thinks in relief.

"I suppose so," the first guard agrees. He steps aside and lowers his spear.

"Ride on, girl," he says. "Get that wedding shawl. We don't want your princess to ruin *another* wedding to Prince Amir."

The guards join in laughter again. This time the joke is quite to the point, she thinks. And no one in Veridue or Dhagabad would have dared to make it, especially in front of a girl so close to both royal courts. Only in Bahdra, an independent city, can people joke freely about the neighboring rulers.

"You probably won't make it through the next guard post," the man calls after her. "They lock up at night. But you can stay in a tavern next to it."

"Yeah, the Desert Lion—they would love to have a witty girl like you spend the night!"

"Unless, of course, you are in such a hurry that you are willing to ride straight through the desert." The guards laugh again, obviously thinking it a great joke. "It is a much shorter way, you know."

"Thanks," the princess throws over her shoulder, sending her horse back into a trot.

Through the desert. It doesn't sound like such a bad idea. At night the desert cannot be all too perilous. And it really is a much straighter way, as she remembers from her geography lessons. If she keeps going in the right direction, she should be across it by morning. And then she will be safe. Her pursuit will never think of following her into the sands. Most likely they will think that she is hiding somewhere in Bahdra and will keep searching for her, giving her plenty of time to reach home unnoticed.

Ride Through the Dunes

She rides out of sight and turns her horse off the road, straight into the dunes. Their silvery mounds, awash by moonlight, look like the still waves of a strange sea.

The stars in the clear night sky shine like jewels over the dune sea. The light, warm breeze caresses her, taking away all her worries and leaving her feeling clean and pure, like a child. She feels drunk with this new sense of freedom, with riding through the desert, alone, all her duties and obligations left behind in the noisy city of Bahdra. She feels like a nomad, a free desert spirit who can come and go as it will, without having to answer to any man. *Free.*

She recalls her lessons with the sage Haib al-Mutassim on reading the stars to pick the right way. As far as she remembers, Dhagabad lies almost directly to the north, with a slight incline to the west. That should be right toward that small star between the constellations of Houri and Desert Spring. Left and down from the constellation of the Prophet.

She has never cared much for her geography and astronomy lessons, preferring history and arts. Now she wholeheartedly blesses the sage's tediousness as a teacher. One never knows when lessons might come in handy.

She rides for a couple of hours, judging by the change in the position of the moon and stars. The sand is now stretching in every direction. The horse's hooves are sinking into the sand with every step, making the progress slower. Behind them she can see a trail of hoofprints slowly vanish, smoothened out on the surface of the sand by the strengthening gusts of wind.

It may take longer than I thought to cross this desert, the princess realizes.

She remembers that in her anxiety to get away she completely forgot about bringing any supplies with her, such as food or water. In her captivity she hasn't eaten much the whole previous day, and her stomach is now starting to rumble.

She searches the horse's saddlebags for some supplies she can use. All she finds is a timber box, a length of rope, and a set of climbing hooks. A strange combination. The owner of the horse must be quite an unusual person. Unfortunately, he didn't store anything in the saddle that might help her out in her situation.

Maybe I should get back to the road, she thinks. *I should be well past the guard post already.*

She tries to remember how exactly the road goes in this area. It should be off to the west, almost parallel to the way she is traveling. The city of Dhagabad, on the other hand, lies directly in front. Should she try to get off her way, or risk it and go straight?

She can tell that the horse must be tired as well. They usually cross the desert on camels, she remembers. They do that because camels can go much longer without water and because they are much more fit to tread on the sand. The horse is probably tired and thirsty. Also, it doesn't have as much at stake as the princess. While she herself might be able to last without water for a day to save herself, the horse may not be willing to do the same. She has no idea how horses are about water. Which probably means it would be safer to get back to the road.

She picks a course westward, left of the Houri constellation that has now moved higher in the sky, hoping to get some time ahead of the possible pursuit by hitting the road farther along. She even considers dismounting to give the horse more rest. But this horse is very big. Its owner must have been a large man, a warrior or a merchant with lots of weapons and armor. Compared to him, the princess's weight should seem like nothing to the huge beast.

After another two hours of riding she starts to get worried. There is still no sign of the road, or any change in the landscape. The stars have faded, and the sky behind her is getting lighter as the dawn approaches. Her mouth is dry, and the emptiness in her stomach makes her feel weak.

She remembers that on the map the road is making large loops to avoid the protruding areas of sand. She cannot remember exactly where these protruding areas are, but she is sure she must be riding along one of them.

Just a little bit longer, she whispers, patting the horse on the back, feeling the need to reassure the poor animal she might have led into trouble. She feels fatigued after spending a sleepless night and a day full of worry. She had originally planned to rest after reaching the road. But now even the sand dunes begin to look attractive. In spite of the wind, rising stronger and stronger in its gusts, it seems so appealing to stop the horse, to slide off its back, to rest just a little bit on the soft, warm sand.

The princess doesn't notice how she dozes off in the saddle, leaning forward onto the horse's neck.

She wakes up with a start. It is light around her. The sun rising over the desert looks dim through the clouds of sand, raised by the strengthening wind. Sand creaks on her teeth, fills her hair, rasps on her skin, making her feel even drier. Her tongue seems to be swollen in her dry mouth, and moving it is painful.

She sits up to realize that she is no longer riding a horse. In her sleep she must have fallen off. Or, the horse threw her off to make walking easier. It must have happened very recently, too. Quite probably the fall is what woke her up. The trail of hoofprints disappearing behind the dune crest looks very fresh. As she watches, it recedes, smoothened over by the wind, leaving a mere depression in the sand.

She must find the horse! She is lost without it. And the horse cannot be far.

Through clenched teeth, she tries to make a sound she has heard grooms use to call horses—half-wail, half-whistle. But her throat is so dry and her tongue is so swollen, she cannot produce any decent sound.

She scrambles to her feet, ignoring the fatigue that makes her sway and lose her footing, and runs over the crest, along the disappearing horse trail. In her weak state, with the deep sand that seems to purposely try to catch her feet, running feels more like crawling. However slow the horse is moving, she will never catch it at this pace.

She stops, trying to suppress her panting. Breathing alone hurts enough. How could she have fallen *asleep* riding a horse? What is she going to do?

The road, she remembers. If the horse has been keeping the same direction during her sleep, she must be really close to the road now.

But what if the horse was just walking in circles and they - didn't move much since the middle of the night? What if the horse turned back where they came from to look for its master?

Don't panic, she tells herself. She has read that horses have a natural instinct to find their way to safety. Which means that the horse, whether it has been going backward or forward, was most likely taking her to safety.

All she needs to do is follow the horse's trail, and she will soon reach shelter. And water.

But she is so weak. So thirsty.

Water.

Walk, she tells herself. The wind is getting so strong that the horse's trail is not even visible anymore. If only she gets over that dune over there. The wind must be less strong there. And she might even see the horse walking away. She may even see shelter, or at least the road, which now seems like a haven of safety. Except that it is getting increasingly hard to see anything in the rising clouds of sand. Even the sun is becoming a blur in the thick haze. She cannot tell anymore if she is moving east or west.

Walk.

Each gust of wind—sand in her face—fills her mouth with creaky dryness. It even seems to penetrate her throat, saturating the air she inhales with tiny grains of sand. She cannot *stand* the sand anymore.

Hasan had to spend two thousand years buried in sand. Was he feeling as much pain as I do now? How could he survive it?

Hasan...

She suddenly remembers that in the books she read about the desert nomads, they used to survive through sandstorms by tying scarves around their faces, so that the sand got filtered out before they inhaled. They even did the same thing to their horses.

With weak fingers she pulls off Sadie's head shawl. The

276

wind almost tears it out of her hands, but she manages to hold on to it and tie it around her face, creating a kind of sand mask. It makes it even harder to see anything, but there is not much to see among the twirl of sand anyway. And it does seem to be easier to breathe.

She stumbles as her tired foot hits the crest of a dune. A strong gust of wind knocks her over. Unable to struggle for her footing anymore, she rolls down the dune, clouds of sand rising all around her. She is not sure where up and down is anymore. Everything seems to be made of sand.

Rise, she tells herself. *If you don't get up, you will be buried alive in minutes, just like the horse's trail. No one will ever find you.*

She cannot breathe anymore. Her dry, swollen tongue seems to occupy most of her mouth. The remaining space is filled with sand.

Light fades from her eyes as she gets knocked over again and rolls to a standstill in a ravine between the dunes. Sand covers her, its warm weight getting heavier and heavier on her legs, her chest, her face. Breathing becomes impossible. As her lungs struggle for air, she begins to hear the darkness around her fill with noises and whispers, many voices reaching her across time and space. Among them she slow beat of a *tama domga* grows louder and louder until it overpowers all the other sounds, filling her ears with its deep musical rhythm.

Hasan, she thinks. She tries to whisper his name, but her lips don't seem to obey her anymore. She whispers it in her mind anyway, over the *tama domga* sounds, in a hurry to speak her last farewell before sinking into oblivion. *I love you, Hasan. I forgive you for abandoning me here to die. I will love you to my last heartbeat.*

Prisoners of the Desert

*T*hea senses a deep, inaudible thud as the last block of the pyramid wall slides into place. They are sealed. There is no way out now. They have been buried alive, inside a pyramid tomb that King Amenankhor ordered built around their temple. Unable to destroy it, he ordered the Temple of the Great Goddess to be buried forever inside a tomb.

Moving in Dance, Thea joins her thoughts with all the other priestesses, dancing together in the great hall. They are dancing here for the last time—dancing until they die and are finally embraced for eternity by the mother goddess.

She senses another shape next to her fall down in exhaustion. The girl Aelana. It was brave of her to stay with them until the end and not leave to go back home like some of the other apprentices chose to do. Amazing that she survived in Dance much longer than even some Mistresses did. In her last breath she has become a full priestess and a Mistress, Thea thinks. Not that it matters now. But in some higher sense it does.

Have peace, Sister Aelana, Thea says in her mind as she feels the girl's soul leave her body as clearly as if it were a part of Thea herself. It *is* a part of her now, just like all the women in this hall are. They are all one creature of the goddess, moving in the last steps of the Sacred Dance. It will soon be over.

Thea half-sees half-senses Aelana's body pierced by shafts

of light, and her light-encased shape rise off the floor in the exact position in which Aelana has stopped her Dance. The step of rebirth, the pose of a reed. The light flashes in the air, projected onto a wall. It happens in a single moment, just like it did for all the other priestesses. Aelana's body is no longer lying on the floor. It is now embedded into the wall of the chamber, forming a mural of a dancing figure, the next one in a row of dancing figures already covering the wall. Each of them a priestess who died in Dance.

There are very few of them still standing in the hall. Very few spaces remaining on the wall. When they die, they will all turn into murals to complete the dancing circle.

She senses Riomi fall down next to her. The pain of the loss is so strong that Thea almost falters in her next movement. But she calls herself back to calmness. She will join Riomi soon. They will all be together forever on these walls. They will be the keepers of the spirit of the Sacred Dance, buried in a pyramid tomb, but never defeated.

Time seems to pass her by as the others fall down one by one and get projected onto the walls of the chamber. Ngara next. Then Ganne. Then, finally, Tamione. Then—

Only Thea remains now, moving slowly to the beat of the *tama domga* sounding in her head. Alone. The last priestess remaining of the sacred cult, so powerful that even the kings have had to go out of their way to conceal it for eternity.

I am coming, sisters, Thea says in her mind, sending the last farewell to the silent murals on the wall that were her sisters just a short time ago. *Great mother,* she prays. *I am coming to you. Take your humble daughter into your arms.*

Shafts of lightning strike her from all sides, piercing her body with terrible pain. They meet somewhere in the center and then fly apart again, tearing her body into dust. She burns in agony, burns forever in their eternal flame that lifts her and carries her through space, leaving nothing of her human form, taking her spiritual essence into another world...

Hasan raises his eyes from the finished scroll and steps deeper into the heart of the library. The air is thick, and he has difficulty moving through it. He also feels his thoughts drifting, so that he has to constantly remind himself why he is here. He has gotten so used to the ghostly shadows of Abdulla and Galeot-din following him everywhere that he doesn't give them any thought anymore.

I am trapped, he tells himself one more time. *I am looking for scrolls that can help me find a way out of here. But—*

He pauses, wiping cold sweat off his brow. Not for the world can he remember where it is he is supposed to go from here. This library, this temple, is the only world he has ever known. Isn't it?

He is vaguely aware that there is another ghostly world out there. He was so desperate to escape from there into the *real* world of this library that he used a portal to go through and *wander along these shelves, keeping in order the priceless scrolls that hold in them the wisdom of creation and absolute power. You don't want to leave here ever again. If you stay, you will share the wisdom of so many wizards like you, who came before you and became an eternal part of this temple and this desert. In time you will learn everything there is to know about this world, the* real *world that your wisdom has allowed you to penetrate. You will become all-powerful here, in this desert, in this temple that reigns over the sands for eternity...*

Something at the back of his mind keeps nagging him, though—some image that tries to break out of his subconscious. Some time ago he was able to suppress it completely. But now it is becoming stronger and stronger. More and more annoying.

An image.

Someone is dying out there, and this someone keeps sending him insistent messages that are becoming increasingly irritating.

Leave me alone, he thinks. *Mortals die all the time in that imperfect, ghostly world. I have no time to concern myself with such things. My knowledge and powers are growing so fast here that I am rising infinitely above the mortal deeds.*

But the image simply will not let go. Worse than that, it is becoming clearer and clearer. It looks like a young girl trapped in the sands.

There are sands all around this temple. Many all-powerful wizards are trapped in these sands. Compared to them the souls of mortals are as unimportant and insignificant as the grains of sand itself. Why does this girl think she can bother you, an all-powerful spirit, with her silly needs? Who does she think she is?

The image is becoming stronger. Dimensional. The girl is falling down, buried in the sands. The image is so vivid that it somehow finds its way through the lines of the scroll he is reading, occupying his mind more and more.

She turns her face to him, her bothersome dark blue eyes bringing unnecessary color to this dim, colorless room. She looks ugly compared to the elegant beauty of the scrolls. Her hair is full of sand; her face is scratched; her dry, swollen lips cracked and bleeding. He sees her lips move, forming a word he seems to recognize. The lips move and move, inaudibly pronouncing this word even as life fades out of her weak, mortal body, even as sense fades out of her bothersome blue eyes.

She is saying a name. A vaguely familiar name. And although her lips are barely moving, the name sounds clearly in his head.

Hasan.

Who in the world is Hasan?

Hasan, I love you.

Hasan, I am dying.

I will love you till my last—

—heartbeat.

Light fades from her sapphire eyes and they close for the last time.

No—

I need to see those eyes again.

There is reason in her eyes.

Reason for—

—living.

Gul'Agdar!

Hasan wakes up with a snap. Princess Gul'Agdar is dying! While he has been away in the library for gods know how long, she has been left without his help. She has come to harm. She may be already dead.

He needs to get out and help her.

Now!

With all the strength of his absolute power, with all the strength he has absorbed by reading these scrolls, with all the strength of his enormous need, he creates a blast of energy that shakes the ancient temple down to its foundation. Amid the falling scrolls flying in every direction, he focuses all this power into a single spot, shifting time and space to create a portal back to the mortal world.

He condenses all his being into a single streak of energy that pierces time and space like a needle, blasting away all obstacles in its path.

The desert looks empty. The recent sandstorm has thoroughly swept through the dunes, eliminating all traces. For a chance observer there is no way to tell what happened here this morning, when the storm hit so unexpectedly at this time of the year. But Hasan knows exactly what he is looking for.

How in the world did she end up here?

He turns his body into a sheet of air, flying horizontally over the dunes, searching for a familiar sight.

Over there, in that cleft between the dunes.

By the position of sand he could swear this cleft was much deeper only yesterday. Probably deep enough to bury half a dozen of riders, let alone one fragile young girl traveling on foot.

What happened? He materializes into his human shape as he sweeps over to the sand cleft.

He is still floating over the sand. He doesn't want to put any additional weight on the princess buried under there.

Buried *alive.*

She is alive, he tells himself, directing enough energy

through his palm to blow away the sand. *She* must *be.*

She *cannot* die on him now.

It takes effort to direct his thoughts away from the terror, to keep removing the sand gently, so that he doesn't damage the fragile body underneath.

After a few minutes that seem like centuries, he sees a flap of brownish cloth. The face is buried deeper beneath, but what he sees of the body is clad in a brownish Veriduan garment. A serving girl outfit.

Maybe it isn't her? he thinks in an uprush of wild hope. *Please, let this all be a mistake! Let it be someone else!*

But he knows it cannot possibly be anyone else. Only the special link he has with the princess could have brought him back from the deadly place he was trapped in. Only her dying thoughts of him could have been strong enough to penetrate the barrier between worlds, to awaken inside him the power to achieve the impossible.

For the second time the princess's wholehearted wish has freed him from the bonds of the ancient desert, the place that imprisons the djinns.

She possesses incredible powers. She *cannot* possibly die like this.

With shaking hands Hasan pulls the lifeless body free of the sand. He lowers himself on the dune crest, cradling the princess in his arms, searching for any spark of life that he can enhance, can blow into a steady flame by joining it with his absolute power.

He doesn't seem to find anything. She is dead.

No, he tells himself, forcing away the rising panic. *She is not dead. Not unless you give up on her.*

She has never given up on him. She has *taught* him never to give up, however impossible the cause.

Hasan knows that no amount of absolute power can bring back the dead. He forces the knowledge away. Of all the useless things he knows, this is perhaps the most useless one of all right now.

Breathe.

She needs to breathe.

He forces her mouth open and carefully blows a breath of air in there. He almost chokes. Her mouth is full of sand.

Her *lungs* are full of sand.

He extends a palm over her mouth, freeing his hand of any powers except one: drawing sand.

A magnet can attract metal to itself. His hand is now capable of attracting sand.

He turns around. Doing a thing like that in a desert full of sand is extremely foolish. He needs to take her to a safer place, where there is no sand. Where there is plenty of water to quench the princess's thirst if—*when*—she finally comes back to life.

Holding the princess tight against himself, he rises to his feet and steps forward all the way from the desert to the Halabean range, to a small hidden valley where there is no sand, where the trees grow freely along a clear mountain stream that forms a small, secluded lake on its merry way down to the lands beyond.

Still cradling the princess in his lap, he moves his magnetic hand over her mouth and watches the sand fly out and stick to it, until there is no more sand left inside her body.

Now, breathe, he tells her. He blows another mouthful of air into her cleared mouth. *Inhale.* Then he pushes her chest down with his hand to release the air he has blown in. *Exhale. Breathe.*

His hand finds something on her chest, under her clothes, that feels warm to his touch. A small, oval thing.

He lowers the princess onto a soft patch of grass and opens the top of her Veriduan outfit to reveal a bluish stone pendant on a delicate silver chain.

The Stone of the Elements.

The surface of the stone is clear, but a single blue beam pulses in its semitransparent depths, pulses with warmth that is looking for a way out, into the princess's chest.

The stone is helping her. It is breathing life into her! If the stone is alive, it means that somewhere, deep inside this coma, the princess is alive too.

Thank you, Zobeide, Hasan whispers, blessing his old friend who has tried to ruin all his plans, sided with his enemies, and almost killed the princess in the process. Whatever her intentions, thanks to her the princess now has the aid of the Elements, who do not let their chosen ones die easily.

Water, Hasan remembers. *The princess is the Chosen of the Water.*

He walks knee-deep into the lake and lowers her limp, lifeless body into the cool water. Then he sits down next to her, water now coming up to his waist, supporting her with his palms, watching her float in front of him, motionless on the mirror-still surface of the lake.

He reaches out to touch her brow, putting himself into a trance where his energy flows into her, for a while blending them into one. Through half-closed eyelids he can see the Stone of the Elements pulse with a blue beam of energy, making the water around the princess glitter with a blue glow.

Hasan calls absolute stillness to his mind, directing all his powers into this bluish, glowing water encasing the princess's lifeless body. He closes his eyes, focusing on their energy link, forgetting everything in the distant stillness that now unites the two of them.

He forgets the flow of time around them. He doesn't realize anything except his hand on her cold brow.

And then, gradually, he starts to feel warmth under his fingers. At first he cannot even tell if this warmth comes from him or from her. Not until he feels her stir.

The current, pulling her floating body away from his reach?

With a start, he comes back to his senses. And meets the look of her dark blue eyes, still hazy, but quite alive.

"Hasan," she whispers with her dry, cracked lips. She tries to smile, but her face muscles don't quite obey her yet. Still, the smile in her eyes makes his heart leap.

"You—you came back for me, Hasan," she whispers. "You saved me."

"You are the one who saved me, princess," he says gently. "If it weren't for you, I would never have been able to come back."

There is a question in her eyes, but she seems to have no more energy left to speak. She awkwardly tries to turn over, to move, to submerge into the water.

Hasan gently pulls her back into his lap, once again cradling her like a baby. He takes a cup out of thin air, fills it with water, and carefully puts it to her lips, helping her to take the first, unsteady sips.

The water fills her with energy, the Stone of the Elements on her neck now blazing with a blue flame. *Gul'Agdar, the Chosen of the Water,* he thinks. *Water means life, especially for those dying in the desert. But for the princess it seems to mean infinitely more than that.* He knows that the ones chosen by the Water can use its aid in more ways than any other human could. And now it is obviously helping the princess, bringing her back faster than any other known remedy would.

She drinks for a long time, getting stronger and stronger with every sip. Then, finally regaining her ability to move by herself, she leaves his side and submerges into the lake, half-swimming, half-bathing in its cool, clear waters.

Seeing that she is now capable of helping herself, Hasan steps out of the water to the soft, grassy glade and sits there, relaxing, recovering from the fight that has shaken him much more deeply than he thought possible.

She is alive, he tells himself. *Alive. And you have blown so much energy into her that she will emerge out of these waters completely well. Relax.*

A shadow falls over him, and he turns to see Gul'Agdar stepping out of the water, her long, wet hair clinging to her body.

Naked body?

She is holding her Veriduan garment in front, not to let him see her. From behind the garment she looks at him with the shy mischief of a child who knows it is doing something improper and yet is unable to resist the temptation.

Seeing the stare of his widened eyes, she lets out a laugh.

"I cannot stand this Veriduan outfit anymore," she says. "Can you give me a bath sheet, please? And turn around, if you could."

"Right away, princess," he calls out, still a little dazzled, and lets a light, silky bath sheet float up to her, at the same time turning away as modesty dictates.

He can still see her, of course. Or, rather, be *aware* of her with his magical senses. But in this game of decency, invented by humans, it really doesn't matter much.

All dried up, wrapped in her bath sheet, she comes up to him and lowers herself on the grass.

"Thank you for saving my life, Hasan," she says, serious again. "I thought you wouldn't come."

"As I mentioned before, princess, the thanks really belong to you," he replies. "If it weren't for you, I would have been trapped forever in the ancient desert."

"Is that why you didn't come before?" she whispers, her eyes wide.

"Yes."

"Not because you didn't want to? Not because—"

She slides forward to bury her face in his chest, flinging her arms around him. She clings to him as if her life depends on it, her body shaking with sobs.

He gently puts his arms around her.

"Of course not, princess," he whispers into her hair. "I would never abandon you."

"Oh, Hasan." She raises her face, wet with tears, to him. "I thought—I was afraid—"

She doesn't finish the phrase. Their lips move closer to each other and meet in a kiss that leaves them both momentarily breathless.

She draws away from him just a little bit, but her body doesn't quite seem to obey her anymore, seized by a dreamy terror of doing something so desirable and so forbidden. She feels drowned in his closeness, in his juniper smell, in the gentle passion of his strong embrace that leaves her longing for more.

More closeness. More passion.

More.

Oh, gods, what am I doing, almost naked in his arms?

More...

She never meant for this to happen. In the depths of her soul, she has always wanted it, yes. But she has feared it even more. The bond between them has been so special that she was afraid to challenge it by mere physical closeness. But his scent, the feeling of his body against hers, is so overpowering she loses all reason. A being has awakened inside her and is now driving her actions to fulfill the most desirable, the most forbidden thing she has ever known.

At least part of her wants to think that she is not responsible for her actions right now. The other, daring, part wants to revel in every bit of this new, wonderful sensation, as breathtaking as falling off a cliff. Her body seems to be moving on its own, overtaken by the same, primal force that has just drawn their lips together, beyond reason, beyond any conscious thoughts.

More. More...

She lets her bath sheet slide off, leaving her naked in his arms, her skin burning under his caressing hands. She trembles in this outburst of passion. Her excitement is so strong that it overtakes her completely, so wild she is afraid it will tear her apart. Something deep inside her is frightened. But the new Gul'Agdar—the being that has emerged victorious from the bonds of rejection, captivity, and certain death—doesn't care anymore.

"Hasan," she whispers, and the words coming out of her mouth burn like fire. "I want to be with you. I want to be *yours.*"

His eyes answer with tender passion, and she senses his clothes evaporate like smoke, leaving his muscular body breathtakingly naked next to her. Throwing away the last of the boundaries, she drowns herself in his closeness. For a while, she has no conscious thoughts. Only passion that drives her actions, bypassing her conscious mind. Then she slowly draws away, meeting his eyes again.

More.

"Hasan," she whispers, shivering with his closeness that makes her head swim. "I—"

His eyes are filled with such a mixture of passion and gentleness that it melts her heart to look into their flaming depths. Whatever the consequences, she cannot stop now. She will never forgive herself if she does.

"Princess," he says gently. "You don't—"

"Don't speak," she whispers, drawing him close, her own breath burning her as she seeks his lips like a desert wanderer seeks a drink of water. As their lips meet, she feels his hands caress her, moving down her back, his fingers touching her, sending shivers through her body. He lowers her down onto the silky bath sheet amid the soft grass, the sharp smell of which mixes with his smell of juniper, rising to her head like incense fumes. She feels her head swim as she wraps her legs around him, finally, once and for all, letting go of any possible control.

His smell—

His skin, so smooth under her burning fingers—

His muscle, so hard underneath, tensing in excitement that matches her own down to a single breath—

Don't stop, she begs him in her mind, her desire so strong that it fills her eyes with tears.

We are so close—

We are together—

I want for us to be together like this forever—

His touch, as he moves in to the ultimate closeness, turns everything else into a blur—a blur of ecstasy where his hands find the exact spots that make this ecstasy reach ultimate limits, where they move in a powerful rhythm to the same powerful beat.

Together—

Her body moves on its own, far ahead of her mind in its dazzled state where it doesn't seem to know, or care, about reason. Her lips between kisses form words that might or might not make sense on their own, but to her serve as a way to release her ecstasy that is so wonderfully unbearable that she doesn't want to let go of it, ever.

Or, perhaps, all she is letting out are moans, while these words exist somewhere in her head, unable to find their way out, to be uttered by her burning lips that are so busy with things that have nothing to do with speech.

I love you, Hasan—
I want you closer—
I want to be one *with you—*

And then she soars in the clouds of ecstasy that defies anything physical, defies pain, suffering, and even death itself. She soars in her happiness that she wishes never to end...

Till my last—
Heartbeat.

The Dancer

*I*n Dimeshq, inside the dark room in the heart of the royal palace, two figures stir and awaken from their death-like sleep, in which their minds have traveled across time and space to another world. They look at each other, barely visible in the darkness, their eyes gleaming, their faces pale.

The man on the left moves, straightening up in a gesture of impatience.

"He escaped!" the man exclaims. "What went wrong, Abdulla?"

"The girl," Abdulla observes darkly. "Their link. Lady Zobeide warned us about it."

"Yes... but... how could she penetrate the ancient desert?" Galeot-din insists.

"How could she have freed a djinn?" Abdulla retorts.

A pause follows when the two wizards collect themselves, shaking off the final bonds of their magical dream.

"Let's talk to Zobeide," Galeot-din suggests. He is angry. And afraid. Perhaps no less angry and afraid than Abdulla. But, having once acknowledged his inferiority to his court mage, he cannot afford to put his anger before Abdulla's. Later, perhaps, when they achieve their goals of becoming all-powerful and free. Only now, after their failure to contain Hasan, nothing short of killing him would save Galeot-din and Abdulla from the haunt of the wind with many voices...

To Galeot-din's surprise, Abdulla doesn't argue. He merely waves a hand to summon a magic mirror out of thin air. They both wait impatiently for Zobeide's face to appear in its depths, hanging in front of them in the air like a perfect portrait in an oval frame.

"What happened?" she asks with a frown that makes her look like an angered goddess of beauty.

"He escaped, lady," Abdulla says, for once willing to be the one to deliver the bad news. "Maybe you were wrong and he is not all-powerful after all?"

"You never know," Zobeide says. "I might have been wrong. But the desert did keep a hold on him for a while, - didn't it?"

"Yes, but the girl was somehow able to use their link to bring him back. At least that's what it seemed like."

"I thought that she might prove to be a problem." Zobeide's frown becomes deeper. "I wish she had died in the challenge of the Elements, like she was supposed to!"

"I guess we do have to take the girl into account after all," Abdulla observes coldly.

"Have you at least learned what you wanted from the True Library?" Zobeide asks.

"Not enough. I wish I knew how the little bitch managed to get to him!"

"She almost got herself killed," Zobeide says. "She sent her dying thoughts to him. Nothing short of that would have worked, I believe."

"I thought she was stored away safely, waiting for our ally Caliph Agabei to collect her as a bride," Abdulla says.

"She did something none of us could have expected from her," Zobeide says. "She managed to run away."

There is a strange light in her eyes that Galeot-din cannot quite recognize. She certainly seems different from their last conversation. But how?

"Wasn't there a way for you to interfere?" Abdulla presses on.

"Perhaps there was," she says coldly.

She is no longer our ally, Galeot-din realizes. She *admires* what the princess managed to accomplish. Perhaps she is also secretly glad that Hasan, her former lover, has escaped such a carefully laid trap. And, of course, she is fully aware of the powers behind them, the powers that make Abdulla and Galeot-din so terrified.

She never was a good ally, anyway, Galeot-din thinks bitterly. *She was probably always looking for ways to break this improbable collaboration.* What possessed him to trust her, the most deceitful of all women, in the first place?

"Why didn't you interfere, then?" Abdulla asks, his voice so terrifying in its quietness that it makes Galeot-din's skin creep with terror.

Across the distance of the magic mirror the coals of Abdulla's burning eyes meet the cool emerald of Zobeide's. Galeot-din, who has wisely chosen to turn himself into a silent observer, watches this clash with fear. Things like this have been known to shatter magic mirrors, to unleash powers that could cause destruction of entire cities, not to mention eliminating chance observers on the spot. But, even more importantly, he sees something in Zobeide's eyes, in the way she carries her head, that looks too much like triumph.

"You—you *wanted* him to escape," Abdulla whispers in suppressed rage.

"I have fulfilled every promise I made to you, Abdulla," Zobeide says, her voice ringing with force. "I was not, however, prepared to interfere with powers I know nothing about. The girl was able to free him once. She has now freed him again. If you want to eliminate Hasan, you will have to deal with the girl yourself."

"And I will," Abdulla hisses, no longer bothering to appear in control. "I know exactly how to deal with both of them."

He turns and walks away from the mirror into the depths of the room, leaving Galeot-din face-to-face with Zobeide. She is angry, Galeot-din can tell. But underneath this anger she seems to be, in some strange way, relaxed.

He has his own score to settle with her. But it will just have to wait.

"Where are they now, Zobeide?" he asks. "Where are they

headed?"

"The situation has become too dangerous for me to take sides, Galeot-din," Zobeide says, her composure back. It seems to him that in the glance she throws at him there is, among other things, regret. "I know that you and Abdulla have to follow the Voices of the Wind. But for me the choice is not clear. I will not tell you any more."

She sweeps a hand in front of her face, and the mirror shatters into many tiny droplets that hang in the air in front of him like gray mist. Only Abdulla, being the one who summoned it, can remove the mirror completely. But Zobeide has, finally and determinedly, severed the contact.

"Let's go," Abdulla says from the depths of the room, his voice, at least outwardly, back to normal. "We have no time to lose. Let's pay a visit to our ally, Caliph Agabei."

"The caliph?" The question freezes on Galeot-din's lips as realization suddenly dawns upon him. Their backup plan. The caliph of Megina possesses a djinn. And a djinn may well be the only power in this world that equals, and possibly exceeds, the power of Hasan.

The only power in this world sufficient to get rid of him once and for all.

They sit together on the sunlit grass in front of a shimmering lake. Leaning against Hasan's shoulder, feeling the warm smoothness of his skin next to hers, the princess tells him of all her misfortunes since the time he saw her last, right to the point where she fell into the cleft between the dunes and lost consciousness.

Despite being happier than she ever remembers being before, a gnawing feeling keeps bothering her, of something that happened and she is not telling him, something that for some reason escapes her grasp. Something that happened at the very end, after she slipped into semiconsciousness. But what?

She doesn't want to think about trouble now. She is alive and safe. She is with Hasan. She has just shared with him such intimacy, such ultimate closeness, that even if she died right now she wouldn't regret a thing.

But she is not going to die. She is going to *live*, with Hasan by her side!

She rubs her cheek against his shoulder and raises her face to the sun, catching little rainbows into her half-closed eyelashes.

"That fat woman was so strange," she says. "I still don't know what she wanted with me. Maybe if it wasn't for her and this Odo who chased me in the shadows, I would have stayed in the Oasis instead of rushing out into the desert."

"She is most likely a slave-trader," Hasan says. "One of those who sell young girls. There are a lot of them in Bahdra. In any big city, as a matter of fact. You must have looked like easy prey to her—lost, obviously foreign to these parts. And ... beautiful."

His hand caresses her hair and slides down along her back. She shivers with pleasure. Is she dreaming, or is it really happening to her?

"I—I am so happy, Hasan," she says. "Whatever happens to us later, I am happy right now."

"So am I," he whispers, so quietly that she almost doesn't hear it. Nonetheless, she senses these words in the touch of his skin, in the set of his head, leaning so close to her that she can imagine she can almost read his thoughts.

She couldn't *really* think of reading his thoughts, of course. Even though they are now so close, even though she is now initiated into magic, he is so much older and wiser. But in her new, happy state she doesn't want to think about it.

"What happened to you, Hasan?" she asks. "Where have you been?"

"I was... back in the ancient desert." His voice wavers with the old pain. "I... almost got trapped in there for eternity."

"Why? My grandmother went there and returned, and she wasn't even a very good sorceress."

"The desert is designed to trap the all-powerful wizards. That is the sole purpose of its existence. Well, almost."

"Then why did you go there?"

"I was looking for information about djinns. And I was stupid enough to overlook the obvious—if the powers that contained me before are focused in the desert, it may not be the best place for me to go."

His voice reverberates with such pain that she feels the need to comfort him. She reaches up and gently touches his cheek, turning his face to her.

He smiles.

"If you hadn't called me back, princess," he says, "there would have been no way out for me. Ever."

"I don't even know how I did it," she says thoughtfully. "I remember thinking about you—but I always do, anyway." She flushes and turns away with a quick smile, embarrassed by speaking her feelings aloud.

"It was your dying thought of me, princess," he says slowly. "I believe nothing short of that could have brought me back."

It sounds terrible, put this way. And yet—isn't this how magic works, answering your wish at the time of greatest need?

She stirs in his arms, shivering under the light mountain breeze. Where does she get this heavy feeling, now that she should be so happy and carefree? Why does she have a sense that this feeling is somehow linked to her time in the desert?

"There is something else that happened then," she says slowly. "Something terrible. Somebody died, I think."

She frowns, trying to recall what happened. She does remember calling Hasan's name. She has been doing it very often lately, anyway. But afterward—did she just slip into unconsciousness? Or did she first witness something terrible, someone else closely linked to her, suffering and dying in front of her eyes?

She sits up sharply, staring into space.

How could she forget somebody so close to her that they almost feel like one?

Thea.

"What happened?" Hasan asks, looking into her suddenly pale face.

"Thea," she whispers.

Thea. Before slipping into unconsciousness, she witnessed the symbolic burial of the ancient Cult of the Great Goddess. She knew about this before, from Hasan. But she never knew that the cult had been buried *alive.*

Just like she was buried alive in the sand.

The cult was buried along with the priestesses, whom she grew to know like sisters, whom she witnessed falling in Dance to be projected onto the walls in the great dance hall, to become the eternally dancing murals, forever circling in the dark depths of the temple. She *felt* Thea's body being torn apart by shafts of lightning as acutely as if Thea's body were her own. And at that moment a part of her, the part that has become very important to her in the past few months, died as well, together with this priestess of the Dance—the woman whose life she has been observing in such detail through the peephole of the dreams that somehow transported her through time and space all the way to ancient Aeth.

"We have to go to the Temple of the Dance," the princess says urgently.

She is not sure why, but she knows they must go there. To see the faces of the murals and to finally learn if her dreams have been true, or if they have just been a figment of her tortured mind. To find Thea among them and finally see her face-to-face, to learn what the woman through whose eyes she has been watching the world looks like. To *know* whether the horrible end of the Temple of the Dance she witnessed in her dream is really what happened.

She doesn't know if, or how, she is going to learn that, but she must go there anyway!

"Let's go, Hasan!" she says, jumping to her feet. "Oh." She looks down her naked body. Then she meets his eyes, and a smile surfaces out from under her concern. "I didn't mean... like this," she adds hastily.

"What would you like to wear?" he asks, looking up at her with mischief.

She throws a dreamy look at his naked form. It is so tempting to stay here just a little bit longer, enjoying the closeness she has dreamed of for such a long time. She reaches out to him and he takes her hands, springing lightly to his feet and enfolding her in an embrace. *So close.*

"Can you get that blue dress for me?" she finally asks, letting go. "The one from the Island of the Elements. It should be somewhere in the house where I was kept—in Bahdra." She suddenly realizes it could be anywhere by now. After her escape was discovered, who knows what could have happened in that distant house on the outskirts of Bahdra.

"Here you are, princess," Hasan says, holding out the silky blue cloth for her.

She takes it from him and slowly puts it on, enjoying the cool breath of silk on her burning skin. She catches Hasan's eyes on her, merry sparkles dancing in their depths, and blushes. Somehow it feels different to see him naked when she herself is fully dressed.

"Your hair, princess?" Hasan asks. He makes a casual shrugging movement and suddenly appears to be fully dressed in his usual white shirt and pants of dark silk.

"No, I want to keep my hair loose," the princess says absently. She has never worn her hair loose before. Now, after so many significant changes in her life, it somehow seems appropriate.

There is something else she needs. Something that belongs to the Temple of the Dance much more than she does.

"Hasan," she says. "Can you get my *tama domga* for me, please?"

The princess sets her foot on the sand and holds her breath, looking around. Everything is exactly as she remembers it from her last trip here with Hasan, almost three years ago. The streak of greenery by the water, pushed back by the sands of the Aethian desert that run away toward the horizon in smooth, yellow waves. Dark pyramid cones on their surface, grouped close together in the setting sun, throwing long shadows across the sands toward the Great River, hidden in the greenery of the reed thickets.

All around them—sands.

Another part of her remembers this place as it used to be in her dreams—perhaps the way it was a long time ago, during the times of Aeth's glory, when the greenery beside the river spread much wider, pushing the sands of the desert farther away. When, just downstream from this burial site, there was a big and noisy city that rose in place of Thea's hometown, and which has now left no trace whatsoever of its existence two thousand years back into the past. When, instead of these pyramid tombs, there was nothing but a grassy plain to surround the Temple of the Great Goddess, rising its proud, harmonious shape straight into the Aethian sky.

The princess feels a lump in her throat and hastily swallows it, blinking away the familiar tingling under her eyelids.

"Which pyramid, Hasan?" she asks.

As soon as the question leaves her lips, she realizes that she knows the answer. That midsize pyramid, behind the large and obtrusive one that looks older than the others. She remembers that the oldest pyramid built here partially shielded the temple entrance from the first beams of the eastern sun. All the later pyramids were built level with it or behind it. There are no more pyramids to the east of the temple.

"Take us in, Hasan," she asks, and a moment later feels the half-familiar sensation of submerging into the cold, heavy mass of gray stone, to emerge in the absolute darkness on the other side of the pyramid wall.

With infallible instinct, Hasan realizes that she needs silence right now. Answering her thoughts before she has time to speak, he summons a giant lantern to float above her head. In its wavering light the princess looks at the smooth, elegant shape of the temple building, surrounded by a single row of columns. Once again, she shakes from the memories of what she has witnessed happening behind these walls through her dream link and swallows another lump in her throat.

Clutching the *tama domga* in her hands, comforted by Hasan's presence behind her, she makes her unsteady way through the temple door.

Memories overwhelm her. Thea, pushed through this door for the first time in her life, crouching, terrified, on the floor of this entrance hall. Long *tadra* exercises in one of the side chambers, whose door is now hidden by the shadows of the passage. First encounter with the Mistresses and their test. The Last Dance in the giant dance hall over there, behind that door.

The princess carefully walks over to the door and pulls it open.

The lantern over her head produces less light than the hall's usual illumination of torches, but she still gets a momentary sensation of suddenly stepping into space, with no floor or ceiling, no top or bottom, but the endless mirrors reflecting the endless spiral patterns of the endless universe. She takes her first, uneven steps over the smooth surface, feeling it so inappropriate to walk in this hall, designed solely and entirely for Dance.

The murals of dancing figures on the walls seem to be watching them. As she and Hasan approach the first figure, closest to the entrance, the princess gasps.

Looking straight at her, head bent in the pose of the morning breeze, is the face of Eilea, which has become so familiar to her in her dreams. The full lips of her inverted crescent mouth, the narrow, upturned eyes that appear to be laughing when her mouth is twitched in scorn, create the impossible divergence of lines, forever making this disdainful, unfriendly face beautiful, the face that draws eyes and turns heads even among the crowd of young, beautiful girls. No girl, for there is wisdom shining in these sharp eyes that pierces even the layers of dead old paint. The wisdom of a Mistress of the Dance, shining through the mural that was painted by no human hand.

She reaches out to touch Eilea's upturned palm and almost imagines that she feels warmth coming through the cold stone wall. She is sure the priestess's soul is trapped right here, under this surface. But how can she ever hope to release her?

Grasping Hasan's hand, so reassuringly real in this eerie place, the princess moves along the row of familiar figures frozen in the continuous poses of the Dance. She recognizes them all. She knows most of their names, except for some young apprentices who weren't in the temple for long before the evil will of the Aethian kings buried the ancient cult, trapping the priestesses in the walls. Her heart falls as she recognizes the faces of Thea's close friends, the ones who were beside her through the centuries of training. It feels as if she is seeing these familiar faces through a window into the past, freezing them through a span of centuries. Painted, true. But somewhere beneath the paint she can sense their beings, imprisoned in stone, waiting for their time to get out and rule again in this once-so-lively place.

Holding her breath, the princess passes the pale figure of Mistress Tamione; Ganne, elegant like a statue of olive-colored jade; Ngara with her heavily built body and a mass of dark braids.

Everyone the princess has grown to know so well in her dreams is here. There is only one face she cannot find. The face she has never really seen before, because she has been looking at the world through its eyes. The face she is sure nevertheless she will immediately recognize, because there is so much they have been through together that she feels forever a part of this person.

Thea.

She stops, a thought half-formed in her head—realization of something she should have figured out a long time ago, if her mind weren't so overwhelmed by her urge to take a look at the Hall of Dance.

True, she doesn't know what it felt like for those priestesses to turn into murals. But there is one thing she is certain of: their bodies haven't been turned into dust by the piercing shafts of lightning. The light that hit them has encased their bodies to project them onto the walls. Whatever it felt like, through Thea's eyes it didn't look like the torture of being pierced through and torn apart into something insubstantial. Very different from the agonizing horror she shared with Thea.

It is quite possible that Thea's fate was different from the fate of her friends. It could just be that her last sensations were similar to what happened to Hasan at the critical point in his life when he realized that he had just learned everything there is to know about this world.

When his body was torn apart by shafts of lightning and he turned into a djinn.

Could it be true that Thea is a djinn? That she is still suffering in the ancient desert Hasan escaped with such difficulty, waiting for someone to bring her back into this world? Or, serving somebody who has gone into the desert and picked up her container to obtain himself an all-powerful slave?

The thought that strikes the princess leaves her momentarily breathless. She slowly turns to Hasan, who is watching her intently.

Thea. The name that means "Dancer" in the ancient Ghullian. Later on she called herself Shaina, which means "Dancer" in the old Aethian dialect. And then she merely started calling herself "Dancer" in whatever language she was addressed.

What if—?

Caliph Agabei's slave, Shogat.

"Hasan," the princess whispers, forcing her lips to form words through the shocked stillness that encases her body. "Does the name Shogat mean anything in any language you know?"

"Yes, princess," he says, puzzled at the look of horror in her eyes. "It means 'Dancer' in Agrit. Why?"

The Final Battle

A soundless thunder shakes the foundation of the ancient temple. A blaze of light momentarily fills the giant hall and fades, leaving behind the dark outlines of four human figures. As the light reaches normal levels, as the princess's eyes regain vision after the blow they have just taken, she makes out the faces of the newcomers. They are all familiar to her, except one—a dark, handsome man with a black beard, his eyes shining brightly in his pale, haughty face. On his left she sees the nervous, boyish Abdulla, Hasan's former apprentice, who almost killed her and Hasan in this very room during their last visit to the temple. She shivers under the look of his dark eyes, but she is no longer afraid of him. She knows that Hasan is stronger, especially now, when he has been set free and he doesn't need her command to defend himself anymore.

She also knows the pair on the right—Caliph Agabei and his djinn, Shogat—and it is Shogat who draws the princess's full attention.

It feels like seeing a long-lost sister after too many years of being apart. She looks into Shogat's huge eyes, and a familiar lump rises in her throat, tears ready to escape her eyelids. She suppresses the urge to rush up to the djinn and hug her, recalling their shared memories of the times long gone.

Shogat's eyes slide over the princess with indifference.

She doesn't recognize me, the princess thinks. *Or perhaps she doesn't know about my dreams. Is it really possible she simply doesn't know? How did our fates get entangled this way?*

"Thea," she whispers, stepping toward the former priestess of the Dance.

The sound of this name makes Shogat's muscles twitch. Her eyes focus on the princess, then slide to the *tama domga* in the princess's hand. The princess wants to step closer, to say something, but she is interrupted by the dry, harsh voice of Abdulla.

"You have escaped the desert, Hasan," he says. It seems to the princess that inwardly Abdulla is watching her, and this unseen gaze makes her feel uncomfortable. She edges closer to Hasan.

"I am afraid we cannot let it end like this," Abdulla continues.

"Why do you want me imprisoned, Abdulla?" Hasan asks. "Is it really about the True Library, or is there something else?"

"I don't see any harm in telling you," Abdulla says. "After all, you won't be with us for long." A flicker in his eyes makes the princess shiver. *He* cannot *do anything to harm Hasan. Can he?*

"Of course," Abdulla speaks, "the knowledge you could have obtained for us in the desert is invaluable, but there is much more at stake here. You see, the Wind itself has made us its accomplices in containing you. In return for our help the Voices promised Galeot-din and me the powers we could only dream of."

The Wind? The Voices? What are they talking about? A glance at Hasan tells the princess he knows exactly what Abdulla means. His neck is tense, face distant with the echoes of his old pain.

"I wouldn't trust the Voices of the Wind if I were you," Hasan says, his voice so cold that the princess shivers.

"You should learn to trust, Hasan," Abdulla mocks. "Your desire to be on your own is what originally led to your downfall."

"Suit yourself, Abdulla." Hasan shrugs. "But in your place I would ask myself: why would the Wind offer to give you and Galeot-din the powers it has denied anyone else?"

"Because we made a pledge to rid the world of the likes of you, Hasan!" the man indicated as Galeot-din says.

"There *are* no likes of me, your majesty," Hasan says with a slight bow.

He must be a ruler of some land, the princess thinks. *But for some reason the mention of his title is making him flinch. Why?*

"It has nothing to do with trust, Hasan," Shogat says. "The Wind has found its way into their dreams. It will haunt them forever if they don't fulfill their pledge." Her deep voice rings under the ancient vault, reverberating in the strings of the *tama domga* the princess is still clutching in her hand.

All heads turn to the djinn, who briefly meets the princess's eyes and subsides into silence.

"Enough!" Abdulla says impatiently. "We came here to rid the world of you once and for all, Hasan, and this is exactly what we are going to do."

He turns to Agabei.

"Caliph," he prompts.

Agabei steps forward with a solemn look that makes the princess's heart quiver. *What are they going to do? How can they rid the world of Hasan if he is all-powerful? What does the caliph have to do with it?*

She suddenly remembers that the caliph was to be her new groom after she was kidnapped in Bahdra. She steps closer to Hasan, as if she, with her feeble strength, could protect him from harm.

"Shogat," Caliph Agabei says slowly, his words ringing clearly in the giant hall. "I wish for you to fight Hasan to the death!"

Before the echo of the terrible words dies out, the hall shakes with a blast of energy that lifts the princess off her feet and throws her against a wall, right between the dancing figures of Riomi and the apprentice Aelana. She feels their warmth-within-cold, deep inside the stone wall at her back, encase her in their protective closeness as she watches, as if in a nightmare, the events unraveling in the giant hall.

Hasan and Shogat stand motionlessly in front of each

other. They don't appear to be doing anything, but their bodies are shuddering, as if the blows they are taking are coming from the inside. A glowing cocoon of force surrounds them, crackling with the intensity of its charge. It seems certain that whoever tries to approach them will be fried on the spot.

Across the cocoon, the princess can see the figures of Caliph Agabei, Abdulla, and the third man they call Galeotdin. They are watching the scene with alertness that suggests they can spring into action any second.

Hasan should win, the princess thinks desperately. *He must win. He can't lose now, when everything is going so well. He is, after all, not only all-powerful, but free, and therefore he possesses more strength than Shogat.*

But the other, more reasonable, part of her knows that the answer is not as simple as that. No one has yet compared the strength of a free, all-powerful wizard and a djinn. It is possible that by gaining his freedom Hasan has become just a tiny bit less powerful than before. Besides, even if he does win this impossible duel, it will leave him so weak that the three wizards who came here to destroy Hasan for a reason she doesn't understand can easily finish him off.

Oh, gods, she thinks, her heart seized by terror. She cannot *bear* to lose Hasan, not like this, not after what has happened between them. If he dies, she simply won't survive it.

She has to do something.

Go to the caliph and plead him to stop the duel? In his own twisted way he does seem to care for her. He has been willing to go through a whole lot of trouble to marry her. He probably offered a large bribe to the sultan of Veridue to make him arrange her kidnapping—that of his son's own bride. Besides, he can't really want to lose his djinn, Shogat, in this terrible battle. For even if Shogat survives, she will surely lose all her strength in the effort.

If Shogat's and Hasan's powers are truy equal, they will both die.

Oh, gods.

The princess scrambles to her feet and struggles to the other side of the force cocoon, where the three figures are standing motionlessly, observing the battle. It feels like walking chest-deep in water. She is still clutching the *tama domga* in her hand, more out of habit than from any real need.

Inside the cocoon, Hasan stumbles and slowly regains his balance. Shogat's hands rise in a gesture that seems to send another blast of energy through Hasan's body, making him shake on his now-unsteady feet.

Shogat is winning. Oh, NO!

As the princess covers the last few paces to the three wizards, she sees Shogat momentarily thrown back to her knees. The priestess of the Dance scrambles up like a cat, regaining her posture in a split second.

No. This can't be happening!

The wizards glance away from the battle and slide their cold gazes over the princess's flustered face. She ignores the other two, directing her full attention to Agabei.

"Caliph," she pleads, forcing her breath to calm down enough to allow her to say more than one word in a row. "Why are you doing this?"

"Stay out of this, princess," Abdulla warns her. The steel in his voice makes her shiver.

She does her best to ignore the warning and grabs the caliph by the arm.

"Please, caliph," she begs. "Order them to stop! This duel may kill Hasan, true, but Shogat will die too! You don't want to lose your djinn, do you?"

Caliph turns his face to her, and she suddenly sees the pain in his eyes.

"I'll find another djinn," he says in a hollow voice.

"This is none of your concern, princess," Abdulla says in a tone that makes her freeze.

He is using magic on me, the princess realizes. *He wants to stop me. Which means that he is, for some reason, afraid of my interference. And that, in turn, means that there is something I can do to stop this. But what?*

"Caliph," she says again, leaning closer to catch Agabei's eyes. *What can I do?* she thinks frantically. *Appeal to the caliph's feelings for me, supposing they exist? But how?*

"Don't say I didn't warn you, princess," Abdulla says coldly.

She feels a wisp of air grab her and raise her off the floor.

"Don't harm her," the man called Galeot-din warns. "You might trigger some link between them again."

"No harm, I promise," Abdulla says, his eyes fixed on the princess. She feels a whirlwind raise her higher to the ceiling and carry her around the force cocoon back to the wall where she used to be, between the figures of Riomi and Aelana. She is gently lowered to the ground, but the whirlwind stays, encasing her, caressing her with a tingling touch. The sensation is not altogether unpleasant, she has to admit. But the air hold leaves her completely helpless.

Hasan, in the center of the room, stumbles and falls down to one knee. He is resisting something that seems to be pushing down on him with great force. A small stream of blood runs down from his nostril, sharply visible against his deadly pale skin.

Blood. Of course. He is human now. He can bleed, unlike Shogat, who is nothing more than spiritual essence. If Shogat dies, she will probably just dissipate. Whereas Hasan can bleed and feel pain like any human does. He will die in agony, and the princess will have to watch it, helpless to do anything to help him.

Unable even to hold him in her arms, to kiss him one last time!

Shogat is showing no sign of dissipation. She hasn't even faded one single bit. She is pressing down on Hasan with force that is visibly shaking his now-human body.

I need to do something, the princess thinks. *Quickly!*

She tries to get up, but the wall of air, summoned by Abdulla, is holding her right where she is. Can she move her arms, at least? Yes, it seems so.

Shogat's figure in the circle wavers and stumbles back, allowing Hasan to get shakily back to his feet. Even from this distance, the princess can see sweat glistening on his forehead. He is weakening. But Shogat's movements also seem to lose some of their sharpness. The djinn is also wearing out. *What, oh what will happen to them?*

While she wholeheartedly wishes for Hasan to win this duel, she cannot bear the thought of Shogat perishing in it as well. This woman, this spirit of an ancient priestess of the Dance, has become so close to her. They have been bonded together for so long now. Will they lose each other before they really have a chance to meet?

Do something, the princess urges herself. *Think.*

She summons all the logic she still can. Abdulla has her trapped in this wall of air. All she can do is move her arms, while remaining in her sitting position. All the actions she can take right now are restricted by her limited freedom of movement.

She realizes that her hand is still clutching something that she has been holding against all odds, despite all the horrible things that have happened in this hall since she arrived here with Hasan such a short while ago.

Moving with difficulty inside her limited space, she raises her hand higher, so that the thing she has been clutching comes into full view.

Her *tama domga.*

The ancient instrument that has been returned to its proper place after more than two thousand years of absence.

Feeling as if some invisible force is moving her hand, the princess leans the *tama domga* against her knee and starts to beat the complex, sixty-four-step rhythm of the Sacred Dance.

Tum-tumm... Tum-tumm-tumm... Two pairs into four... Tum-tumm-tum-tumm... Tum-tumm-tum-tumm-tumm-tam... Two six-teens into thirty-two... Tum-tumm-tum-tumm-tumm-tam ...Tum-ta-ta-tamm-tum-tum-tamm... Tamm-tammm-tammmm ...

You don't want to kill this man in front of you, but your body and mind move on their own accord, all your power unleashed by the will of your mortal master, who wished for you to enter this duel to the death with a wizard whose power seems to equal your own.

You know that you can possibly kill him, for his power is weakening and his human body is already showing signs of wear. You know that this duel will most likely kill you too, for every spell you throw at him takes away a bit of your power. The impartial part of your mind wonders what will happen when a djinn is killed, for such a thing, to your knowledge, has never been done before. A larger part of your mind also questions the decision of your master, who gave an order that will most likely rid the world of two unique beings whose powers are too great to be ignored.

It has been so long since you were last in this hall, at the moment of your transformation into a djinn. You are acutely aware of your sisters around you, their dancing figures watching you from the walls in what can hardly qualify as comprehension, but which surely sends signals straight into your soul. They are alive, somewhere inside these walls. Their essence is what keeps these walls intact after more than two millennia. It seems unfair that your first deed after your return to this temple has to be this needless act of death.

It has to be the Dance.

It has to be...

The Dance.

And then you hear the deep, low beat of the **tama domga,** *as if the goddess has heard you and answered with a miracle, suddenly awakening the ancient cult under this silent vault.*

As if the murals, the souls of your trapped sisters, have come alive to play for you, to remind you that there are forces in the world greater than your imprisonment, greater than the need to fulfill the foolish orders of your human master.

Forces of the Dance.

The deadly spell about to be unleashed at your opponent freezes on your fingertips. You pause as your body unfolds itself into the first shape of the Dance.

The pose of the morning breeze.

Face up, palms outward, one leg raised in a smooth, flowing movement that resembles the movement of a snake coiling up from the reeds to meet a new day.

Tum-tumm... Tum-tumm-tumm... Two pairs into four... Tumtumm-tum-tumm... Tum-tumm-tum-tumm-tumm-tam... Two sixteens into thirty-two... Tum-tumm-tum-tumm-tumm-tam ...

The Final Battle

Tum-ta-ta-tamm-tum-tum-tamm... Tamm-tammm-tammmm...
*Entranced, you hear a barely audible click as the metal bracelets
of slavery on your wrists snap open and fall down in a shower of
sparks, mixing with the old dust that has somehow found its way
into this hall through countless centuries of its existence.*
Through countless centuries of the Dance.

A soundless thunder shakes the ancient temple. The princess
awakens from her trance, feeling that she can now move
freelly and nothing seems to hold her anymore.

It is over.

Oh, gods! Hasan!

She jumps to her feet, forcing herself to look, to keep her
eyes open even in the face of the unthinkable.

The center of the hall is empty. Where is everybody? What
happened?

"Princess?" says a voice by her ear. A dear, familiar voice.

"Hasan." She turns to look into his smiling, gray eyes. "You
are... all right?"

"Never better!" he says with the mischievous grin that she
loves so much.

"Oh, Hasan!" She steps forward and sinks into his arms,
too shaken up to say anything intelligible. *Hasan is alive!* She
doesn't know how, but he is alive and well. It means that she
can go on living, too. It means—*oh, so much!*

His face, looking down on her, is pale and drawn. His
hands are shaking. He is not as well as he claims to be.

A new uprush of alarm seizes her. Is he hurt?

"Oh, princess, you are such a worrier," he says with a
laugh. "I feel wonderful!"

"I've seen you feeling better," she says, forcing a joke to release some of her tension. She doesn't feel like laughing.
"Have you won the duel? Where is everybody?"

"They are all here, don't worry, princess. And no, I haven't
won the duel. But you have."

"Me?"

He doesn't have time to answer before another shape appears next to him. A priestess in a long gray tunic and a snake necklace, her hair tied into a smooth knot at the back of her head.

Shogat, the Dancer. Or, as the princess is more used to calling her, Thea.

There is something different about her now, but the princess cannot quite catch it.

"Thea?" she breathes out. "Are you all right? What happened?"

"You have freed me, Gul'Agdar," Shogat says, raising her hands up to her face.

That's what's different, the princess realizes. *There are no metal bracelets on her wrists.*

She meets the priestess's eyes, tears trembling on her eyelashes.

"Thank you," Shogat says. "I am now forever in your debt."

"But how—? What—?" The princess stumbles, fighting the urge to fall into the older woman's arms. It feels as if a part of her soul has been released. It makes her feel too overwhelmed. The changes in her life are coming too fast.

"You have released me through Dance," Shogat says. "You are quite a *tama domga* player, you know. How did you learn? I thought this art was long lost. And how did you know my ancient name?"

"I know all about you," the princess breathes out.

"Your dreams," Hasan whispers beside her. "Thea— Shogat—the Dancer... The two of you have shared a dream link. But how—?"

Shogat slowly turns to him, realization dawning upon her.

"My mas—former master ordered me once to open your dreams to magic," she says. "I came and triggered your female side of magic. Of course, I didn't give you any exact dreams. But what happened—"

"She has been reliving your life, Shogat," Hasan says. "To learn magic the way you did."

"That means we are... sisters of the Dance," Shogat whispers, looking the princess in the eye. She steps closer and throws her arms around the princess in a tight embrace.

It feels to the princess like coming home. For a moment the two of them seem like one. She buries her face in Shogat's shoulder, catching the sweet, vaguely familiar scent of Shogat's skin, having now acquired a human touch to it.

The scent of myrrh.

That is how it all started, she realizes. On the day when she woke up and there was myrrh scent in the air near her bed. Only a few months ago, but which now seems more like a lifetime.

Of course, it really started long before that, when she opened Hasan's bottle on her twelfth birthday. Or earlier, when her grandmother went to the desert and found Hasan among the sands. Or even earlier than that, millennia ago, when Hasan and Shogat were ordinary people learning their first lessons in magic.

"How much do you know about me, Gul'Agdar?" Shogat asks, drawing away and looking at the princess with a new expression in her eyes.

"Everything," the princess says. "From the day your mother tied you up on the river bank and Eilea and Ganne collected you in the morning. I know how you learned the Dance. How you met Sel. How your son was born and sent away across the river. How your temple was buried and you became a djinn."

A flicker in the depths of Shogat's huge eyes momentarily shifts her features in response to those memories. It seems to the princess that she can sense the deep feelings arisen by her words. *Sel.*

"I guess it is possible," Shogat says slowly, looking into the distance. "For how else could you have learned all these things to the point where you could have freed me from my eternal slavery? Time in the dream world flows differently. It can perhaps fit centuries of my lifetime into a few months' worth of your dreams, Gul'Agdar. I wonder—"

She stops abruptly as the three wizards approach them. All of them, even Abdulla, are staring at the princess with wonder.

"How did you do it, girl?" Galeot-din demands.

The princess senses Hasan's hand tighten its grip on her arm and smiles inwardly. *These wizards are wishing me harm,* she thinks. *They are upset at me. But with Hasan and Shogat by my side I am protected so well none of them can touch me.*

She looks Galeot-din straight in the eye and answers from the depths of her heart. "I don't know how I did it, your majesty, but I am glad it's over."

She notes the flinch in the strange man's face when she pronounces his supposedly honorable title.

I should ask Hasan about this one day, she thinks. *As well as about many other things.*

It feels wonderful to know that she will have a chance to talk to him about this for as long as she likes. It creates such a peaceful feeling inside her. She absently smiles at Abdulla, who is piercing her with his fiery gaze.

"It seems to me that the two of you are in for an intriguing conversation with the Voices of the Wind," Shogat says matter-of-factly to Abdulla.

Abdulla's face twitches in an expression uncomfortably similar to agony. The princess has no idea what are these Voices of the Wind they are talking about are, but if it is frightening Abdulla so much, it must be something truly horrible. She is not quite sure she *wants* to know.

Caliph Agabei, however, doesn't seem to be hearing them. Hollow-eyed, he is looking at Shogat with such longing that the princess, observing him, shivers.

"What of us, Shogat?" he asks hoarsely.

"I am not sure what you mean, caliph," Shogat says coldly.

The caliph steps closer and reaches out to touch her, but she draws away with such repulsion that Agabei's arms weakly drop to his sides.

"You are not going to abandon me, Shogat, are you?" he asks, his voice ringing with plea.

"Just think of me as a casualty, caliph," Shogat says, her full mouth twitched in scorn. "It wasn't clear what the outcome of the duel would be, was it? In fact, it seemed most likely that both Hasan and I were going to die. Why don't you write me off as a former slave who died, fulfilling her master's wish to fight a hopeless magic duel?"

Agabei raises his tortured face to her, and his eyes, to the princess's amazement, fill with genuine tears.

"Please, don't leave me, Shogat," he whispers. "I cannot live without you."

"You should have thought of that when you ordered me to fight Hasan to the death, *master*," Shogat says, putting so much hatred into the last word that it seems to charge the air around her.

She must have endured so much pain in his service, the princess thinks. *How terrible it must be to exist solely as somebody's slave.*

She steps away from them, closer to Hasan, to feel his reassuring warmth beside her and his protective hand on her arm.

The movement, however small, attracts the caliph's attention. The eyes he raises to her are full of such passionate anger that the princess recoils from him into the safety of Hasan's embrace.

"It is all your fault, Princess Gul'Agdar!" the caliph exclaims, his voice cracked with despair and fury. "But this isn't over! I am not done with you yet!"

He throws another passionate glance at Shogat and lets his accomplices, Abdulla and Galeot-din, lead him away.

"He will soon calm down," Shogat observes coldly, watching them go. "He always does."

She turns to the princess and Hasan, and her expression changes. Despite the millennia that have passed since that day, she looks strangely similar to the eight-year-old girl that her mother tied up on a riverbank to wait for her destiny almost three thousand years ago.

"I am free," Shogat whispers. "I am *home*. Among my sisters..." She sweeps her gaze over the silent murals.

"They are all in here," the princess says quietly.

She steps forward and presses the *tama domga* into Shogat's hands.

"I think you need it now more than I do... Mistress Thea," she says.

Their eyes meet in a last, long look.

"Good-bye and thank you, sister," Shogat says, lips only.

She nods to Hasan beside the princess and turns away, walking across the hall and disappearing into the deep shadows of the Temple of the Dance.

It is dusk outside, and the stars are shining like jewels in the transparent blue of the evening sky.

"Let's go down to the river," the princess says, taking Hasan's hand. It feels so good to be near him, to feel his warmth at her side, to inhale his light juniper smell. She wishes they could forever remain like this.

"Of course, princess," he says with a laugh.

She feels a gust of wind momentarily take her breath away, throwing back her loose hair and making everything inside her leap and fall down in a terrifying gasp. In one step they have covered the distance all the way from the pyramids to the barely visible edge of the water.

"You—you should have warned me, Hasan!" the princess laughs out. "You could have scared me to death!"

"I thought you wanted to get there faster," he replies with false innocence, his eyes alive with dancing sparkles of laughter.

They settle down among the reeds, among the floating smells of earth, lotus, and wet grass.

"They must be beside themselves, looking for me in Dhagabad and Veridue," the princess says. "They probably think I am dead. Do you think I should keep it this way?"

"It depends on what you want, princess," he replies. "Just like it has always been."

"Oh, Hasan. I hate it when you are so serious! If nothing else, you could definitely read thoughts. You know what I want, don't you?"

She throws her arms around him and looks into his laughing eyes. The smell of his skin is maddening. She feels her mind clouded by it to the point where she once again can lose control over her actions.

"You know what I want right now?" she whispers. "I want to have a sheet to lie on, right here, among the reeds."

"Your wish is my command, princess," he whispers, holding her close, even as she feels the bumpy ground under her give way to the airy softness of a silk sheet.

She moves closer to Hasan, until his face becomes blurry in front of her unfocused eyes. Then, she gives in to the overwhelming feeling that rises in her, the feeling she never wants to end.

The night deepens around them, and the Great River Ghull majestically carries its slow, turbid waters past the endless banks.

About The Author

Anna Kashina grew up in Russia and moved to the United States in 1994. She has a Ph.D. in molecular biology and is a published author of fantasy and historical fiction in Russia, Germany, and the US. She lives in Philadelphia, PA, where she is combining her successful career as a scientist and her passion for writing

Did you enjoy *The Goddess of Dance*?

Read more about the princess and Hasan in

The Princess of Dhagabad,

available from **Dragonwell Publishing.**
www.dragonwellpublishing.com

Also by **Anna Kashina**:

Mistress of the Solstice,

upcoming from **Dragonwell Publishing** in early 2013

Mistress of the Solstice
by Anna Kashina

I stood beside my father and watched the girl drown. She was a strong one. Her hands continued to reach out long after her face had disappeared from view. The splashing she made could have soaked a flock of wild geese to the bone. She wanted to live, but there was no escape from the waters of the Sacrifice Pool.

I looked at my father's handsome profile. His pale face, awash with moonlight, looked magnificent. The power of the Solstice enfolded him. It made me proud to be at his side, his daughter, his head priestess. He was the one who mattered. The only one.

The girl's struggle ceased. The rippling water of the lake stilled, glittering in the silvery light of the near-full moon. We watched the flicker of the glowing candles set in the flower wreaths as they floated downstream. A few of the wreaths had already sunk — bad luck for their owners, who would most likely die before the next Solstice. Maybe one of them belonged to the next Sacrifice Maiden?

I felt my father stir next to me, as he too peered into the amber depths of the lake.

"A fine sacrifice, Marya," he said to me. "You did well."

"Yes." I closed my eyes to feel the familiar calmness wash over me. I was detached. I didn't care. I didn't even know her name.

My eyes still closed, I sensed my father throw off his cloak and stand naked, his arms open to the cool night breeze.

"Bring her to me, Marya," he whispered.

I stretched my thoughts, seeking out her body tangled in the weeds on the bottom of the lake, seeking the spark of life that still remained there, trapped, beating in terror against its dead shell like a caged bird. I reached for it, brought it out, and gave it to my father. I sensed the moment the two of them became one, her virginal powers filling him with such force that the air around us crackled with the freshness of a thunderstorm.

He sighed, slowly returning to his senses. I kept my eyes shut until he found his cloak on the damp grass and wrapped it around his shoulders, once again becoming himself. The Tzar. The immortal. The invincible.

The undead.

We could hear people singing in the main glade. The celebration was at its full. Soon they would be jumping over the bonfire. As the night reached its darkest, quietest hour, they would break into couples and wander off into the forest. "Searching for a fern flower" they called it. Fern has no flowers, of course. But searching for it made a good excuse for seeking the solitude of the woods. Besides, blood of virginity spilled on the Solstice night glowed like a rare, exotic blossom of true passion. Those who found their fern flowers tonight were blessed by Kupalo.

I could hear the whisper of every leaf, every tree, and every flower in the forest. This was the night when the powers of Kupalo roamed freely in the world; this was the night when everyone's mind was clouded by Love.

Except mine. Love had no power over me. My mind was free.

Also from **Dragonwell Publishing:**

www.dragonwellpublishing.com

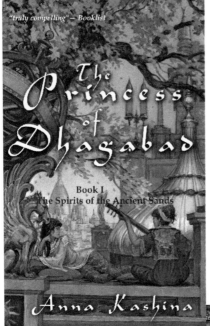

ONCE UPON A CURSE

PETER S BEAGLE, NANCY KRESS,
PATRICIA C WREDE, CINDY LYNN SPEER,
LUCY A SNYDER, SIOBHAN CARROLL,
IMOGEN HOWSON, AND ANNA KASHINA

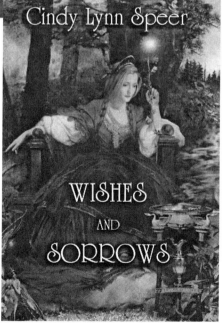

Cindy Lynn Speer

WISHES

AND

SORROWS

Visit our web page

www.dragonwellpublishing.com

to order our books and sign up for our newsletter

Follow our blog at

dragonwellpublishing.wordpress.com

to meet our authors and participate in our giveaways

CPSIA information can be obtained at www.ICGtesting.com
Printed in the USA
LVOW061933051012

301678LV00009B/12/P